Amelia

Amelia

LAURA STARR

Printed in the United States of America

Publisher's Cataloging-in-Publication Data

Names: Laura Starr, author.
Title: Amelia / Laura Starr.
Series: City of Roses Collection
Description: Bend, OR: Starr Publications, 2025.
Identifiers: LCCN: 2024923040 | ISBN: 979-8-9913092-0-2 (paperback) | 979-8-9913092-1-9 (ebook)
Subjects: LCSH Women journalists--Fiction. | Portland (Or.)--History--19th century--Fiction. | Coming of age--Fiction. | Historical fiction. | BISAC FICTION / Historical / General | FICTION / Women
Classification: LCC PS3623 .A96 A64 2025 | DDC 813.6--dc23

First Printing, 2025
Second Printing, 2026

Contact: starrpublications@yahoo.com
www.laurastarrwrites.com

Chapter One

Riverside, Oregon
March 1898

"You must be pleased with yourself, Amelia," Diane said. "This family is certainly the laughingstock now."

Amelia Hughes shrank against the thinly padded carriage seat, twisting her handkerchief around her fingers. Her younger brother, Horace, sat on one side of her, seemingly oblivious to the situation. Her older brother, Cedric, stared out the window, tense but separate from her as well. She was isolated from all of them. Even her father, across from her, sat stiff and silent as her mother berated her.

She knew she'd messed up. But it wasn't as if she'd meant to become disheveled. She really had been enjoying herself, talking to the maid. But to her mother, having a daughter enjoy herself was the height of embarrassment.

When they arrived home, Diane immediately started complaining to the maids about Amelia's latest blunder as they helped her with her hat and wrap. Her brothers disappeared upstairs to change, and Amelia knew they'd be gone playing baseball all day. Their father, Richard, retreated to his study with an unlit pipe. Amelia sneaked into the library, stopping the door from clicking shut. Sighing, she settled down and tried to read, but her mind wandered to the fact that Cedric was moving away soon for his apprenticeship. She, however, wasn't so fortunate.

Moments later, her mother entered the library, pausing at the threshold to scowl at Amelia. Biting her lip, Amelia debated acknowledging her mother. She chose silence instead, counting the seconds as her mother approached and sat down.

"Are you trying to ruin my reputation? Is that it, Amelia?" Diane's voice was sharp.

"No, Mother," Amelia replied meekly, closing her book.

"Humph. That's a likely answer." Diane pulled her handkerchief through her free hand. "I'm not sure how I'm supposed to believe you when you so willfully disgraced me this morning."

"But I only asked the butler what it was like to…"

"Only!" Diane threw her hands in the air. "I'm afraid to know what you would think constitutes a terrible disgrace if that is an *only* act. Have you no shame?"

Amelia pressed her lips together, tears filling her eyes as her mother continued.

"I've done everything I can to teach you to act right. Even in private you can't sit properly!"

Amelia immediately sat up straight, pinching her handkerchief.

"It's a little late to sit like a lady now, don't you think?" Diane pressed. "You might as well slump over until your shoulders touch your knees. There's no one here but me, and I know very well that you don't care a whit about what I think."

"That's not true!" Amelia gasped.

"It clearly is! I'll decide what to do with you, young lady. Don't think you're getting off easy this time," Diane snapped and stood abruptly. "I don't want to see you until breakfast tomorrow. I can't stand the sight of you."

Amelia's shoulders drooped back down. She pulled her feet up onto the chair, tucking her skirt around them. A tear trailed down her cheek before she bowed her head and cried.

After a long and miserable night, Amelia reluctantly crawled from bed, setting her book aside and righting the bed linens. Several minutes of unsuccessfully trying to pile her unruly red hair on top of her head led to a groan of frustration, and she moved to get dressed instead. When the clock chimed the half hour, she hurriedly brushed and plaited her hair, finishing with a neat bow. Her mother would disapprove of the style, but she would be more upset if Amelia arrived late to breakfast.

Amelia kept her gaze down as she joined her family in the dining room. The silence after her father's prayer was deafening, and Amelia grew so uneasy that she couldn't help but glance at her mother.

As if she'd been waiting for Amelia to look at her, Diane spoke. "It's clear that you're completely hopeless at learning how to behave properly. I've done everything I possibly can to give you the best instruction and motivation." She paused, arching an eyebrow.

"Yes, you have, Mother," Amelia lied, hands clenched in her lap.

"Indeed, I have. But you simply will not learn," Diane scowled. "So, I wash my hands of you. You'll go live with my sister in Portland. I doubt that she will have any success, but I simply cannot take another day of your insubordination. You'll catch the 1:30 train today. You can take one suitcase."

Stunned, Amelia could barely breathe. "Father?" Her voice was only a whisper, but he flinched.

"Don't look to him for help!" Diane snapped. "You're going, and I won't hear one more word about it."

Amelia sank back into her chair. *Is Father really going to let me be sent away?* As the meal progressed in silence, it became apparent that he wasn't going to intervene. She sat woodenly in her chair, staring at her plate.

"If you're not going to eat, you might as well leave the table. I cannot abide eating my meal in the company of a statue." Her mother's voice was filled with disgust.

Amelia hurried to her beloved room where she'd spent hours reading, dreaming, and hiding from her mother. When the door closed behind her, she leaned against it and let her tears come again.

To: Angela Barrington
635 Avery St
Portland, OR
From: Diane Hughes

Angela,

As you know, for the past few years I have had trouble with my daughter. She outright refuses to behave as a young lady of society should. You can't imagine the many disasters that have embarrassed our family.

This latest one is not to be borne though. When we arrived at a party hosted by the Grants, she immediately started talking with the butler. Not an hour later, she was in a corner, talking with a maid! Her dress was mussed, and her gloves were off. I was mortified. She looked as if she were the maid! I could not bear the humiliation and told her to leave immediately. The frightful thing walked as slowly as possible. I just knew she was wanting everyone to get a good look at her disheveled state, so they'd think I'm to blame.

The girl is lazy and refuses to improve, so I wash my hands of her. When you've given up on her, as I'm certain you will, send her to work in a grand home. Perhaps seeing what she could have had will make her regret her stubborn ways.

Respectfully,
Diane

Chapter Two

During one of Aunt Angie's rare visits, she'd told Amelia about her home in Portland and the neighborhood around Avery Street. "The families living there now," she'd said to her young niece, "are descendants of those who originally settled Portland."

"I bet they're wonderful," Amelia recalled saying. Her aunt had nodded and pursed her lips. "Some are," she'd agreed.

Amelia replayed this memory as the open carriage turned up Avery Street. The entire trip had been emotionally exhausting. She'd sobbed through most of the train ride, her feelings ranging from desolate, to abandoned, to completely forgotten. Then, as she stepped off the train, an overwhelming sense of dread took over. She was headed to a new home in a new city, where she only knew one person. True, she loved her aunt, but the whole thing was devastating. She was only fifteen years old. What did her mother expect?

Now, though she was so worn down, Amelia almost felt calm. She even let out a small laugh at the sight of an older woman in a passing carriage, her nose high in the air, a small dog in her lap. Stifling her giggle, Amelia leaned forward toward the driver. "Excuse me, Henry. Which house are we going to?"

"That one just up the lane, Miss Hughes. The white one with the rose bushes out front."

Leaning to see, a young gentleman caught her attention. He was assisting an elegantly dressed young woman into a carriage. His hat was tipped, and his cane hung on his arm. Amelia turned in her seat and watched as she passed. He glanced up at her and smiled. Embarrassed at being caught staring, she quickly turned around, her cheeks blazing. *I wonder who he is.*

As the carriage slowed she looked up at the place that would be her new home. She opened the door of the carriage and stood, ready to step down, when Henry called to her to wait. "I'll help you," he said.

A carriage coming down the road drew her attention. Inside was the same stylish couple from a moment earlier. The gentleman was dressed in a gray suit which paired well with his companion's pink dress. A parasol protected the lady's fair skin while her black hair caught the sunlight. Her hat with its broad brim was angled just so, allowing the gentleman to draw near. Amelia blushed but couldn't look away.

"Miss Hughes?" Henry's voice jolted her from her stupor. She turned and tripped on the seat, catching herself on the side of the carriage. "Careful now, we don't want you falling before you see Mrs. Barrington," he said kindly.

Cheeks burning, she accepted his hand out of the carriage. "Thank you." Her mind went back to the handsome couple. "Do you know who those people were, in the carriage just now?"

"Why, that was Miss Georgia Fossit, and young Mr. Harrison James with her," Henry said. He closed the door behind Amelia, then moved to the back of the carriage to unload her luggage.

Tucking away the information, Amelia nodded, wondering what to do next. She pulled her handkerchief out from her sleeve and wrapped it around her finger. Realizing that Henry was too busy to notice her hesitation, she decided to at least go up on the front porch. The pathway was lined with small rose bushes, while larger bushes bloomed on either side of the wide porch. Smiling at the welcome, she turned to look back at Henry just a few steps behind her, holding her bags.

"Welcome, Miss Hughes," a voice said. "Please come in."

She turned to see a tall older man holding the door open for her. "Thank you," she smiled. "You must be Walter?"

"Indeed, Miss Hughes. It's a pleasure to meet you. Mrs. Barrington is waiting in the salon."

Amelia nodded, taking in everything about the two-story entry hall as she followed Walter. She knew her aunt was rich but hadn't been aware that she was this well off. Even the wallpaper and ceiling were more opulent than any she'd seen in Riverside.

"Miss Hughes, ma'am," Walter announced. He stepped to the side, motioning for her to enter.

As Amelia walked into the sunny room, her nervousness eased as her aunt greeted her. Aunt Angie's brown hair was piled on top of her head most becomingly, and her green eyes shone with love.

"Amelia, I'm so glad to see you again," Aunt Angie said. "Did you have a good trip?" She hugged her niece close. Amelia took a deep breath, savoring the subtle scent of roses.

"I suppose," Amelia said against her aunt's shoulder. "I read for most of it, or tried to at least." When Aunt Angie stepped back and looked at her, Amelia added, "I did cry, some. But seeing you makes me feel better."

Amelia found herself in another hug. She reveled in it just as much as the first. She'd always loved spending time with her aunt. Now, if she could forget the reason why she was here, she was sure she could be quite happy. The moment the thought crossed her mind, her mother's admonishments came back to her. She pulled away.

"Oh! I'm supposed to give you this," she said, and took a wrinkled envelope from her apron pocket.

"Hmm. Thank you," Angie said. She took the envelope but barely gave it a glance. "Why don't you freshen up. Then we'll enjoy some tea."

"That sounds lovely," Amelia agreed.

"Very good. Grace will show you to your room." Aunt Angie picked up a small bell from a side table and rang it. Almost immediately, a maid came and curtseyed in the doorway. "Grace, please show Miss Amelia to the blue room, and help her change for tea."

"Yes, ma'am," the girl said, her voice sweet but formal.

Amelia hesitated and looked at her aunt, uncertainty filling her.

"I'll be right here when you come back," Aunt Angie reassured her. "Go on, now."

Amelia eyed the maid as she followed her through the house. Grace's brown hair was in a tight bun under a small lace cap. Her black uniform, white apron, and sturdy black shoes were rather plain.

Grace glanced at Amelia when they neared the top of the staircase, and Amelia quickly turned her attention elsewhere, blushing. "This home is fancier than any I've ever seen," she said, hoping to distract the maid from the fact that she'd been staring at her.

Grace nodded politely. As they strode down the hall, Amelia knew that what she'd said was true. Even the railing was polished to a high sheen, and the wallpaper was so detailed that her eyes widened in awe.

"Here we are, Miss Hughes," Grace said, then paused. "Miss? Are you feelin' all right?"

Amelia took a deep breath. "Yes. I'm just…tired." The fear that had settled in her throat made it hard to talk. She'd felt so much braver when she'd been with her aunt.

"It's all right, dear. You'll be able to rest after tea." Grace's voice was soothing. Amelia relaxed, although she found it funny that Grace called her dear, since they were probably the same age. "Ready now?" Grace asked.

Amelia forced a nod as Grace opened the door. The room was decorated with peacock feather wallpaper and mahogany furniture. The rug spanned most of the floor, touching the bed on one side and the wardrobe on the other. A washstand, dressing table, and chair were set along the far wall. Once her attention landed on the full bookcase, her eyes lingered there. In awe, she walked toward it and caressed the covers and spines of book after book.

"It's just so pretty, isn't it?" Grace said, smiling.

"It is," Amelia agreed. "Are you sure this is the room she meant for me?"

"Of course, miss. Now let's get you changed. Then you can have your tea." Grace opened the wardrobe.

"Did you unpack my bag?" Amelia asked. "I could have done that."

"It was no trouble at all. How about this one?" Grace pulled out a pale yellow dress.

Amelia reluctantly agreed, trying not to grimace at the bright, ruffled dress. It wasn't just distaste for the dress holding her back; she wasn't used to changing with someone in the room.

"Can I help you change?" Grace asked gently. "I'm used to helping my sisters."

Amelia smiled uncomfortably but agreed, turning her back to the maid. Grace kept up a running commentary on her siblings back home, easing Amelia's discomfort as she tucked a few curls back into place and declared Amelia ready to see her aunt again.

Downstairs, Angela Barrington clenched the letter in her hands, angry beyond words. She'd been upset enough this morning at the arrival of a sparsely worded telegram from Diane. As she skimmed the letter a second time, Angie could barely believe what her sister had written. "...*The girl is lazy...refuses to improve...I wash my hands of her.*"

For Diane to speak so of her own daughter! Angie was more ashamed of her sister than she'd ever been, and there had been ample opportunities over the years. Disgusted, she tossed the letter in the fire then called for her butler. Walter appeared quickly, bowing just inside the doorway.

"Yes, ma'am?"

"It appears that my niece will be living with us for the foreseeable future," she said. "Please let Ms. Dean know." *The poor housekeeper will fret for a week that she couldn't prepare properly, but what's done is done.* Angela sighed.

"Of course, ma'am."

"And store Amelia's luggage in the same place as mine."

"Luggage, ma'am? Miss Hughes came with one trunk."

She lifted her eyes toward the ceiling. "Oh, Diane, what a trial you are." Then she addressed Walter again. "Very well, we'll have to outfit her ourselves, won't we?"

Walter bowed. "The staff will do everything we can to help her settle in, ma'am."

Angie glanced at the fire to check that the letter was gone. "Thank you, Walter. She's had a tough break. I aim to…" but she stopped as Amelia entered the room.

"Aunt Angie, that room is beautiful!" Amelia said, walking in with a bright smile. Angie nodded at Walter who slipped away. "I'm glad you like it," she said to her niece.

"Like it? I love it. It's perfect."

As they settled into matching embroidered chairs, Angie watched her niece admire the room. She knew without a doubt that Diane had not done her best with the girl, not even close. Her sister had been too busy trying to keep up with the ladies of the whatever-the-newest-society was. She'd never done any real training with her own daughter.

Angie could see that one thing the girl didn't lack was spunk, once she got past her fear of failure. Perhaps that explained part of why Angie had always had a soft spot for Amelia. She'd been the same way years ago. She had wanted to explore the world and discover as much as possible. Yet, she had been frightened of what her family, and of course what society might say.

She poured them both cups of steaming mint tea. "It was always my favorite guest room," she said. "That was the first room I decorated."

"You decorated my room?" Amelia asked.

"Indeed. I was worried about how well I would do on ours, so I chose a guest room first. As if that would mean any less work and cost if we had to do it over." She chuckled, then handed the teacup and saucer to Amelia. Her humor faded as she watched her niece struggle to handle both items.

Amelia moaned at the rattle of cup against saucer. "I'm so sorry. Mother is always telling me to hold them properly, but I never seem to manage it. They always feel like they are going to break somehow."

"You'll learn. For today, how about you set it on the table there and pick it up only when you want it." Angie pulled the tea tray toward her to afford more room on Amelia's side of the low table. She wanted to laugh at the look of relief Amelia gave her, but merely smiled.

Amelia did as Angie suggested, and carefully slid the saucer and cup onto the table…not without several rattles. "Thank you," she said. "I'd hate to break your china. It's so lovely."

"People are more important than possessions," Angie replied. "I'd far rather have you here with me than have a whole cup and saucer."

Tears filled Amelia's eyes. "Really?"

"Really," Angie said gently. "So, what do you think of the city?"

Amelia dabbed her eyes with her handkerchief. "It's loud, and there are people everywhere. But I love all the trees. They sort of soften things. And I just love all the roses and lilacs! They smell so wonderful. I took deep breaths as we passed rows of them."

"It is a busy city, but you're right, the trees and flowers make it a beautiful place to live. All these people mean that there are plenty of diversions. There's always something going on if one's in the mood to be out of the house."

"Oh, I'd love that," Amelia breathed. "Back home, we don't have much for entertainment. Just small parties that the mothers put on. And they're never much fun."

"I can imagine," Angie agreed, remembering how her mother had loved those kinds of parties as well. "I'd planned on going to the theatre on opening day this weekend. Would you like to join me?"

Amelia clapped her hands together in excitement, fairly bouncing in her chair. "The theatre? I'd love to go! I've heard so much about it."

"Good. We'll plan on it then."

Angie watched Amelia eye the teacup and wondered if she'd like another sip, but her niece kept her hands in her lap. She could tell the poor girl was nervous. She was probably afraid to break the cup.

"Would you like a tour of your new home?" Aunt Angie asked, thinking a little movement might do the girl some good.

Amelia nodded eagerly and clasped her aunt's arm as they left the salon.

～◡◡〜

"It's so beautiful," Amelia said, admiring the painted wallpaper in the hallway and the crystal chandelier.

"Thank you, dear." Aunt Angie turned them so their backs were to the front door. "To the right is the dining room. Down the hall is the kitchen and back door. To the left is where we were. That's the salon. I do almost all my entertaining in there."

"It's a wonderful room," Amelia said eagerly.

"I'm glad you think so." Aunt Angie led them toward the hallway that passed along the stairs.

As they walked, Amelia peeked into the dining room. "Do you ever have enough guests to fill this table?" she asked, awestruck. The table spanned the length of the room. The backs of the chairs were curved and etched, lending another touch of elegance.

"When your uncle was alive, he loved to have grand parties," Aunt Angie said, her voice turning wistful. "You should see the ballroom," she continued, motioning toward the pair of double doors on the other side of the room.

Amelia gasped and skirted the table. As she opened one of the doors, her mouth dropped at the sight of the room's tiled floor, tall windows, and empty candelabras. There was even an orchestra balcony at the other end of the room. She turned back to her aunt. "This seems like something out of a dream," she said.

"It's especially stunning by candlelight," Aunt Angie said. "Come, let's continue."

Amelia took her aunt's hand, excited to see the rest. She couldn't believe that this lovely house was going to be her home.

～～～

It was late that evening when Angie finally settled into bed with her book. She was completely worn out. She hadn't realized how quiet her days had become since losing her husband a decade ago. She closed the book, then her eyes.

"God," she said aloud, "you know it's going to be quite the adjustment having Amelia here. I ask for guidance and patience in the coming days. She's a good girl, just uncertain of herself. You know Diane has a way of bringing that out in others."

She felt a nudge from her conscience. "Forgive me for speaking of my sister that way. She's Your child too." Then she paused, taking a few breaths. "Amelia is young, and I hate to admit it, but I've been feeling rather old lately. Give me the strength to keep up with her."

Angie sighed. She'd barely reached forty and was already feeling like she was past her prime. Was this normal, or was something the matter with her?

Her attention strayed back to her niece. *How can I help ease her transition? What would she enjoy that would take away the sting of being sent away from home?* She opened her appointment book, hoping to find inspiration. Instead, an appointment marked for the next day distracted her. Sighing at her forgetfulness, she set the book aside and went to inform her niece before it got too late.

"Amelia?" she called and knocked softly on the closed door.

"Yes?"

Angie entered and grimaced at the position her niece was in. "How can you sit like that?"

"It's the most comfortable to write in," Amelia said. She looked down at her crossed legs and shrugged. "It keeps the headboard from digging into my back if I lean against it." She pointed at the pillows in a stack behind her. "Pillows aren't ever enough to soften it."

Angie nodded, not sure what to say. "I wanted to tell you that I have an appointment in the morning. I'd take you with me, but alas…"

"Oh, I don't mind staying here," Amelia said. "I know you didn't expect me."

"You're a dear. Thank you. I'm glad to have you here, and my leaving you tomorrow doesn't imply otherwise. Once I'm back, we can do whatever you like."

"All right."

She started to leave then paused. "How are you feeling about all of this?"

Her niece bit her lower lip. "Being with you is wonderful already. And this house is beautiful." Angie nodded, waiting for more. "But…it is hard to be away from home…and from Father and Cedric especially…and my friends. I miss it." Amelia's eyes filled with tears.

"It's all right to miss home…and to cry. This is a big change." Angie prayed for the right words. "I'll always be glad you're here with me, and I want you to feel comfortable talking to me when you're homesick. Okay?"

Amelia nodded, brushing tears away.

"I'll let you go back to writing," Angie said. "Don't stay up too late."

"Aunt Angie…" Amelia groaned.

"It had to be said," Angie laughed. She closed the door and went back to her room.

Chapter Three

Amelia leaned back to savor the feel of the sun on her face. There was something about planting flowers on such a gorgeous day. Sighing happily, she looked over at her aunt's gardener, Marc. Her mother would have screeched at her for being out like this, but she was having a wonderful time.

"Miss Hughes!" The call distracted her, and she almost dropped the small plant she was holding. She set it in the hole she'd dug then looked up, wiping a length of hair from her face. Grace stood nearby. "Mrs. Barrington is waiting for you in the salon. Mrs. Grey is visitin.'"

Amelia blanched. "Oh no, I forgot." She stood in a rush. "Marc, I've got to go." She turned quickly, almost running into Grace. She barely heard the gardener's farewell as she dashed between the flowers onto the path. She bunched her skirts in her hand and hurried through the kitchen, then down the short hall that led out to the foyer.

Grabbing hold of the hallway doorframe, she slid to a stop, gasping for air. Walter caught sight of her, and they shared a smile. He inclined his head, his humor at her frequent tardiness apparent.

Taking a deep breath, Amelia stepped into the salon. Aunt Angie and another woman were already enjoying tea. At her entrance, both ladies looked up.

"Ah, there you are Amelia. This is Mrs. Edith Grey, the wife of our pastor. Edith, my niece, Amelia Lynn."

Amelia smoothed her palms on her apron and stepped forward to grasp Mrs. Grey's hand. Then she quickly hid her hand behind her back, mortified at the dirt smeared all over it. "Oh no. I…it's very nice to meet you, Mrs. Grey."

The older woman smiled. "Amelia Lynn, my husband and I have heard so much about you from your aunt. I look forward to getting to know you better."

Amelia relaxed under Mrs. Grey's calm voice and pleasing demeanor. "Thank you, Mrs. Grey. I am sorry about the way I look. I've been gardening."

"That's all right, Amelia," her aunt interrupted. "Perhaps you could make yourself presentable, then come back and join us for tea?"

"Thank you, Aunt Angie. I'll be back soon."

Once she freshened up and returned, Amelia couldn't help but think how Mrs. Grey was exactly how she'd always pictured a pastor's wife to be. Nothing like Mrs. Smark from back home, who was wrinkled from frowning at everyone and everything. Mrs. Grey wore a gown of dusky blue with touches of lace at the collar and sleeves. Her hair was arranged artfully with a sprig of flowers tucked in. It took no time at all for Amelia to like her.

"So, Amelia, what do you think of the City of Roses?" Mrs. Grey asked.

"I haven't gotten out much, but from what I've seen, I like it a great deal."

"Have you been to the park yet? There are benches throughout where you can sit and enjoy the scenery and take in the scents of roses everywhere." Mrs. Grey's eyes widened in excitement. "Perhaps we could make an outing of it soon. What do you think, Angie?"

"It's a great idea, Edith. I've been meaning to take Amelia there."

Aunt Angie served her as they continued making their plans. The tea service was highly polished, and the miniature cakes were artistically arranged on gold-edged plates. Amelia relaxed in the easy friendship of the two women, carefully balancing her teacup and saucer.

"How long have you been here?" Mrs. Grey asked.

Amelia set her teacup down gently. "It's been a few days now."

"We've been settling in and enjoying our time, haven't we?" Aunt Angie smiled.

"Oh, yes. It's so different from home," Amelia said. Then she paused, unsure if she should continue, even as both ladies waited expectantly. She took a deep breath and went on. "I can't wait to go to the opera house this weekend…and to see the skating rink. Aunt Angie and I have been making a list of books we want to read too."

"Indeed, Amelia is a lover of words," Angie agreed. "And you know that I can never get enough time to read. It's been fun to share."

"That's one thing I've never been able to enjoy… reading," Mrs. Grey said with a smile. "Have you been to an opera before?"

Amelia shook her head. "Riverside didn't have a theatre. I've always wanted to see one."

"It will be fun to take you with me," Aunt Angie said.

Amelia sipped her tea then carefully set the cup on the saucer.

"Did you hear that George Macdonald is coming for a reading next month?" Mrs. Grey asked.

"No, I hadn't! But we'll certainly have to add it to our calendar." Aunt Angie waved her personal maid, Marie, over. "What day is the event, Edith?"

"The afternoon of the fourth or the fifth," Mrs. Grey said. "You'll have to contact Mrs. Taylor for precise information. I wasn't planning on going, and didn't note the details."

"Marie, make a note to ask Mrs. Taylor about the author event," Aunt Angie said. "And you might as well mark it down on the fourth or fifth."

Marie moved to the small desk set to comply with Aunt Angie's request.

Mrs. Grey turned to Amelia. "What else do you enjoy, dear? Perhaps we can have you meet some girls your age with similar interests."

Amelia shrugged, jostling her teacup and saucer. "I read and write, mostly. I haven't tried very many things, really."

"What do you write?"

She smiled, her nervousness easing. "I like to write about what I've seen. I think it would be so fascinating to be a journalist…to actually get paid to go to events and different places, and to interview people. Think of what you could see in a job like that!"

"You make it all sound quite interesting," Mrs. Grey said.

"Writing and journalism are Amelia's passions," Angie said fondly.

"I can tell. Are you interested in pursuing them when you're older?"

"I'd love to." Amelia's eyes sparkled, but a frown quickly replaced her exuberance. "Mother would never approve.

She says ladies don't have careers. We don't *go traipsing* around the world alone." She slouched as she reflected on her mother's disdain for her dream.

"Perhaps not," Mrs. Grey sighed. "But I don't see why that should stop you from *your* dream. There must be ways to maintain propriety as a journalist. Don't you think, Angie?"

"Indeed," Aunt Angie agreed. "If you want it enough, we can help you figure out a way."

Amelia couldn't believe what she was hearing. She sat up straight and beamed at the two ladies. "Thank you. You've given me hope."

Their answering smiles filled her heart.

⁓⌣⌣⌐

Amelia just stared up at the opera house, the night already feeling magical. A tug on her elbow drew her attention. She pulled her gaze to Angie, who stood several steps ahead of her. Blushing, she caught up with her aunt. "I'm sorry, it's all just so beautiful."

"It's all right, I'm always a bit in awe of it myself," Aunt Angie said as they entered.

"Oh," Amelia breathed, looking around at the splendor of the hall. She began to say something to her aunt, but someone called out her name.

"Angela! It's so good to see you! How are you?" The loud voice easily carried across the noise of the crowd. Amelia turned with Aunt Angie to greet the newcomer.

"I'm well, Mrs. Detrid," Angie said. "And you?"

"I'm simply wonderful. I'm so excited to see *The Wedding Day*. It's been my favorite for years." Mrs. Detrid spoke as if sharing a great secret, even though her voice was just as loud as before. Eyeing the woman's elaborate gown, Amelia realized anew just how poor her dress must look. She'd hated putting on the pink thing for her first opera attendance, but her only other option had been to stay in. And she wouldn't miss this for anything.

Gripping the offending skirt between two fingers, she focused instead on the crowd. Mostly older people filled the hall, but she did spot a few younger faces as they disappeared into the theatre.

Her aunt bid Mrs. Detrid goodbye, and they moved on. The theatre dazzled Amelia with its splendor. Once they found their seats, Amelia leaned back to observe the audience.

"Aunt Angie, look! Georgia Fossit is here!" Amelia tapped her aunt on the shoulder, pointing across the room. "I saw her on my first day here."

"It's not ladylike to point," a woman sniffed at her from the row behind.

Amelia dropped her hand onto her lap immediately, her face burning.

"You'll see Miss Fossit most places we go," Aunt Angie said. "But did you see that young woman near the back wall? That's Miss Sarden."

Amelia looked where her aunt indicated. A girl about her own age stood with what appeared to be her family, in a dress that very much resembled the one Amelia wore. Nothing about the girl appealed to her.

She immediately sought out the fashionable Georgia Fossit again. "Can you introduce me to Miss Fossit?" She leaned closer to her aunt, not wanting the rude woman behind them to hear her.

"I don't know her, dear. Besides, I'd much rather you befriend Miss Sarden. I've heard good things about her."

"Oh," Amelia groaned.

Her aunt turned to speak to a woman sitting on her other side. Looking around, Amelia's heart fairly stopped when Harrison James started walking down the aisle. He was far more handsome than she remembered. He scanned the room and paused when he noticed her. Smiling broadly, he winked at her before moving on. She smiled back, cheeks flushed, envious as he stopped next to Georgia. How she wished she could join them.

⁓⌣⌣⸁

Eyes alight during intermission, Amelia entered the powder room, which was lavishly decorated with mirror stations with small tables and padded stools before each one. Most of the stations were occupied, as women reapplied lipstick and needlessly patted their hair.

Amelia sat in one of the empty stations and bit her lip, not wanting to place her purse on the table. To her, it was far too shabby for this environment. She set it on her lap then moved to catch it as it slid off the slippery fabric. She raised her knees, balancing on her tiptoes to keep her purse from slipping again. Turning her head, she checked the updo that Marie had guided Grace into styling. It was the first time she'd been allowed such a grown-up hairstyle, and she loved it. She patted a curl pinned just above her ear, pretending to tuck the pin in a bit more, then did the same to the other side.

Her aunt had declared that she was still a little too young to use lipstick, so Amelia bit her lips to darken them. When her gaze dropped to her dress, she frowned, her joy stymied by the pink and lace. *I look like a little girl in this dress.*

As she moved to stand, her toe caught the hem of her skirt. She lurched forward, barely catching herself on the table of the next mirror station. Her purse flew to the floor and ejected everything in it. Laughter ensued as Amelia pulled her skirt from under her foot, then knelt to pick up her things.

"Who's that on the floor? Doesn't she know how to behave in company?"

Amelia grabbed the last of her items and looked up. Georgia Fossit stood a few feet away, snickering. *There's something not very nice about her smile.*

"I tripped and dropped my purse," she said as she stood.

"Look at that dress," another woman trumpeted. "She's probably a maid." In a false undertone, the woman asked, "Did Mrs. Barrington feel sorry for you, dear?"

Another woman piled on. "My neighbor did that for her maid once," she said. "She told me later how it ruined the girl for any sensible work. She had to fire her a few weeks later."

"This one here is acting above her station for sure," a third voice added.

Amelia stood rooted to the spot, horror filling her. She looked to Georgia Fossit for help, but she only smiled and walked to a mirror station. The slight pressure Georgia exerted against her arm as she moved past freed Amelia from her daze.

As she hurried from the room, the laughter redoubled when she nearly collided with another woman who was entering at the same time. Amelia's cheeks flushed even hotter now. She moved quickly until she found an empty spot against the wall. People walked past her without a glance. She breathed deeply, trying not to cry. Sighing from the embarrassment, she entered the theatre and made her way back to where her aunt was talking with some women. She'd feel so much better once she was near Aunt Angie again.

~⁓~⁓

After enthusiastically applauding with the rest of the audience at the end of the play, Amelia followed Angie from the theatre. She threaded her arm through her aunt's, wishing she could sing like the sopranos. She wondered what it would be like to be an opera singer, and to live such an exciting life.

"Excuse me, Amelia. I'll only be a moment." Aunt Angie released her arm and took the hallway that led to the powder room.

Amelia bit her lip to keep from calling out after Angie. She let the crowd carry her into the lobby until she found a place to stand near a candelabra.

That one is acting above her station, for sure. The jibe ran through her mind and made her wince. A high-pitched giggle drew her attention. It was Georgia Fossit, laughing and leaning against Harrison James. Amelia admired his dark wavy hair and blue suit. She desperately wanted to meet him.

As she scanned the room, her eyes fixed on a tall man near the lobby's double doors. His black suit fit him well. Her gaze widened as she studied his clean-shaven square jaw and sideburns that weren't fashionably prominent.

He's so handsome! I wonder who he is. She continued watching as he drew nearer the doors, then looked away quickly as he turned toward her. Her cheeks burned. She kept her eyes on the other side of the lobby, searching for Harrison James, but couldn't resist looking one more time at the other man. He stepped aside to allow his companions to exit the building first.

Amelia sighed and longed for someone that attentive. She couldn't wait until she was allowed to date. She imagined Harrison James taking her out to dinner, then to the opera. She sighed again and almost missed the fact that Georgia and Harrison were headed her way. She straightened her shoulders and pretended not to notice. While she wanted Georgia to acknowledge her, she didn't want to look like she was begging for the socialite's attention.

"Have you found any more messes to clean lately?" Georgia asked.

Amelia blushed and smiled a little, uncertain what to say.

"This is who I was telling you about, Harrison."

He brushed his hair out of his eyes and smiled at her. "I'm Harrison James. This is Georgia Fossit. And you are?"

"Amelia Hughes." She curtseyed. "I'm glad to meet you both."

"This is obviously her first time at the opera," Georgia giggled. "Can you imagine?" She leaned against Harrison. "I've been coming for years." Harrison nodded and shifted her direction. It was subtle, and Amelia was sad to see it.

"Not everyone grows up hearing the great singers, Georgia," Harrison said. He smiled at Amelia. "I'm sure you had other pastimes?"

"Back home, we held dances occasionally," Amelia said shyly.

Georgia laughed. "Oh, Miss Hughes, that doesn't compare at all."

Amelia blushed, embarrassed that Harrison was laughing as well. "I know that," she began to say. "It's just…"

"Come, Harrison," Georgia said. "I want to talk to Harriet before we leave."

Neither said goodbye, and Amelia frowned. That introduction hadn't gone at all how she'd hoped. But Harrison James had talked with her, and seemed interested until she'd said something silly.

"What's brought on that frown?" Aunt Angie asked as she walked up.

"Oh, nothing," Amelia said.

"Do you mind meeting a few more people? Or would you rather go home directly?"

"I think I'd like to go home," she answered. The glamour of the evening had faded. All she could think about now was curling up with a good book.

∼⌣⌣⌐

A few days later, Amelia sat on a sun-warmed bench in the garden, savoring the scent of roses and lavender. She fingered the satin gloves in her hands, wishing she could forget the last several days. Mainly her embarrassing introduction to Aunt Angie's friend, as well as falling in the powder room. She dearly wanted to do things properly, but everything was so new. She never knew when she'd make another mistake.

And then to act as if a small-town dance was the same as going to the opera! she chastised herself. *You're not in Riverside anymore, Amelia.* Her cheeks heated again, her eyes filling with tears. She tried to blink them away as Aunt Angie walked toward her.

"Are you excited for Mrs. Bobbin to arrive soon?" Angie asked. "She'll have so many fabrics to choose from." Angie paused when she saw Amelia's expression. "What's the matter, dear?"

"I keep messing up," Amelia said. "I'm always embarrassing myself. And I embarrassed you when your friend was here," she added miserably.

"I wasn't embarrassed," Aunt Angie reassured. "I did the same to my mother so many times." Angie sat down beside Amelia and took her hand. "I just had an idea. It might be helpful, but only if you're interested. What do you think of having deportment lessons? Just to help you get your feet under you."

"Oh, please!" Amelia smiled broadly, relief filling her. "I'm always so worried that I'm going to do something wrong. Yes!"

"I'm sorry that you've been so concerned. I wish you had told me. I'll look into lessons for you, especially since you like the idea so much." Aunt Angie squeezed Amelia's hand. "It's been less than two weeks since you arrived. Be sure not to put too much pressure on yourself. And remember, a lot of society's rules are just plain silly. That's why I ignore some of them."

"I tripped in the powder room at the theatre the other night," Amelia admitted. "The ladies in there laughed at me. It was so embarrassing."

"Ah, so that's why you came out in such a mood."

Amelia nodded, frowning. "I could hear them laughing as I left." Her cheeks heated. "I never want to feel like that again. I'll prove that I'm just as good as they are."

Aunt Angie met Amelia's declaration with silence. Amelia felt herself calming. Her breathing slowed. She began to feel silly for being so upset in the first place. Still, she knew what she'd said was true. She wouldn't give anyone a reason for talking to her like that again.

Finally, her aunt spoke. "I understand, Amelia, but I want to caution you. No matter what you do, there will always be someone who will find fault with it. You'll never be happy if you're constantly looking for validation from the outside. You must know who you are, and who you want to be. And you must keep those two things always in your view."

Aunt Angie's words filled Amelia for a moment. Then she pushed them away. *I'll show them.*

Amelia could barely contain her excitement as Mrs. Bobbin and her assistants unpacked piles of luxurious fabrics in Aunt Angie's room. Amelia felt a little self-conscious as they recorded her measurements, but she enjoyed everything else. A whole new wardrobe was taking shape in Mrs. Bobbin's notebook—evening wear, tea and afternoon dresses, night-gowns, undergarments…so many options that Amelia began to forget all they decided on.

"The current style of sleeve is a double puff that can either be brought in at the elbow, or, if done at the wrist, make a beautiful wide bishop," Mrs. Bobbin said. "If you like, we can put some epaulettes of lace or frills over the puffs."

The selection of fabrics, ribbon, and lace couldn't have been finer. There were many choices of linen, seersucker, flannels, and woolens. But the fabric Amelia could not resist was a brocade of olive, with a floral pattern that subtly caught the light.

"You have fine taste, Amelia," Aunt Angie said. "Silk brocade is one of my favorites as well. Perhaps an evening gown?"

"Oh yes, please," Amelia said. She fingered the swatch of fabric, her eyes alight.

"Hmm, yes, with a trim of black, no…brown perhaps?" Mrs. Bobbin's voice was muffled as she dug through a mound of material on the table. Soon they'd planned everything out. Mrs. Bobbin and her assistants folded, wrapped, and carried the fabrics out in trunks to the waiting carriage.

"Now remember," the seamstress chided, "it will be much longer on your end than mine until these are done. No pestering, you hear?" With her unorthodox farewell, she sailed out of the house. Amelia stared out the door. Her aunt's chuckle startled her out of her shock.

"If anyone else issued that warning, they'd be thrown out of town," she said. "But when you're the best, that's how it goes." She shrugged. "Don't worry, Amelia. Before you know it, Mrs. Bobbin will be back for a fitting. I take it you're happy with what you selected?"

"Yes!" Amelia took her aunt's arm as they walked to the salon. "I can't believe all you bought for me. There's so much!"

"I'm glad you like it. These things should last you a couple of years at least." Aunt Angie paused to look at her. "You know what I realized yesterday? You need a dedicated place to write. You can't always contort yourself into that horrible position on your bed."

"It's comfortable, though," Amelia said, hoping to ease her aunt's concerns. "That way, I can write until I fall asleep." She smiled just thinking about how much she loved the feeling of her eyes closing while she tried to scribble down a few more words.

"Yes," her aunt said, "but eventually, you'll want to write during more civilized hours. You'll be glad you have a desk. You can use Uncle Miles' desk in the library if you like."

"Can we go look now?" Amelia asked eagerly.

When they entered the library, Amelia sighed in happiness. It had a very masculine feel to it. Shelves of books lined three of the walls. On the fourth wall, a tall window overlooked Avery Street. A large desk stood in front of it with a leather chair pulled close. Amelia ran her fingers along the edge of the mahogany, taking in all the things that were precisely laid out on its surface—a feather pen, an ink bottle, and a stack of papers under a paperweight.

Excited, she looked to her aunt, only to find Angie in deep contemplation. Her fingers also touched the desk, in a light caress of remembered affection.

"Aunt Angie?"

Her aunt sighed and smiled sadly. "He spent so much time here. I can almost still see him sitting in the chair."

"Are you sure about me using it?" Amelia asked. She hated to think of leaving this magnificent desk, but she didn't want to hurt the most generous and loving person she knew.

"He'd be glad you were using it. He would have chided me for letting it sit here unused all this time anyway. Now it's yours to enjoy."

"I'll be very careful. I won't hurt it, I promise."

Aunt Angie touched her cheek tenderly. "I know, Amelia. You're a thoughtful girl." Aunt Angie stepped back and tapped the stack of papers. "Let me or Ms. Dean know when you're getting low on paper. We'll order more."

Amelia thanked her, waited until she was alone, then sat down at the desk. She couldn't believe that this desk was hers to use. It was far more than she'd ever dreamed of having.

Chapter Four

Come see the incredible event of the balloon ascension! Mr. Wyse will ascend at half-past ten on the morning of April third! For only fifty cents, you will get a close-up view of the take-off in a special enclosure. Do not miss this spectacular sight!

As Amelia read the announcement aloud, excitement washed over her. She'd been looking forward to this since she first came across the advertisement. They'd learned about these newest flying contraptions in school. Being from a small town, she hadn't expected to see one in person.

She folded the advertisement and put it in her purse, catching a glimpse of the huge woven basket before the crowd swarmed around it. She followed Aunt Angie out of the carriage and across the rough grass toward a roped-off section where a handful of elites stood with a full view of the goings-on.

Everyone watched the men finish the necessary preparations before the ascension. They opened the hydrogen gas tanks, and slowly filled up the balloon with a hiss. As it grew larger, exclamations from the crowd mounted. It took a good half hour before the balloon stood straight. By then, Amelia was so excited about the take-off that she thought she might burst.

A girl about Amelia's age stood next to her, smiling. She leaned close to Amelia. "I'm so excited! I've been waiting for one to come to town!"

"I know! They never came to my hometown."

"Where are you from?" the girl asked.

Just as Amelia was about to answer, a young man whose spectacles reflected the sun stepped in front of the crowd. He motioned for quiet before announcing, "Ladies and gentlemen! In just a moment, Mr. Wyse will show you the wonder of the balloon! He will ascend to thirty thousand feet above us, and fly to Hander's field, twenty miles away."

The crowd cheered as an older man, dressed in a fitted coat and outrageous checkered pants, bowed repeatedly before climbing into the tall basket. After much maneuvering, the balloon slowly started to rise off the ground. Amelia gasped along with everyone else—it really was going to fly! Soon Mr. Wyse was just a speck inside the basket. The wind took him toward Hander's field. It was a long while before the crowd dispersed. They'd just watched an unbelievable feat. *How will I write about it when I get home?*

<div align="center">~~~</div>

That afternoon, Amelia envied her aunt's calm as they waited for Mrs. Hartly, the deportment teacher, to arrive. She pressed her hands against her blazing cheeks to cool them. She couldn't do anything about the knots in her stomach, though the smile Aunt Angie sent her eased her tension somewhat.

Walter greeted their guest, and Amelia hurried to put on her gloves. Realizing too late that her aunt was already standing, and that Mrs. Hartly was in the room, Amelia rose, fumbling a little as her foot caught the hem of her gown. She could feel her cheeks flushing even more as she curtsied. "Pleased to make your acquaintance, Mrs. Hartly," she said meekly.

"And I'm pleased to make yours, Miss Hughes. I look forward to working with you."

Tea came, but Amelia's nerves remained stretched thin.

"Miss Hughes," Mrs. Hartly began, "I've heard from Mrs. Barrington why you want deportment lessons. But I'd also like you to tell me."

"Well, I…" she began, but couldn't find the words.

"It's all right," Aunt Angie said. She handed Amelia a cup and saucer. "Her mother was hard on her in company. She gets a little…"

"Please, don't apologize for her, Mrs. Barrington," Mrs. Hartly said, kindly but firmly. "She's a grown woman now. She must learn to comport herself properly. That is why I am here, isn't it?" She kept her eyes on Amelia. "I am not an ogre, Miss Hughes. I hope we can get along, and that you will, overall, enjoy our time together. I have no desire to remind you of past experiences." She fell silent and waited, sipping her tea.

"Thank you, Mrs. Hartly," Amelia finally said.

"You're quite welcome. I can come across as terse, but you'll just have to get used to me. And I to you. Now, Mrs. Barrington, was there something you wanted to say?"

Aunt Angie smiled and shook her head. "I'll let you start your lesson. Excuse me." Amelia watched her aunt leave, then pulled her gaze back to her new teacher. She was terribly uncomfortable without her aunt, but she also wanted to learn.

"Allow me to explain what etiquette is," Mrs. Hartly said. "It is often described as correct behavior, but I much prefer to think of it as common sense. The intent is to make life run more smoothly and pleasantly. As for knowing these rules, keep in mind that it's mostly about what is appropriate for a certain situation. I'll teach you to follow these guidelines so you'll feel comfortable and confident wherever you go. Now, to return to my earlier question, what is your goal in learning from me?"

"Well, I want to fit in here," Amelia admitted. "Everyone seems to know just what to do or say, and I don't. There are so many things that I've already done…"

"Ah. You've gotten those looks of disdain, haven't you?"

Amelia nodded, feeling embarrassed all over again.

"Walk to the doorway and back to your seat, if you will," Mrs. Hartly instructed. Amelia stood, looking at Mrs. Hartly curiously. That lady simply raised an eyebrow expectantly. Amelia tried to walk as gracefully as possible, then sat back down.

"Hmm…do it again. This time, try keeping your chin level with the ground, and step lightly. Don't tromp around." Her voice was kind, but Amelia flinched.

"Do I walk that badly?" she asked.

"Do you need to watch every step you take?" Mrs. Hartly countered.

"No."

"Unless the terrain is uneven, and you find it necessary to pay constant attention to the placement of your feet, you should not be looking downward. Look in front of you. Try again."

Back and forth Amelia walked, trying to follow Mrs. Hartly's instructions. By the end of the half hour, she'd walked the length of the room countless times, focusing on her speed, footfall, and posture. Her assignment was to walk ten minutes a day with a book on her head until their next lesson.

Preparing to leave, Mrs. Hartly took her hat and gloves from the maid, then turned once more to Amelia. "You've done well for your first lesson," she said. "Retraining yourself to do the most basic tasks takes time and commitment. But I get the feeling that you have what it takes. I'll see you Thursday next. Good day."

"Good day, Mrs. Hartly," Amelia gushed, then went straight to her room, worn out. Daydreaming, she imagined herself as a belle of society. She'd make such an impression that Harrison James would fall madly in love with her. She smiled and sighed, thinking of how handsome he was. She was sure she'd never seen a more handsome man in all her life. Unless it was that tall man from the theatre. She still had no idea who he was, or whether she would ever meet him.

The morning sky was dim and overcast. Angie tied her robe and left her bedroom, heading to the library. It was the tenth of April. Ten years ago, her beloved Miles passed away. Her vision blurred, and she blinked away tears. She wasn't ashamed of crying, even this many years later, but she'd rather not fumble her way down the stairs. Her slippered feet made no sound on the thick rugs as she paused outside the open doorway of the library, noting a dim light coming from inside.

Did a maid forget to douse the light? Stepping into the room, she breathed a sigh of relief and amusement. Her niece lay curled up on the chaise, a book next to her as if it had landed there on its own. Clearly the girl had fallen asleep reading. Thankful that Amelia's candle hadn't started a fire, Angie rescued the book from its precarious position. She smiled slightly at the sweet innocence of the sleeping youth, then turned to the mahogany desk.

This was where she always felt Miles the most, where she could still see him sitting with his spectacles balanced on his nose and a frown on his forehead. He'd always frowned when doing figures, no matter how well they aligned. Angie sat in the chair and lovingly placed her hands on the desk. How many times had she joined him in this room to read while he worked, just to be near him? How often had they sat in front of the fireplace and talked about the children they would have?

They'd had too few years together. *How I miss your gentle guidance and loving care.* She could use both these days. Too often lately she'd had the feeling that something was terribly wrong with her body.

"Aunt Angie?" Amelia asked, her voice rough from sleep.

"Did I wake you?" Angie asked in reply, tamping down her loneliness and fear.

A soft knock preceded Susan, one of the maids, who efficiently set about serving them hot chocolate and croissants. Without a word, she curtseyed and left the room.

Sighing, Angie savored the sweet concoction. "It's been ten years since Miles passed away. I always sit in here to pray and remember him."

"I'm so sorry, Aunt Angie. I didn't realize. Do you want me to leave?"

"Only if you want to," she said. "I enjoy the company."

Amelia cradled the mug in her hands. "Will you tell me about him?"

Angie smiled and wiped a tear away. "He was the most generous man. He'd take me to Europe if I so much as hinted at wanting to go. One time I said how interesting it would be to tour Spain's museums. He had us leaving in two weeks!" Angie chuckled and sipped her hot chocolate. "He taught me to forgive, and how to love unconditionally. Much of who I am is because of him."

Her voice softened, and she almost forgot who she was speaking to. "We used to dream of having children," she went on. "I would talk about a boy to be his heir, and he would dream of a little girl with curly hair and an undaunted spirit. I thought I was pregnant a few times, but…" A sharp pang speared her. Blinking, she looked over at her niece. "You're much like him, Amelia. He would have loved you and counted you as a daughter. As I do."

"I don't remember meeting him," Amelia said.

Angie shook her head. "I'm sorry to say, you never did. He wanted to meet you and Cedric." She grimaced and looked down at the desk. "He loved you from a distance." She wasn't going to tell her niece that they'd been forbidden to visit. Diane lifted the ban after Miles' death. As far as Angie was concerned, Diane had only done so in the hopes that Angie would leave her wealth to her in the event of her own passing. The thought brought her anger and pain.

"I wish I could have known him," Amelia sighed. "I never thought about how much you must still miss him."

"Thank you, Amelia," Angie smiled sadly. "Such a loss is life-changing, but I can't let it keep me from living. I can sense him here in this room…even though ten years have passed." She couldn't believe it had been so long. Yet to her heart, it'd been a lifetime since she'd seen him or held him close.

The sun brightened the room as they sat in silence. Having enjoyed their drinks and pastries, the two went their separate ways. By early afternoon, Angie had lain down for a nap with a headache, her heart still yearning for her husband.

A few weeks later, Mrs. Bobbin arrived with Amelia's new wardrobe. Amelia was excited to see each outfit and the different ways to wear them. Her favorite was still the green brocade, but a day dress made her pause—a brown brocade silk with blue flowers. The sleeves were puffy from shoulder to elbow, then fitted down to her wrist. Her favorite part was the high silk collar. She felt so grown up in it, she hardly wanted to take it off. Feeling Mrs. Bobbin's gaze on her, she hurried behind the screen. "I'm sorry, it's just so lovely."

"No, no child, don't apologize for appreciating one of my creations. So many of these socialite women are impossible to please. That's why I charge so much." A hoarse cackle, and then her aunt's light chuckle, made Amelia smile.

"Oh, I like this one," Grace whispered as she buttoned up the back.

"I love everything she made," Amelia whispered. "I've never had clothes like this!" She ran her hands down the front of the beaded chiffon skirt.

"Come out and show us, Amelia Lynn," Aunt Angie's voice interrupted them.

"Yes, ma'am." Stifling a giggle, Amelia stepped out from behind the screen, holding the sides of her skirt out. "Isn't it beautiful?" Her aunt agreed wholeheartedly.

Taking the next outfit behind the screen, Amelia waited for Grace to undo the buttons. "I'll be able to do this one myself," she said. Grace nodded as she took the beaded dress away, then left Amelia to change alone.

Amelia buttoned the shirtwaist up the front, loving how the puffed sleeves tapered down toward her wrists, similar to her other new outfits. However, this shirtwaist was much plainer. Next, she pulled on the simple green skirt and marveled at the scalloped hem, just a few inches off the floor. She added the matching jacket, buttons cinching around her waist. She stepped out from behind the screen and pretended to be holding a pen and pad of paper.

Aunt Angie smiled. "You look like a true reporter."

"Journalist," Amelia playfully corrected.

"Ah, does Miss Hughes wish to be a journalist?" Mrs. Bobbin inquired as she circled her, checking the fit of the outfit, just as she'd done with the others. She motioned for Amelia to remove the jacket.

"Yes," Amelia said. "I've wanted to be a journalist ever since I was a child." She pulled the sleeves off with a bit of difficulty.

"Hmm." Mrs. Bobbin inspected the sleeves of the jacket and shirtwaist. "I'll let these sleeves out a bit." Then silence stretched for a few moments while Mrs. Bobbin marked where to make the adjustments. She moved onto the shirtwaist. "It could be an interesting job, I suppose."

"I think so," Amelia enthused. "Getting to go places and meet people that you wouldn't otherwise. Writing about it so others can get to know them as well, even if they are in another town or state! Just imagine," she sighed.

"You've found Amelia's passion, Mrs. Bobbin," Aunt Angie said with a smile.

"Sad to say, but I can't see any man hiring a young girl like you, Miss Hughes. They are territorial about their professions."

Amelia sighed again. She knew how hard it was for women to enter the newspaper world. Her mother and even her father had said so on countless occasions. She didn't like to think about how unlikely her dream was to come true.

Angie saw the light go out in Amelia's eyes at the seamstress' words. She knew Mrs. Bobbin hadn't meant to be negative. She may have been as forthright as they come, but she wasn't cruel. The bigger problem was that what she'd said was painfully true. Men didn't like women encroaching on their jobs. Most still held the belief that women belonged in the home.

"You're right, Mrs. Bobbin," Amelia spoke. "Very few women have managed to make it as journalists."

"You never know if you don't try, Amelia Lynn," Angie cut in. Amelia didn't say anything, just moved behind the screen to try on the last of the dresses. Angie was concerned though. Would her niece really give up on her dream? If she did, what would she replace it with? Pushing her worries aside for a moment, she smiled in approval as Amelia walked out wearing an elegant party dress of silk and lace. *What if it's society that Amelia focuses on instead*? A dart of dread shot through her. She was determined to do something that would encourage Amelia not to give up on her dream before she'd even tried.

By the time Mrs. Bobbin left, Angie had hit on an idea. Leaving Amelia still admiring her new wardrobe, she went to send off a request as soon as possible.

～⁓～

Angie rarely took advantage of her social status, but this was one of those times when she knew it would come in handy.

Now, the trick would be convincing Mr. Fletcher, the owner and editor-in-chief of the *Oregonian*, to give Amelia a chance. It wouldn't be easy, but Angie had a feeling she'd be successful. Seeing as Mr. Fletcher had been eager to meet with her, she didn't think he would want to insult her with a refusal.

As the carriage took her across town, a question ate at her. What if her darling niece rejected this opportunity? Had Amelia been caught by the glimmer of society already? Resolutely, Angie put the doubt out of her mind. Amelia was a sensible girl. She had nothing to worry about.

She entered the offices of the *Oregonian* and was surprised by the hustle and bustle. People yelled across the room and hurried between desks. She paused and continued toward the glass-enclosed office at the end of the room, where a heavyset man sat behind a desk. "Forgive my intrusion," she said, opening the office door, "but the young man at the front told me to come straight in."

"Of course, Mrs. Barrington. Please, have a seat. I'm Mr. Fletcher." He waved a hand toward a chair in front of his desk.

"Thank you for taking time to meet with me. I'm sure you're very busy."

"Oh, not at all, ma'am. It's no trouble for a lady such as yourself. What can I do for you?"

"I'm sure you've heard this before, Mr. Fletcher, but my niece has talent."

"Yes, yes. I'm sure she does."

"And she aspires to be a reporter one day," Angie said then corrected herself, "I'm sorry, I mean a *journalist*."

"Naturally, naturally."

"In light of that, I brought a piece she wrote." Angie pulled out Amelia's written description of the balloon ascension.

Mr. Fletcher fairly snatched it out of her fingers and scanned the paper. "This is quite good…quite good. There are several structural errors and… well…it is quite good, I assure you."

"I'm glad you think so. I was hoping that you could perhaps find a place for her here. She's still young and needs to learn the ins and outs."

Mr. Fletcher rubbed his hands together, his eyes darting around the bustling newsroom. "We could put her with Larry, or Frank. No, no that won't work. Maybe with Stanley." After a few more mumbling attempts, he shifted his focus back to Angie. "We can do that, Mrs. Barrington. As you say, she's not ready for a writing job, but there are a few places we could put her. Naturally, I'll need to meet her. Not to imply that she isn't a credit to you, ma'am. I'm sure she is, sure she is."

"Thank you. Amelia will be so excited when I tell her." Angie stood, preparing to leave.

"Of course, of course. Did you know that my wife has always longed to be part of the circles that frequent the Portland Hotel? But new money is looked down on, you know." He shuffled some papers and moved a pen to a small cup. "It's a constant conversation in our home, you understand, her wanting to be a part of it. Her heart is set on it, you see."

"I'll send her an invitation to accompany me the next time I go, if you think she'd accept?" Angie smoothly accepted his request for a favor. She was only glad that it was something as simple as this.

"She'd be beside herself, I assure you," Fletcher said. "This week, perhaps?"

Angie smiled, not surprised that he was pushing her for a specific day. "Of course," she agreed. "I hadn't planned on going this week, but I'm sure I can fit it in. And I'll bring Amelia in next week. Perhaps Monday?" If he could play that game, so could she.

"Yes, yes. That will do." Mr. Fletcher nodded, clearly done with the meeting.

"Until then, Mr. Fletcher. Thank you for your time."

"Anything for you, Mrs. Barrington." He bowed but didn't move from behind his desk. His manners apparently only went so far.

Pleased with the meeting, Angie stepped out onto the sidewalk, excited to share the news with Amelia. She was heading to the park to meet her niece and Edith directly.

"Mrs. Barrington!" a voice called behind her.

"Ian!" she said with pleasure. "What are you doing here?"

"I have a meeting with Mr. Fletcher," Ian said. A tall young man, his blue eyes were as kind as his smile. He was well dressed as always, with his watch tucked in his vest pocket. She knew that he treasured the watch, as it used to be his father's.

Angie nodded toward Fletcher's office. "He's a slippery one."

"I've worked with him before," Ian said with a smile. "I've come with an offer he won't be able to refuse. It's been weeks since I've seen you. Are you free for dinner tomorrow night?"

"I'd love to. How about Friday instead? I'm attending a play with my niece tomorrow night."

"Ah, I wasn't aware you had guests. We can postpone. I wouldn't want to take you from your niece."

Angie waved her hand. "She lives with me now. That's partly why you haven't seen me lately. We've been getting settled in. It would be good to get out."

"If you insist. I'll pick you up at seven?"

"That will be wonderful. I'll see you Friday."

The friends smiled a last goodbye then turned, one to the carriage and the other toward the building beside them.

Amelia strolled the shaded path, savoring the faint smell of the flowers. The park was quickly becoming one of her favorite places. As much as she liked the bustle of the city, she found the park's slow, easy pace soothing. As she walked, she held her parasol at just the right angle, and looked for Mrs. Grey. She followed another curve in the path and smiled in delight at the group ahead of her.

A short distance off the path, a group of elites was gathered, all a few years older than Amelia. She was excited to see Georgia and Harrison among them.

Amelia straightened her shoulders and twirled her parasol, hoping they would notice her. Georgia was flanked by two young women who, despite their own beauty, seemed overshadowed by her striking presence. The women held parasols at angles to block the sun, while a half-dozen young men vied for their attention. As Amelia approached, she reminded herself to breathe and avoid staring at Harrison.

Georgia Fossit called out to her first. "We were just talking about you, Miss Hughes." Her greeting stopped all the conversation around her. Her deep voice with the southern drawl sounded exotic to Amelia. "Weren't we, girls?" she added. Her friends nodded and smiled on cue, although one looked confused at the assertion.

"That's so kind," Amelia said. "It's lovely to see you again."

"I simply couldn't stand being indoors any longer. I just had to come out and see everybody," Georgia smiled at Harrison as she spoke.

"You know I would've come directly to you had I known you craved my company," Harrison smiled, one eyebrow arched. "Lucky for us, we seem to know each other's very thoughts and desires."

"Oh, Harrison, you mustn't tease me in front of Miss Hughes," Georgia scoffed. "She isn't used to such society."

"We could help her with that," Harrison said. "Invite her to your party Monday." He eyed Amelia briefly. "She's pretty enough to be in your entourage."

Amelia flushed at his words and attention. She could scarcely believe what was happening. Georgia paused, then reached her hand out to Amelia, pulling her closer.

"What a wonderful idea! You must come! It's my first party this spring. You don't want to miss it. Daddy doesn't care what we spend on them, so long as I have fun. And I always have fun at my parties," she winked. "Say you'll come. Yes? It just won't be right without you there."

Ecstatic at her first party invitation, Amelia readily agreed. She was immediately ushered into a chair in the middle of the group, and included in the conversation. Harrison attended the brunette next to him, who blushed and stepped closer. A stab of jealousy filled Amelia. She turned away, focusing on Georgia as she talked about the last party she'd attended.

～ ～ ～

As the carriage pulled away, Angie tilted her parasol over her shoulder and savored the peace of the park, even as she started looking for her niece. No redhead was in view, so she continued her stroll. She greeted those she knew and waved at a few people who were too far away for easy conversation. Edith stood several feet up the path talking with Mrs. Detrid.

As Angie moved toward her, she heard Amelia's voice. Scanning the groups nearby, Angie frowned when she saw what group Amelia was part of. She waved to get Amelia's attention. The girl smiled and waved back.

Motioning toward Edith, Angie waited for Amelia to join her. When Amelia only nodded, Angie turned and sighed, feeling suddenly tired. As Angie drew closer to Edith, she reflected how a person didn't really *talk* with the flamboyant Mrs. Detrid, but merely listened and waited until the women left in a rush. She caught Edith's eye as she came to her friend's rescue.

"I just saw Mr. Detrid down the path talking with Mr. Whitmore," she said. "I was surprised…I didn't think you were on speaking terms with that family."

"Oh, that man!" Mrs. Detrid frowned. "He refuses to avoid them. I must go and intervene. Farewell!" As she scurried away, the scent of her perfume caused Angie's eyes to water. Waving at the smell with her fan, Angie looked at her friend and chuckled. "I thought that would do it. How are you, Edith?"

"Thankful that you came along when you did," Edith said. "She wasn't about to let me loose before telling me all about her new damask curtains. Anyway, I'm doing well, enjoying this wonderful weather! How are you? Where is Amelia? You haven't left her home on a day such as this, have you?"

"No, she fell in with some friends," Angie said. Her tone left no doubt as to how she felt about Amelia's new friends. "I'm doing fine, although tired. I'm hoping the fresh air and sunshine will revive me."

"It's not often that you mention being tired," Edith said.

Swallowing a measure of guilt, Angie shook her head.

"I haven't been sleeping well since the anniversary of Miles' passing." Tears began to fill her eyes.

Edith slipped her hand through Angie's arm, and the two started up the path. "I was praying for you that day," she said. "I'm sorry I couldn't come visit. I'd intended to, but things kept happening."

"It's quite all right. I appreciate the prayers, and the intent. It helped having Amelia here this year." She couldn't resist turning to check on Amelia again. The James boy was standing rather close to her niece. A knot of unease settled in her stomach. She sighed as she turned away. "I don't like it, Edith. They are hungry wolves, and she's the sheep."

"Oh, Angie. That's a bit harsh, isn't it? I know young Georgia is used to getting her own way, and the James boy is just as bad as she is, but it's not like they are going to *eat* Amelia."

"Not literally, of course," Angie said. "Amelia has been getting starry-eyed with society. I'm afraid that those two, especially, will turn her head even more." Angie spoke with a mother's love and concern. "She'll get swallowed up in the glittering world they live in. Then she will turn around one day and wonder where her life went."

Edith tsked under her breath and squeezed her arm against Angie's. "That temptation is there for every young woman these days. We'll pray she's able to keep her eyes on what's important, and not get turned by the shallow things the world offers."

They claimed a nearby bench and admired the view. Angie was glad that just down the sloping hill, she could see the group Amelia was in.

"I was surprised not to see you at the fundraiser the other night," Edith mentioned.

"Amelia and I decided to stay home," Angie explained, skirting the truth. "We were both worn out from the day. I trust the fundraiser was a success?" Feeling a little uncomfortable with the tiny lie, she turned the direction of the conversation. This had been the only reason she was nervous about meeting Edith today. She knew her friend would ask about her absence at one of their favorite events. The diversion worked, but as Edith talked about what would happen with the raised funds, Angie told herself sternly that she was going to have to tell Edith soon.

⌒‿‿◞

"I have some news for you," Angie said as she met Amelia on the pathway near the carriage.

"I have news too!" Amelia beamed. "Miss Fossit invited me to a party. Can you believe it?"

"Well…that is exciting," Angie said, worried about this development. "You've got an appointment with Mr. Fletcher to start a job at the *Oregonian*."

"What?" Amelia squealed. Angie smiled, pleased by her niece's reaction. They climbed into the carriage, then Henry started them home.

"You'll have to work hard, but you'll be on the right track for it. Mr. Fletcher said you'll work with one of his journalists."

"When do I meet with him?"

"Next Monday."

Amelia's face fell. "Next Monday?"

"What's wrong?"

"That's the day of Miss Fossit's party."

"Oh…well…we'll have to send her your regrets," Angie said. "I'm sure she'll invite you to another party."

"I suppose," Amelia said. "But what if she doesn't? She's very particular about who she invites to her parties. The fact that she asked me to one is…I don't think I can miss it. I couldn't, not now that I've accepted."

As Amelia listed all the reasons for attending a frivolous party, Angie struggled to maintain her composure. The girl was young and enamored with society. She hadn't seen how it treated those among its inner circles. Ironically, Angie knew that Diane would be proud of Amelia lately. Her sister had always wanted to be one of the elite, but life hadn't turned out that way for her. To have her daughter in high society would make her proud for the first time in Amelia's life. However, this didn't lessen Angie's own disappointment or her frustration.

"Miss Fossit is the sort of person who seeks to put others down so she can feel superior," Angie began, doing her best to remain calm. "She doesn't care about others, except in the sense of manipulating them to get what she wants. Society is full of people like her, Amelia…eager to bring you near, and just as eager to watch you fall."

"She's not like that!" Amelia burst out. "She likes me. She said that it wouldn't be right if I'm not there." She took a breath. "You don't understand, Aunt Angie. I've wanted to be a part of high society for so long!"

"No, you haven't," Angie said, speaking sharply now. "Don't forget, I've been a part of high society for many years. I know firsthand how people take advantage of you. It's not all glamour and prestige."

"Stop!" Amelia's eyes were closed, as if trying to block out the harsh words. "You're wrong! She's my friend. They're all my friends. You don't understand."

Chapter Five

Angie sighed as she watched Amelia leave for the party. *That girl's stubbornness matches her mother's.* She'd hoped that Amelia would change her mind, and they could go to the *Oregonian*. Instead, she'd chosen to attend the garden party where Miss Fossit would manipulate and control her. Angie wondered what she was going to do if her niece continued down this path. She sighed again, then shifted her focus to her monthly meeting with Ms. Dean.

"The new undercook is slow to start in the mornings," Ms. Dean said with a grimace. "And she's had to be woken a few times this past week."

Angie nodded, making notes in her household notebook. "It's always hard on the girls who are new to service. We both know that."

"I do, ma'am, but it's been a month now."

"That's not so long to accustom oneself to a new situation."

Ms. Dean pursed her lips but moved to the next topic. "These are the items that will need to be ordered soon. Some will have to come from Boston if you want something of quality."

Angie accepted the neatly written list. "Our serving platters are still serviceable, but other than that, it looks satisfactory." She handed the list back. "Are there any staff concerns we need to address?" She wondered at the uncharacteristic hesitation of her housekeeper. "What's happened?"

"There is one matter that is of utmost concern to me, ma'am. It seems Grace has formed an attachment to Miss Amelia. I'm aware that this is often the case for upstairs maids, but it worries me. I've spoken with her, but I think it would be best to move her back to downstairs duties and replace her with Susan. She's a quiet, efficient girl, who's been trained as an upstairs maid. She'd do well for the young mistress."

Angie slowly nodded. "I admit that I anticipated your concern. But I don't share it. Grace is a positive and calming influence on Amelia, and I'm pleased that they are becoming friends."

"Forgive me, ma'am. But they are from different worlds."

Angie held up a hand to stall the argument. "I know how you feel on the distinction between staff and employers. And I've always given you free rein in that regard. But in this case, I must override you. I want Grace to remain as Amelia's personal maid so long as the situation pleases them both." She spoke kindly but firmly. "Grace is an exceptional girl, and I'd love to see her fulfill her desire to be out of service."

Ms. Dean nodded stiffly, closed her notebook, and left. Angie sighed. Sometimes, Ms. Dean's East Coast training made things difficult.

⁓ ⌣ ⌣ ⌐

Amelia climbed the sloped steps to the Fossits' back garden, determined to let excitement prevail over her scattered nerves. This party could launch her into the circles that she desperately wanted to be a part of. And the girl who could help her get there was surrounded by a flock of admirers, preening at the attention.

"Good afternoon, Miss Fossit," Amelia greeted. The older girl's beauty suddenly made her feel dowdy, as if her dress wasn't at the height of fashion.

Georgia glanced at her. "I need you to entertain Mr. Sarden," she said. "He's over there, next to the drink table." Georgia waved a ringed hand toward a gangly young man with unfashionably long hair and a suit that didn't fit right. "I've told him to wait there for you."

"But we've not been introduced!" Amelia protested. She couldn't believe what Georgia was asking. To introduce herself to a young man? To anyone? Mrs. Hartly had been quite strict when she'd instructed her on 'imposing oneself.'

Amelia forced herself in the direction of the drink station, toward the young man who was nervously tugging at his collar.

As she wove through the milling crowd, she glanced around, wondering how to escape this situation. To her relief, Harrison was stepping around a loud young woman who was waving her glass wildly about. He smiled when he saw Amelia. "Quite the party already, isn't it?" he exclaimed. "How come you don't have a drink?"

"I've just arrived."

"Well, you're already behind! You must catch up!" He handed her a fluted glass and exchanged his own for a fresh one. "Drink up."

Amelia sipped at the pale pink beverage. It was too sweet, but she took a second sip anyway, earning a smile from Harrison.

"It's good," she said.

"Of course it is," he proclaimed. "Only the best around here. Now, let's romp a bit, shall we?" Harrison took her arm and smiled expectantly.

Amelia glanced at Mr. Sarden, still waiting for her. His curly hair kept flopping over his forehead, despite his attempts to brush it back. She quickly turned back to Harrison. "Yes, let's!"

They wandered the grounds before Harrison led her to his friends congregated under a large, open-sided tent. Couches, chairs, and a myriad of tables sat upon a large rug. "This giant is Mr. Carl. Next is Mr. Halper, Mr. Green, Mr. Peal, Mr. Tenkington, and Mr. Douvre," he said, waving a hand toward each. The young men nodded as Harrison introduced them, their gazes a variation of amused, reserved, or outright bold.

"Well, Harrison, who exactly is this delightful young thing?" Mr. Peal asked. He was tall, although nothing compared to Mr. Carl, whom Harrison had called 'a giant.' Still, Mr. Peal's long frame dwarfed the chair he sat in.

"This is Miss Amelia Hughes," Harrison said. "She's Mrs. Barrington's niece."

Three of the young men sat up at that news. One even straightened an errant collar. Their smiles brightened, until Harrison added quietly, "She's off limits, boys."

"But…" Mr. Peal protested.

"And how do you find our city, Miss Hughes?" Mr. Carl asked, shooting a glare at his friend.

"I like it very much," Amelia said. "It's quite different from home, but it suits me, I think."

"I think it does too," Harrison agreed.

Amelia found it hard to breathe when he kept his gaze on her. She smiled, wishing she had the courage to slip her arm back through his.

Georgia Fossit appeared serene, but was inwardly seething. She'd planned everything meticulously, especially looking forward to spending the day with Harrison. However, he'd sauntered away without a word, leaving her frustrated. When he wanted to, that man could charm the birds out of trees. He could also be equally exasperating.

To keep the newcomer Amelia Hughes out of her way, Georgia had brilliantly planned for Eric Sarden to escort her. Sarden's father was the chief financial officer at the bank, and she was forced to invite the son. Now Georgia was irritated that this plan had gone awry. Amelia wasn't with Eric. Instead, she'd gathered quite the crowd of admirers, Harrison among them.

Georgia didn't see Amelia Hughes as a threat in any way, and knew Harrison wasn't serious about anyone. Still, she was not going to be ousted by some upstart from the country. She strolled around a group of guests and choked on her drink when she saw Harrison standing far too close to Amelia. *I must do something.* Harrison was hers, after all. How dare *that girl* come between them. Harrison was the richest young man in the area, with the smile and *joie de vivre* to go with it. She clenched her jaw, plotting how to salvage the situation before others saw the two of them like that.

Georgia set her empty glass aside and fingered the handle of her parasol, watching Harrison guide Amelia through the crowds. She could tell he was at his most charming, complete with his smile cast downward, and his hand at Amelia's back. Continuing her stroll, Georgia smiled at anyone she passed, edging closer to her target. As she walked, she admitted to herself that she just might have to befriend the girl. By the time she was close enough to see the adoration on Amelia's face, and the glint in Harrison's eye, she knew what to do. She accepted a new drink and started to move past them. At the last second she spilled the lemonade on Amelia's dress.

"Oh no!" she exclaimed. "You'll want to get that washed off immediately." Before Amelia could respond, Georgia shooed her in the direction of the house.

Harrison's deep chuckle caused her to turn around. "Very subtle, Georgia," he said. "She never knew what hit her."

"You looked positively tortured with such a country girl," she said with a smile. "Come, let's mingle." She was more than pleased when he laughed and offered her his arm. "Just remember, I don't jump at your bidding, Georgia. I jump only when I jolly well want to."

She ignored his warning, thinking how easily he'd transferred his attention to her, and changed the subject.

～～～

Amelia wiped off the worst of the spill, then headed back outside, thankful that the pattern of her dress mostly hid the stain. She sighed, hoping Harrison wasn't upset with her for leaving so abruptly, or Georgia for that matter.

The day had gotten warm, and Amelia was grateful for her straw hat's large brim. She headed for the drink station, hoping for something different than what Harrison had given her. The sweet taste still lingered in her mouth. As the server offered options, Amelia settled on a strawberry lemonade.

"Miss Hughes?"

"Yes?" Amelia turned with a smile.

"I'm Eric Sarden. Miss Fossit said you'd introduce me to your friends. I've not been to these types of parties much. I've been waiting for you." His eyes were large for his thin face.

"Yes, Mr. Sarden, I've been looking for you." The lie came easily, as she wasn't about to admit that she'd been avoiding him all day.

Amelia accepted her drink and waited. Her companion stood by her side, turning his empty glass around in his hands. Finally, Amelia suggested they walk through the maze. Sarden hurriedly agreed and started off without her. Nonplussed, she stared. She hadn't realized just how accustomed she'd become to the nicety of a gentleman escorting her. She wasn't going to go wandering after him, though. She waited, then simply snapped her parasol open when he appeared at her side.

"I'm ever so sorry, Miss Hughes. I completely forgot myself. And then I couldn't find my way back. I kept getting turned around, you see." His too-high voice grated on her nerves.

"How do you ever hope to make it through a maze if you can't find your way in an open lawn?" she asked.

He grinned, showing a slight gap between his front teeth. "I'll just have to trust myself to your guidance. And if all else fails, we can trail after another group. Never fear, we'll make it out again." He offered his arm, motioning with his other toward the maze. She accepted, but wondered how any man could be comfortable trailing after strangers in order to get where he needed to go.

She vaguely listened as he explained his life-long difficulty with navigation. "It gets worse when I start thinking about something I've read in a theology book," he added, laughing at himself. How could she be stuck with someone like this? She'd hoped to spend the day with Harrison.

After several minutes of turning toward one dead end after another, they stopped at an intersection. "We do seem to be lost," Mr. Sarden complained. He put his hands on his hips, jutting his jacket out at odd angles. Amelia held in a huff as she turned around.

"Let's see if anyone else is nearby."

"Capital idea," he grinned, hurrying to follow her. Hearing voices around the next turn, Amelia slowed to let the poor young man catch up to her. She may not be fond of him, but she didn't want it to look like she was running away. The laughter grew louder as they turned the corner. She smiled at Mr. Carl and a few other young men she'd met earlier.

"Miss Hughes!" the dark-haired youth said, his eyes darting toward Mr. Sarden.

"We seem to have gotten lost," Amelia said. "Can we join you?"

"Of course! We've got Harper with us. He's done this maze dozens of times. We'll be out quick as a wink, just you watch." Amelia sighed and stepped further away from Mr. Sarden.

⌁⌁⌁

"Come join us!" a girl called out, then dashed over and claimed Amelia's arm, tugging her toward a large tent. Amelia tried to remember her name, but she'd lost it amidst all the people she'd met during the day. She caught Mr. Sarden's eye and motioned to the tent. Ignoring his frown, she turned back around and picked up her pace. Perhaps Harrison would be in the group. Seeing him, her breath caught in her throat. The girl who held her arm followed Amelia's gaze and giggled loudly. "Isn't he just the handsomest?" she gushed. "I've been half in love with him forever. He barely knows I'm alive though. How'd you get him to notice you?"

Amelia shrugged. "We met soon after I moved here. He's always been the perfect gentleman."

"Oh, he's got the most polished moves around," she said, then abruptly turned her attention elsewhere. "George!" she called out, then left Amelia without another word, rushing off to latch onto the arm of a boy.

"Are you sure you want to be with this group, Miss Hughes?" Mr. Sarden asked, suddenly at her elbow. "I've heard they're not the most welcoming, and besides…"

"Miss Hughes!" Harrison beckoned. Feeling smug, she quirked an eyebrow in Mr. Sarden's direction and walked away.

Immediately, the conversation between Harrison and his friends swept her in. People moved in and out of the group, wandering their way through the open-sided tent. After a time, Amelia's excitement began to falter. Harrison was deep in conversation with Georgia, a drink in his hand, his cheeks flushed.

Still, she enjoyed watching him, he was that handsome. *Would it be terribly bold to join them?* Just as she was about to, one of Harrison's friends, another person whose name she'd already forgotten, stepped next to her.

"You look like you're having fun," the young man smiled.

"Georgia throws the best parties," she said, wanting to sound like she'd attended several. "I can't remember your name though."

"I'm Peter Peal," he said, then sidled even closer to her, his eyes roving her face. "You are a pretty one."

She took a step away from him. "I think I'll get another drink."

"Don't be shy." He grasped her arm. "I know a spot where no one will bother us. What do you say?" He rubbed her cheek with his thumb.

"Get away from me!" Her demand emerged as a loud whisper. Her shock at his suggestion made her throat tighten and her heart pound wildly in her ears. If only she hadn't been so eager to join this group. She leaned stiffly away from him as he kept hold of her arm.

"Don't be such a snob," he frowned. "I know the girls Harrison likes. They aren't stingy with their favors." He put an arm around her, drawing her shoulder against his chest. "I'll give you a better time than he ever could."

Her cheeks burned and she wished he'd let her go. "This isn't proper! Let go of me!"

～⌣⌣◠

Harrison laughed at Georgia's story and drained his glass. Looking around for a fresh drink, he smirked when he saw Peal working his charm on some girl. Once he caught sight of her red hair, his humor faded. He handed his glass to the nearest person and headed straight for the lout. *How dare he touch Amelia!* Anger flared when he saw the look on her face.

"Peal!" Harrison growled as he grabbed the young man's shoulder.

Peal yelled, turning abruptly to see who was assaulting him. "What are you doing?" he glowered.

Harrison shoved him backward. Peal pushed Harrison's hands away and smoothed his jacket.

"We're just having a little fun," Peal said. "What's your problem?"

"Didn't I tell you she was off limits?" he snarled, resisting the urge to punch his smirking face.

"How do you know she wasn't liking it?" Peal taunted. Harrison clenched his jaw and glared at him.

"Stay away from her, Peal." He didn't move until uncertainty shone in his friend's eyes. Then he turned to check on Amelia. She hadn't moved, but her eyes were wide. "Are you all right?"

"I'm fine," she whispered. Her gaze darted around the tent. He took her arm and walked her toward the edge of the crowd, aware that everyone was watching.

"I'm sorry. I didn't think he'd...I told them not to. Are you sure you're all right?" He put an arm around her waist. Her hands shook as she clutched her handkerchief, and her cheeks were deeply flushed. As attractive and alluring as Amelia was, how dare Peal push where he wasn't wanted!

"Miss Hughes, shall we go?" a high pitched voice asked. Incredulously, Harrison watched Eric Sarden step next to Amelia and offer his arm. "I think we've had enough of this group," he added, sending an accusatory glare toward Harrison.

Amelia accepted the too-thin arm. "Thank you, Mr. Sarden," she said. Before she walked away, she turned to Harrison. "Thank you, Harrison. I...uh...very much appreciate your assistance." She was still flushed.

Harrison felt powerless to stop her as she walked away from him. Watching her disappear into the crowd, he finally started back a few steps, still the center of attention. The first thing he saw when he turned around was Georgia's scowl.

Chapter Six

Upon hearing Walter greet Amelia, Angie set her pen down with a frown. She hadn't expected Amelia to be back for several more hours. These types of parties usually lasted until well into the evening. She took a deep breath and debated whether to greet her niece or stay where she was. She wasn't feeling well enough for any kind of conflict. But why was the girl home so early? Perhaps the party hadn't been all she'd expected?

As Angie stood, she steadied herself on the back of the chair, then walked across the room. Before getting to the door, Amelia entered. Angie's heart skipped a beat. Her niece's cheeks were bright red, and her eyes flashed.

"What's wrong?" Worry propelled Angie toward her. "What happened?"

"He ruined everything! Now everyone is going to think I'm a prude and Harrison won't talk to me anymore." She paced the room, pulling out her handkerchief.

"Slow down, Amelia. Come, tell me what happened." Angie sat in the chair nearest her, unwilling to test the strength of her legs.

"That disgusting boy ruined the whole party," Amelia declared. "It was going fine until he...until he..."

Angie worried exactly what this boy had done.

"He expected me to just...oh, Aunt Angie, I felt so disgusting when he implied...but then Harrison was there. He was so mad!" Amelia fell silent. She walked slowly now, twisting her handkerchief around her fingers.

"And then?" Angie asked. It didn't sound like anything more than unwanted attention, but she wasn't sure. She was surprised to hear of Harrison James' intervention. It showed a certain amount of honor.

"Oh, Harrison was sweet…he was worried about me," Amelia gushed. "He apologized."

Susan came in and delivered tea, curtseyed, and left the room. Angie poured out two cups, sweetening hers with sugar, and Amelia's with honey. She stayed silent as Amelia paced the room, and waited until the girl was ready to talk. After a few minutes, Amelia sat down and balanced the cup and saucer easily. Angie allowed a smile, knowing what a struggle that simple act had been for her niece only a few months ago.

"I was with a group of Harrison's friends," Amelia began. "One of them came over to talk to me, but he stood too close." Her eyebrows lowered. The flame on her cheeks was receding. "I wasn't worried until he suggested we go…somewhere…together. When I told him to get away from me, he told me I was a snob. That's when Harrison came over."

"And he did nothing else?" Angie asked.

"Well. He said some other things about favors and…" Amelia shuddered, rubbing her arm. "I'm not sure he would've left me alone if Harrison hadn't intervened."

"He didn't touch you anywhere inappropriate?" Angie asked. Amelia shook her head, and Angie felt the tightness in her chest ease. "Who was it?"

Amelia grimaced. "Peter Peal. I thought he was handsome, so I ignored how close he was at first. But then he made me uncomfortable."

"It sounds like you handled it well," Angie said. "And now you know to avoid this young man."

"I don't know how Harrison is friends with him."

"You said that Harrison was mad at Peter?" Angie asked.

"Yes. I thought he was going to punch him, right there in front of everyone."

"I'm impressed by his unexpected chivalry. I'm glad he intervened."

Amelia smiled. After a moment, Angie asked, "Are you feeling any better?"

"I am," Amelia sighed. "Thank you for listening, Aunt Angie."

"I'm always here to listen, Amelia." An odd feeling overcame her, and she carefully set her cup and saucer down. "I'll be right back."

Angie forced herself to walk calmly to her bedroom. She leaned against the door as soon as she closed it. She felt exhausted, as if all her energy was seeping out, leaving her more drained than she'd ever felt. She closed her eyes, as the unexpected exhaustion overtook her concern for her niece. She wasn't sure what was causing her symptoms, but something wasn't right. So far no one had seen her during one of these episodes. She'd even been able to hide them from Marie, but she worried about what might happen when her luck ran out.

Angie focused on her breathing. She willed her mind to relax, even as she slid all the way to the floor. She was too weak to stand. A quarter of an hour passed while she sat there, immobile and vying for calm. When she started to feel a little stronger, she worked to stand upright. Her knees remained weak, but she was able to make her way to her washstand.

She dipped a cloth into the tepid water to wipe her face, then checked her reflection in the mirror. *Will anyone be able to tell what had just happened?*

Satisfied, she returned to the salon. She felt guilty for leaving Amelia so abruptly, but she'd come to recognize the symptoms that preceded one of these episodes. She shook her head at her own foolish pride.

Pleased to see Amelia engrossed in a book, Angie eased into her favorite chair and leaned her head back. Her strength had mostly returned, but an overwhelming tiredness came upon her. She turned her thoughts back to what had happened at the party, and decided that some blame could be laid at the Fossit girl's feet. She'd been pampered so much that she behaved like the princess of the city. She'd only gotten worse as she'd reached her teenage years, and the boys began flocking around her. Angie shook her head at the way that girl's social life had been managed… mismanaged, as it were. She was determined to do better than that for Amelia, if only her niece would recognize the maneuverings that high society played, even out here in the West.

It was quite late that night when Angie peeked into Amelia's bedroom. It seemed Amelia had been able to do what Angie hadn't—fall into a sound asleep. Walking to the side of the bed, she lightly touched the blanket, and began to pray quietly.

"You know I've come to love her as a daughter. Thank You for protecting her today, even if it was the James boy who intervened. Help her see the selfishness that pervades high society. Bring her new friends and guide her down the

path she should take in life. I'm worried about her friendship with Georgia Fossit. That girl is shallow through and
through. Forgive me for speaking of one of Your children like
that. Only You know Georgia's heart."

Angie paused, taking the time to get her breath back,
which seemed to take longer than normal these days. "I
place Amelia in Your hands," she continued. "For You love
her far more than I do, and You know what's best for her.
Guide me as I help her through these days. Amen." A sense
of peace filled her as she finished. She kissed her niece's
forehead before leaving the room. Perhaps now she'd be
able to sleep too.

In the morning, Angie sat opposite Amelia in the library,
picking up a book of poetry. "What did you find to read?"
she asked.

"*Lorna Doone*," Amelia replied.

"That was one of Miles' favorites," Angie said. She noted
that Amelia looked calmer than yesterday, but there was still
something different in her expression.

"It docs look more worn than the others," Amelia
remarked.

Angie eyed the leather-bound book. "That particular
shelf was where he kept his favorites," she said. "He liked
being able to pick one at random and know that he'd enjoy
the story from beginning to end." Her tone grew wistful as
she remembered many evenings in this room, Miles reading
in the chair where Amelia now sat, glasses perched on the
end of his nose.

"Do you want me to put it back?" Amelia asked softly.

Angie shook herself out of the memory. "No. He would've liked sharing them with you." She'd just opened her book when a letter came. Unfamiliar with the handwriting, Angie opened it, glancing at Amelia before reading it.

Mrs. Barrington,

Please forgive my presumption in writing to you. I want to apologize for not being able to protect Miss Hughes better. I'm terribly scatter-brained, and am afraid that this tendency left your niece open to unwanted attentions. I regret not insisting that we find better companions. I understand that she'll not want to see me again, but I'll always think fondly of her.

Sincerely,
Eric Sarden

Compassion for the boy filled Angie, and she moved to the desk to write a reply. She agreed with him that Amelia would have no wish to see him again, but was impressed by his eloquent letter and apology. Assuring Mr. Sarden that the only one to blame was Peter Peal, and that she would be forever grateful to Mr. Sarden for the assistance he gave to her niece, she sealed it. *I hope that's the last of this incident.* Eyeing her niece, who was engrossed in a story, Angie wondered how much of an impact this situation would have on Amelia. Would the girl have to see Peal regularly?

Swallowing her worry, she stood to move back to her chair, but a sudden onslaught of fear made her breath catch. Her body was weakening. She walked carefully to the door, wanting to run so Amelia wouldn't see her like this, while feeling the urge to crawl. How had her body become so frail?

She made it a few steps before she had to lean against the wall. She prayed fervently for strength, but when her knees weakened, she slid to the floor. The sounds of the house faded as her breathing grew shallow. *Please.* She willed her mind and body to relax. As minutes passed by, she remained immobile.

"Ma'am?" Walter inquired softly. "Are you all right?"

She opened her eyes, wanting to tell him she was fine. But, since she was sitting on the floor, hugging her knees, she doubted he would believe her. Finally, she mustered the strength to nod. "I will be," she offered.

"You're not so young that sitting on the floor is common, ma'am," Walter said. "Neither are you old enough to be falling and breaking your hip." He sat down in the middle of the hallway, his long legs crossing awkwardly. "That means something is wrong."

"Walter, you don't have to sit with me," Angie said. "I'm fine."

His white bushy eyebrows rose at her words. Angie smiled apologetically at him. "Mrs. Barrington, if you don't mind, I'd like to be quite open with you?" She nodded. He continued. "I've noticed some things over these past months. At first, I thought they were to do with Miss Amelia joining the household, but then I remembered that I saw some of these things before she came. And they've increased, even though she has settled." Angie stared at the tops of her knees. She'd never thought Walter might notice.

"I've not said anything because it's not my place to, ma'am," he spoke quietly. "But there's something the matter with your health. And if you've not seen a doctor yet, you'd best do so. You're much too young to be feeling the way you have been."

Her eyes filled with tears. "I don't know what to say, Walter."

"There's no need to say anything, ma'am. If I may be so bold as to add that we care about you, and want to see you healthy."

She nodded and reached out a hand. She waited while he debated whether to take it. When he did, she held on tightly. "You've been a dear friend, Walter. I hope you know that."

"And I will be for many years to come. Are you able to stand now? I hear Miss Amelia moving about in the library."

She started to tell him of her suspicions, but he'd already risen and moved to assist her. She sighed in relief that her knees were a bit stronger. He walked her to a couch in the salon. Before he could leave the room, she called to him. "Walter. Could you…not mention this to anyone?"

He turned back and looked at her a moment before answering. "I'm the soul of propriety, ma'am."

The following weeks were quiet. Angie and Amelia spent as much time together as they could. Neither felt much inclination to be out and about, although they did attend the events they'd already agreed to. Mostly, they spent their days at home, reading their favorite authors and taking tea in the garden beneath a large tent the maids set up. The calm was just what they both needed. Then a letter from her sister spoiled things for Angie.

She tapped the folded the pages against her knee. Her sister had always possessed a talent for causing upheaval. Angie eyed Amelia, who was engrossed in *Pride and Prejudice*. She supposed she should tell her. Sadly, she knew the sooner she replied, the sooner Diane would insist on coming.

Forgive me for my uncharitable thoughts, but I can't imagine having Diane here. She'll undo all the improvements I've started to see in Amelia. And she will notice that I'm not feeling well. Angie shivered. Diane would inevitably pick on her about her weakness…and she would know just how to make her words cut as deeply as possible.

Diane is Your child as well, Angie continued, *but she is such a trial.* It wasn't a particularly reverent prayer, Angie realized, but she knew God wanted her to be honest with Him. Her feelings toward her sister had been a topic between the two of them for many years now.

"Amelia?" she called aloud. Her niece stirred but didn't respond, she was that wrapped up in the novel. Angie waited until Amelia turned the page and tried again. This time, Amelia looked up at her, eyebrows raised. "I have something to tell you," Angie said. She was pleased to see her niece put her book down. Her manners had really improved these past months. "How would you like to have a debut for your sixteenth birthday? There will be dancing and dinner…and a new party dress. What do you think?"

"You really want to do that for me?" Amelia's eyes shone. Angie nodded, then tapped the letter on her lap. "Your mother suggested it." *That's a generous way to put it isn't it?* "If you like the idea, we can go all out, whatever you want." She was amused when Amelia bounced out of her chair and hugged Angie's neck instead of answering.

They sent a maid to bring fresh tea and Angie's writing box so she could start making notes on what they needed to do. Angie let her niece ask questions about debuts until the tea arrived. "Planning will be rather rushed, if we hold it in July," Angie said, "but it will be a wonderful opportunity for you to learn the necessary skills on how to be a good hostess. While I don't want you getting lost in the glamour of high society, it would be good for you to learn."

Angie paused and sipped her tea. "In this society, Amelia, being a good hostess is imperative. You must know how to throw a party for any occasion and how to deal with the problems that will arise, from planning the party, to handling a rude guest during it. Strangely enough, it will open doors for you. You have a way with people, and we can cultivate that ability. But only if you are willing to learn."

"I'm willing, Aunt Angie! I'm so excited!"

Angie smiled. "I'm glad to hear it. You won't always enjoy the process, because it can get tedious, but if you work hard, you will learn and do well."

～ు ⌐

The days that followed became a whirlwind for Amelia. Not only was she planning her own debut for the beginning of July, but she also attended several others. Her status as Angie Barrington's niece meant that she received every party invitation of the season, but she only went to the ones that her aunt and she agreed on together.

While each event was thrilling, Amelia paid special attention to the details. That helped her decide what she wanted at her party. For example, she learned that she *did not* want to serve fish, like the Carl family had at their youngest daughter's party. Conversely, seeing how the outside lighting created an enchanting feel at the Spurlins' place, she decided she wanted to do the same at her party.

True to her aunt's word, Amelia discovered that much of the planning was tedious. Still, during the entire day of Mrs. Bobbin's visit, as they planned her party dress, Amelia was walking on clouds. She also enjoyed marking every invitation acceptance that came in from her long guest list. And sometimes, it was just as satisfying to mark that someone *wasn't* coming. Overall, most people planned to attend, and Amelia started to get nervous at the numbers. What would it be like to have all of these people looking at her?

Her debut was a week away when her dress arrived. Amelia breathed out a sigh of pure happiness as she pulled it from its wrappings. It was pale blue crepe arranged over matching silk. The short sleeves were covered with pleated gauze pulled up with bows of ribbon. Bands of dark pink ribbon ran around the waist and to the hem with bows and tufts of flowers.

"Try it on, Amelia," Angie insisted. "We need to make sure it fits properly."

Amelia laughed and moved behind the screen to change. They'd had two fittings before now, and she couldn't imagine it not fitting perfectly this time. She slipped the sleeves over her shoulders and waited while Grace laced up the back.

"Oh, it's lovely, it is," Grace whispered.

"You'll have to try it on tonight! It'll look wonderful on you too!"

"Oh I couldn't…"

"You will too!" Amelia argued. Once Grace finished, Amelia walked to the center of her room, unable to resist a small twirl.

"That is lovely on you, Amelia." Her aunt's compliment made her flush.

"Thank you," she breathed. "I don't want to take it off, yet I'd hate for something to happen to it!"

Her aunt smiled at her, understanding. "Let's head to the park for the afternoon, what do you say?"

"That's a great idea!" It didn't take long for Amelia to change back into her day dress, which suddenly seemed far less beautiful than it had when she'd put it on this morning. Their carriage was waiting for them as they left the house, Henry ready to assist.

"The sunlight feels wonderful, doesn't it," Aunt Angie commented, turning her face to the sun. Amelia agreed but couldn't stop thinking about her new dress or the upcoming party. Music floated from an open window of one of the houses. "Are there any new plays out, Aunt Angie?"

"You miss it already, do you?" Aunt Angie chuckled. "They're rehearsing a new one, so it should be out come summer."

"It's just so thrilling," Amelia said. She played with the ribbons on the end of her parasol handle.

"It is indeed," Aunt Angie agreed. "It's always been one of my greatest enjoyments here in the city." Her voice softened. "Your uncle always took me on opening night."

"You loved him very much, didn't you?" Amelia asked.

"Oh, yes. He was such a wonderful man. He brought the best out in everybody."

When Angie fell silent, Amelia worried that she'd upset her. But soon her aunt was talking about a book that was coming out next month. Amelia sighed in relief and relaxed. Everything was just fine.

Ladies and gentlemen strolled along the rose-lined paths, while children ran about playing. Those in carriages drove slowly, often stopping to indulge in gossip. The park was never loud or raucous, even with crowds. In all, it was an idyllic place to spend a few hours. Today, though, the calm was deceptive. Gasps of delight could be heard, and then the rustle of skirts marked the passage of news moving from person to person. The coming-out party for the niece of Angela Barrington had become the thing to talk about.

Rumors about Amelia had started flying as soon as she and Angie had been seen about town together. The stories ranged from outrageous to scandalous. Some claimed that she had been orphaned, and that Angie had taken her in to raise as her own. Others said emphatically that she was Angie's secret daughter, not her niece. Angie paid them little mind, knowing how the gossips could be. *Oh, how their tongues will fly once they find out about my illness.* She shuddered. Her personal hell would be dissected by these pitiless women. She'd once been one of them, and she knew exactly how it would go. It had been a teaching of Pastor Grey, several years ago, that made her realize the futility of trying to live in the make-believe world of those around her—a desire she hoped Amelia would forgo as well.

A waving handkerchief pulled Angie from her thoughts. She directed Henry to stop the carriage near Edith, and noticed Amelia looked just as pleased to see her friend.

"Hello Edith! Will you join us?" Angie called out. Henry assisted Edith into the carriage, her parasol hanging from one arm.

"I know it's unseemly to not come down to you," Angie said. "I hope you don't mind."

"Not at all," Edith said. She hugged Angie, then settled in next to Amelia. "The ladies are all buzzing like mad today, so it's refreshing to be away from them."

Angie returned Edith's smile. "Drive on, Henry." She wondered if this latest development might be too much for young Amelia to accept without being further drawn into society. They would know in a few days' time, Angie mused.

Overall, the time since Amelia had come to live with Angie had been wonderful. Visiting parts of the city and sightseeing made for wonderful memories. Amelia's delight reminded Angie of when she had first left her small-town existence, and her own wide-eyed wonder. Yes, it was good that Amelia had come, even if it seemed there was still so much to teach her, not to mention so many things to undo that Diane had drummed into her.

"Angie, are you not feeling well?" Edith asked. "I don't think you've heard a word we've said." She leaned forward to touch Angie's arm.

"I'm sorry. I was lost in thought," Angie said, hiding a small lie inside of a truth.

Edith sent a shocked look at Amelia, but her eyes twinkled merrily. "She scandalously invites me into the carriage instead of coming down, and then all but ignores me. I'm not sure if this is to be borne, Amelia."

"Perhaps she was thinking of a scoop of ice cream, Mrs. Grey," Amelia laughed. "It is very distracting." Her voice was full of innocence, but her face betrayed her hopefulness.

"Ah, I couldn't blame her if she was on such a warm day," Edith agreed. "And it has been such a long time since I indulged in it myself. I think we should make her wish come true. What do you say, Amelia? Shall we spirit her away in her own carriage?"

Angie laughed and told the driver to head to the ice cream parlor. Pushing away her fears and doubts, she focused on enjoying this time with her niece and friend.

Chapter Seven

The sun streaming through the lace curtains illuminated a throw draped across a small chair. Amelia stirred at a knock on the door.

"Miss Amelia? Your aunt has called for breakfast in her room." There was a long pause, then, "Miss Amelia?"

"Mmph," she yawned. "Yes, thank you, I will be there shortly." Amelia slowly sat up, muttering about early breakfast times. Stretching, she caught sight of her debut gown and grinned. "It's tonight," she whispered, not wanting to break the spell that the dress had cast. What made the day even better was that her mother had telegrammed yesterday with the news that she'd gotten ill and wouldn't be able to come.

Once prepared for morning, Amelia fairly floated to her aunt's room.

"Well, I can see you're excited for tonight," Aunt Angie said. "But I have news for you. Adelina Parri will be attending."

"The opera singer accepted?"

"She did! I wanted to surprise you," Aunt Angie said.

"I just never dreamed…" Amelia began, shaking her head in wonder. "It will be wonderful to meet her. But didn't you say she doesn't attend parties anymore?"

"She's come to my parties in the past, but I haven't thrown one in quite a while now. Just enjoy the day and don't worry."

Before she knew it, Amelia was running her hands over the smooth bodice of her dress, admiring the way it fit her. No longer was she the skinny awkward girl who had arrived months ago. Tonight, she felt grown up, with her hair arranged by Marie's experienced hands, and a host of people coming in less than an hour. Turning to see the back of the dress, Amelia smiled. This was going to be a wonderful night.

"Amelia? May I come in?" A light tap at the door accompanied the request. At her affirmation, Mrs. Grey slipped into the room. "You look beautiful, my dear. That dress does wonders with your hair. Are you excited?" At Amelia's smile and grimace in quick succession, Mrs. Grey laughed. "Don't worry, you'll be fine. Remember, almost every woman in this room has been in your shoes. They may whisper and twitter behind their fans, but there's compassion among them. Relax and enjoy yourself."

"Thank you, Mrs. Grey. Have you seen Aunt Angie? She looks ethereal in her dress."

"Not yet," Edith said. "I'm on my way to see her next." She smiled mischievously. "I just couldn't wait until the party to see you two. I told Pastor Grey that I was coming early, whether he came with me or not."

With that, she slipped out the door. Amelia realized she already felt less nervous about the rest of the evening thanks to Mrs. Grey's visit. She let Grace finish doing the row of tiny buttons up her back.

"When I was younger, I'd read in the newspaper about the socialites' debuts," Amelia shared. "I would dream of what mine would be like…if I ever had one. I always imagined a sparkling ballroom with an orchestra, guests dripping with jewels. I would be wearing the most spectacular gown.

But before it could be quite perfect, my mother would be there too, telling me not to trip on my dress, or to twist my handkerchief. And then I'd give up the dream because my mother had completely ruined the magic of it. But this is different." She clasped her hands in childlike wonder. "It's even better than what I'd dreamed. Just look at this dress!" She couldn't resist gently pulling the skirt out so it fell perfectly around her again.

"And what's better is that Mrs. Barrington knows you won't fiddle with your handkerchief," Grace said. "And, well, if you trip, you'll give everyone a great show of the underside of this dress. So, mind you don't trip going down those stairs."

"Grace!" Amelia spun around and tried to glare at her maid, who was quickly becoming a dear friend. When their eyes met, they both broke into laughter.

"Feel better now?" Grace asked.

"Yes," Amelia beamed, then impulsively reached out and hugged Grace. "Though I do wish my father was here."

The murmur of guests milling about the hall made Amelia's hands clammy as she eased her bedroom door closed. Her plan to be downstairs before guests arrived was obviously doomed. She moved along slowly, hoping to see her guests before she reached the steps. Her mother would be appalled if she knew Amelia was doing such a thing, but walking into a crowd was too much to bear.

As she gazed over the railing, her eyes widened in amazement. Everyone was dressed in their finest. The women's jewels and rustling skirts stood out against the men's dark suits. Noticing her aunt glance up the stairs, Amelia took a deep breath and pulled her gloves on firmly before walking down. She willed her knees to remain strong, and held her chin level as she felt the thrill of being the center of attention.

She joined her aunt at the receiving line and welcomed each guest. Greeting Georgia and Harrison was the highlight, although she was disappointed that they'd come together. Just as she spotted Eric Sarden and what she assumed was his family, Aunt Angie leaned over to whisper in her ear, "Mr. Sarden is a good young man."

Amelia's voice was higher pitched than normal when she greeted him, but she hoped no one noticed. As he walked away, she decided that he certainly wasn't interesting or handsome. She scanned the room for Harrison, and found him leaning against the wall with a drink already in hand. Amelia was pleased he'd come and hoped he'd ask her to dance. Then another guest arrived, pulling Amelia from her daydreaming.

～ ～ ～

Outside, stepping down from the carriage, Ian Hayworth adjusted his long coat and resolutely made his way to the front door of the Barrington house. He avoided these types of functions, but when the invitation came, there'd been a note from Angela telling him he couldn't wiggle his way out of it. She *expected* him to be there.

His lips twitched into a smile. One thing he could count on was that Angela always knew how to get him to do something. Only twenty years old, he was years her junior, but their friendship was like none he shared with any other woman. With his own mother gone, he considered her a surrogate of sorts.

Walking up to the crowded entryway, he handed his coat to the waiting maid. He spotted Angela at the head of the receiving line, where she stood with a young woman he assumed was her niece. He bypassed the other guests and reached her side quickly, waiting as she greeted another couple. Before the next guest could step up, he touched Angela's elbow to gain her attention.

"Ian, you're here!" she turned to him. Her smile lit up her face.

He bowed over her hand. "As I promised to be," he said. "Quite the turnout."

She laughed, eyeing the line. "And they're all here at once."

Ian glanced at a lady still waiting in line. She was trying to simultaneously glare at him and smile at her hostess. "I'm upsetting your other guests," he said. "I'll talk to you soon, yes?" he asked, though he assumed Angela's hostess duties would keep her busy all evening.

"Of course," she said. "And I expect one dance with you." Her grin told him she knew how he hated to dance, but didn't care.

He bowed over her hand again and stepped back. Before he'd turned toward the ballroom, Angela had transferred her focus to the put-out matron, soothing her with an eager welcome. He was glad that Angela's niece had been talking with another young woman. He wasn't ready for that particular introduction yet, though could not say why. It wasn't like Angela would try to play matchmaker. Or would she?

"Mr. Hayworth?" a woman said. "I'd like to introduce you to my daughter…" He missed the girl's name due to a nearby loud cackling laugh. Rather than prolong the conversation, he smiled and bowed over both ladies' hands. "A pleasure," he said.

"I'm sure you don't remember, but we met at the Spurlin party. You promised my daughter a dance." The woman smiled, then her daughter mirrored the same look. Ian forced a tight smile in reply.

"You must be thinking of someone else, madam," he offered. "I'm sorry your daughter was left without a partner, but as you can see, there are plenty of eligible gentlemen this evening." He waved his hand to hopefully fix their attention on any other man in the room. But it was useless. The mother had her sights on him.

"Mr. Hayworth, please. As if you're not an eligible choice," she tittered, and the daughter echoed the sound. Ian could not stand it when women tittered.

He looked directly at the daughter. "It was a pleasure to meet you," he said, "and I hope you have a pleasant evening." He bowed and left them. As he did, he reached for his pocket watch and rubbed it absentmindedly.

Escaping mothers who were set on capturing a husband for their daughters was something he loathed, which was largely why he avoided parties like this. He wove through the crowd to the refreshment table. Barely ten minutes through the door, he already had disappointed one mother. Angela was going to owe him big time for this.

⌒‿‿⌒

Slipping her shoe off, Amelia carefully wiggled her toes, trying to get feeling back into them. The last dance had been long and painful, as the young man had clearly forgotten that her feet were only for her to walk on, not for him to dance upon. Wincing, she slipped her shoe on and scanned the room for her aunt. Spotting the sprig of flowers in Aunt Angie's hair, Amelia sighed in relief and moved past the last few people between them.

"Amelia, I'm glad you've found me," Aunt Angie said. "Allow me to introduce you to Mrs. James. And of course, you know her son, Harrison."

Bowing to the petite Mrs. James, she almost missed the gleam in Harrison's eye. As they murmured the appropriate greetings to each other, she was drawn in by his gaze.

"Amelia? Are you all right?" Aunt Angie's voice seemed far away.

Dragging her eyes from Harrison's felt nearly impossible. When she did, the rest of the room came into focus again… Mrs. James staring at her oddly…Aunt Angie looking worried…and Harrison smiling broadly.

"Would you care to dance?" he asked, hand outstretched. Hardly daring to breathe, Amelia slipped her hand into his. They walked to the dance floor. She set her hand on his shoulder as he rested his upon the small of her back. Once the music began, he led her through the dance, never stepping on her toes or hesitating.

"It's nice to finally dance with you," he said as he spun them two steps to the right.

"What do you mean?"

"I've been wanting to dance with you since we first met. But I could hardly ask you at the park." He smiled down at her. Being in his arms as he smiled made him more appealing than ever. Amelia blushed.

"Did you not want to dance with me?" he asked playfully. "Am I a terrible dancer, then?"

"Oh no, you're wonderful," she said, "...a wonderful dancer." Her heart pounded as he pulled her closer.

"You're quite wonderful yourself, Amelia."

She couldn't think of anything to say in response. They completed their dance in silence, but she could feel him staring at her whenever she looked away, which she did by sheer force of will. Mrs. Hartly had drilled into her that it was too forward to stare into a man's eyes.

At the end of the song, Harrison led her from the dance floor but paused at the edge of it. "Will you save the quadrille for me?" he asked.

"I beg your pardon?" She'd been so focused on calming her racing heart that she barely heard him. She tried to ease her hand out of his, but he caught it closer to his gray jacket.

"Will you save the quadrille for me?" His voice was low and inviting.

Stepping back quickly, she let out a small laugh. "Oh, of course," she smiled, feeling as if the night could not be more perfect. He kissed her hand before leading her back to her aunt. Feeling silly for the way she'd reacted, she resolved to keep her head the next time she saw him, no matter how his brown eyes drew her.

The ball was filled with gaiety and dancing. Amelia savored every sight and sound, taking joy in knowing that she was the reason for the revelry. She'd joined a group of young elites in talking about dresses, parties, and some of the men. When one of the girls announced that Adelina Parri had arrived, Amelia excused herself and moved toward the ballroom entrance. It would be a huge gaff on her part if she wasn't there to greet such an important guest.

The crowded room made it difficult for her to hurry. She slipped past the mingling groups but misjudged the space between two men. Just as she was about to collide with one of them, someone caught her elbow.

"Watch out!"

The whispered warning barely registered in her ear as she struggled to maintain her balance. Once her feet were under her again, Amelia looked up at her rescuer. Harrison stood close with a grin, his hand still cupping her elbow. "I just saved you from having to grovel for the next month." He guided her a few steps away, nodding back to one of the men. "He forgets nothing. Where are you headed?"

"I need to get to the doors," she said, flushed. "I'll die if I don't get there in time." Her whole arm was tingling from his touch.

He quirked an eyebrow and offered his arm. "We don't want that to happen, do we?" She slipped her hand in his bent elbow and was amazed to see a path open ahead of her as he guided her across the room.

"When in a room like this, the key to getting anywhere is having a gentleman guide you," he said. "No slight intended, Miss Hughes," he added, although she made no move to object. "It's just the truth of society. A woman alone will take the whole of the evening just to reach the other wall, but put her on the arm of a man, and *voilà*! She arrives."

Amelia couldn't help but admire that they reached their destination just as he finished talking. Bowing, he gave her a cocky smile and left just as Aunt Angie greeted Mrs. Parri. Adelina was a sight to behold. Her dress, made of the finest silk and embroidered along the bodice and hem, testified to her wealth. The bright red contrasted with the more commonly chosen colors, including rich hues that served as backdrops for elaborate shawls and jewelry. Amelia wondered if Adelina Parri intentionally wore such colors, so different than the other women.

"I'd like to present to you my niece, Miss Amelia Lynn Hughes," Aunt Angie said. "Amelia, this is Mrs. Adelina Parri. We've been to hear you sing several times. Isn't that right, Amelia?"

Amelia curtsied, praying her knees wouldn't betray her. "It's one of my favorite things about the city."

"Oh, you are a dear, Amelia Lynn," Mrs. Parri exclaimed. "And just like a china doll too. Angela, she could have been your daughter."

Amelia smiled. She'd heard this sentiment often, especially this evening. It was a lovely compliment, but it also triggered the longing that she truly was her aunt's daughter. Not for the fine things around her, but for the fact that only with her aunt did she feel she was loved no matter what she did. *Even if I chose a frivolous party over the newspaper.*

"It does look as if your debut has been a success, Amelia Lynn. I apologize for being late." Adelina's lilting voice lifted above the noise of the crowd.

"I can't believe you came," Amelia blurted, then immediately looked at the floor, cheeks flushing.

Aunt Angie's hand clasped hers. "We're delighted you came, of course. Let me call for some refreshments." Angie motioned to a nearby server.

"I could never miss one of your parties, Angela. You've always known the proper way to entertain." Adelina claimed a tall glass from a tray, scanning the crowd. "How would you like box seats at *Robin Hood*, Amelia?"

Amelia gasped. "I'd like that very much. Thank you, Mrs. Parri."

Adelina nodded, then leaned in. "A determined young man is heading your way. A word of caution, his mother is a schemer, and his father a gambler."

The next moment, a young man spoke. "May I have the next dance, Miss Hughes?"

She offered him her gloved hand and they headed for the ballroom.

⌣⌣⌣

"Adelina, I wish you wouldn't spread gossip to Amelia," Angie admonished.

"It's the truth, isn't it? She needs to be prepared. This society is cutthroat, as you well know."

Angie sighed. "I know, but she's already experienced enough."

"She must learn how to handle herself."

The brisk tone made Angie glance at her friend in concern. "Has something happened?"

A moment passed as Adelina finished her drink and stared at the empty glass. "Life is hard, and you've got to make what you can of it, that's all." Angie waited for her to say more, but Adelina excused herself and disappeared into the crowd. Angie frowned, said a quick prayer for whatever her friend was going through, and mingled with her guests. When she spied Amelia coming off the dance floor with flushed cheeks, Angie met her halfway and took her niece's hand. "Are you all right?"

"He had the nerve to laugh when I told him I want to be a journalist!" She lowered her eyebrows, imitating the young man. "'Women don't write, Miss Hughes. They are meant to be managing a home.' The cheek!"

Angie laughed softly at the impersonation, and was surprised that Amelia admitted her ambitions. "I'm afraid you'll have to get used to it," she said. "That's the feeling around here."

"I know," Amelia sighed and took her arm. "Can we go eat now? I'm starving."

"Yes, splendid idea," Angie agreed. That dreaded weakness was hounding, despite her attempts to ignore it.

⌒﹏﹏⌒

"Have I introduced you to Ian yet, Amelia?" Angie asked as they left the dining room.

"Who?

"Ian Hayworth. You've heard me talk about him. He's around here somewhere." Angie searched the room and found him standing as far back from the crowd as he could. "There he is."

Amelia followed her, even though Angie was sure she would have preferred to join her friends again. Angie wondered if maybe Ian might catch her niece's eye, although she'd never dream of pushing the two of them together.

"Have you come to claim your dance?" Ian asked. "You're going to make everyone here think I'm completely lacking in manners."

"I'm sure they're already convinced of that by the way you've managed to avoid their maneuverings," Angie replied, laughing. "I just ate, so I'll wait a little bit to dance. I've come to introduce you to my niece, Miss Amelia Lynn Hughes. Amelia, this is Mr. Ian Hayworth."

Ian turned from Angela and took her niece's hand. Truth be told, he'd been watching her some through the evening, hoping to get an idea of what type of girl this niece was. So far, he wasn't very impressed, though she did seem to genuinely care for her aunt. "Miss Hughes, it's a pleasure to meet you."

"Mr. Hayworth," Amelia curtsied. "I've heard a lot about you."

"And I you. How do you find our city?" he asked.

"It's beautiful. And there are so many things to do."

"Amelia and I plan to attend *Robin Hood*. Would you care to join us?" Angela asked.

"I would, thank you. I'd already planned on going, but it would be more enjoyable in your company." Realizing he'd left Amelia out, he nodded to her, hoping the gesture would suffice. *Is Angela playing matchmaker?* His shoulders tensed.

"Hearing Mrs. Parri sing again will be divine," Amelia said. "The moment I heard her voice, I realized I'd never heard true talent before. That was the first time Aunt Angie took me to the opera. It was so thrilling. I dreamed of being an opera singer for at least a fortnight after that." Her eyes shone at the memory. "Until I realized how much work it is, anyway." She laughed and smiled at him.

Ian smiled in response, but was saved from answering when a waiter paused with a tray of fluted glasses. Directly on his heels came another waiter with a strained smile. Angela turned as the server reached her elbow, speaking too low for Ian to hear.

Ian and Angela had formed their unlikely friendship two years ago. At first, there had been some scandalizing gossip about them, but it eventually faded. He knew Angela had been lonely before Miss Hughes came along, and that she genuinely enjoyed having her niece living with her. But he readily attributed the underlying strain on Angela's face to the task of having to manage an emotional young woman.

His sympathy for Miss Hughes vanished, and his disdain for people so self-absorbed that they made others suffer began rising to the surface. No matter the reason she'd been sent to live with her aunt, she hadn't any right to cause pain to Angela.

"If you'll excuse me, Ian, I must see to something," Angela said.

"Not at all," Ian said. As he bowed to them both, he noticed the look of relief on Miss Hughes' face. The women went in opposite directions—Angela to solve whatever crisis had arisen, and Miss Hughes to join a group near the doors to the garden, with Miss Fossit holding court in the center. He shook his head. One spoiled girl always reigned each season. From the little he'd heard, Miss Fossit took to the role with a vengeance.

Ian retreated to the corner again to wait to fulfill his promise to dance with Angela. After that, he decided, as another matron led her daughter toward him, he would leave.

Georgia fluttered her fan, observing Harrison watch Amelia draw near their circle. The look in his eyes was enough to make her want to scream at the redhead to leave them alone. But as it was the young upstart's debut, she supposed that wouldn't be proper.

As Amelia joined them, Georgia leaned against Harrison. "I'm dying for a dance," she crooned.

"I do believe that was a subtle hint for me to ask you to dance," Harrison returned.

"There was nothing subtle about it, Harrison," Georgia laughed. She glanced at Amelia as they walked past, pleased to see a frown on the girl's face. If Amelia would simply accept that Harrison was Georgia's, there wouldn't be any problem between the two girls.

"I'm going to venture a guess that you don't care for Miss Hughes," Harrison commented as they swung into the dance. Georgia pretended not to notice that he pulled her closer than proper.

"You're wrong," she said lightly. "I like her. She's sweet and pretty."

"A trifle too pretty for you to be comfortable with, though, isn't she?"

"Do you think she's pretty?" Georgia asked bluntly, keeping a smile in place. "After all, you rescued her from Peter Peal not long ago."

His laughing eyes met hers. "I know better than to answer a question like that." Before she could deny it, he shook his head. "Never fear, Georgia. I won't be getting pulled into anything like a wedding noose anytime soon."

Pleased by his statement, yet also dissatisfied, Georgia focused on how good they must look together. Given enough time, she was sure he would realize how mutually beneficial it would be for them to become a couple. She had far more to offer him than the young redhead.

Ian sighed and straightened his cravat just to have something to do with his hands. Glancing over the crowd, he checked that his pocket watch was properly in his vest pocket, and the chain draped from watch to buttonhole.

The party was at full swing. He was exhausted, but he knew he couldn't leave until his dance with Angela. He couldn't see her from his spot near the wall, and resigned himself to enter the crowd.

He was glad Angela didn't put up with the popular entertainments and activities at her parties. Those types of things tended toward the riotous and even vulgar. All the same, it was a lively group. He passed a circle of gossiping women, hoping they wouldn't spot him. Once he safely skirted them and rounded the corner, he breathed a small sigh of relief. A group of men called out to him. He smiled and joined their circle.

"Not dancing tonight, Hayworth?" Eric Sarden's father asked.

"Actually, I'm just on my way to find Mrs. Barrington," Ian said.

"I tried to court her a few years after her husband died," grumbled an older gentleman named Kilenny. He glared at Ian from under heavy eyebrows. "I was as civil as could be. The woman didn't give me a second of attention."

"We're just friends, sir," Ian replied.

Kilenny harumphed. "I should hope so. You're young enough to be her son."

"Come now, Kilenny," the elder Sarden interrupted. "Mr. Hayworth hasn't done anything to you."

"He just better watch himself with Mrs. Barrington," Kilenny barked.

"Mr. Kilenny, is it?" Ian said. He eyed the older man and kept his voice mild. "My friendship with her is of no concern to you. Besides, I don't see how you have any authority to threaten me."

"I didn't mean it like that," Kilenny protested, his eyes popping. "I beg your pardon," he said, then hustled away, wiping his forehead with a handkerchief.

"Don't mind him," the elder Sarden said. "I'm sure he didn't mean anything by it. He was truly taken with the lady. I think he still holds some affection for her."

Ian frowned. "Very well. Thank you." Ian nodded then looked around. The rest of the group had fallen silent during the exchange. "Well, gentlemen, I'm off to find the aforementioned lady. Good evening."

The men nodded in turn as Ian walked away, still bothered from the encounter. He'd never imagined Angela having an admirer, though it made sense. Finally, he spotted her talking with a few other women. He timed his approach to the end of the song. When she turned to him, he held out a hand.

"Are you ready for our dance?"

"I'd be honored," she said.

He led her to the dance floor. Waiting for the music to begin, he eyed her critically. Yes, she was still beautiful, despite the slight shadows under her eyes.

"Is something the matter?" she asked softly.

"I met an admirer of yours a moment ago." When the music filled the room, they began to move to it. He led her in a simple set of spins and steps.

"An admirer?" she repeated doubtfully.

"Mr. Kilenny?" he said. Angie's cheeks reddened as Ian chuckled. "Forgive me. I didn't mean to embarrass you," he said.

"You most certainly did, Ian. But I do the same to you occasionally. I suppose it's fair."

His grin widened. He didn't question her, even though he dearly wanted to know more of the story. As they circled the room, Angela followed his guidance in an easy and natural way.

"You haven't lost your elegance," she said. "You're still a wonderful dancer."

"Thank you. It's because I so rarely employ it," Ian quipped. They laughed and finished the dance. He started to ask if she wanted to dance again, but hesitated upon seeing her flushed cheeks. "Shall we find a spot to rest?"

She nodded, looking relieved. He tucked her hand in his arm and led her to an unoccupied table in the next room. Ian pulled a chair for her, and signaled to a waiter at the same time. He sat in the seat next to her. "Are you not feeling well?"

She waved her hand in dismissal. "I haven't planned a party like this in ages. I forgot how much work it is." She smiled at him. "What do you think of my Amelia?"

"She seems quite devoted to you," he said.

Angela's face softened. "She is. She's become like a daughter to me."

Ian nodded and couldn't help but search the crowd for the girl. He quickly found her red hair standing out among blondes and brunettes. She was dancing gracefully, a smile on her face as she answered her partner. He watched her, suddenly fascinated. He didn't know how long he sat like that, but when he turned back to Angela, she was smiling at him.

"She's young and enamored with high society right now," Angela said quietly. "But she's already learning that it's not all it seems. She'll mature soon enough."

Ian forced himself not to look back at Amelia. "No offense, Angela, but you're not allowed to play matchmaker. You know how I feel about that."

"I was just…no, I won't say that," Angela said. "I couldn't help myself, Ian. You didn't see your face just now when you were watching her. But let me promise you something." She paused as he waited. "I will never play matchmaker between the two of you."

Sincerity shone in her eyes. Ian nodded. "Thank you, Angela. If she turns out to be half the wonderful woman her aunt is, I don't know how any man will be able to resist her."

Angela's cheeks turned a lovely shade of red. Ian smiled. Just because she was like a mother to him didn't mean she didn't occasionally need a compliment. While she exchanged glasses with a passing waiter, he chanced a glance back at Amelia. She was no longer dancing, but was on the arm of Harrison James, a ridiculous grin on her face. A passing dart stabbed at him and he frowned. There was no way he was jealous, not of that young dandy, nor of the young girl on his arm. Sighing, he decided that he'd best bow out of the party as gracefully as he could, before he made a fool of himself.

He bid Angela good night and moved through the crowd, disturbed. He couldn't have been turned by the sight of a pretty girl, could he? She was a flirt and clearly caught up in high society…just the type of girl he'd avoided for all these years. No, Amelia Hughes would never be anything more to him than the niece of his dear friend.

Two hours later, Angie sat down, trying to mask her weariness. The debut had gone splendidly, aside from the normal crises along the way. Tonight had reminded her why she hadn't thrown such a gathering in years. After losing Miles, she didn't enjoy them as she used to, though she was glad she had done so for Amelia's sake. The girl had enjoyed it immensely.

Only a handful of guests remained, and Angie could see the staff starting to discreetly clean. A loud burst of laughter turned her attention to the small group still stationed near the garden doors. Georgia Fossit was leaning against Harrison James, but her other hand was stretched out to lightly touch another young man's arm. Other than Amelia, only one other young woman remained. Neither looked pleased about Georgia Fossit monopolizing both men.

Angie's mood sank as she watched. She hoped that soon, Amelia would understand what type of people these were—wolves in sheep's clothing, just as the Bible said. Not wanting to dispel her good mood, she focused on the success of the night. She'd done something for her niece that Amelia would remember for the rest of her life. For tonight, that was enough.

Amelia,

I hope the two of you had a wonderful time at your debut, which I suggested. I hope you did not do anything too embarrassing, though that seems like a high hope for a clumsy, uncaring girl like you.

I look forward to hearing all about the debut, and if any young men have asked to call on you yet. Amelia, don't you dare refuse an eligible man. Keep your hands folded, your mouth closed, and sit up straight. Let him do the talking. Heaven knows that if you start running your mouth about writing for a paper, he'll run for the nearest exit. I expect to get a letter from you soon, young lady.

Diane

Chapter Eight

The next morning, Amelia closed her book, restless from keeping vigil near her aunt. She was getting concerned about Angie, who had gotten such a bad headache at breakfast that she needed assistance to her bedroom. She'd been sleeping ever since.

Amelia sighed and decided to respond to the invitation for the James' gala, then to start writing thank-you notes. She had to word each note differently so as not to offend anyone. When she couldn't focus any longer, she leaned back and looked at her two piles. One was on the floor in crumples, full of ink blotches and misspelled names. The other sat on the large desk, ready to be sealed.

The clock softly chimed the noon hour. Her aunt still hadn't stirred. Amelia reached for a blank sheet, dipped her pen into the pot of ink and slowly etched across the page. She described her debut in detail, just like she'd done with so many other parties. She felt a thrill as she signed her name with a flourish. After that, she snuck out of the room in search of food, and was relieved to find that a delicious lunch was already waiting.

"Mrs. Barrington is awake and wantin' you," Grace told her half an hour later. Amelia nodded and hurried up the steps. She entered Angie's bedroom when her aunt's soft call came.

"I hear you watched over me," Aunt Angie said, standing at the washstand. She wiped her face with a wet cloth and moved on to fixing her hair. "That was very sweet of you."

Amelia blushed. "I was worried about you."

"You're a dear, Amelia Lynn," Aunt Angie smiled tenderly. "I see that you worked on the thank-you notes." She motioned toward the pile on her desk.

"I didn't get very many done, but I wanted to surprise you. Will you look over them?"

"I'd be glad to," Aunt Angie answered. "Would you like to go on a drive with me?"

"That sounds like a lovely idea! I wasn't sure what I was going to do after lunch. Do you want to eat first?"

"I probably should," Aunt Angie said, then moved toward the door. "Will you ask Henry to have the carriage ready in an hour?"

Angie seemed back to her normal self, and Amelia put aside her worry that her aunt shouldn't be exerting herself. She left the room and delivered the message to Henry. In less than the planned hour, she and Angie gathered their gloves, hats, and shawls. Amelia admired the hat her aunt chose. It had a large brim and a length of tulle that Angie tucked below her chin. Amelia chose her current favorite hat, a small one with ribbons and feathers.

Once they were on their way, Aunt Angie smiled. "Did you respond to Mrs. James' invitation?"

"Yes, although I didn't send it," Amelia answered. "I wanted you to see my reply first."

The carriage pulled into the park, shading them from the summer sun.

"Angela! Angela!" someone cried. Angie cringed at Mrs. Detrid's overly friendly voice as she hailed her from the lawn. She directed Henry to pull over near her. When they stepped down, Mrs. Detrid extended a heavily ringed hand to Angie, while the other held a beribboned parasol. Amelia compared the two women's attire as they talked. Both outfits spoke of wealth that she'd never imagined before coming to the city, but Amelia preferred the quiet statement of her aunt's wardrobe.

"You are either thinking about clothes or a man, aren't you, Miss Hughes?" the outlandish Mrs. Detrid prompted.

"Oh, I was thinking about my new dress," Amelia said.

"You had Mrs. Bobbin make them, I assume." Mrs. Detrid said, eyeing Amelia's dress. "She makes the most divine creations. I'm meeting with her about one for the party I'm throwing come winter. You simply must come so you can see it. I declare, that's Claire Jard over there, isn't it? I must talk to her. You'll forgive me, won't you Angela?" In a whirl of ribbons and skirts, Mrs. Detrid hurried away.

"That is typical of one of the most influential women you'll ever meet," Aunt Angie said sardonically.

Amelia chuckled. "She is rather vivacious."

"Well said. You've already learned that in this society, one forgives a lot to maintain one's social standing. In some rare cases, I agree. In others, well…it is ridiculous what's swept into the shadows."

"There's so much beauty in society as well though," Amelia observed.

"That's true. Just don't get so blinded by it that you forget to watch for the negatives. It can be a slippery slope."

"I'll try," Amelia promised.

The two strolled arm in arm toward the pond, their parasols shading them, until Henry was finished setting up their chairs. Then Amelia steered them back in his direction. "Have you heard of the new book out by Jules Verne?" she asked her aunt. "It's a story of a young girl who travels to find her missing father. Could we purchase a copy and read it next?"

"Are we really almost done with *The Invisible Man*?"

Amelia relaxed in the chair, gazing at all the people. "Yes. Can you believe it? I can't decide if Griffin's insane, or someone to be pitied."

Their conversation stayed on Wells' book, as it did every time they were near to finishing a novel. If pressed, Amelia would admit to finding poetry boring, but her aunt loved it, so they read Longfellow, Dickens, and Poe. In return, they read her favorites, the likes of Wells, Kipling, and Alcott. After half a year of reading with her aunt, Amelia had read more than most young ladies her age. Aunt Angie liked to remind Amelia that reading so much would benefit her. She'd been exposed to more diverse thoughts, beliefs, and ideas than she would have been otherwise.

"I've been thinking about something," Amelia said once they were done discussing the book. "You were right about some of the people here." Sharing this confession was harder than she'd expected. "Do you think we would be able to schedule another meeting with Mr. Fletcher?" She'd been trying to gather the courage to ask, but had always swallowed the words before they left her mouth.

"I'd love to tell you that we can, but I'm not sure he'll be open to it," Angie said. Even though she'd spoken softly, Amelia felt the sting of her words. She closed the parasol and leaned it against her chair so she could clasp her hands together between her knees.

"I was so caught up in the excitement of being here that I lost myself for a while," she said. "I am trying though. I still catch myself longing to be part of Georgia's crowd…and to have Harrison…" Then she stopped. A blush raced across her cheeks. "Well, to be courted, and all of that."

"That's understandable," Angie replied. "We all want to be loved and appreciated. But I worry that you'll start to believe your beauty is only skin deep. You're so much more than how you look. You have a lot to give, Amelia, but you must know what you want. Originally, I set up the meeting with Mr. Fletcher hoping it would pull you out of the artificial world you'd cocooned yourself in. If you'd like to meet with him, I suggest you write and ask him yourself. Apologize for cancelling previously, and ask if he has time."

"I'll do that," Amelia said, perking up. "I want to at least try. What if I put in some examples of my work?"

"It wouldn't hurt. You've got talent. You should write more pieces like the one about your debut."

Amelia smiled, blushing. Her aunt continued. "By the way, Mrs. Hartly informed me that you've no further need of her instruction," she said. "You've learned all she can teach you. She asked me to pass on her best wishes for your future."

"I can't believe it," Amelia said, leaning back in her chair. "She was a great teacher, but quite strict. I'm glad to have taken lessons with her, but not sad to be done with them."

Silence fell for a few moments. Amelia enjoyed the sounds of quiet.

"I expect that we'll soon be getting requests for young men to come calling on you," Angie said unexpectedly, breaking the spell.

Amelia felt some of her contentment slip away. "What?"

"Well, that is a large reason, normally, for giving a debut," her aunt explained. "But since that wasn't our purpose, there's no pressure to accept anyone."

Amelia bit her lip, wondering if Harrison would send such a request. "I don't…I don't think I want to…"

Aunt Angie reached over and patted Amelia's hand. "I don't blame you. Let me know if that changes. Until it does, I'll just refuse any requests. You won't have to think about it at all."

"Thank you," Amelia smiled. "I'm glad we came to the park."

"I am too, but I'm ready to go home now."

"Is your head hurting again?" Amelia asked. "If so, we should go right away." She stood up quickly. Her aunt's soft laughter slowed her.

"I'm fine," Angie said, waving. "Everyone will think someone's died if you keep rushing about." Amelia's laughter rang across the park. They decided to walk slowly back to the carriage, once again arm in arm.

～⌒～

After their meal, Harrison and Georgia lingered at their table at the Portland Hotel. As usual, the food and service were excellent, and the atmosphere just busy enough to produce a low murmur in the background. Georgia was quite the picture seated across from him, and the rest of the day looked promising.

"I hear you've been attending a lot of the Whitmores' parties," she said, eyeing him carefully.

"Celene knows how to throw a good party," Harrison smiled. "I've seen you there once or twice, haven't I?"

"You know I don't go there," she frowned. "She's not a lady, Harrison. I'm scandalized that you're friendly with her."

He smiled again. "She's easy to be friendly with."

Georgia's eyes widened. "Have you no shame talking about another woman like that to me?"

"Listen, Georgia. You're fun to be around, but I'm not committed to you…or to anyone." He held his hands up. "If that's what you're wanting, then I'm out of here."

"I thought you liked me!" Georgia pouted.

"You're about the most beautiful girl around," he said, and meant it. She was more gorgeous now than when she'd first caught his eye. Her black hair and sparkling blue eyes were perfect compliments to her pale skin. "So don't go spoiling it, okay?"

"What do you mean, 'about the most beautiful girl'? I don't like backhanded compliments."

"Oh, Georgia." He drained his wine glass, then waved it at the waiter, who moved toward him immediately, wine bottle at the ready. Georgia accepted another glass as well, but Harrison halted him. "I'll take the Cabernet Sauvignon instead." He'd only ordered the Moscato because Georgia preferred it, but there was no way he was drinking another glass of that stuff.

"Very good, sir." The waiter bowed and left.

"We were going to have a nice day together," she said. "Instead…you're…"

"No," he cut her off. "Don't." He leaned forward and set his glass down. "You're the one who brought up Celene, then acted as if we're committed to each other. I've never once indicated that I'd be the type of man to settle down, Georgia. And you know it."

"I just didn't expect you to speak so…" She paused. Harrison raised his eyebrows at her, waiting. "Openly…about Miss Whitmore. You caught me off guard, that's all." Then she smiled slyly. "You do tend to do that to me, Harrison."

He nodded, though he wasn't convinced. She'd been acting proprietary of him lately, ever since Amelia arrived in town. He looked at her as she sipped her wine. *Has Georgia Fossit grown jealous?* The very same flirtatious, fun-loving Georgia who never cared one whit what girl he looked at… until Amelia arrived. Georgia played with hearts like he did, but in her own way. That was one reason why they got along so well. They didn't get caught up in the game like others did.

Harrison waited while the waiter filled a fresh glass. Once he sauntered off, Harrison decided to tease Georgia a little. "I'm looking forward to seeing Amelia at my party," he said. "Did you invite her to yours?"

Georgia looked at him sharply, then covered her grimace almost immediately. He wouldn't have seen it if he hadn't been watching so closely. *Ahh… jealous indeed.*

"I'm surprised you give her any attention at all, Harrison," she mocked. "I've heard that she's practically engaged to that Eric Sarden." She raised her eyebrows meaningfully.

"Why should that stop me?" he challenged. He kept an eye on her as he finished his glass, then signaled for the check. He paid and stood to offer Georgia his arm. She smiled sweetly and allowed him to lead her out of the restaurant.

"Shall we go to the museum next?" she fawned.

"No, I don't think so," he said softly, without hesitation.

"But Harrison! We'd planned…" Her drawl was more pronounced when she was upset. Normally, he laughed at her pouting. Not today.

"I don't appreciate getting played, Georgia," he commanded. "It's a fact you well know." He stopped in front of the building and waited for his carriage. "When you decide to pull your claws in, perhaps I'll come around. But that's the only way I'll be back. I don't care how gorgeous you are. You aren't putting a noose around my neck." He watched a flush cross her cheeks, then pulled her arm from his and turned toward the valet. "Call a cab for Miss Fossit."

His carriage pulled up a moment later and he stepped toward it. A sharp, "Harrison!" stopped him. He turned to see Georgia, her eyes snapping as she stood two steps behind him. "You are not leaving me here like this!"

It was a demand…an order. Today, Harrison was done with those. "I've requested a cab for you," he said. "You'll be able to get home just fine on your own." He climbed into his carriage and directed his driver to 635 Avery Street.

❧

Amelia slipped a note to Mr. Fletcher, along with a copy of the description of her debut she'd written, into an envelope. Before sending it, she asked for her aunt's feedback. Handing it to Angie, she sat on the edge of the chair opposite and waited.

"This is worded very well," Aunt Angie said.

"You think so? I don't need to…"

Walter, entering the doorway, unknowingly interrupting her thought. He bowed as Amelia and Aunt Angie turned their attention to him. Before he could speak, Harrison stepped around him, grinning widely.

"Mr. James!" Amelia curtsied. "How good to see you!"

"I decided to visit you and Mrs. Barrington," he said. "I hope you don't mind?" He bowed over each of their hands, appearing sure of his welcome.

"You're always welcome here, Mr. James," Angie offered. She motioned to the cluster of chairs they'd just been occupying. "Please, have a seat."

"I hope I haven't interrupted anything, coming in such an uncivilized manner?"

"You've pulled me away from the piles of paperwork I've been arguing with," Angie laughed. Amelia and Harrison smiled at each other, then the three of them settled into seats. Amelia tried to slip her papers and envelope onto a side table without Harrison seeing.

"Writing love letters?" he asked.

"Oh, no. I…" Amelia's cheeks flamed.

"Come now, who's the fellow you're writing to?" he toyed. "I will have his name."

"How's Georgia?" Aunt Angie interjected, seeing her niece's discomfort.

"She's fine," Harrison said off-handedly. In a moment, tea arrived, and Aunt Angie served them.

"Have you heard that the Trendles lost everything, and are moving in with his parents?" Harrison asked.

"Oh, that's terrible!" Amelia exclaimed. "What happened?"

"The old man blew it all on a bad horse bet." Harrison shook his head in disgust. "He could have doubled his money easily! All he had to do was bet on Lookout. Everyone knew he was going to win. But instead, he bet on Sir Waller. I say it served him right."

"Indeed," Aunt Angie said. "And how is your mother?"

"She's all right. In the throes of planning her gala," Harrison said. "Father couldn't care about the gala, except that it reminds people how influential he is. That's all he cares about, really, making sure people know he's the one at the top." Harrison took a drink of tea. "Well, he'll see that he can't dismiss me. I'm up there with him, whether he wants me or not."

Amelia couldn't believe Harrison had come to visit them like this. *He seems so at ease here.* She smiled, imagining many afternoons spent like this.

"The Fossits are throwing a small dinner party next week," he said casually, looking at Amelia.

"Do they always entertain so frequently?" she asked.

"I think they'd entertain every evening if they could get away with it," he replied.

Their conversation flowed easily for the next few minutes as they finished their tea. When he was done, Harrison set his cup and saucer down on the table, with hardly a rattle. He smiled at Amelia, then turned to Angie. "Thank you for your hospitality, Mrs. Barrington. I'll take my leave."

"It was a pleasure," Aunt Angie said. "We'll see you at the party then?"

"Of course," Harrison agreed, standing. Amelia and Aunt Angie stood as well and walked him to the door. Once he was gone, they headed upstairs to decide what dress Amelia should wear for the James' party.

Chapter Nine

Ian fingered his watch chain as people streamed into the theatre. The day had been so hectic that he'd worried about making it this evening. But he'd committed to seeing *Robin Hood* with Angela, and he wasn't going to miss it. Part of him wished that it were only her joining him, but he supposed he had to get used to her niece tagging along.

"Excuse me, Mr. Hayworth?" The voice was high-pitched and quieted the people around them.

Ian flinched. "Madam?"

"Forgive me for intruding, but I'm Mrs. Riley. This is my daughter, Willamina." Mrs. Riley, was a short woman whose hat jiggled with her every movement. The tall beribboned contraption seemed like it was going to topple from her head at any moment.

He looked over her shoulder, prepared for an similarly beribboned and squat daughter, but his eyebrows rose as he took in the sophisticated woman before him. She was not much shorter than Ian, and her poise added to her beauty. An embarrassed smile crossed her lips when their eyes met. She curtsied, and although she spoke so softly he could not hear her, he was fascinated by the way her lips formed his name.

He bowed in response. "Miss Riley," he said.

"I'll leave you two to get acquainted," the mother smiled triumphantly, then left in a rustle of skirts. His usual frustration sparked as he watched her leave, but he quelled the urge to say anything.

"Forgive my mother, Mr. Hayworth," the younger Miss Riley offered. "She's overeager, and nothing I say can deter her. If we may speak for a few moments, I can bid you farewell. I promise I won't bother you again." Her voice was just loud enough to carry to him, and its deep tones were soothing.

He frowned. "This is an interesting ploy to gain my interest, Miss Riley. I admit that it's not…"

"Oh, I'm being earnest!" she said. "I'm horribly embarrassed every time my mother foists me on an unsuspecting gentleman. I have no wish to interfere with your plans." She glanced over his shoulder. "There. Mother will be satisfied. Thank you for your forbearance. Good evening." *Even her departure differs from her mother's.*

As she walked off, Ian searched the crowded hall for Angela, his fingers going to his watch chain again. In the time that he'd been talking with Mrs. Riley and her daughter, the room had filled considerably. He stepped closer to the wall to allow space for a pair of young women who walked toward him. Even so, they passed by uncomfortably close. He smiled when he spotted Angela approaching.

"It seems these plays are drawing more crowds than ever," Angela remarked. "Especially young women."

"Now, Angela," he teased before focusing on his friend. "How are you doing? You looked quite worn out last time I saw you." He scanned her face. She looked well, but there was a new tightness around her eyes.

"You should know better than to say something like that to a woman," she teased. Then her smile faded. "The debut wore me out more than I expected, but I'm feeling better now."

"I'm glad to hear it."

Amelia arrived and slipped her hand into her aunt's as she stepped next to her.

"Miss Hughes," Ian bowed.

"Mr. Hayworth," she said, then immediately turned to her aunt. "I ran into Mrs. Detrid again. That woman…"

"Amelia…" Angela's voice was calm, but held a warning. Ian was glad when her niece grimaced and stopped talking. Angela turned back to him. "How have you been, Ian?"

"I've been well," he said. If he could just ignore Angela's niece, this evening would be more enjoyable. "We're working on finding a new location for the orphanage. It's taking up most of my time. I visited my sister Dorothy and her boys last evening." He smiled in remembrance of the boys' exuberance when he'd arrived with a stack of new puzzles for them.

"I'm glad to hear the orphanage will be moving," Angela said. "The condition of that building you're in right now is disgraceful."

"I agree, though I'm still trying to convince the board that a new building is a financially prudent investment."

"If you end up being short, you know I'll gladly help make up the difference," Angela offered.

"You've already donated so much."

"Getting those children a better home is more important than having money wasting away in a bank," she said. Ian smiled. Her way of talking sometimes reminded him of his mother.

"Thank you," he said. Feeling as if he should engage her niece, he turned to Amelia. "Are you excited to see *Robin Hood*, Miss Hughes?"

She turned from watching the crowd. "Oh yes! I've been hearing so much about it. I've heard the lead is a wonderful actor."

"I've heard the same," Ian said. "Although I don't think I've seen him in anything before."

"This is his first time coming to the West, apparently," Angela said. "The crowds are practically singing his name, if you can believe the articles in the newspaper."

"Well, I guess we'll see if we're singing when we leave in a few hours!" Amelia said, laughing. Ian checked the time.

"Speaking of which, shall we head in?" he asked.

"Lead the way," Angela said. She slipped her gloved hand into the crook of his arm, letting him lead her toward the theatre. He felt a little guilty pulling her away from her niece, but it was entirely appropriate that Miss Hughes walk behind them.

⌒⌄⌄⌒

"I think Friar Tuck was the funniest person up there," Amelia said as they walked out of the theatre.

Ian offered Angela his arm, and she took it, ignoring the exhaustion that nipped at her. "What did you think of it, Angela?" he asked.

"It was most amusing," she said. "And I can see why people are so enthralled with the lead actor, though I've forgotten his name. Did you enjoy it?"

"I did," Ian replied. Angie smiled but didn't pursue the conversation. If she wasn't so tired, she would invite him over for coffee, but all she could think about was climbing into bed.

"Angela! Yoo-hoo!" a voice rang out. It was Mrs. Detrid, of course. Angie turned, sighed quietly, then smiled.

"Good evening Mrs. Detrid," she offered.

"I do declare…" Mrs. Detrid said, scanning Angie walking with Ian. She pulled her hand from Ian's arm, setting him free from what was likely to be a long and boring conversation. She wasn't surprised when he quietly excused himself not two minutes later.

Free of Angela and her niece, Ian wove through the crowd, keeping an eye on Miss Riley who stood alone near the wall. "Miss Riley?" he called out.

"Mr. Hayworth!" she said. She glanced around, then relaxed after a moment.

"Did you enjoy the play?" he asked.

"I did," she smiled, a welcoming one that made him return it. "And you?"

"Very much. I always regret not coming to the theatre more often."

"Mother loves it, so I often find myself attending the same play multiple times. That's not to say I don't enjoy it!" She rushed to explain, her hand fluttering. "I do of course. That is to say…" she petered out, her attention drifting past him.

Feeling as if his time with her was ending, he asked the first thing that came to mind. "Can I call on you tomorrow?"

"What?" she looked back at him, her eyes wide.

"Can I call on you tomorrow evening?"

She darted a glance behind him and leaned closer. "I'm engaged. Mother doesn't know."

He bowed, not letting his disappointment show. "Good evening, Miss Riley."

The sound of taffeta nearing reached him as he walked away. Aside from the disappointment, he was unsure how to feel as he moved to rejoin Angela. He'd met someone that was interesting enough to pursue, but she was unavailable. He did admire the fact that she'd told him straightaway.

Sighing, he returned to Angela. Perhaps he should be content with his friendships. Especially his friendship with Angela, which held no surprises.

Chapter Ten

The day of the James' gala meandered by in pleasant diversions. Amelia fingered her gray silk dress reverently as they entered the mansion. The chiffon overlay slid through her fingers, the miniscule beads that were sewn all over catching the light. She followed Aunt Angie's lead as they greeted Mr. and Mrs. James, along with Harrison. Then they made their way through the crush of people. As they did, Amelia reached for her aunt's hand. Peter Peal was in attendance. Flustered, she did not notice that they'd reached a table occupied by Edith and other ladies. Before she could greet them, Mr. Douvre asked her to dance. She eagerly agreed, letting him lead her toward the dance floor.

~⌣⌣⌣~

"I'm surprised you're here so late," Edith said to Angie. "I thought Amelia would be pushing you out the door."

"Oh, she was. I just didn't let her push too hard," Angie smiled, skirting the truth. A flute of champagne appeared in front of her, but Angie shook her head.

Edith frowned. "You look a bit worn," she said. "Come, sit." Edith guided them toward her table. Angie waved a hand dismissively.

"I'm sure that I'll be back to normal soon," she said.

"Have you talked to a doctor?" Edith asked, leaning forward. "It could be something serious. You mentioned being tired a few months ago."

"Oh, I'm sure it's nothing," Angie said, and cast about for another topic. The last thing she wanted to do was reveal just how terrible she'd been feeling these past months. "I did want to ask your advice about Amelia. I know you struggled with your daughters years ago, and their wanting to be a part of society. How did you keep them from it?"

"I'll allow you to change the subject, but please think about seeing a doctor," Edith said. "You never know." After taking a sip of tea, she continued. "Our daughters weren't too drawn to those circles, so it wasn't a large concern. We kept them as busy as we could. Of course, then the young men started calling, which became its own distraction," she smiled. "Recalling those days makes me glad that all three of my girls are married and settled. They were busy."

Angie nodded. Then she confided another worry. "I think Amelia's developed an attachment," she said.

"Is it not someone suitable?"

Angie was grateful for how her friend got right to the heart of the issue. "I'm not sure that it is. Plus, she's still so young."

"She's the same age I was when I got married. And the same goes for many of these women here," Edith paused. "Is the boy really so incompatible?"

Angie searched the crowd, but couldn't find Amelia. "Only time will tell," she said. "I don't think so. I'm worried about seeing her hurt. She's grown so much since she came, but is still so insecure."

"We all were, one way or another," Edith said. "Some still are. But she's not nearly as meek as she used to be. Look how tall she's standing. Remember how she used to slouch?"

"She is more confident," Angie agreed.

Their conversation turned to Edith's recent trip to meet her newest grandchild. Her husband hadn't been able to go with her, due to an illness of one of their parishioners.

"We've made plans to visit again in a few months," Edith said. "Oh look, Amelia's dancing with Harrison," she exclaimed. "She's practically floating."

They watched the young couple finish their dance, then pivot toward Edith and Angie's table. Amelia's hand was tucked in Harrison's arm. If her smile was a little too bright, Angie hoped no one else noticed.

Bowing to each in turn, Harrison greeted them, and assisted Amelia into the chair next to Angie. Amelia took Angie's hand, and Harrison joined them, engaging in a lively conversation. A server stopped near his chair, speaking softly into Harrison's ear. Harrison nodded then rose. "Forgive me ladies, but my mother is asking for me." Before he turned to leave, he looked at Amelia. "May I claim another dance with you?"

"I'd like that," she said. Harrison gently kissed the back of her hand, then bowed to all three of them.

"Well…he seems to be rather taken with you, my dear," Edith said. Her words brought a smile and a flush to Amelia's cheeks. Angie raised an eyebrow as Edith's gaze flew to hers. She appreciated the understanding that filled Edith's face. Her friend didn't say anything further on the topic. Instead, they watched the comings and goings of the revelers.

"How are you feeling, Aunt Angie?" Amelia asked.

"I'm fine," she offered. Eager to change the topic, Angie asked, "I saw you talking with Miss Fossit earlier. How is she doing?"

"She was discussing the latest fashion," Amelia said disinterestedly. "Lately though, I've been wishing she could talk about something more real."

"Like what?" Edith asked.

"The suffrage movement or…something," Amelia said and accepted a glass of punch from a passing waiter.

"There's a group of women forming that want to help those less fortunate," Edith said. "I'd intended to ask if you'd like to join us. Our first meeting is in just over a week."

Amelia's eyes widened. "Of course we would! Oh, Aunt Angie, you agree, don't you?"

"I agree to nothing without learning more about it," Angie said. "I'll go, and then we can decide." Turning to her friend, Angie added, "No offense meant, Edith."

Edith waved her apology aside. "I assume the first few meetings are going to be figuring out just what our goals are, how we fund them and so forth."

"Then it's settled," Angie said. "I'll attend. Then I'll know if it's something we want to be a part of."

"Yes, Aunt Angie," Amelia answered with a frown. She became restless as she sat with Edith and her aunt, but then livened up again when Harrison returned for another dance. After that, Angie was pleased to see Amelia join Eric Sarden's sisters for a time. Still, she was concerned about how much the James boy hovered around her niece. Thankfully he had the good sense to not ask Amelia for a third dance. Two in one evening led to gossip and speculation. A third would have been downright scandalous.

As the party was ending, Harrison joined a group of men in the drawing room for a round of cards. He greeted them and noted that the more influential of them, such as Mr. Fletcher, Mr. Ladd and Mr. Boggs, were present for his father's popular game.

He lit his cigarette and settled next to Maddox Lancer at the game table. He'd met Lancer a few months ago at a Whitmore party. While he was a bit abrasive, Harrison liked that the man knew how to have a good time.

Peter Peal sat on his other side and nudged him. "I see you haven't tired of the Hughes girl yet," he smirked. "She's making you work for it, huh?"

Peal's suggestion turned Harrison's stomach. "You're drunk," Harrison said.

"She's a bit of a snob though," Peal went on. "You've got to go gentle with her. Otherwise…"

Harrison clenched his tumbler, feeling his blood start to boil. "Watch yourself, Peal."

"It was just a bit of fun," he said.

"Did you not learn anything from me that day?"

"She probably fits in your arms real nice," Peal grinned. "But I'm guessing you know that by now, don't you? Girls like that don't take long to convince."

Harrison stood so quickly that his chair crashed behind him. He grabbed Peal by the shirt. "Don't talk about a lady like that," he growled. "Get out!" He shoved Peal backward into the upturned chair. The other men hurriedly grabbed their drinks, moving to the sides of the room. Cursing, Peal leveled himself, barely pausing before charging Harrison.

Harrison shifted his stance. At just the right moment, he swung at Peal's gut, doubling the man over. Stepping forward, he grabbed Peal by the shoulder and yanked him close. "Had enough yet?" Harrison asked, his face close to Peal's.

"That's enough," Mr. James' voice boomed from the other side of the room, cutting the tension. "Mr. Peal, you'd better leave," he said.

Harrison let go of Peal. He knew his father would throw him out too if he kept at it.

Peal straightened with a wince and glared at Harrison. He walked to the table, found his drink, and swallowed what was left of it. "This isn't over, Harrison."

When he was gone, Maddox slapped Harrison on the back. "One heck of a show there, James! I'll have to remember that you've got a wicked left hook."

Harrison shoved Maddox's hand off him.

"That was one professional-looking match," Mr. Ladd added. He shifted his gaze to Maddox as he spoke. "I don't know anyone who could have handled it as well as that."

Harrison returned the salute, then nodded at the other men who were sharing in his triumph. He kept an eye on Maddox, though, seeing the anger building in the man as he was dismissed by the others. Maddox glared. "I'll have you know that I..."

"Don't be a fool, Maddox," Harrison muttered.

"What's that?" Maddox snapped.

"I said," Harrison began casually, "...that I certainly hope Peter is all right."

Maddox squinted suspiciously at Harrison. The dealer called out deuces wild for a game of sevens, then dealt the cards.

"What do you say, Harrison? Want to test your mettle?" Maddox tipped back in his chair, dark eyes gleaming.

"Let's keep it to cards, gentlemen," Mr. James said sternly. His eyes lingered on his son for a moment. "My drawing room has seen enough damage for one evening."

Maddox glowered but let the matter drop, to Harrison's relief. He wasn't afraid to scrap with the obstinate fool, but he wasn't in the mood. His mind kept going back to what Peal had insinuated. *The way that lout talked about Amelia. If he ever bothered her again…*

Harrison forced himself to relax and glanced around the table, reading each man's reaction to their cards. He'd learned from his father how to read a man. Play continued, and he finished off his bourbon. As it slid down his throat, a flash of Peal's hands on Amelia's waist burned in his mind. He coughed, choking on the last of his drink.

"Can't handle a man's drink, can you?" Maddox sneered. "There's some champagne over there."

Only one man chuckled at Maddox's insult, but he stifled it quickly.

"I was just thinking how easy it would be to knock you flat on your back," Harrison said calmly.

Maddox half rose out of his chair. "How dare you!"

"Mr. Lancer! It's your turn," Mr. James once again intervened. He shot an exasperated glance at his son. "Hold your tongue, boy."

The game continued in near silence. It took the dealer's calm voice announcing the next play before anyone relaxed enough to start talking.

Harrison kept one eye on his cards, the other on Maddox. He was starting to rethink his choice not to fight him. His hands were getting that familiar itch to lay someone flat. When Maddox lost another round, Harrison almost said something, but a look from his father stopped him. Instead, he merely smiled and drained his refilled glass.

Maddox threw his cards down, rounding on Harrison. "What's the matter with you? Don't you have any pride?"

At that, Harrison dropped his cards and sent a punch right to the side of Maddox's head. The blow was swift and sudden, dropping Maddox back into his seat. The chair tilted, dumping the burly man onto the floor, where he sprawled, unconscious.

Harrison poured another shot of bourbon and downed it. "I'll bid you good evening, sir," he said to his father, stepping over Maddox as he left the room, ignoring the calls of the men to play another round.

"Harrison, that was downright impressive!" David Carl said. He'd followed Harrison to the front hall. "You didn't even let him get a shot off!" The fellow was wide-eyed, and none too steady on his feet.

Straightening, Harrison looked down his nose at him. "Sometimes, the only response is to outright flatten them."

"Then why didn't you do that to Peal? You could have belted him just like that."

Harrison shook his head, stepping to the side to regain his balance. "You don't do that to friends. Not unless you've got a good..." He stopped, once again picturing what Peal might have done to Amelia. "I guess I have a good reason, don't I? Hey." He turned to David suddenly. "What do you know about Georgia's garden party?"

"I know you laid claim to Amelia Hughes. A right shame too, she's..."

"About Peal."

"He didn't do anything."

"Have you seen them together again?" Harrison felt sick just asking it.

"No," David said. "Why are you so worked up about this?"

"I don't trust him. You know what?" He motioned to a maid for his things. "I'm going to go ask him. You want to come along?"

"Oh, I don't think so, Harrison," David shook his head, backing away from him. "That sounds like trouble."

The maid walked up, carrying his coat and hat. He took them from her with a wink. She was a cute thing with a smile that seemed as good as…

A flash of Peal holding Amelia intruded in Harrison's mind. He scowled, startling the maid. Brushing past her and David Carl, he left the house, intent on making sure Peal never thought about touching Amelia again.

<h1 style="text-align:center">Chapter Eleven</h1>

Gray morning light lit the room as fear propelled Amelia from bed. She threw her robe on then hurried into the hall, turning toward her aunt's bedroom. Only then did she realize the noises that had wakened her were coming from the entry hall. Looking down, she was surprised to see Walter attempting to help a hollering, flailing Harrison up from the floor. Occasionally she caught her name in the deluge of words.

"It's Mr. James," Grace said, joining her at the railing. "He's wantin' to see you. Walter tried to tell him that it's too early for callin', but Mr. James wouldn't listen."

"I'd better go down and see him then," Amelia said. Despite the spectacle, she felt a blush rise. *Harrison wants to see me so badly that he called this early?*

"Oh, but Miss Amelia, this isn't proper!" Grace's voice squeaked in shock. "You're still in your nightgown!"

Amelia waved her concerns aside, ran her hand along the braid that hung over her shoulder, and started down the stairs.

Walter had finally gotten Harrison back to his feet, and kept both hands around his arm. "Miss Amelia, I told him that it's far too early to be calling, but he's insisting that he sees you. Perhaps you can persuade him to return at a more reasonable hour?"

Before she could respond, Harrison leaned toward her. "Amelia, I'm so sorry." He lurched, but Walter kept him from falling. "I made it right though. It's all okay now."

Amelia frowned. "Perhaps we should go sit down?" She led the way into the salon and waited until Walter left the room before looking at Harrison. He sat slouched in the chair across from her. "You have to believe me, Amelia, I didn't…but I've made it right." He ran his hand through his hair, causing it to stand on end on one side.

"What are you going on about?" Her voice dropped to a whisper.

"Peter…Peter Peal," Harrison frowned. "The lout!"

Amelia shuddered at the look that crossed his face. "What did you do?" she whispered, then caught sight of his scraped knuckles. The blood drained from her face. She sank heavily into a chair.

"He won't touch you again. I want you to know that." Harrison swayed but caught himself on the arm of the chair. As he stared at her, she noticed his eyes were bloodshot and uncharacteristically hard. "You didn't deserve that," he went on. "I couldn't handle the thought that…" He ran his hand over his face. "You're safe now."

Amelia touched the edge of her robe, unsure what to say or do. A part of her wished she'd listened to Grace and stayed upstairs. She couldn't believe what she was hearing. "I don't know what to say," she finally offered.

Harrison grunted and pulled a metal flask from his jacket pocket. "Peal is a cussed fool," he said, then tilted the flask to his lips.

"Mr. James!" Aunt Angie strode into the room, her voice stern. Her entrance startled Amelia from her shock at Harrison's behavior. "I will thank you to watch your language, and put that vile flask away while you are in my house."

Harrison nearly dropped the flask, splashing liquid down his jacket. "Blast it all!" he exclaimed, jumping up and swiping at the drops. "Look what you made me do!"

"It's time for you to leave," Angie snapped. "You're not in any condition to be around my niece." Angie stepped next to Amelia, who took her aunt's hand, thankful for her presence.

"I came to tell her…" Then he stopped and attempted to slip the flask into his jacket.

"You came drunk, Mr. James," Angie corrected, "and well before the proper hour." She called for Walter, then looked pointedly at Harrison.

"Thank you, Harrison, for the message," Amelia said gently. She wasn't sure what to think about what he'd said, but he looked so upset at her aunt's dismissal that she felt she had to say something. "I'm grateful for your…assistance."

As he nodded, his eyes flicked over her briefly. He started to say something, but Walter took his elbow. "Right this way, sir," he intoned.

Amelia didn't know what to make of any of it. Part of her wanted him to stay, while another part of her was glad he was leaving. She stayed with her aunt as they watched a stoic Walter lead him away.

"Well, I'm glad *that's* over," Angie said, sitting down once she heard the door close. "I never thought I'd have such a thing occur in my house."

Amelia blushed and chewed her lower lip. Her hands were tight in her lap as she stared out the doorway. "It has been a singular experience," She offered. Aunt Angie chuckled and rang the small bell for tea.

"You do have a way with words, Amelia," she laughed. "What did he have to tell you that couldn't wait for propriety?" Her mouth twitched. "Or sobriety, for that matter."

"He apologized and said that he took care of Peter Peal… that he would never touch me again." Amelia took a shaky breath as a shiver ran down her spine. That this should come so soon after seeing Mr. Peal again was just too much. "I didn't know what to say or do! He was drunk! His knuckles were all bloody! Why would he…I don't know what to think." Resting her head in her hands, she bent over her knees, hiding her face.

"Perhaps a cup of tea will help calm you," Aunt Angie offered. "It should be here in a moment. We must try to… I mean…"

Amelia sat up at the disjointed words. Her aunt was rubbing her fingers absently. Were they hurting again?

"I know it's been a whirlwind for you since coming here," Angie went on. "The challenges you've faced have been more than either of us expected. But I feel we need to make some changes in how you spend your time."

Amelia was immediately distracted. "I know you don't like my friends," she began, then stopped as her aunt sat forward.

"I'm going to ask you two questions," Angie spoke. "I want you to think them over before you answer. First, how do you see yourself right now? And second, what type of woman do you want to be?"

"That's not what I was expecting," Amelia said, avoiding her aunt's gaze. "Right now, I feel like I'm failing. I like being in society, but I've started noticing the things you warned me about." She blinked back tears.

"It's all right," Aunt Angie said softly. "It's a good thing, even though it's hard. As for my second question, who do you want to be?"

"I've known who I want to be since I was a little girl," Amelia replied. Her voice grew stronger. "I want to be a journalist. I want to be confident, pretty, and independent. I don't want to look to someone for approval. I want to make my own decisions."

"You made me completely forget what I was going to say," Aunt Angie said, her voice suddenly thick with emotion. "You can travel, write, and be independent. You are already beautiful. As for confidence and being able to make your own decisions…those will come with time. But I do have a piece of advice. Only let words that are good and true into your heart. Some will seek to tear you down. You will have to learn how to tune them out. Miles used to tell me, 'Be a duck, Angela, be a duck.'"

"A duck?" Amelia asked, unsure.

"He meant I should let negativity roll off me. You should do the same. Don't let it steal your joy and dreams."

"Like my mother," Amelia said.

Aunt Angie sighed and grasped Amelia's hand. "Your mother has always been very caught up in appearances. You'll run into all sorts of people who will try to tear you down. When you choose your friends wisely, it makes such a difference. I didn't learn that lesson until later in life."

A comfortable silence fell as they enjoyed tea and pastries the maid brought in. Before they parted, Amelia brought up her mother again.

"Mother's words keep playing in my head," she said. "Right now, I don't know which side will win, the person I want to be, or the side that Mother created."

"You're so much more than what she sees in you," Aunt Angie remarked. "Remember that. By the way, did you request a meeting with Mr. Fletcher?"

Amelia blew out a breath toward the ceiling. "Yes. He said that while his wife had a wonderful time at the club with you, he didn't have time to meet with me…but to be sure to give you his regards."

"So, what are you going to do?"

"I don't know. I thought of writing him again, or perhaps trying to speak with him in person. But I just don't know." Amelia rubbed her temples, wishing she had taken her aunt's advice when the chance first arose. If only she'd gone to meet with Mr. Fletcher, then everything she was dealing with now would not be happening. Harrison would have never come over drunk. *Harrison.* She recalled how he looked that day at the party. Then last night, when they danced not once but twice. And how he'd smiled at her. But then the image of him this morning intruded. His red eyes, wild hair, crumpled clothes, bloodied knuckles. What did he think of her now? Would he think she was the type to…?

She didn't realize she'd spoken aloud until her aunt answered. "I don't think so," Angie said. "As much as I don't trust him, he was clearly upset at what happened to you. And he obviously did something about it. Whether we agree with his actions or not, I would say his opinion of you is high… higher than it's ever been for any young woman, I imagine."

Her aunt's tone was dry. Amelia decided not to ask her what she meant by that. A part of her knew Harrison was a flirt, and also a bit egotistical. But, she'd been drawn to him ever since the first time she saw him. He had always been so kind to her. She couldn't imagine him being anything other than a gentleman.

Eventually, her mind shied away from his display this morning, refusing to examine it past the fact that he'd been worried about her.

~⁓~

The girl has stars in her eyes. Angie sighed and left her niece to her daydreams, as she pondered the situation. She would never forgive herself if Amelia ended up with such an untrustworthy young man. However, she knew just as surely that Diane wouldn't have one doubt about pushing Amelia toward Harrison James. She wouldn't care about his character until after the wedding, if ever. All she would see was that he was rich, handsome, and charming.

Angie shook her head and added some sugar to her tea. *There has to be something I can do to nip this infatuation in the bud.* She'd hoped the rumors surrounding the James boy were empty, but after seeing the state he'd been in, and the look on his face after he took in Amelia's appearance this morning, she had no doubt that most of the rumors were true. *Perhaps all of them, for that matter.* She'd always known he was manipulative. Considering how he'd been raised, he hadn't stood much of a chance to be otherwise. *He'll rise to the top no matter who he steps on to get there.*

Angie grimaced when she thought of Amelia being someone Harrison crushed in order to achieve his goals. She took a sip of tea, and almost dropped the cup in surprise.

"What's wrong?" Amelia asked.

"Apparently, I added more sugar without topping it off first. It's entirely too sweet," Angie laughed. "I just had an idea. What if you politely thank Mr. Fletcher for his response, but leave it at that. Then, go apply at some of the other papers around town?"

"I could take some of my articles with me as samples!" Amelia's excitement rose as they discussed where to try first. Before long, she hurried up the stairs to get ready for the day.

Ian's mind raced through his prepared speech as the men gathered, greeting each other before settling around the table. He sat near the elder Mr. Sarden, nodding as the representative of the bank prepared for the meeting. On Ian's other side sat Mr. Halper, a businessman who regularly donated to charitable endeavors. Next to him was Mr. Detrid and then Mr. Carl, men who'd inherited their wealth and were generally opposed to helping others.

Mr. Sarden gained their attention with a quick rap on the table. "Gentlemen, on behalf of Ladd & Tilton Bank, thank you all for coming. This is a significant endeavor we are pursuing. God is grateful for your kindness to the needy among us."

"God has nothing to do with it," Mr. Detrid said. "It's my pocketbook that's going to suffer."

"But is it not God that has so blessed you that you can even be here among us?" Mr. Sarden asked mildly in reply. Ian appreciated his friend's calm rebuke. Then Sarden continued. "You all know why we are here. Allow me to turn the floor over to Mr. Hayworth."

"Gentlemen," Ian began, "while we are sitting in our homes with every imaginable comfort within reach, twenty-five children are living in a home that is falling around them. They don't know it, but they deserve better. They should have every opportunity to succeed, but how can they when they don't have basic necessities? Before they can start learning, they must be fed, well-clothed, and warm! As you know, we've found a building, and while the owner is willing, he'll only sell if we pay a premium price."

As Ian shared the figure, exclamations broke out from among the men. He waited as Mr. Sarden emphasized the significance of their endeavor, fingering his watch chain while the men discussed the price and value of the building. He took his watch out, glancing at the time and the picture on the inside. Half past eleven. They'd been there fifteen minutes and had gotten nowhere.

He returned the watch to his vest pocket.

"I say we pass on this deal," Mr. Detrid said. "The owner has been too demanding. This is far above the price we agreed on."

"There's plenty of real estate available," Mr. Carl said. "I'm sure we'll find a better match."

Ian clenched his jaw as despair rose inside him. How could they not understand the urgency to secure another location before winter? He shifted in his chair, ready to object when a raised hand stopped him.

It was Mr. Halper, an elderly man with plenty of influence. "I think what these men are saying, is that we've discussed, at length, the purchase of a building for Nettleville. I fear that if we cannot decide soon, it will imply that one cannot be made, and we'll need to shelve this project for the time being."

Are we doomed to wait another year before we can move? Ian waited for Mr. Sarden to say something. When he didn't, Ian took a deep breath. "You bring up a valid point, Mr. Halper," he said. "In light of that, I propose a trip to Nettleville, to illustrate the points I've made here. In the interest of moving this along, we'll commit to making a decision before dispersing today."

"Why should we waste our time by going there?" Mr. Detrid asked. "I have other things to do!"

"I agree," Mr. Carl said. "It seems to me that if Mr. Hayworth were serious about this project, he'd be better prepared."

Ian's heart dropped. Did he truly seem ill-prepared and inexperienced to these men? Before he could speak again, Mr. Sarden raised his hands, bringing quiet to the room. "Please, gentlemen," he said. "Would it not be better to go and have this resolved today, than to sit here for another meeting or two before we make this decision?"

Some grumbled objections, but the men finally agreed. A shuffle followed as they put on their coats and hats and called their carriages.

As Ian led the men into Nettleville, he hoped Mrs. Lardish was ready for them. To his relief, she was just entering the hall.

"Mrs. Lardish, allow me to introduce you," he said. "Gentlemen, I'd like to introduce Mrs. Lardish. She is the reason Nettleville has stayed open. This is Mr. Sarden, Mr. Detrid, Mr. Carl, and Mr. Halper."

The men nodded and doffed their hats in turn.

"Thank you for coming to see us," Mrs. Lardish said. "I've sent the children to play outside, so it won't be too noisy. First, I'll show you their classrooms. Then we'll tour the kitchen and bedrooms."

Ian was impressed with how she handled them, although he wasn't surprised. She'd been at Nettleville since it opened in 1886. As she led them through, she explained various limitations and struggles they faced. She didn't whine or beg, just shared how they were consistently short on funds and necessities. She also relayed what they taught, along with success stories of children who had grown and were now on their own.

Walking between rooms, Mr. Carl cleared his throat. "If you're doing so well improving their lives, why worry about a new location? It seems to me as if…"

"Oh, come now, Jerry," Mr. Detrid interrupted, his mood clearly altered from earlier. "This place is about ready to fall around their ears!"

Ian hid a smile. To hear it coming from someone else, especially Mr. Detrid, was proof that perhaps his plan was working after all.

"Even so," Mr. Carl sniffed, "if they simply economized more, they'd be fine, I'm sure."

"We're quite economical, I assure you," Ian countered. "It's almost impossible to heat this drafty building, which is why we have rounds of sickness every winter among the children. We lost two little ones last winter alone."

"Let's head back downstairs," Mr. Halper suggested. "It's much too cramped up here."

When they'd gathered in the largest classroom, Ian waited and prayed.

"Well, gentlemen, what do you think?" Mr. Sarden asked.

"I still believe the requested price is too high," Mr. Detrid said. "But after seeing this place, it might be worth it to get these children into a better situation."

As an agreement circled the room, Ian felt a wave of relief. Despite his inexperience and the disinclination of at least two of the men, they'd done it. This old building would soon be a bitter memory.

As Ian shook hands with each man, he sent a prayer of thanksgiving heavenward. The children would have a warm place come winter.

An hour later, Ian stepped through the door of *The Gazette*, tapping his advertisement against his finger as he scanned the room. Everything was the same as always, from the rhythmic thumping of the printer, to the errand boy bringing in the owner's lunch from the diner across the street.

A well-dressed younger woman was talking with the owner, George Thompson. Ian waited several paces back. He wasn't trying to eavesdrop, but couldn't help overhearing their conversation.

"I'm sorry, miss, but we aren't in need of a woman writing recipes," Mr. Thompson said. "Now, if you'll excuse me, we're quite busy."

Mr. Thompson stepped aside, noticed Ian waiting and nodded toward him. Ian waited, not wanting to intrude. The woman swung her bag around in front of her, and began pulling pages out of it. "But sir, if you look at these samples I've brought, you'll see that I can do more than recipes and fashion. I know that I'd have to prove myself, but..."

"Miss, I gave it to you plain. Now you're making a nuisance of yourself." Mr. Thompson crossed his arms, frowning at her. "I have a paying customer waiting, so I'll ask you again to move along."

The young woman squared her shoulders and raised her chin, making Ian sure Mr. Thompson was about to get severely reprimanded. Instead, she nodded once, tucked the papers back into her leather case, and thanked the newspaperman cordially. Ian's eyebrows rose and his admiration grew.

When she turned around, her eyes met his with a spark of recognition. He was stunned. "Miss Hughes?" he blurted.

Amelia stopped in surprise, her cheeks reddening. "Mr. Hayworth. Good afternoon." She swallowed hard, glancing nervously between him and the door.

Ian couldn't speak, unable to believe that the poised young woman before him was Angela's niece. She'd readily spoken ill of an acquaintance at the theatre, and now she'd not thrown a fit at a stranger? How had she changed so much in such a short time? When he didn't speak further, she slipped past him.

"Well, Mr. Hayworth, back with a coded message for that nephew of yours?" Mr. Thompson asked. "I hope you don't mind, but I always like to try and figure them out myself, at day's end." The newspaperman grinned, his hands clasping the front of his ink-stained apron.

Ian fingered his chain, not liking the difference between how Mr. Thompson treated Miss Hughes and himself. Smiling rather stiffly, he handed the piece of paper across the counter. "I don't mind at all, George. I'll warn you though, I've been thinking of coming up with a new one, as this is getting too simple for the boy."

"Ah, throw him a curveball," Mr. Thompson chuckled as he read the message. "This will be four cents, please."

Ian counted out the change, adding enough for the day's paper. "I'll see you next time." As he left, he wondered what the chances were that Miss Hughes was still in the area. She'd shown a level of maturity in there that he hadn't expected. When he spotted her through the front window of the diner, he debated going on his way. Instead, he walked across the street, waving off his driver. He tucked the paper under his arm and opened the door to the diner, not sure at all what he was doing.

⌒～⌣~◦

Amelia flushed when she saw Ian Hayworth enter the diner. Hoping he was there for some reason other than her, she sipped from her heavy mug, grimaced at the bitter taste, and set it back down just as he walked over.

"Not a coffee drinker, Miss Hughes?" he asked.

"Not this coffee, anyway." She didn't tell him that this was her first cup, or that she'd hoped they'd have proper tea. "You're welcome to stay," she said.

"Thank you." He sat down across from her and placed his hat on the corner of the table. When the server approached with a smile, he ordered a black coffee, along with two slices of apple pie. "You must try their pie," he said once the server left. "It's some of the best I've tasted."

"And what if I don't like it?" Amelia asked. She was surprised by how calm she sounded, sitting across from someone she barely knew, conversing as if they were friends.

"Then I'll eat both slices," he grinned. Then he straightened. "I apologize for my rudeness a moment ago. I was surprised to see you."

"Oh," Amelia said. She picked up her coffee, tried another sip, then set it down. "It's quite all right."

"I was dropping off a coded message for my nephew. My sister subscribes to *The Gazette*. I like to give him a puzzle from time to time." He smiled at her.

She had the impression he was hoping she'd reciprocate and tell why she'd been there. Gathering her courage, she explained, "I've been job hunting all morning. Each place echoes what Mr. Thompson said. They notice that I'm not a man, and won't consider my writing."

Amelia had felt so hopeful and excited this morning. Now, having been turned away from each paper she'd visited, her frustration was mounting. She had just about decided to head home, except thinking of home made her remember Harrison's visit. She frowned.

"Are you all right?"

Ian's gentle question drew her back. Amelia flushed. She'd forgotten he was sitting with her. "I'm quite all right, thank you," she said stiffly. When a flash of disappointment crossed his face, she felt a stab of guilt. Sighing, she answered honestly. "I've had some hardships lately. I'm trying to move past them, but I'm finding it difficult to put them out of my mind completely."

Ian nodded in understanding, "I'm sorry to hear that."

The slices of pie arrived, and Amelia sighed in relief. She'd never been that vulnerable with a man before, and wasn't sure how to carry on the conversation. They ate their slices quietly. Amelia was surprised by how good it was. She peeked a glance up at Ian.

"You were right about the pie," she said. "It's delicious. Thank you."

"You're welcome," he smiled.

Amelia blinked at the way his smile transformed his face. *Has he always been so handsome?* Suddenly feeling awkward, she started to plan a way to graciously leave.

"Do you need a ride?" Ian asked. "This neighborhood isn't the best."

"I'm all right," Amelia answered.

"If you say so. I know Angela would want you to be safe."

Harrison's voice rattled through her head. *He won't touch you again. I took care of it. You're safe.*

As if through a fog, she heard Ian's voice say her name. "Miss Hughes?" She shook her head, and he came back into focus. *What's wrong with me today?* She blinked, suddenly noticing how blue his eyes were.

"I'm fine," she said sharply, wincing at the sound of her own voice.

"Of course," Ian said with a stiff smile. "I'll be on my way then, Miss Hughes." He put his hat on, nodded and left.

Alone again, Amelia felt lower than she had all morning. She debated about going after him to apologize. When she moved to pay the bill, she realized that Ian had left enough money for both slices of pie and their coffees. She slipped her shawl over her shoulders and headed outside, quickly scanning the street. She spotted Ian a little way down and hurried after him. He'd paused by a carriage, talking to the driver.

"Mr. Hayworth!" she called, buttoning her glove at her wrist. He turned toward her, and she held out her hand, eager to make amends. "It seems now I must apologize to you. You have my regrets."

Only when he'd gripped her hand did she realize she'd not put on both of her gloves. The one she'd offered was bare, and his hand held hers perfectly.

"You're quite forgiven, Miss Hughes. It seems it's been a day for both of us to be out of countenance. Good day." Before she could form a reply, he tipped his hat and climbed into his carriage.

Chapter Twelve

Angie sighed as Mrs. Taylor called the first Ladies Aid Society meeting to a close. *I'm so tired.* She nodded at Edith, who was talking with Mrs. Taylor, and started making her way out of the house. She'd invited Edith for tea and wanted to arrive early to make sure everything was ready. She smiled at those she passed, hoping to avoid conversation. She'd almost reached the front door when Mrs. Detrid stopped her.

"Angela, I thought I'd missed you."

"Mrs. Detrid, how are you?" Angie asked. She wondered if the lady ever noticed that she never returned the sentiment of first names.

"Oh, I'm right as rain, Angela," Mrs. Detrid replied. "I was worried about you, having missed the last two debuts, although Amelia was there. She said you were fine, but I just knew something was wrong."

"I'm quite all right," Angie remarked. "Thank you for your concern."

Mrs. Detrid grabbed her arm. "There's speculation…"

"I'm quite well," Angie said, stiffening. "I must be on my way."

"Well," Mrs. Detrid released Angie's arm. "I was merely concerned for your welfare. If this is the thanks I get, I'll not be bothering you again."

"I'm sorry, Mrs. Detrid. I didn't mean to offend." Angie would like nothing better than for the woman to avoid her in the future, but her conscience couldn't allow it. "I was sorry to miss those events, but something unexpected came up. Thank you for your concern, and for taking time to speak with Amelia at the parties."

Mrs. Detrid nodded. "Very well, Angela. I hope nothing untoward has occurred, but I won't ask. A woman has the right to secrets, and it's clear that you are keeping yours close. Good day."

Angie left Mrs. Taylor's house, troubled by the interaction. There was no way she was telling that gossiper the reason she'd been absent from the parties. The news would spread through town before day's end.

Angie climbed into her carriage and suppressed a shudder. *Grant me more patience for Mrs. Detrid. And guide my tongue.*

Weakness hit her like a wave as the carriage went on. She leaned her head back and closed her eyes. By the time she was home, she felt a little better, but her movements were sluggish. She set her things on the table, picked up a waiting letter from Diane, and entered the salon.

Angie regretted how slowly she'd been able to get downstairs and intervene earlier this morning. She still could not believe Harrison James had shown up in such a state! Shaking her head, she wondered how Amelia's job search was going. She was impressed by the girl's decision to go today. Perhaps if Amelia was away from Georgia and her friends long enough, she would lose her infatuation with high society. *Please, let it be true.*

Angie slid two pages from the envelope. Before she read them, she wondered if she should put it off until she felt better. Letters from her sister were never pleasant. Diane had learned the tactic of making people feel small from their mother. When Angie left her hometown for good, it was the bravest thing she had done up to that point. Her family had been suffocating her. She knew she couldn't stay any longer. The day after her eighteenth birthday, she bought a one-way train ticket to the city, and never looked back.

She returned her mind to the moment, unfolded the letter, and began to scan it with dismay.

…I require Amelia home no later than the 20th of August to attend a wedding. She may bring one personal maid. Cedric will accompany her on the return trip on the 5th of September, and will stay with you until his classes start at university, which will be just over a fortnight…

It continued, but Angie set it on her lap. *Amelia is to be gone for a fortnight.* Angie had no intention of arguing the matter. After all, Amelia was Diane's daughter, not hers. The timing of this could've been better, given today's events. Hopefully Amelia would have time to process this latest fiasco with Harrison before she left to deal with her mother. It was less than a week until she'd have to leave.

Hearing the front door open, Angie set the letter aside and stood. "Welcome, Edith," she said as her friend walked in. "Tea will be here shortly."

"Thank you," Edith replied. "So, do you think the group has potential?"

Angie answered, but was only half attentive to the conversation. Her mind was still on Diane's letter. If there was one thing Diane was exceptional at, it was disrupting other people's plans and peace of mind.

"Edith, she's ruined everything," Angie burst out. "How can Amelia heal if she has to put up with her mother's manipulating?"

Edith served tea and listened patiently as Angie explained. Once Angie had spent all of her words, she sat quietly, exhausted. Worse, her throat was closing, cutting off her oxygen. She took short breaths, hoping it would pass quickly.

"I don't mean to be insensitive, Angie, but surely you knew Amelia would eventually have to go home for a visit?" Edith continued when Angie didn't answer. "I know you're concerned about what happened this morning, but this fear seems to be more than that."

Once her throat eased, Angie sighed. Her friend was right. Her fear was more than what she'd claimed. "I've been having some problems breathing," she admitted, "as well as this exhaustion. I started coughing last night too…" She trailed off at the look on her friend's face.

"Have you talked to a doctor?"

"It's been several months since I saw him last." Even as she spoke, she knew she'd been fooling herself.

"And you're feeling poorly today?"

As Angie nodded, tears sprung to her eyes at the admission. Edith summoned a maid, and instructed her to send for a doctor immediately. Her concerned gaze stayed on Angie the whole time.

～∾∿

Dr. Luke Martin watched Angela stir. He waited until she opened her eyes before speaking. "Angela, I need to check your pulse. Will you lie still?" At her nod, he gently held her wrist, checking her pulse, while also noting how pale she was, and the shadows under her eyes.

"What happened?" Angela asked in a strained voice.

Dr. Martin didn't answer until he'd finished counting. "You fainted just as Edith sent for me, as I understand it. How do you feel?"

"Weak. Chilled. It's hard to breathe. And thirsty."

He made note of her checklist, as well as the fact that she'd listed her symptoms. Most patients wove their answer through a story, or lengthy descriptions. He'd found that people who kept close tabs on their bodies gave answers in lists. His heart ached at what this might mean for Angela.

"Those are all understandable," he said. "The last one will be easy enough to remedy, if you don't mind, Mrs. Grey." Dr. Martin nodded toward the pitcher of water, which Edith carried over to him. He turned back to Angela. "Do you check how you feel before doing something?"

"Yes," she murmured. There was a wealth of information in that one word. Setting aside his notepad, he took her hand again.

"I'm concerned that this has apparently been going on for a few weeks. Is that correct?"

"About eight months," Angela admitted weakly.

He shook his head, frowning. "You know you should have called me the first time you had trouble breathing. But we'll move on from here. I trust you'll call me in the future." His tone left no room for arguing.

He first met Angela when she was a new bride, and had cared for her over the years. The days of her husband's illness and death had been some of the hardest of his career. He started to speak again, but footsteps banging up the stairs made him pause. He stepped back when Angela's niece flew through the doorway. She didn't stop until she'd fallen to her knees beside the bed, quickly grabbing Angela's hand.

"Are you well?" she inquired anxiously.

"I'm fine," Angela whispered.

Dr. Martin turned away and looked out the window. Moments like these didn't need an audience. Aside from that, it hurt to see the look of fear in someone so young. He wasn't certain what he could do to help Angela, but he would do all he could. He'd leave the rest in God's hands.

A few minutes later, Amelia sat on the bedside and held Angie's hand as she listened to the doctor. She knew Aunt Angie hadn't been feeling well, but didn't know how serious it was. *Can I be the companion she needs?* Lifting her chin, she took a deep breath, pushed her doubts away, and focused on what the doctor was saying.

"Listen to what your body is telling you. It will let you know when you need to rest. Don't push yourself…or you'll make it worse."

"How much time do you think I have before…" Aunt Angie's voice faltered.

"That depends on how the consumption progresses. I'd say in the next few months, you'll be quite limited in your abilities. I'm sorry, Angela, but if there are any plans you've made past that, you might want to change them." The kindly doctor grasped Angie's hand for a moment. "I'll be back in a few days."

Amelia was surprised to see such familiarity between them. He turned toward her. "I'm glad you're here with her," he said. "Bless you."

Offering thanks, Amelia shook his hand. Wrinkles around his eyes evidenced that he was a happy man, despite the pain he must have seen during his years serving people. His spectacles lent him a distinguished look, and his hair stood on end. His persona spoke of honesty and caring. All in all, Amelia decided she liked him.

With one last squeeze of her hand, he released her and turned to leave. Amelia stared blankly at the spot where he'd stood, wondering what she was supposed to do next.

"I'll show you out, doctor," Edith offered. "Amelia, I'll be right back with some tea." When they were gone, Amelia felt her aunt shaking. She wrapped a shawl and her arms around Angie's shoulders, and held her silently. Tears rolled down her cheeks.

Edith entered quietly some moments later with the tea tray. Amelia accepted a cup from her. Tears burned her eyes. *Is Aunt Angie really going to die? Can I be the companion she needs?*

They sipped their tea in silence. Amelia felt like they were each biding time, waiting for the other to speak. She had no idea what to say. She felt like crying or screaming. She was determined to be the support her aunt needed, though her heart was so broken that she felt overwhelmed.

"Can you help me lie down?" Aunt Angie asked after finishing her tea. Amelia and Edith moved to help her, eager to assist her in any way they could.

That evening, Amelia sought solace in her room, but the day's events were too much to handle. Her thoughts bounced between the doctor's diagnosis, Harrison's visit, and the rejections she'd encountered at various papers. Eventually, she focused on Ian's gentleness, and the feel of her hand in his. Maybe she'd misjudged her aunt's friend as being a stick in the mud. Besides, she realized something. Ian was the handsome man she had noticed on her first trip to the theatre. How had she not recognized him immediately?

～⌣⌣⌣～

"Does yours say the same as mine?" Amelia tossed the letter away from her and chose a pastry from the small table between them.

"Diane insists that you go home for a visit," Aunt Angie said, speaking in a bit of a rasp.

"I feel like a raincloud has settled over me, Aunt Angie," Amelia admitted. "Do you think we could put it off? I don't want to leave you right now."

"I doubt I'd be able to persuade her," Aunt Angie said uncertainly. "Besides, it is a good time for you to go…before I get worse. Selfishly, I'd like to have you here with me as I decline…"

"I'll be with you every day, no matter what!" Amelia promised.

"Thank you, Amelia Lynn. That means so much. I should have thought of you going home before this. I just didn't want to, I suppose."

Amelia couldn't think of anything to say. Her heart was heavy, and her eyes burned. Excusing herself, she hurried upstairs to her room. She found Grace waiting for her.

"Are you all right, Miss Amelia?"

"I should've known it would happen," she stammered. "I'm worried Mother will keep me there…and I'm so happy here. I can't leave Aunt Angie right now!" Her fears rushed out, leaving her breathless. She lay on the bed, completely miserable. Sitting upright suddenly, Amelia's face lit up. "You'll go with me, won't you? It wouldn't be quite so hard if you are there."

"If your aunt agrees."

"She will, I'm sure of it."

At first, Amelia kept away any thoughts of returning home. At the start, she'd been too homesick for her father and Cedric. Later, the inevitability worried her. A fortnight felt entirely too long to be gone from Aunt Angie, but as usual, when it came to her mother, she didn't have any say in the matter.

⌒‿⌒

"This cannot continue," Ian said as he paced the large sitting room in his sister's home. "All of you must leave."

"He felt horrible afterwards," his sister confided. "He apologized and had the maid get some ice…and really was the sweetest the rest of the evening."

Her words didn't reassure Ian in the least. He kept his back turned to his sister, to avoid having to look at her bruised cheek. He stopped in front of a window and stared into the dark night. His reflection stared back at him, but he focused on his sister's reflection instead. She sat with her head bowed, her hands covering her stomach.

The pose was so similar to one from years before that he felt as if he was looking into the past, when she was pregnant with Hugh. He remembered their conversation then…

"Why don't you let me help you get away from him?"

"I decided that I'd had enough. But then I found out… I'm pregnant."

"Please, come live with me. You'll be well looked after during your confinement. You could live at the Manor in a year or so if you wanted."

"No. I won't deprive this child of having a father, or burden him with the scorn of having a single mother."

"Doesn't he have a right to a healthy mother? To a life without…"

"I've made my decision, and you won't talk me out of it."

Her words that night so closely mirrored what she said when they argued about her marrying Maddox in the first place. The memory caused him to flinch. He and his father tried talking to Dorothy about the types of charges Maddox had been running up in town, as well as the claims he'd been making of the wealth he'd soon have. But Dorothy said it was her money. What did they have to be upset about? She did not see the point of their argument, even as they tried to explain their fear that Maddox expected a larger dowry.

Ian sighed. The same determination that had gotten her into this marriage was keeping her in it. He snapped back to the present when Leo, her third, ran into the room, "Mama! I can't find my…"

As soon as the boy was gone again, Ian spoke. "Your husband's reaction afterward doesn't excuse his actions."

"I'm aware of that, Ian. But it won't happen again, he promised it wouldn't."

Hearing the exhaustion in her voice, Ian moved to her side, picking up one of her hands as he sat down. His sister was once again choosing the wrong path. He knew he couldn't stop her. He searched her face as he rubbed his thumb over the back of her hand. All he could see was that same dogged determination…and fear. "Ah, Dorothy. If I weren't bound to silence…"

Before he could finish, she lifted her chin defiantly. Her tired, shadowed eyes sent out sparks. He leaned back. They stared at each other, siblings caught in a tide of consequences and regret. He squeezed her fingers, worried at how pale and drawn she was.

"I've not changed my mind," she said stiffly. "My boys enjoy good standing in society and will be able to do whatever they please. They have a good name."

"But not a good father," he bit out. Unable to say what he wanted, he released her hand and stood. Looking down at her, he frowned. "I'll bid you good evening." He felt as if he was going to explode. He didn't want to be around his sister if he did.

"Ian, please," she reached out for him, but he ignored her plea and left the room in long strides. The maid quickly had his coat and hat ready for him.

"Uncle Ian!" Hugh slid to a stop by his side, his hair tumbling across his forehead. "Did you talk to her?"

Ian slapped his gloves in his hand and reached for the door. "I did. But it didn't do any good."

"You can't leave!"

The panic in the boy's voice stopped him. Closing his eyes for a second, he prayed for patience. "I can't stay. I'm not abandoning you in this situation. I just can't think straight right now. Do you understand?"

"I think so." The boy was obviously shaken, but Ian could do nothing more than grip his shoulder in a silent farewell before leaving.

～⌣⌣๏

Agitated, Ian didn't notice the roses in bloom, nor the way their scent filled the air while he waited outside of Angela's house. His mind was full of the past and the present. Nothing had changed, other than Maddox's behavior growing worse.

"Mr. Hayworth," Walter bowed to him.

"Is Angela at home?" He struggled to speak around the tightness in his throat.

"Yes, sir. Let me announce you." Walter bowed and left Ian standing in the entry. His regard for propriety made him pause, but his anxiety to see his friend overcame it. He'd made it to the other side of the room when Walter came back out of the salon. "Right this way."

The butler held his hand toward the open doorway and left. Grateful for the man's consideration, Ian entered the salon silently and found himself unable to summon a smile.

"Ian? What's the matter?" Angela asked, standing, and drawing near.

"I came to…" He dropped heavily into the closest chair and hung his head in his hands. She put her hand gently on his shoulder. He sighed. "Forgive me, Angela. I didn't mean to come in such a state and…" He ran his fingers through his hair, uncertain how to continue. "I've just come from my sister's."

"Ah," Angela's voice was gentle. "Has something happened with her husband?" She took the seat next to him.

He nodded. "In a way, yes. The man is a brute."

"You've known that for a long time."

"Yes." He stood up, unable to remain still. "And she knows it as well. But she refuses to do what's best for her and the boys, which would be to leave him. She maintains that it's better for her children to have a father, even if he is a scoundrel and an abuser."

"What's happened that has so upset you? Not to diminish the situation your sister's in, but this isn't new."

He groaned. "I went over to see her after getting a distressing note from Hugh. He claimed that Maddox hit her last night, knocking her onto a side table. When I asked her about it, she didn't deny it." Saying it out loud tore his heart further. His voice broke. Blinking tears away, he looked at her. "And then she told me why he hit her. She's pregnant again." Tears ran down his face.

"Oh, Ian." Angela's voice was a whisper.

Chapter Thirteen

Leaving Aunt Angie at the train station that morning was so hard that Amelia already felt like she'd been gone for days. The rain falling in sheets all night before she left only added to Amelia's loneliness. Now, with the train getting closer to Riverside, she only felt worse. Sadly, Amelia knew that if her mother hadn't been waiting on the other end of this trip, it might have felt like a fun adventure. Instead, the knot in her stomach grew as the train slowed and pulled into the small station.

Amelia looked out the window at her rain-soaked hometown. Riverside was not as isolated from the city as it seemed. It was actually trying to catch up with modernity, including electricity and even some automobiles. Still, as she scanned Main Street's modest, faded buildings, Amelia felt a twinge of disappointment. Only the sight of Cedric among the throng with his large umbrella made her smile.

She introduced him to Grace as a porter brought their luggage. Cedric, with his bright red hair, freckled cheeks and lean frame, led them to the nearby carriage and assisted them in. Then her brother tipped the porter and climbed aboard, snapping the reins and setting the horses moving.

Amelia peered out at people they passed, wondering if she'd recognize anyone. Everyone was bundled up against the rain, making it impossible to see faces. Home or not, the town seemed foreign somehow. She slipped her arm into Cedric's as they rode.

"Mother has cleaned everything from top to bottom," he said. "And you know she only does that for special visitors." Cedric slapped the reins again. "How's Aunt Angela?"

"She's…doing well." Amelia didn't like misleading her brother, but her aunt wasn't ready to tell anyone about her diagnosis. "We've read so many books these past months. We are going to start *The Jungle Book* when I get home."

Amelia quickly glanced at her brother when the word *home* came out of her mouth. She wanted to see if he'd caught her slip, but he didn't seem to have noticed.

"Leave it to you to tell me how Aunt Angie is by mentioning what you're reading," he teased. Grace chuckled, which prompted Amelia to glance at her.

"You don't have to agree with him, Grace," she said. "You're *supposed* to be on my side."

"You've always said how you can tell if you'll like someone by what they're reading," Grace reminded.

As they turned onto a narrow street, Amelia fell silent. Their house was near the other end of this road. The knot in her stomach was growing bigger. If it weren't raining, the street would be busy with neighborly visits. As it was, everything was quite empty.

Amelia pulled her arm from Cedric's and twisted her handkerchief, rehearsing her greeting to her mother. As they pulled in front of the house, she brushed a hair from her forehead and accepted Cedric's assistance from the carriage. Standing in front of her childhood home, she tucked away her handkerchief and led the way onto the porch. *I can't do this.*

Inside and settled, Amelia sat across from her mother. She took a deep breath to calm herself. She could faintly hear Grace being led to the kitchen for tea and wished she could've joined her. Instead, she was relegated to her mother's salon, listening to the gossip from the past year, even though she'd already heard about it through their letters. She scanned the room a little, not wanting her mother to catch her, and noted the new embroidered cushions as well as a new portrait of Horace in the center of the mantel.

Amelia's throat tightened, and she quickly looked down at her teacup. She couldn't bear to look at the oh-so innocent smile on her younger brother's face. At a lull in the recitation, she set her teacup down, heart pounding. "I brought you a gift, Mother," she said.

She retrieved the hat box from the front hall, but in her hurry, it hit the doorframe and slipped from her fingers. Just catching it, she blushed before placing it next to her mother on the settee.

Sighing, Diane opened the lid, pulling out a hat made in the latest fashion. Clusters of flowers were gathered at the front of the wide brim, while a ribbon wrapped around the base. Diane's eyes widened for a moment before she grimaced. "Is that all you could do for me?" she muttered as she dropped the hat back in the box. "I suppose I should be glad that you thought of me at all."

"But, Mother, it's a lovely hat. I thought you'd be pleased."

"I might wonder why I get only a hat when your whole wardrobe is all the rage of fashion. Your own hat for instance!"

Amelia's hand went to her head. "I'm sorry. Aunt Angie got it for me. Here, let me take it off." Her fingers desperately sought the hat pin, hidden among the adornments. She couldn't remember where she'd pinned it.

"Oh, well…if your aunt wished it, then you must have it," Diane said bitterly. "And wear it to flaunt over your family as if you were better than us now, I dare say."

"But that isn't it at all," Amelia said, wincing and pulling her hands down quickly. The hat pin stabbed her, and blood started to pool at the end of one finger. "I'm sorry you don't like it. I ordered it specially for you. I was quite anxious that it wouldn't be ready in time." Amelia realized that she was practically begging her mother to like her gift. Deliberately setting her shoulders straighter, she wandered the sitting room, trying to regain her composure.

"Sit down!" Diane said sharply. "You're making me nervous, pacing like that."

Amelia sat again, her back ramrod straight even though she wanted to curl into the cozy chair. Sipping her tea, she tried to focus on what her mother was saying, but her mind trailed off. How would she ever make it through the coming afternoons, when she'd be confined to this same chair as her mother entertained.

"I see you've finally learned to sit properly," Diane said, her voice less stringent.

"Yes, Mother," Amelia murmured.

"That puddle you left in the entryway will probably ruin my floor."

"Sorry, Mother."

"Why you came on a day when it's raining like this is beyond me. Why, when Mrs. Smark's daughter came home for a visit, she came on the most beautiful day. We were all able to stop by the house and wish her well. No one will be coming by to see you, I dare say."

"No, Mother, I suppose not," Amelia said, looking out the window. She didn't see how the rain was her fault, but she kept her opinion to herself.

It was another hour before Diane sighed and looked critically at Amelia. "Go rest until your father gets home."

"Yes, Mother." Amelia stood then paused, gathering her courage. "Can Grace stay with me in my room during my visit?"

"You want the maid to sleep in your room?"

"I do," Amelia said, her voice shaking from nerves.

"It seems my sister is failing, but I'm hardly surprised." Diane set her teacup down and shook her head. "If you want to sleep with a servant girl, go right ahead. Although I can only imagine what the neighbors will say when they hear about this."

Amelia thanked her mother and hurried from the room. Upstairs, Grace was already in Amelia's old bedroom, unpacking the bags. Amelia lay on the wide bed and happily abandoned all images of refined womanhood as she relaxed.

"I've decided something," she said to Grace. "While we are here, we're the same. It's silly anyway, all the stuff you do for me."

Grace paused in airing out the fine dresses. "It's my job," she protested.

"I know. But wouldn't you like a break?"

"Well..."

"Good. It's settled. We'll help each other get ready."

Amelia walked with her arm in Cedric's as they followed their parents into the reception hall. The wedding ceremony was over. Now all she had to do was survive the reception. Cedric released her, waving at a friend across the hall. Amelia sighed and watched him go. She wasn't given long to regret his absence, however, as Diane turned to her.

"I must introduce you to some people," her mother said.

Hiding a frown, Amelia obediently followed her mother, even though she was sure she knew everyone present. They stopped in front of the Smarks, whom Amelia had known for as long as she could recall. The fact did not deter Diane from reintroducing her.

"You remember my daughter, Amelia, of course," Diane said. She held her hand toward Amelia as if displaying her.

"Of course," Mrs. Smark said, stiffly. "That dress is truly lovely."

Before Amelia could respond, Diane jumped in. "Mrs. Bobbin, in Portland, made it."

Mrs. Smark nodded and inspected Amelia's dress, a gleam in her eye. "I've obviously heard that her creations are the best, but I'd never seen one in person."

"The lace is a clear example of the quality of her work," Diane said. She pulled Amelia's hand toward her to show off the lace that edged the long sleeves.

As the conversation continued, Amelia stood silently. Diane wasn't interested in having her contribute. She just wanted her daughter to stand there and smile. They continued on around the reception room…Diane greeting person after person, showing off Amelia like a prize, then moving along. Soon, Amelia was exhausted from talking about nothing but her wardrobe. She sighed in relief as they reached her father. Diane nodded then hurried away alone.

"You're making her proud," Richard Hughes said. He patted Amelia's hand, which she'd tucked under his arm. Amelia smiled then looked away. She watched a young couple dancing and imagined it was her with Harrison. *How wonderful to be anywhere but here.*

"Do you mind another introduction?" her father asked.

"I suppose not," Amelia smiled. Her father led her toward a short man whose middle was his widest point.

"Mr. Grote, this is my daughter, Amelia. She's home for a visit."

Mr. Grote's small eyes assessed her from behind round glasses. "A pleasure to meet you, Miss Hughes." He jerked his chin upward, tugging at his collar as he did so.

"I'm pleased to meet you, Mr. Grote," she said.

"Mr. Grote and I work together," Richard clarified. "He's a clever man at business."

Mr. Grote laughed and rubbed at his chin. "As if you aren't just so, Richard!" Turning to Amelia, he asked, "Have you got your father's mind for business, young lady? Or are you focused on something else?"

"Oh, Mr. Grote, you know it's highly inappropriate for a young lady of breeding to be in business!" Diane interjected, butting in as if she'd been part of the conversation from the beginning. Grote swallowed, jerked his chin again and nodded.

"Just so, madame," he offered. He turned to Amelia. "A pleasure, Miss Hughes."

As he left, his short legs taking surprisingly long strides, Diane scoffed. "That man wouldn't know *true* society if it walked up and slapped him in the face," she said. "Amelia, I want you again. Come."

Diane snapped her fingers. Richard squeezed Amelia's arm before releasing her. She wished she could stay with him longer, but her mother was already waiting for her several feet away. Fighting the urge to scurry over, she walked sedately to her mother's side. Diane turned on her heel, sweeping through the room with her head high. A knot of dread tightened in Amelia's stomach as they drew closer to the newlyweds, Jane and Michael.

"Mrs. Hughes!" Jane said graciously. "Thank you for coming."

"I'm pleased to have been invited," Diane said, then added a self-satisfied smile. "The placement of the flowers is perfect, I must say."

"They do look wonderful, don't they?" Jane said, giving the flowers a quick glance before spotting Amelia. "Amelia? Is that you?"

"Yes, I'm back for a visit."

"You look wonderful! Who made your gown?"

"Thank you. Mrs. Bobbin of Portland."

"I wanted her to make my wedding gown, but she was too busy."

Amelia smiled and admired the girl's wedding gown. "It's stunning, whoever made it. You look beautiful."

Jane blushed and started to speak.

"Amelia's whole wardrobe is made by Mrs. Bobbin," Diane cut in, before the bride could continue. "And her hats are…"

"Thank you, Mother," Amelia interrupted. She flushed in embarrassment, then in fear that her mother would scold her for interrupting her like that.

"She doesn't like when I boast about her," Diane said, patting Amelia's hand. The bride nodded knowingly and smiled. Amelia couldn't remember a time when her mother had ever said anything so positive as to be considered a boast.

The days soon took on a rhythm that mostly depended on Diane and the weather. While Amelia's new wardrobe struck a spark of envy in her, Mrs. Hughes was determined to make as many people as possible jealous of her now stylish daughter. Amelia smiled and nodded wherever her mother took her but found no joy in any of it.

As much as Amelia tried to stay focused, her aunt's diagnosis hung over her like a cloud every day. Finally, one afternoon, she retreated to her bedroom, unable to hold back the tears of hurt for her aunt, and a genuine homesickness for Portland. She wiped her eyes and took a calming breath as Grace entered.

"I have just the thing to cheer you up," Grace said as she set an envelope on the bed.

"It's from Aunt Angie!" Amelia sat up and read the news hungrily. "Mrs. Parri is singing next month at the club and has sent us personal invitations!"

"How exciting!" Grace exclaimed. "Is Mrs. Barrington doing well?"

"She says that she is, but she wouldn't really say anything else in a letter. I do worry about her. Her hands have started shaking so much." Amelia's excitement faded.

"I've noticed that," Grace admitted.

Has she fainted again? Amelia wondered. *How much longer until...?* She took a deep breath and refocused on the letter. "We'll be back home shortly."

"Better not let Mother hear you call Portland *home*," Cedric said. Amelia looked up and saw her brother leaning against the doorframe of her room. She hated it when either of her brothers snuck up on her.

"You did so in the carriage as well...the day we arrived," he went on. He took a few steps into the room. "I agree though...this isn't home. Even though my job at the mercantile was tough and my room a literal closet, it was still better than being here. Being back wouldn't be so bad if Mother didn't hover so. Living there, I became my own man. At first, I resented our parents for sending me away, but it prepared me for life outside of this house. And now that I'm eighteen, I'll be heading to university."

Amelia stared at him. How could the brother she'd left earlier this year be so grown up?

"I'm glad for you," she said.

"Don't look so surprised," he smirked. "You've changed too, although she's taking that away from you, bit by bit."

"What?" She glanced quickly at Grace. "Have I changed?"

"Since we got here? Yes," Grace said softly.

"She's a force of nature, our mother," Cedric continued, then looked at Grace. "I suspect you're not as meek as you seem either." She flushed at his comment.

"Cedric!" Amelia chided. "How impertinent can you be?"

"I meant nothing by it," Cedric replied. "Mother can bend anyone to her will. I was merely stating that I think Grace has chosen the quiet way of dealing with it."

"Well, she is my better," Grace nodded. "It's only right that I remain deferential."

"No one is your better," Cedric said forcefully. "You're as much a lady as my sister here. Maybe more so." Before either could respond, footsteps rang out on the stairs. All three tensed. Cedric moved toward the doorway. When it turned out to be a maid going about her chores, everyone breathed easier.

"Let's see if we can take a walk," Amelia suggested, setting aside Aunt Angie's letter. "I'm ready for some fresh air."

Half an hour later, they were on their way, with Cedric driving. They remained silent until they were well clear of the house.

"Amelia Lynn?" a young woman's voice called out as they rode. "I declare, it is you! Hold up, Cedric!"

"Prudence!" Amelia exclaimed. Her friend was still waving them down, her face lit up in excitement as Amelia rushed to catch her in a tight hug. They talked until Cedric cleared his throat loudly several times.

"Can't you chatter away another time, Amelia?"

"All right, all right. We must get together for tea soon!" Amelia said before bidding Prudence goodbye. Once back in the carriage, she turned to Grace.

"Prudence was my sworn enemy when we were six years old," Amelia laughed. "But then Mr. and Mrs. Smark moved into town and their daughter started school with us. We became friends out of necessity."

"The enemy of my enemy is my friend," Grace offered.

"Exactly," Amelia laughed, shaking her head. "Mr. Smark is the banker, so Mother insisted we do our duty and have them over. Luckily, she couldn't stand Mrs. Smark, after she made a remark about the carpet in the parlor."

They soon arrived at their destination, a quiet corner of the town's park. With fall on its way, the trees were ablaze with colors. Amelia looped her arm through Grace's, and they followed the meandering path. As they walked, some of the worry and stress that had been weighing her down began to ease. The park was so familiar, yet Amelia felt oddly detached from it, as if seeing it for the first time through different eyes.

"I used to come here to read under that tree," she said, gesturing to a grand oak.

"It's a peaceful place," Grace acknowledged.

Amelia nodded, her mind drifting to the mix of elation and guilt she used to feel whenever she'd sneaked away from her mother. "Just a few more days and we'll be going home to Aunt Angie. It doesn't feel right being gone for so long, even though Mrs. Grey is with her." She squeezed Grace's arm gently. "Although, I'll miss our nightly talks."

"Oh, we'll still have them," Grace reassured her. "Just at a different time of day, is all."

In the evening, Amelia sat on the front porch with Cedric, discussing their upcoming trip to Portland. The sun was getting low, and the neighborhood was quiet. She was relieved that there were only a few days until they left. She would most likely spend them packing everything properly, so her mother wouldn't shame her for poorly packed trunks.

Amelia sighed. *As if anyone cares about that.* Her nerves were worn thin. She was looking forward to the calm environment of her aunt's home...her home.

"You know what we were saying about home, before?" Amelia spoke quietly to her brother. Cedric nodded. "Aunt Angie's *is* home…now. I don't think I'll ever live here again. There's no reason to."

"Especially if you get married there," Cedric teased.

Amelia chuckled. "I don't know when I'll marry, but it won't be for a long while. There's too much I want to do and see. Besides," she said airily, brushing a curl from her cheek. "I haven't met anyone that I'd consider for a husband."

"You've never met anyone that took your breath away, even for an instant?" Cedric asked quietly. "No one you felt safe with, even if you'd only known them for a short time? Or someone you felt knew you better than anyone?"

Cedric's questions took her back to a moment of holding hands…brilliant eyes looking at her like they truly knew her. She shifted in her seat and glanced at her brother.

"I'm not surprised," he grinned. "It can hit you from out of nowhere, little sister."

"What can?"

"Love." He looked toward the horizon again.

"I never said I was in love!" Amelia protested. "If I were, do you think I'd be going to every newspaper I can think of to find a job?"

He turned to her in surprise. He was about to speak when their mother's voice preceded her through the screen door. "Doesn't Angela have more than enough money to keep you?" she shrilled. "If you're too much of a burden for her, you can keep yourself here."

Amelia stood quickly. "Mother, that's not…you misunderstand…"

"I misunderstand?" Diane shrieked. "I sent you there to learn proper etiquette and meet a rich young man! With Angela's position, you can have your pick of the bachelors there. But instead you're traipsing about, begging for a job… like a commoner!" Diane ended with a sneer.

Cedric stretched his long legs in front of him. "Mother, calm down," he said. "If she wants to work, what's wrong with that? She can still get a rich husband."

"A man of class isn't going to be looking for a wife who's gone all day," Diane protested. "He wants her home to host lavish parties and look after his interests. His peers would laugh at him if he even thought of marrying a *working girl*." Diane's cold words struck Amelia in the heart. "As for love… ha! I'd like to see how much *love* can help anybody when they're out of money and can't afford wood to feed the fire. Or food to curb their appetite. It's far better to marry for practicality than for something as fleeting and fanciful as *love*."

This time she addressed both her children, skewering them with her gaze. "Love is for children. Grow up, both of you."

Cedric stood and turned to lean against the railing. "If you haven't noticed, we have grown up. And we don't think love is what you say."

"And who would you have fallen in love with, Cedric?" Diane sneered. "It's certainly not been any of the girls around here. You've not stood up with the same girl twice this whole fortnight."

He shoved off the rail and turned away from her. Amelia wished she could do the same, but she'd never had the courage to ignore her mother when she was in one of these moods.

"We weren't speaking of anyone specific," she said, trying to stay calm. "It was more about the *spirit* of love." She willed herself not to think of the handshake that came to mind a moment ago. Her mother would see any shift in her expression and pounce on it.

Diane's heels rang sharply as she joined them on the porch. "I would've done anything to have the opportunity you have. I didn't have the chance to live in lavish comfort so I could find a suitable husband while my family lived in squalor."

"This is what you call squalor, woman?" Richard's angry voice cut in from the bottom of the porch stairs. "If this is squalor, then I certainly married the right woman…one who nags her children night and day but doesn't offer one word of thanks to her hard-working husband! You deserve to know what true squalor is!" He turned and left without another word.

Diane spun on her heels back into the house, leaving Amelia and Cedric in shock. Their father had actually raised his voice to their mother. In all their years, he'd quietly ignored and humored his wife by turn. When they'd run to him as small children, grieved by something she'd said or done, he would remind them to be as good as they could be so they wouldn't upset her. Never had he confronted or reprimanded her.

Eventually, Amelia and Cedric settled back in their seats, somber and quiet. In the silence, Amelia decided that she wouldn't marry for anything but the deepest love…and that she would never leave her fate in anyone else's hands but her own.

***

Diane was in fine form the morning of their departure, admonishing and scolding them for not having things prepared to her standards. Amelia, Cedric, and even Grace sighed in relief as they boarded the train and settled into the private car Aunt Angie had reserved for them.

After spending the first hour of the trip in silence, Amelia set aside her book, which prompted Cedric to do the same.

"Are you excited to see your family again, Grace?" she asked.

"Of course," Grace nodded. "I'm always happy to see them."

"That's a rare thing, you know," Cedric said softly.

Amelia understood the longing in his voice. "We have Aunt Angie. I know you'll love her like I do."

He nodded, watching Grace as she embroidered. "I remember the first time I realized that not all families were like mine," Cedric said. "I was relieved and sad at the same time." He glanced at Amelia. "Tell me about Aunt Angela."

"Well, she loves to talk about theology, books, poetry, and so much else. She'll play cards if you want to stay in, or she'll take you to the theatre…or the park." As Amelia spoke, her heart began aching to be back with her aunt.

"What do you think of her, Grace?" Cedric asked.

"She's the kindest, most gentle soul. I've never met a better person."

"Never?" Cedric asked pointedly, leaning forward. Amelia smiled and looked away. She was getting the feeling that her brother liked Grace. She only turned back when Cedric spoke again.

"What sort of house does she live in?" he asked.

"A beautiful two-story, with a wraparound porch," Amelia answered. "There are so many guest rooms. There's even a large ballroom no one ever uses, except for my debut. The library is wonderful and has many books. It's truly the best room in the house."

"You didn't mention the garden, salon, or kitchen, though," Grace added. "Or the fact that you can catch the streetcar just a few blocks away."

"I didn't know about the streetcar," Amelia admitted. "Let's see, what else? We don't host much, mainly Edith and Mr. Hayworth."

"Aunt Angela has a beau?" Cedric asked.

Amelia laughed. "Ian's a friend of hers." She focused on Grace's movements as she started another flower. "Should we have lunch?"

"I'll serve it," Grace said, moving to put away her embroidery.

Cedric stood and pulled the basket down. "No need for that. It's not like we're incapable of emptying a basket on our own."

"Mr. Hughes, really, I can do that."

Cedric offered her a playful wave, then set the basket down near his sister. Amelia opened the lid and pulled out the prepared lunch. "I don't normally argue with a lady, Miss Grace, but if you insist on this conversation, I'll be forced to do so," he said. He sat back down and accepted a sandwich from Amelia. She was curious as to who would win this friendly argument, but tried not to be obvious about it.

"It's a simple meal to be shared among friends," Cedric went on. "And when you're with friends, you share the duties."

Amelia set a sandwich next to Grace, then pretended to be engrossed in unwrapping her own. "And I'd dearly like to consider you a friend," Cedric continued. Amelia peeked a glance at the two of them.

"I'd like that too," Grace said, smiling shyly.

With her niece and nephew due to arrive within an hour, Angie couldn't focus on anything. She'd already apologized to Maud, whom the whole house referred to as "Cook," when she stood and wandered away from the desk as they planned the weekly menu.

"All right," Angie said. "What do we have left to plan?"

"Just next Saturday, Mrs. Barrington," Cook replied.

"Do you have anything you can easily put off for the next day?" she asked. "I was thinking of taking Amelia and Cedric to the theatre. We might eat at the Portland Hotel. But I'm unsure if Cedric will be interested in that." She trailed off, frowning.

"How 'bout a stew?" Cook suggested.

"That sounds good. Let's have a quiche for breakfast. And how about leftovers from Friday night for lunch?"

Cook nodded, writing in her chicken scratch on the butcher paper to fill in Saturday. "That does it then. I'll leave ya to pace now," Cook teased as she gathered up her things.

Angie laughed and shook her head. She couldn't wait for them to arrive, yet she was nervous about hosting her nephew. He'd been so young when they'd seen each other last. If she was honest with herself, she was worried about the sort of young man he might have become. Would he upset the rhythm of their house? She said a quick prayer for calm even as she heard the front door open.

As she moved toward the entry hall, she glanced at the clock. They were right on time. Her heart swelled at the sight of them. Amelia took off her coat and hat, smiling at Walter. Grace ducked around the corner of the room toward the kitchen. Cedric stood still, looking around the room in astonishment. She stepped forward to greet them.

"Welcome home, Amelia," she said. "And Cedric, welcome!"

"Aunt Angie! I've missed you so!" It did Angie's heart good when Amelia turned and hurried toward her, arms outstretched. Their hug was tight and long. Angie smiled at Cedric over Amelia's shoulder, noticing his attention stayed on Grace as she disappeared down the hall.

He turned as if caught doing something wrong. "Thank you, Aunt Angela. Thank you for having me."

"Please, call me Aunt Angie. It's a pleasure. I missed getting to see you grow up. You've turned into quite the young man." His blush was sweet, his smile wide. Angie held out a hand. "I'd offer a hug, but as I don't know if you're comfortable, I'll settle for a handshake."

"I think a hug would be just fine," Cedric laughed. Angie realized he was as nervous about their reintroduction as she was, which settled her some. She gave him a quick, tight hug, smiling up at him, amazed at how tall he was.

"Would you two like to get settled first or have some tea?" she asked.

"I'd love to wash my face, if you don't mind," Amelia said, already heading upstairs. "I feel so filthy after that trip. Cedric, come this way, I'll show you your room."

Cedric smiled then followed his sister. Turning back toward the salon, Angie decided that she might as well pour a cup of tea for herself while she waited. Now that they were here, she could finally relax.

◦~◦~◦

Angie paused in her bedroom doorway, waiting until Grace and Cedric bid each other farewell and parted at the top of the stairs. Grace had a rosy glow as she entered Amelia's bedroom. Angie smiled and walked slowly to that same room. She'd keep an eye on them to make sure Grace never felt uncomfortable with Cedric here, but it seemed plain that the young people were interested in each other.

"Amelia, what do you think of playing Minister's Cat this evening?" Angie suggested. "With Cedric here, it'll be more fun."

"That's a great idea," Amelia agreed.

"Good, it's settled. Grace, would you mind seeing that it's set up for us after dinner? I'd like it to be a surprise for Cedric," Angie said. "Oh, and Amelia, I'd like to introduce Cedric to Ian. What do you think?"

"If you like. You know Mr. Hayworth much better than I do."

"I think they'd get along well. I'll invite him for Friday night," Angie said. She noticed that now, Grace was not the only one who was flushed. Amelia was as well.

"How are you feeling?" Amelia asked. "Have you seen Dr. Martin again?"

"I'm all right," Angie answered softly, drawing close to her niece. "I saw Dr. Martin while you were gone. I'm still in the beginning stages." When Amelia's eyes filled with tears, Angie hugged her and excused herself. She feared she hadn't answered very well. Still, thinking about her diagnosis had become too much for her. She would need to settle some things before too long. For now, she focused on enjoying her time with her niece and nephew.

Chapter Fourteen

A few mornings later at breakfast, Amelia's patience with her brother's constant folding and refolding the newspaper had nearly reached its limit. She was about to say something when he spoke first.

"Did you hear the *Free Press* is looking for a reporter?"

Her frustration vanished instantly, and she leaned forward.

"What else does it say?" she asked.

"That they've been a small weekly paper for twenty years, and recently moved here. They're eager to grow their readership in the Rose City."

"It might be worth going to talk to the owner, Amelia," Aunt Angie suggested.

"I'll do that right after breakfast."

Amelia finished eating and ordered a carriage. Dressed in a white blouse, deep green skirt, and matching jacket, she pinned on her hat and hollered goodbye to her aunt and brother.

On the ride, she practiced what to say, occasionally glancing out the window as they drove across town. Her nerves began to override her excitement. Still, when she stood looking at the small one-story building, she felt this was her chance.

She adjusted her grip on her portfolio, crossed the street, and entered the building. Her heart pounded as she looked around. It smelled of ink, paper, and dust. Immediately, she sneezed, which brought a man forward.

"Beg your pardon, miss," he said. "My son just took to dusting, and he's stirred up everything." He wiped his hands on a towel, inspecting her fine clothes as he walked closer. "What can I do for you? Are you needing to place an advertisement?"

"No, sir. I've come because I read that you needed a reporter. You see, I've brought some samples of what I can do." She pulled a handful of pages out of her portfolio and handed them to him. "I don't mind what I do here, I just want experience. And I know I can improve."

The man lifted his hand, halting her rush of words. Amelia bit her lip. He glanced through the pages, then flicked his gaze back to her. "Would you be the young lady that's related to Mrs. Barrington? I believe I saw your picture in *The Oregonian* the other day." He scanned her outfit again. "The article talked about your return."

Amelia nodded self-consciously. "Yes, I'm Mrs. Barrington's niece, Amelia Hughes. I arrived with my brother from visiting my family in Riverside."

The man nodded and thumbed through the pages. "If I understand correctly, your aunt is quite well-to-do."

"Yes, sir." Amelia shifted on her feet, impatient to get back on topic. "As you can see, I can do more than just write recipes and how-to pieces, although if that is what you need, I'd be glad to write those."

"You can write, Miss Hughes," he said. "And if you take instructions, you can learn to write well." He shot a glance at her face. "I've never thought of employing a lady. But you're eager, and you have the means to make it work. I've owned this paper for years, but haven't been able to make much of it. Moving here to the city will be the break we need."

He handed her pages back to her. "I'm Lionel McFarce. That's my son, Brock. He helps keep the place clean." Mr. McFarce grimaced at the dust that lingered in the air. "Well, once we get it set up right. It'll take a few days. Come back on Monday for your assignment. In the meantime, look these over." He grabbed a small stack of papers and set them on the counter.

"What areas should I pay particular attention to?" Amelia asked as she put the papers into her bag.

"Note how we do things. The type of news we cover, that sort of thing. With you being so highly connected, you'll cover the Society Page."

"Thank you, Mr. McFarce. I won't let you down. I'll see you again come Monday," she confirmed, trying not to squeal in excitement. After they settled on a time for her to arrive, Amelia strode out of the building toward Henry and the carriage. She couldn't wait to get home and tell Aunt Angie and Cedric. Her brother may not understand why she wanted to work when she didn't have to, but he'd still be excited for her. Her aunt, of course, understood. She'd be thrilled.

⁓⸜⸝◠

Angie moved her black checker and waited for Cedric to take his turn. Her enthusiasm for the game itself was limited. It was the company of her nephew she truly valued. The days had been good ones, but they were passing quickly. Having missed out on Cedric's early years, Angie was savoring the opportunity to connect with him as he matured into a young adult. He was headed to the University of Washington in two weeks. She knew the experience would change him even more.

"King me," Cedric said, smiling. Shaking her head at his obvious satisfaction, she did so, then eyed the board.

"You did warn me that you're good at this game," she said. Cedric chuckled.

"My friends and I used to play all the time."

"Aunt Angie!" The holler from the front of the house drew both their attention. Cedric rolled his eyes.

"She still yells all the time, huh?"

Angie smiled. "She's gotten better about it," she said. "It sounds like she's excited though." She waited until Amelia entered the salon before responding to her niece. "You sound happy."

"You are looking at the newest journalist at the *Free Press*!" Amelia squealed.

"Oh my! Congratulations! Come, tell us all about it," Angie insisted.

Amelia sat next to her. "The owner, Mr. McFarce, is very nice. He's got a son, Brock. They're a small paper, but they're hoping that a move to the city will help them grow. Mr. McFarce has big plans. He wants me to come back Monday. I'm just so excited!"

"I never would have guessed," Cedric said dryly.

Angie smiled at the typical brotherly comment. "It sounds good, Amelia. Are there any other workers? Any secretaries?"

"I don't think so. It's just the two of them, Mr. McFarce and his son." Amelia was still bursting with excitement. "He said I'll get my first assignment on Monday!"

"I can't wait to hear how your first day goes. I am a little worried though, that you'll be there by yourself."

"The owner and his son will be there."

"Aside from them. I'd be more comfortable if there were another woman in the office."

Amelia groaned. "If I wait for that, I may never get a chance to work at any paper!"

"She has a point," Cedric chimed in. "It's a man's profession."

Angie looked between them and sighed. "I'll pray about it." She held her hand up to forestall Amelia's protest. "I know this is a big opportunity, but I must remember my responsibility for you, Amelia. Let me pray about it."

"Yes, Aunt Angie." Amelia stood and left the room, looking a little sulky as she did.

Angie finished her game with Cedric, who remained silent. "It was nice to see her so excited," he finally said. "For a little bit, at least."

Angie nodded, thinking about Amelia's sparkling eyes and bright smile. "I hated to do that to her, Cedric. But she's a young girl joining a world neither of us know anything about. I must reach a level of peace before I can agree to this."

He nodded, ran his hand through his hair, nodded again and left the room. Troubled by the direction the afternoon had taken, Angie walked slowly to her room, determined to start praying right away. This wasn't something to take lightly.

⌒◡◡◠

Amelia had taken to spending large parts of her afternoons in the tent in the backyard. It was a comfortable place to relax, filled with couches and tables. But three days after meeting

Mr. McFarce, she wasn't finding it as calming as normal as she awaited her aunt's decision.

Something else was troubling her as well. She was unaccountably nervous about Ian Hayworth coming over. She hadn't seen him since they'd shared coffee and pie, weeks ago. With her nerves getting the better of her, she sent for Grace.

"You called for me, miss?" Grace asked when she arrived in the yard.

"You know you don't have to call me that. I'm just Amelia." She set down her embroidery and patted the cushion beside her in invitation.

"Yes, miss." Grace dropped a quick curtsy but grinned unrepentantly. "What do you need?"

"Aunt Angie still hasn't told me if I can work at the *Free Press* yet, and Monday is only three days away." Amelia slumped back into the cushions, looking defeated.

Grace took a quick look around the yard before sitting. "Least she hasn't said no," she encouraged.

"That's true," Amelia conceded. "I really want this job! It's not like anything's going to happen."

"Amelia," Grace chided.

"I know," Amelia reluctantly shook her head. "That's wrong of me. I just want this so badly!"

"Mrs. Barrington knows that. And she wants the best for you. Be patient," Grace advised.

Amelia sighed and sat up. She pulled her handkerchief out to twist around her finger. "Ian Hayworth is coming for dinner tonight."

Amelia began recounting her various encounters with Ian, from their first meeting, right up to the newspaper office and the diner. "And now he's coming tonight, and I don't know how to act. He's so stuffy one minute. And then the next…he's…I don't know." She put her handkerchief away. "Anyway, he's not coming to see me. He's coming to meet Cedric." She nodded as if that changed everything and picked up her embroidery.

"It's rather simple, I think," Grace offered. "You just have to be courteous. He's Mrs. Barrington's guest and friend. Aside from that, let his behavior guide you. He's one of the truest gentlemen I've met."

Distracted, Amelia stuck her finger with the needle and quickly put it in her mouth. "I'm not courting him, Grace, goodness. It's just this evening that I'm worried about." Feeling the throb of pain ease, she checked that the bleeding had stopped.

"That's right enough. But I still say what I said. Men that are true gentlemen are rare enough, like your brother."

"What about my brother?" Amelia looked at her maid and friend, trying not to smile.

Grace waved her hand, obviously flustered. "I'd best be gettin' back to work. Ms. Dean wouldn't like to find me sitting here when there's work to be done."

She hurried off, passing Aunt Angie on the path. Amelia sat straighter as her aunt settled where Grace had been a moment earlier.

"I know these past few days have been a trial for you," Aunt Angie began. "Thank you for bearing up under them with such patience."

Amelia felt a dart of consternation, thinking how much she had chafed under the delay. And how just a few minutes ago…

"Although I'm still concerned about it," Aunt Angie continued, "I don't see any reason why you can't give the job a chance."

Amelia flung herself at her aunt, hugging her tightly and saying thank you repeatedly.

"I want you to be aware of your surroundings," Aunt Angie said. "If you ever feel worried about the situation, leave and tell me immediately. Understood?"

Amelia agreed without hesitation. Her heart was soaring. She was going to start her first job on Monday!

All evening, Amelia noticed that Ian looked the same as before, though a little sterner. It was as if in the intervening weeks, he'd forgotten how to smile. She covertly watched him as he laughed with Cedric and Aunt Angie. Perhaps it was just her nerves that made her perceive him differently. Uncertain, she followed her aunt as their group retired to the salon. As they sat down, Angie mentioned there was another women's meeting coming up.

"When is it?" Amelia asked, leaning forward eagerly. "I'd like to go with you."

"It's not until Wednesday, I believe. I'd enjoy your company, you know that." Aunt Angie smiled, and Amelia leaned back, pleased. She glanced at Mr. Hayworth. His lips twitched in what she assumed was a smile before he looked away.

"Don't forget that you've got a job now," Cedric said. "You can't jet away to whatever meeting you like."

She shifted to face Cedric, finding that it put Mr. Hayworth out of her line of vision. She simply couldn't think around him tonight. "I imagine this will be of interest to Mr. McFarce," she remarked. "Besides, how am I to report on events if I don't attend them?" Feeling she had gained the upper hand, Amelia smiled superiorly at her brother.

"Congratulations on your job search paying off, Miss Hughes," Ian said.

"Thank you. I just got it." She smiled at him. *Why does he have to look so handsome tonight?*

~∼∽~∽

When Cedric changed the subject to recent job losses at the mills, Ian was eager to discuss it. He tried not to glance at Amelia as Cedric talked, but his eyes were traitorous…they kept seeking her out. The gaslights along the wall lit her to advantage, and he'd noticed right away that the dress she wore enhanced the color of her eyes.

He forced himself to focus on Cedric, whom Ian found to be an interesting combination of idealism and cynicism. He wished Cedric would be staying with Angela a little longer. He'd like to get to know him better. They were only a few years apart, and seemed to have similar interests. Their conversation ranged from job losses, to the Nettleville orphanage, to the newest plays coming out. If Amelia hadn't been so distracting, he may have enjoyed himself more.

At a pause in conversation, Ian turned to Angela. "I'm afraid that I haven't asked how you've been feeling lately, Angela. Forgive my lapse." He was surprised to see her dart a glance at her nephew.

"I've been feeling fine, Ian. Thank you. And don't fear, I knew it wasn't lack of care on your part." Her smile was sincere, but it lacked its normal openness.

Alarmed, Ian shot a glance at Amelia, who was chewing on her lower lip, looking at her aunt. There was something wrong. He didn't know what, nor did he want to make things any more awkward than he apparently had. He was relieved when Angela suggested a game.

Amelia moved to retrieve the cards from a nearby table. What he hadn't counted on was the game being cribbage, or that he'd be paired with Amelia. She frowned slightly at her aunt's suggestion. Wondering what she could have against having him as a partner, he sighed.

"I've always enjoyed cribbage, but Amelia isn't that fond of it," Angela said. "I try not to torture her with it too much, but with you gentlemen here, perhaps it won't be quite the trial for her."

Ian was enamored with the blush that crept across Amelia's cheeks.

"I enjoy playing with you, Aunt Angie," Amelia said. "It's counting the points at the end of each hand that trips me up. I'm not sure why."

"I can help you," Ian said. He didn't realize that he'd spoken until she looked up at him, the light reflected in her green eyes. A small smile flickered on her lips.

"You'll have to, if you want any chance of winning," she said.

He smiled back at her. "It's not all about winning."

"I'm glad you feel that way, Ian, because I fully intend to beat you two," Angela teased.

Cedric laughed and shuffled the cards, dealing five out to each of them. Play started, and despite Amelia's reservations, she played well, keeping her team only points behind Angie and Cedric. Ian hadn't played in quite some time, but found that the game quickly came back to him. Having Amelia as a partner had its advantages.

Of course, there were also disadvantages, as she distracted him from time to time. In the end, Angie and Cedric won, but they agreed that the game had been fun. As they stood, Amelia moved closer to Ian.

"I'm sorry I wasn't a better partner...the game confuses me."

"You did just fine," he said. "It takes time to get the hang of it. I think our opponents had an unfair advantage, though." His tie suddenly felt tight, but he resisted the urge to loosen it.

"What's that?"

He smiled down at her. "Your aunt knew I wouldn't play as well, since I'd be distracted by your beauty."

His own words surprised him. He held his breath, wondering how she'd respond. He'd never said something so forward to a woman. He relaxed when her eyes lit up before she ducked her head. She moved away without saying anything, and he looked over at Angela, who was still standing nearby.

Her smile was wide. "I'll have you know that I did no such thing on purpose. But now that I know that, I'll be sure to pair you together next time."

Ian glanced away. Even though he was embarrassed, he couldn't help but respond with honesty. "I hope you do."

Chapter Fifteen

"Good morning, Mr. McFarce!" Amelia called.

"Good morning, Miss Hughes. Come around the counter and I'll show you the place." Mr. McFarce waited until she stood next to him before pointing at what he was doing. "I've been preparing the types. You must be exact with your placement, or the whole page will be wrong, which wastes valuable time, ink, and paper. I always check the whole thing over before we go to print. Check twice, print once. Understood?"

"Yes," she nodded.

Brock was near the back of the room, stacking reams of paper on a shelf. He didn't pause in his job, merely nodded in Amelia's direction. His build was like his father's, but where the older man had a paunch, Brock was fit and muscular. They also matched in their black hair and dark eyes.

"Good morning," she called out, not sure how to refer to him. Would both be Mr. McFarce? Neither man said anything, and she supposed she'd have to find out on her own.

"Here's where we store the ink and paper," the older Mr. McFarce said. "We keep the letterpress in these drawers here. You'll notice how they are organized." Then he stopped. "Oh, forgive me for not asking after your aunt. How is she doing?"

"She's doing quite well, thank you." It wasn't the truth, but she couldn't go around telling everyone that Aunt Angie was sick. Her stomach knotted.

"I'm glad to hear that. It would be a pleasure to meet her someday. Perhaps she'll even deign to visit our little paper now that you're here?" he asked hopefully.

"Perhaps one day," Amelia smiled.

Nodding, he moved on, indicating a small desk between two shelves. "That's your desk. It's a mite small, but I hope it will satisfy. Of course, you will be off attending events and the like, so you won't be here all the time."

Amelia clasped her hands in front of her. "It's just fine, Mr. McFarce." She stared at it disbelievingly. *My very own desk.* She tore her gaze from it and realized that he'd walked away. "I do have one question," she called after him. "Rather…I suppose it's more of a suggestion." She couldn't seem to get the words out properly. "There's a meeting on Wednesday that could be of some interest to you and the paper."

"What kind of meeting?" he asked.

"It's the Ladies Aid Society. They are seeking to aid the poor. My aunt is attending, and I thought that I could go with her and report back to you."

"That's a fine idea," he said. "Our readers would enjoy such a feature. Get details on who's there, who leads it…that sort of thing."

Amelia smiled. "Thank you, Mr. McFarce."

"Of course, I'll go over it beforehand," he told her. "I won't be printing anything that doesn't meet standard. Just ask Brock if I let anything less than perfect get printed." They turned to Brock, who was now preparing the letterpress. He ignored them, engrossed in his work. "Ah, that lad gets lost in his own mind. Well, let's get some coffee and get to work. As you can tell, we're a small operation, but we'll grow. That's why we moved here, you know. There's more chance to expand."

Amelia nodded, although she wasn't sure just what she was agreeing to. She certainly didn't know if moving here would be what they needed. Instead of asking, she silently accepted a sturdy cup of coffee, followed him to his desk, and sat in a chair across from him. Sipping the dark brew, she listened as he described what she needed to learn. Realizing that she should be taking notes, she pushed her coffee aside so she could set her notepad on the desk.

"That's good thinking," he nodded in approval. "Take notes as often as you can. You'll never remember as much as you think you will once you sit down at the typewriter. Speaking of which, we need to get you a typewriter. Brock!"

His sudden yell startled her. She banged a knee on the desk, knocking over an open ink pot. The ink ran directly onto her lap. She stood immediately, but all that did was let it run the full length of her skirt, leaving a black trail against the blue fabric.

"Oh," she cried out as the ink puddled on the floor near her bag.

Mr. McFarce stood and quickly moved her bag, then grabbed her notepad from the table where the ink was pooling. "Are you all right?" he asked.

"I'm fine, if you'll tell me where…"

"The privy is just down the hall there," he motioned, as if instructing a child.

⌒⌄⌄◝

With the door closed behind her, she huffed in frustration. *This is not how my first day is supposed to go!* She grabbed the hand towel, then hesitated at the idea of rubbing ink all over it. A quick glance around the small room revealed merely the necessities of a privy. Shrugging, she set to her task, starting at the top of her skirt, and rubbing down to the hem. She wrung the towel out a few times, then eyed her skirt. She'd done the best she could under the circumstances. Sighing, she hung the towel up to dry.

When she returned to Mr. McFarce's desk, he quickly stood. "I'm terribly sorry, Miss Hughes. Is your dress ruined?"

She smiled at his obvious concern. "Perhaps. But it's all right, it's just a dress."

"Determined little thing, aren't you? That's what I like to see. Well, while you were gone, Brock brought out a type-writer for you. Of course, if you have a newer one from your aunt that you'd like to bring, that's quite all right. This one is a bit worn, I'm afraid."

"Oh, it looks just fine, Mr. McFarce. Thank you." Amelia desperately wanted to look it over, but when Mr. McFarce sat back down, she followed suit.

"Be that as it may, our things are a little worn out here at the *Free Press*. I hope that doesn't bother you."

"Not at all," she said. Not knowing what to do with her hands since she didn't have anything to write, she reached for the coffee.

"As I was saying, you'll need to make sure that…" Amelia listened, but struggled to follow the rest of his advice, still embarrassed by the accident.

Having arrived home late from a drawn-out meeting, Ian handed his outer garments to his butler, Austin, and agreed to some coffee in his study. He wanted to relax, but if he was going to convince those men that a wage increase for mill workers mattered, he needed to compile a list of reasons how they would benefit from it. He also needed to check with Austin about the affairs of the Hayworth estate.

Their situation was unusual, he knew. Most butlers weren't also the family's estate manager, but Austin had worked alongside his father for so many years that it naturally continued when Ian inherited. He'd overseen the family estate for only two years, and was still getting used to the full weight of the responsibility. His late father had judiciously protected the legacy he'd passed to Ian. Now Ian was determined to do the same. Even if he never had sons to pass it to, his sister had four boys already.

Ian settled in front of the study's fireplace. The warm glow soothed him after a tumultuous day. Thinking of his sister recalled the previous evening when he'd dined with them. He loved spending time with his nephews. Despite their differing opinions, he and his sister had become close. Dorothy was almost ten years older than him, but since the loss of their parents, he'd made it a point to stay in her life. The benefit of that was a relationship with her and each of her boys. Unfortunately, he could not say the same of her husband. He was a man Ian wished to never see again, if possible.

A door slamming startled him. The voices were muffled, but he was certain he recognized them. He opened the study door just before his brother-in-law reached it. The man reeked of alcohol. Even without that, his bloodshot eyes told Ian all he needed to know.

"Ian, old chap! Have your man pour a glass. We've business to discuss." His voice was too loud, and Ian involuntarily took a step back.

"And what business would that be, Maddox?" he asked, knowing he'd dislike anything the man was about to propose.

Maddox Lancer often pitched sure-fire, money-making ideas, attempting to persuade Ian to invest in them. A year ago, Ian had. He'd done it to show Dorothy that he wasn't hard-hearted. He lost a large amount of money to that doomed venture, and vowed never to do so again. Staring at Maddox, who was now sprawled in one of the chairs before the fire, Ian frowned. He disliked his brother-in-law more and more. The man was everything Ian could not stand…an ill-disciplined, selfish wastrel.

"It's a sure-fire investment," Maddox announced. "I met a man just this evening who's in the middle of…"

Ian quickly tuned him out, thankful Maddox hadn't brought the man over this time. Dealing with his brother-in-law was one thing. Doing so while also appeasing a stranger was another situation altogether.

Shaking his head, Ian relaxed deeper into his chair, and began wondering how to get Maddox out the door before it was too late to finish his paperwork. It invariably depended on his mood. He glanced at Maddox, still speaking enthusiastically about something. What was it this time? A local boarding school, from the sounds of it.

"You won't regret it, Ian, I promise you that," Maddox said, as earnest as always in his appeal. He drained his glass and poured another, leaving the decanter within easy reach.

"You always say that," Ian said. "Remind me, how exactly did the last investment end?" His patience was running short. He rubbed one hand down his face.

"Ah, that was a disappointment," Maddox agreed, shaking his head. "This one is different, I guarantee it. Might even send the boys there once it's up and running! I'm putting in a percentage of my own money tomorrow morning." Maddox rubbed his hands together as he smiled. "We'll make a profit of seventy percent. There's never been a set up like this. And, do you know, Harrison might be joining me. That man has more money than you, and he's willing to chip in. What do you say?"

"Harrison James?" Ian asked. He'd met Harrison on several occasions and had never been fond of the cavalier young man.

"Of course. What other rich Harrison is there? All you lot know each other, don't you? It will make you feel better knowing he's putting in his own percentage." Maddox once again emptied his glass, then refilled it.

Ian eyed the bottle and decided he'd better move this along. "It's quite the opposite," he said. "You see, I don't trust Harrison James. If he's judged it to be worthy of his money, spend your time with him. I really must get to some paper-work. Now, will you excuse me?"

Ian stood. Maddox did not. "Well, he hasn't exactly committed yet," he hedged. "I'm heading to meet him after I leave here. I'm certain he won't be able to refuse this opportunity. And you shouldn't either, you know. As a matter of fact…"

Ian sat down again wearily. The temptation to throw the man out on his ear was strong, and he briefly debated it. But the consequence would mean Maddox would refuse him access to his house and family. He had threatened to do so last year, and Ian knew the man wouldn't feel an ounce of remorse if he ever carried out the threat. Shaking his head, Ian wished Maddox was a better man.

"Actually…forget it, old chap," Maddox said. "It was just a suggestion. I do think you'd get the feel of it more if you talked to Mr. … oh what's his blasted name?" Maddox squinted into his glass, either trying to remember the name, or wondering how his glass had gotten so empty.

Ian took the opportunity to stand, pour Maddox another drink, and then deposit the decanter in the cupboard. As he turned, he ignored Maddox' scowl. "I don't need to speak with anyone," he said. "I'm not going to be investing in anything. I far prefer investments where I'm certain of the outcome, or ones that aid others. In that vein, I do have some important paperwork to get to this evening."

"Aw, don't be like that," Maddox protested. "Can't a man have a talk with his wife's brother without hostility? And without him being deprived of a little drink? If I didn't know better, I'd think you didn't want me here. And that upsets me." Maddox stopped and fixed him with a glare that Ian felt clear down to his toes. "I came to have a gentlemanly talk, but if you're interested in something more physical, why don't you say it?" He stood quickly.

Ian was taller than Maddox, but the man was solidly built and knew how to fight. "I'm tired," Ian said. "And I really need to get some work done tonight. That's all I'm saying."

"You're just not man enough to take me on," Maddox said. "Can't handle a little challenge, eh?" Maddox stepped toward him, his shoulders thrown back.

"I've no desire to fight you. I'll see you to the door." Ian turned and walked away, his senses on alert. Turning calmly, he expected Maddox at his side. Instead, the man had poured himself another drink. Ian clenched his jaw but waited silently. Maddox always had to have the upper hand. If this was the way he wanted to prove he was the bigger man, so be it.

"Your taste in alcohol could be improved," Maddox said, then handed Ian the empty glass. "But I suppose it goes with everything else about you." He glanced at Ian, curling his lip at the sight of his three-piece suit.

"Good evening, Maddox," Ian said.

When the door closed, Ian leaned against the doorway relieved.

"Is there anything you need, sir?" Austin asked.

"That'll be all, Austin. Thank you." Retreating again to his study, Ian sank into the chair and slowly fell asleep, staring into the flames.

The Ladies Aid Society meeting paused for light refreshments after having decided, with minimal argument, to help the Playtin family. Amelia followed Aunt Angie out, joining Mrs. Grey and Mrs. Fossit. Georgia was already there, leaning against the railing.

"I noticed you were taking notes, Miss Hughes," Mrs. Fossit said. "Whatever is that about?"

"I'm writing an article on this meeting, Mrs. Fossit."

"An article?" she laughed and shook her head. "I do declare, Mrs. Barrington, you must involve your niece in some more activities like my Georgia. The poor thing is bored to tears if she's taking notes like a common secretary."

"Actually, she's working for the *Free Press*," Aunt Angie said. "I'm proud of her for finding an alternative to spending all of her days at parties."

Georgia pulled Amelia away from the older women in a sudden rush of excitement. "There's going to be the most divine party in a few days. I'm wearing the most delectable gown. You really should come, Amelia."

Amelia smiled, thinking how it could be fun to go to a party. It had been a few months since she'd attended one. Besides, it would be a chance to see Harrison again. She'd loved dancing with him. With the thought, another came… that of Ian unexpectedly smiling down at her. He was so unlike Harrison, and she'd been drawn to him the last few times they'd met.

"It won't be as great a party as the ones I throw of course," Georgia said. Amelia blinked, coming back to the present. "Of course, no one really has my father's money," she continued. "Except for Harrison's family. They're practically as wealthy as we are." She caught Amelia's gaze, her smile suddenly stiff. "I know how appealing he seems, Amelia, but he's off-limits. He's only paid attention to you because your aunt is rich. The elite must play nice with each other. But don't set your sights on him. You're far too beneath him. Besides, I've heard him say that he cares nothing for you."

Amelia remembered how it felt to dance with him, and how earnest he'd been when he visited her last. Drawing a deep breath to banish the memories, Amelia smiled. "You're too kind. If you'll excuse me." She walked to her aunt without waiting for Georgia's response.

"Are you ready to go back in, Amelia?" Aunt Angie asked.

"I am," Amelia answered, hoping that the rest of the meeting would go quickly. She suddenly wanted to be home.

~‿‿◦

Once they were home again, Angie gave in to the exhaustion she felt. It was far more than she'd expected from simply attending a Ladies Aid Society meeting. Her body was heavy and sluggish. She sat alone in the salon, hoping no one would come in for a few minutes. Amelia had gone to the library to write her article, and Angie knew her niece would be occupied for quite a while.

A cough caught her unaware, then another, each hack painful. She sat back once they passed, clenching her handkerchief. She closed her eyes against the pain. Dr. Martin had warned her about the symptoms of consumption. She didn't want to think about them, but the list parading through her mind increased her fear, causing the pain in her throat to worsen. *What's happening to my body?*

Amelia sat at the small diner table with a sigh. The morning had gone well, if a little slowly. Turning in her first article had been nerve-wracking, but Mr. McFarce didn't seem upset that it needed improving before print. The rest of the time, she'd been struggling to type bills on the old typewriter. She decided to ask Aunt Angie if they could buy a new one.

Amelia thanked the waitress when she brought a cup of coffee and a sandwich. She still didn't care much for coffee, but found she was adjusting to the bitter taste. The sandwich filled the plate and tasted as good as it looked.

"I don't care if he is my father!" Pulled from her contemplations by the loud voice, Amelia realized Brock and another man were sitting nearby.

"What has he ever done for me?" Brock asked. "Right after my mother died, he sent me to an orphanage, Will."

Amelia froze. Mr. McFarce had sent his son to an orphanage? Amelia hadn't heard much about how the institutions were run, but the little she knew caused a shiver to run through her.

"You can't know what it was like. It changes you. He calls me addle-brained, but I still see the children…" Brock slumped back in his chair, catching Amelia staring at him.

She set her sandwich down, wiping her fingers clean. "Forgive me…I didn't…"

"Give the lady a break," his companion said. "You were talking loud enough for the cooks to hear you." The affable man turned to Amelia. "I'm Will Norris. This is Brock McFarce. Might I ask who you are?"

"She's the journalist he hired," Brock muttered, then caught himself and sat upright. "I apologize, Miss Hughes. That was uncalled for." Amelia smiled and sipped her coffee.

"Please, join us," Mr. Norris added. "There's no sense in eating alone." When Brock repeated the offer, Amelia gathered her hat and purse, and moved to their table, surprised when Brock rose to bring her lunch over.

"Did your father really send you to an orphanage?" she asked.

Brock grimaced. "You'd be surprised how common it is."

"Parents don't always want their children to go," Mr. Norris spoke up. "Sometimes the government takes them if they deem the parents unfit in some way."

"The government decides what the label 'orphan' means," Brock said. "The children are taken so they can learn to be law-abiding members of society. That's the general idea, anyway." Brock's face was hard. "You labor for ten hours a day. If you fall behind or make a mistake, you're whipped. If you get placed out with a family, they might beat you, or any number of things. You can imagine the situations that are possible for a friendless child."

Amelia shivered. His tone was hard, and his eyes held a world of pain. "Why hasn't anything been done?" she whispered. It felt like her heart had lodged in her throat.

"Because the people who know don't care enough to act." Brock leaned back like he was daring her to argue. He crossed his arms, his shirt tightening around his shoulders. She hadn't realized how large of a man he was until that moment.

"What trade did you learn there?"

"Bricklaying," he said flatly.

"Why are you working with your father then?" She hesitated, belatedly realizing how personal these questions were.

"It was this, or laying bricks for pennies a day," Brock said. "I chose the lesser of two evils."

Flustered, Amelia choked on her coffee. "Pardon me," she said hoarsely.

Mr. Norris smiled sympathetically. "This coffee's harsh, but it does get one's blood pumping." He leaned forward, eyeing her. "I've not heard of a woman journalist, especially one so pretty, or dressed so fancy."

"I'm just starting out," she said, becoming uneasy with this friend of Brock's. "I suppose I am overdressed. Perhaps you know of a seamstress that specializes in clothing for female journalists?" The words were pointed and unexpected, even to her.

Mr. Norris blinked in surprise while Brock laughed. "You deserved that, and you know it. Miss Hughes is a lady."

"Thank you, Mr. McFarce," Amelia said. "Now I believe I'd best get back to work. Your father will be wondering what's keeping me."

"I think you could do just about anything, and he wouldn't bat an eye," Brock said wryly. "You're the golden goose to him." He smiled, but then frowned and shook his head. "Forgive me again. I spoke out of turn." After paying the tab, he walked away. Mr. Norris bowed, bid her a chagrined farewell and lingered a moment before departing.

Brock's revelation whirled in her head while she paid her own bill and left. Wouldn't people do something if they knew how terribly these children were being treated? What if she could expose the situation?

Suddenly excited, she hurried into the office. Brock stood at the back, leaning against his desk with his head down. Amelia walked toward him.

"Mr. McFarce..."

"Please, call me Brock."

"Brock, I have an idea. What if I exposed the conditions at orphanages?"

"To what end?" he asked.

"If people know, they'll help! We can bring change for those children."

"We?"

She paused, thrown off by his skepticism. "Why not? Your photos could make such an impact! And since you've been there you could, well..."

"Yes, I've been there. Which is why I'll never go back." His eyes flashed. She was sure he was about to say something more when the bell over the door rang out.

He side-stepped her and went to help the customer. She sat down at her desk, stunned by his intensity. *Why won't he help me?* The more she thought about exposing the conditions the children lived in, the more determined she became to do it. She glanced at Brock as she started typing out the last of the bills. She wasn't sure how she was going to convince him, but she would.

Another obstacle would be convincing the senior Mr. McFarce. That one she wasn't as worried about. What man wouldn't want to help children escape such treatment that his son had undergone? She was sure he'd see it as an opportunity to help other families from making the same mistake. Thus encouraged, she focused on her slow task for the rest of the afternoon.

With the pile of papers finished, she turned them in to Mr. McFarce, then took a deep breath for courage. "May I run an idea by you?"

"Of course, anything for you," Mr. McFarce said.

"While at lunch, I had an idea for a story series for this upcoming holiday season. Something to tug at people's heartstrings and encourage them to help the less fortunate." She paused, trying to rein in her excitement. "I could interview the directors of different orphanages in town to show the plight of the children."

Brock stood at the back of the room glaring and shaking his head. Ignoring him, she looked instead at his father, who had a similar expression.

"A bunch of brats wallowing in their misery isn't the type of thing that I want marring the pages of my paper," Mr. McFarce snapped, his voice rougher than normal.

"But sir, don't you see? If we tell people how much the children need assistance…"

"And aren't they getting it by being in the orphanage?" he replied. "No. Stick to the Society Page, Miss Hughes." He picked up his pen again without another glance at her.

Stunned, Amelia looked appealingly at Brock, who simply shook his head and turned away. Hiding her distress, Amelia went back to her desk.

"Aunt Angie, could we buy a typewriter soon?" Amelia asked. "I'm miserably slow on the one at work. It took me hours to type the bills today." She sat with Aunt Angie on the front porch, scribbling down notes about the orphanage idea as they came to her.

"If you need one, we certainly can," Aunt Angie said. "I never had any inclination to get one. But I must ask, why are you typing up bills? Shouldn't that be a secretary's job?"

Amelia swallowed, wishing she hadn't mentioned that part. "He doesn't have one. And I don't mind. I'm there anyway, and I don't have much experience."

"I wasn't judging you, dear," Aunt Angie said. "Are you free to go shopping in the morning?"

"Yes. I only have the golf tournament in the afternoon to attend. Mr. McFarce mentioned that we should set a schedule for me, since I won't be needed there every day." Amelia's attention drifted as she noted another argument for convincing Brock to help her.

Her aunt was laughing. "You didn't hear a word I just said, did you? Well, let's plan on getting you that typewriter in the morning. And we might as well go to the tournament together."

"Oh, I didn't think you were going," Amelia said. She'd never been to a golf tournament before. Having her aunt along would make her less nervous.

"Cedric asked to move our plans to the next day, so I'm free," her aunt said.

"Why would he cancel your plans?" Diverted, Amelia wondered at her brother, cancelling plans with his aunt when he was leaving town soon.

"I didn't cancel them," Cedric said, joining them on the porch. "I merely rescheduled. There's a difference. Besides, I have friends here, Amelia. Quite good ones in fact." He smiled.

"What day do you leave?" she asked, closing her notebook.

"Trying to get rid of me?" Cedric teased. "This coming Wednesday. Classes start the next week. I want to have a couple of days to settle in."

"I can't believe it's so soon already," Amelia mused. "Will you have time to do something with your little sister, or will your 'good friends' be keeping you too busy?" Amelia teased him back.

His eyes shone. "I'll schedule you in. They're pretty understanding."

"Good. I want to go with you to see that new play. Aunt Angie, what's it called?"

"*The Pirates of Penzance*," Aunt Angie said. She stood with her embroidery basket in one hand. "I'm going inside now, but you two stay out here. There won't be many more of these evenings left this year."

They silently watched her enter the house. When the door had closed behind her, Cedric turned to Amelia. "She hasn't told me what's wrong, but it's clear she's not well," he said just above a whisper, his earlier mirth gone.

Amelia pressed her lips together, fiddling with her pen, trying to think of what to say.

"You know, don't you? I can't believe this. You must tell me."

"I can't. She doesn't want people to know."

"I'm not *people*, I'm her nephew." His voice rose, the hurt evident.

Amelia flinched. "You'll have to talk to her, Cedric. I'm sorry. But this is something she should tell you."

"You're growing up, aren't you?" Cedric observed with a sigh, leaning back in his chair.

She let out a laugh. "I'm trying. It isn't easy."

"I don't think it ever is." He tapped his thumb against his knee. "There just comes a time when you realize you can't continue as you were. You must stop acting as if the world revolves around you, and put the hard work in."

"Is that why you decided to go to college?"

He nodded. "Father getting me the job at the mercantile was good for a time. At one point, I thought I could be a salesman, but the work never ends."

"Wouldn't it be different once you were a cashier rather than an errand boy?"

"Maybe. But even they worked long hours, and had to fight to get more than one day off every few weeks." He shook his head. "That's not how I want to live. So, I sent in an application to Washington. I'm going to get an engineering degree."

"It must be exciting, getting to go to college."

"I'm rather nervous, but excited too," he admitted. "I'll get to learn without…" They both grew silent at his almost-mention of their mother. "What about you? You seem to have it made here, with Aunt Angie."

Amelia smiled. "I do. Aunt Angie is wonderful." The constant fear for her aunt flared, but she pushed it away. "And now that I've got the job at the paper, I'm even happier."

"It's nice, being away from home, isn't it?" Cedric said softly.

Amelia nodded. "It is."

Angie waved farewell to Cedric as he boarded the train, glad that she'd gotten this time with him. She was going to miss him, but he promised to write as soon as he was settled. A tear trailed down her cheek at the memory of telling him about her illness last night. He'd sat unnaturally still, asking questions quietly until he hugged her and left the room. She prayed that she'd handled it correctly. She didn't like talking about her illness. It made it too real.

She laughed softly when Cedric popped his head out of a window a few cars down and waved with a cheery smile. *Dear Cedric. How he and Amelia had come out of Diane's house with such zeal for life was clearly a miracle.*

She and Amelia waved exuberantly as the train started slowly chugging away.

"Well, he's gone," Amelia said.

"Will you miss him?"

"I will," Amelia answered, almost sounding surprised. "I missed him before, when I first came here. But I think that was more for something known, and not for him personally." Amelia's tone was introspective. Angie softly agreed and waited. "Now though, I feel like he's a friend," Amelia said softly.

Chapter Sixteen

When the carriage arrived at Nettleville Orphanage, Amelia stepped out, eyeing the worn sagging building that seemed unlikely to survive the winter. She carefully ascended the dilapidated stairs, thinking of Brock's words from weeks ago. They'd sparked something within her—a desire to make a lasting difference. And what better cause existed than aiding children?

She knocked on the door, feeling energized for the meeting. She attempted to rehearse the interview questions, but they skittered away from her when the door swung open, revealing a short, older lady who beckoned her inside.

"Come in, Miss Hughes," Mrs. Lardish said. "You're likely to freeze in that wind. Welcome to Nettleville Orphanage."

"Thank you," Amelia replied warmly. "I have an appointment with Mr. Hayworth. He mentioned I could interview you as well if you have time." She loosened her scarf but didn't take off her coat—it was quite cool inside.

"Ah, of course," Mrs. Lardish nodded. "He told me about you coming today, but it slipped my mind. It's been a busy day. Come this way, I'll show you to the director."

Amelia noted the small, worn jackets that hung from hooks on the wall as she followed, listening as Mrs. Lardish pointed out the names of rooms and children as they passed. "Kitchen…Larry. Infirmary, down that hall…George. School rooms are down there…Mary. Here we are. Go on in but be very quiet." Mrs. Lardish opened a door just wide enough for Amelia to slip through.

She entered, unsure why she suddenly felt so nervous. Was it because of who it was? Still, what met her eyes defied everything she'd been prepared for. Ian Hayworth sat in a rocking chair with a baby in his arms, his jacket over the still form. He hummed an unfamiliar tune as he patted the child's tiny back. His surprise at seeing her was brief. He nodded toward the other rocking chair, then resumed the lullaby.

Amelia walked around the tiny beds, counting three more infants already asleep. She sat slowly, not wanting to wake the children. How long they sat there, she wasn't sure, but the rhythmic rocking, Ian's quiet humming, and the steady breathing of the little ones lulled her nervousness away.

Finally, Ian gently placed the infant in the last vacant crib and tucked a blanket around him. When the child didn't stir, Ian slung his jacket over his arm and looked at Amelia, who was standing, poised to follow him out. It wasn't until they were several feet away from the shut door that she finally exhaled.

"Thank you for your patience, Miss Hughes," Ian said. "Patrick hasn't been sleeping well. We've found that rocking is the only thing that soothes him." He paused, putting his jacket on, transforming into the proper gentleman she was used to, with vest, pocket watch, and starched collar. Still, he seemed more approachable now that she'd seen him in shirtsleeves, rocking a baby. "If you'll follow me to the office, we can talk there."

She followed him silently down the hall, recalling the rooms Mrs. Lardish had pointed out earlier. When she focused on the broad shoulders in front of her, her stomach knotted. No matter how often they'd crossed paths, this was different. She needed to prove she wasn't just a flighty girl caught up in society. *Will he believe I'm doing this because I care?*

She adjusted her grip on her bag as they entered the office and looked around at the cramped space. One small window provided poor lighting where two desks butted against each other, both covered in paperwork. Much of it, from what she could see, was children's artwork.

Ian pulled two chairs out from the desks and turned one for her. "I'm sorry it's chilly in here," he said. "We focus the heat in the rooms with children. I should have lit a fire in advance. In fact, I'll do that right away." He headed for the cold fireplace.

"That's not necessary, Mr. Hayworth," Amelia said. "There's no need, save the wood for the children." She stopped at the look he gave her. "What's the matter?"

"Forgive me. It's nothing." He stepped around her and sat down.

She cleared her throat, striving for a professional tone. "How long have you been the director here?"

"Nearly two years now."

Amelia opened her pen and notebook. "From what I've seen, orphanages are regimented in their daily routines," she said. "What's yours like?"

"We are strict in some things, but I think you'll find that we're relaxed compared to other orphanages," he said. "Mrs. Lardish and I believe in letting children be children…in giving them freedom to play and rest…while teaching them life skills."

"What do you mean by 'life skills'?" she asked. "Teaching them a trade?"

"In a sense, yes," Ian said. "But I know what you're thinking. And believe me, our children are not laboring. Instead, we teach reading, writing, arithmetic, and the Bible.

They have recess and a lunch break. There's time for them to play as well. Naturally, they have tasks they must perform, but they are rewarded. You'll find that we're not slavedrivers here."

Amelia smiled, focusing on her notes. "I'm pleased to hear it," she said. "I've been appalled by what I've found this past month. How many children are under your care presently?"

"We have twenty-eight children," he said.

"You are billeted as having thirty. Did two get adopted?" she asked hopefully.

"One did," he sighed, sadness in his eyes. "The other passed away recently."

"What happened?"

"A young girl came with a high fever, and there was nothing we could do but keep her as comfortable as possible. She'd had no one her whole life and we didn't want her to feel that way at the end."

They sat in silence for a moment, Amelia's fountain pen still as she absorbed this revelation. She took a deep breath then wrote a quick note. From there, her remaining questions went by quickly. Ian answered openly and honestly. When they were through, he suggested a tour.

"And let's see if Mrs. Lardish is free," he said. "She sees to the day-to-day running. I mainly take care of the financial side of things."

"It seems you tend to far more than that, Mr. Hayworth," Amelia said as she stood and shifted her scarf.

"How so?" Ian asked, turning to her, his hand on the doorknob.

"You were rocking a baby to sleep when I got here," she said. "If that's not an indication that you're very much a part of this place, I don't know what is." She spoke softly, suddenly self-conscious as he stared at her. The spark of admiration that lit his face warmed her.

"You've become astute, Miss Hughes. I'm impressed."

"I've been trying to be," she said simply.

Neither moved nor spoke for several seconds. He seemed content to just look at her, and she at him. And she found that she didn't mind in the slightest. Finally, he spoke, breaking the trance. "Let's go and find Mrs. Lardish for that tour, shall we?"

Angie sat in the salon, waiting for Amelia. Even with the afternoon sun on her back, she couldn't shake the heaviness of the day. She clutched her handkerchief as her throat tightened, a sure sign of an imminent cough. Footsteps echoed in the entry hall, and she willed the cough to wait. Unable to repress it any longer, she held the cloth to her mouth and winced. When she was done, she sighed, savoring the air in her lungs. She had never thought that one day, this feeling would be the sweetest thing.

A quick glance at her hands ruined the moment. Her handkerchief was stained with blood. Fear cinched her middle, and airflow became restricted until she began gasping for breath. Through the fog of fear, she heard footsteps in the hall again, light and quick. *Amelia.* Angie closed her eyes against the pain...and the idea of Amelia seeing her in this state. She hated her weakness. Fortunately, Amelia bypassed the salon, talking to Walter before heading upstairs.

A trickle of air coursed through Angie's lungs, then another. A few moments later, she was breathing deeply, willing her muscles to relax before her niece came back down. She tucked her handkerchief into her sleeve, the blood carefully folded to the center.

"I asked Walter to have some food brought to us," Amelia said as she entered the room. She kissed Angie on the cheek, then sat across from her. "I'm so hungry today."

Angie smiled at the girl, and her heart swelled with love for her. As much as she didn't want to be caught having one of her weak spells, she was glad she wasn't alone.

"You had a good day then?" she asked. Amelia nodded.

"That was the first orphanage I've been to where I didn't leave depressed and heartbroken for the children," she said.

"Ian is a kindhearted man," Angie said. Her throat tightened as she spoke, and she said no more. She was pleased as Amelia readily agreed, then went on talking about Nettleville, her eyes shining, her cheeks flushed.

Susan set a tray with several cut sandwiches on the table near Amelia. Angie fingered her sleeve where she'd hidden her handkerchief and wondered what she would tell Dr. Martin. She knew she couldn't put off another visit from him after today's development.

Amelia finished eating and wiped her hands on a napkin. "Shall we finish reading *A Tale of Two Cities*?"

"Yes, let's," Angie agreed.

"Shall I read today? You look worn out, Aunt Angie."

The concern in her voice almost made Angie deny it, but she handed the book over. "Thank you, Amelia. I fear that I am rather weak today," she admitted.

Amelia set the article about the Sardens' holiday party on Mr. McFarce's desk, then turned to her own. She grimaced at the sight of it, swamped with paperwork, pens, and ink bottles. She'd planned to straighten it today but was too tired from having stayed late at last night's party. She couldn't resist singing carols, and had enjoyed herself quite a bit, even if she didn't know many of the partygoers. It was a different crowd for her.

She stifled a yawn then drained the rest of her coffee, no longer shuddering at the taste of the bitter brew. She checked the list of upcoming events and announcements she needed to type up for tomorrow, then sat down and got back to work.

"Is my father in?" Brock asked as he stepped in from the back door, his arms full of wood.

"No, he has a meeting," Amelia answered absently. "I think he'll be back by two o' clock." She returned her focus to properly wording a marriage announcement. Though she'd grown accustomed to Brock's sudden comings and goings, his refusal to help with the orphanage story still lingered in her mind. The last time she pressed him, he threatened to tell his father she was interviewing people against orders—a threat she doubted he'd carry out. Still, it nagged at her. She finally turned to face him.

"You wouldn't actually tell your father about my interviews, would you?" she asked. Her shoulders relaxed when his sagged.

"No, I won't," he said. "But I wish you'd stop badgering me about it. I'm not going to be your photographer on this crusade. Find someone else. Mr. Norris is a decent shot if you want me to contact him for you."

Amelia snorted at his offer and debated pressing the issue. Deciding not to, she turned back to the wedding announcement. Right then, the front door opened, admitting a shivering Mr. McFarce.

"I think it's going to rain," he said. "You'd better head home early today, Miss Hughes."

"Yes, sir. I'm finishing up announcements now."

"Put them aside for a minute. I have something to tell you." He shrugged his heavy coat off and stood near the fire. "Brock, coffee. Miss Hughes, a while ago you came to me with the idea of exposing the conditions of children in orphanages. Do you remember?"

Amelia shared a glance with Brock as he handed his father a mug.

"Yes, sir. You forbade it and urged me to focus on the Society Page." The memory of that conversation still burned, and she'd started to wonder about him. Who could deny the chance to help children?

"I've reconsidered," he said shortly. "It's a fine idea to interview a few directors and show the plight of those orphans. This is the season of giving, after all. We can even ask for donations to be brought here."

Amelia was shocked but nodded. "Thank you, sir." She decided it wasn't lying if she did go to interview the last director.

Mr. McFarce downed the coffee. "Take Brock with you to get some real heart-breaking pictures. He knows the kind the public likes."

That pronouncement could have knocked her over. Brock scowled. "What's going on, Father? We've never done anything like this before."

"And what's wrong with change?" McFarce replied. "It's for the good of the community. Be ready whenever Miss Hughes needs you, you hear? I want to see your best shots for this."

Brock nodded stiffly, looking suspiciously at his father. Amelia ignored him and thanked her boss. "I know I can do justice to the article," she said. "We can let readers know how hard those children have it, and what people can do to help."

"You don't need to sell it to me," Mr. McFarce waved her off. "Of course, don't let it affect the rest of your work. Finish those announcements. Then you can go home. Brock will take you today."

Amelia turned back to her desk. She didn't know what had changed Mr. McFarce's mind, but she was relieved. All her hard work would be worth it, and her article would be published! She was sure it would move people to help once they read about the conditions the children endured. She decided to use Ian's techniques as examples of what other orphanages could do.

Once she finished the announcements, Brock left to hail a carriage for her ride home. On her way out, Mr. McFarce reminded her to attend the suffrage meeting the next evening.

"Of course," she said, not admitting that she'd forgotten about it. She bid him goodbye, pulled on her wool overcoat and gloves, then hurried out to Brock. "You don't have to ride with me," she said to him. "I've done this ride unaccompanied plenty of times."

"If I go back in there right now, he won't be happy," Brock explained. "You'd best let me ride along." He helped her in the carriage then climbed in directly after her, giving her no chance to argue.

"The address is 635 Avery Street," Amelia told him, wondering what his reaction to her home would be. He passed the address on to the driver, then settled into the seat. Noticing the grim look on his face, she chose not to talk about their new assignment. However, when they turned onto Avery, she couldn't take it any longer.

"Can you believe he changed his mind?" she asked. "I'm so excited. This is the perfect time of year. People are going to be more likely to give, don't you think? We can go to Porter's Home for Boys. I've been trying to get in touch with the director. Maybe we can just show up, and he'll have to talk to us. How could he refuse some pictures?"

"Hold on a moment," he said, raising his hand. "You know I've never wanted to be a part of this." The carriage stopped in front of her house. Brock looked out, his eyebrows raising. "This is where you live?"

"Yes."

He nodded silently, climbed down to help her out, and bowed as she thanked him. "I'll be on my way then, Miss Hughes," he said. "I'll see you tomorrow."

With that, he climbed back into the carriage.

<hr>

Ian arrived early to the weekly service, slipping into a seat at the front of the sanctuary. He closed his eyes, seeking a moment of peace. Today marked two years since his parents' tragic accident during their European tour. The pain of their loss still lingered, and the weight of it pressed down on him.

A hand settled gently on his shoulder. The pastor's voice, calm and reassuring, broke through his thoughts. *"Come to me, all you who are weary and burdened. I will give you rest.*

Take my yoke upon you and learn from me, for I am gentle and humble in heart, and you will find rest for your souls. For my yoke is easy, and my burden is light." He paused before he addressed Ian directly. "I know this day is especially hard for you. Remember, you're not alone in this."

Ian kept his eyes closed, focusing on the comfort in those words. A sense of relief began to ease the tightness in his chest. The tears that threatened to spill retreated as he took a deep breath. The pastor gave his shoulder one last comforting squeeze before moving on.

A few moments later, Ian stood and greeted Mrs. Lardish.

"How are you today?" she asked compassionately.

"I'm holding up," he said. "I was just going to search for my sister."

"Ah, Mrs. Lancer," Mrs. Lardish nodded somberly. "I pray daily for that child."

Ian smiled. His sister was nearing thirty years old, yet the lady still called her a child. "Thank you," he said. "I appreciate it."

Mrs. Lardish patted his hand. "Go look for her. I'll see you tomorrow."

He said goodbye and continued his search. The entry was getting crowded when she finally entered with Hugh.

"Dorothy," he said as he approached her.

She turned with a wan smile. "Ian."

He took her arm and escorted her to the sanctuary, choosing an empty pew at the back. He knew she didn't like to sit where she thought people might see and judge her. While he waited for them to get settled, he scanned the gathered worshippers for Angela and Amelia, but didn't see them. Pastor Grey stepped on the dais and started the service.

Angie was weary as she exited the church, trying to hold in her cough until she reached the carriage. The racking cough had gotten much worse, and she knew she couldn't conceal her condition much longer. Nervously, she checked the white cloth in her hand and sighed in relief when it was clean. After pocketing it, she noticed Henry up the path and walked towards him.

"Angela!" she heard a voice call. "One moment, please?" Recognizing it was Ian, Angie turned, her worry replaced with delight.

"How are you?" she asked. Settling his hat back on his head, he stopped before her.

"I'm as well as I can be right now," he said. "I just said goodbye to Dorothy and Hugh." He shrugged, his eyes sad. "How are you doing? And Miss Hughes?"

"She's fine, though a little under the weather today," Angie answered. Feeling a cough coming on, she slipped her hand into her pocket, grasping her handkerchief.

"I'm sorry to hear that," Ian said. "I'd planned to ask if I could visit today. Perhaps I should wait."

"That's a wonderful idea," Angie said. "If we need to, we can relegate her upstairs." She smiled at him, her delight distracting her from the pain. *I wish he and Amelia would form an attachment.*

"If you're sure, then I'll come over directly?" Ian suggested. "I know it's a bit presumptuous, but I can't bear an empty house today."

"You can stay as late as you need," she replied, aware of the day's significance.

"Thank you," he said with a sigh.

She took his offered arm, trying to hold back her cough. Ian waved to Henry to stay in his driving seat, and helped her in. "I'll see you soon, then."

Angie nodded and held her breath until he left. The cough burst out of her painfully. Just as the carriage started moving, a shout caused Henry to stop again. Ian appeared in the opening, obviously concerned.

"Forgive me, Angela, but are you ill?"

Angie sighed, realizing he'd heard her cough. She looked at his earnest, worried face, and knew she couldn't put off telling him any longer. "Yes, Ian…I'm quite ill," she admitted.

Ian had expected Angela to laugh away his worry, perhaps pat his hand like his mother would. Her sudden seriousness nearly broke his heart. Time slowed, and he struggled to breathe. He unconsciously gripped the top of the carriage door. "You're not…" he began, then stopped and shook his head.

"I'm sorry, Ian. I shouldn't have told you like this," Angie remarked.

"Don't apologize! You just told me you're…" His normal reserve forgotten, he stared at her, moved that she'd be concerned about him in a moment like this.

"Come," Angela patted his hand. "Ride with me." He climbed in, then called for Henry to inform his driver to follow them to Angela's home. It took several minutes of the carriage's gentle swaying to loosen Ian's tongue. He lifted his tortured eyes to her.

"You've looked tired lately," he said, faltering, unable to form a thought. Finally, he blurted, "How sick are you?"

"It's consumption," she said plainly. Ian swallowed, trying to push down the pain that threatened to undo him. Having

Angela in his life had been the one thing to soothe the aching loss of his parents, especially the hole his mother left behind. Now, hearing that he was to lose her too drove a cold knife into his heart. He knew he should say something but couldn't think of what. He stared at Angela. The compassion in her eyes eased his despair. She was ill, yet she was worried about him.

"How long have you known?" he asked quietly.

"Dr. Martin came in August. But I've been sick for almost a year now." Ian's stillness told her how much her news hurt him. "I couldn't catch my breath," she went on. "I'd get exhausted doing little things. And now this cough." She coughed as she spoke, then took a few deep breaths before continuing. "I'm sorry to tell you like this. I couldn't talk about it, Ian. I couldn't."

Angie paused and tried to catch her breath again. She was relieved to have finally told him, but when she looked at her young friend, she regretted her honesty. His eyes were wide, and his face had gone ashen. He stared at her, trying to make sense of it all. Before she could soothe him, he reached out a gloved hand and grasped hers.

"I'm so sorry, friend, that you went through all of that alone," he said. "I wish I could have been there."

At those kind words, Angie wept.

⌒〜〜⌒

Amelia stretched and set her book down, relieved she had skipped service to avoid the cold, as she already felt better. After styling her hair in a loose chignon, she grabbed her book and went downstairs to read in the salon until Aunt Angie returned.

"Mr. Hayworth!" She stopped short at the door, surprised to find him in the house.

He turned and bowed. "Good afternoon, Miss Hughes. I hope you're feeling better?"

"I am, thank you." Puzzled, she glanced around the room. It was empty except for them.

"I begged your aunt to let me come home with her," Ian smiled slightly. "She was gracious enough to oblige."

"Aunt Angie is the most gracious person I know," Amelia said. She waved toward a set of chairs and sat down in her favorite.

"I've long believed the same thing," he said. "I'm blessed to call her friend."

They sat in silence, which left Amelia feeling a little nervous. She was used to Ian leading their conversations. She started to ask after Nettleville, but his paleness and stillness struck her. "Are you all right?" she asked. "You look rather ill."

She caught a flash of pain on his face. He started to speak, but then looked past her and smiled as Angela entered. "I asked Walter to have lunch served in here today," he said to her.

"Oh, lovely," Angela replied. "Amelia, how are you?"

Amelia took her aunt's hand as she settled on the settee next to her. "I'm feeling better," she said. "Rest was just what I needed. How was service?"

"Pastor Grey spoke of having faith through trials," Ian answered. "And Mrs. Lardish was as kind as ever."

Aunt Angie laughed. "I adore that woman," she said. They continued talking as Susan entered and set about laying a small table for lunch.

"Mrs. Lardish treats me like she's known me for years," Amelia said. "She's very sweet."

"That is typical of her," Ian said. "She keeps track of my attendance, as if I'm still the little boy who used to run by her on my way outside to play." He leaned back in his chair, a smile of remembrance on his face.

Amelia tried to picture him as a rough and tumble boy but found it impossible.

"She's a genuine soul," Aunt Angie said.

Unable to ignore the hoarseness in her aunt's voice, Amelia leaned close. "Would you like your honey tea?"

Angie nodded in obvious relief. Amelia squeezed her hand and requested the tea be brought as soon as possible. Wondering what Ian would think, she looked at him. As he watched Aunt Angie, a tender yet pained look crept across his face. Lowering her gaze, Amelia realized that she'd crumpled her handkerchief in her free hand. She sighed softly, smoothing and folding it before tucking it back up her sleeve.

"Luncheon is served, ma'am," Susan said. They settled at the small table laden with food. Sunlight streamed in through the large window that looked out to the garden, soothing some of Amelia's worry.

"This was a great idea, Mr. Hayworth," she said. "We'll have to do it again."

"It was rather presumptuous of me," he admitted. "But it was such a beautiful day outside..."

Aunt Angie covered his hand with hers. "It's lovely, Ian."

Amelia stared at their hands, then up into each of their faces. The pain in Ian's eyes was obvious. In that moment, Amelia knew that Aunt Angie had told him about her diagnosis. Some of the burden lifted from her shoulders. She was relieved someone else knew, and that her aunt had another person she could lean on.

Their lunch continued with little talking, just camaraderie and enjoying each other's company. When they finished, Aunt Angie excused herself for a moment. As she left, Amelia stepped closer to Ian.

"She told you, didn't she?"

"Yes, she did," Ian admitted without hesitating. Amelia nodded. "Do let me know if there's anything she needs or wants," he went on. "I'm available any time. Just send for me. I'll get here as quickly as I can." A faint sense of pleading tinged his voice.

"Of course," she agreed. "I know she thinks a great deal of you."

"As I do her," he said. "She's been a good friend to me, since my parents died."

"I didn't know that. I'm sorry for your loss."

"It's been two years. If not for Angela, I don't know what I would have done." He sighed and made an obvious effort to pull himself together. "Forgive me for being so open with you, but today is the anniversary of their passing. I always tend to be…"

"It's all right," Amelia said. "I've been a bundle of nerves these past weeks as well."

It was only then that Amelia realized they'd been talking as friends, their shared love of her aunt allowing them to find solace in each other.

Chapter Seventeen

The rattling of the carriage bounced Amelia's notepad, and she moved to catch it before it fell off her lap. She'd been distractedly watching the scenery go by, reflecting on the past few days. Dr. Martin had prescribed tonics for Angie's racking cough and exhaustion. They helped her feel well enough that, shortly after Thanksgiving, she'd spent most of an afternoon at Edith's. Taking advantage of the time, Amelia recruited the staff to help her decorate for Christmas. Together they made the entry hall, salon, and dining room as festive as possible, and were just putting on the finishing touches when Angie returned. Amelia loved seeing the surprise and pleasure on her aunt's face.

Now she was on her way to meet Brock at the *Free Press*. From there, they were going to Porter's Home for Boys. For the rest of the ride, she steadied herself and focused on preparing for the interview.

The carriage slowed in front of the brick-face building, home to the paper's offices. Amelia tapped the notepad on her knee. Brock climbed in, thanking Henry before closing the door. She watched as he took in the luxurious carriage, his eyebrows raising. He saw her watching him and flushed.

"What will we do if Mr. O'Nell won't see us?" Amelia asked once he settled.

"We'll go back to the office and do our real work," Brock said. He set his camera bag on the seat next to him and rested his hand on it to keep it from falling.

"That's not our only option," Amelia said. "Besides, this is our real work. Your father..."

"My father has something up his sleeve, Miss Hughes," Brock interrupted in a low voice, keeping his gaze out the window. "You'd do well to be careful."

Amelia shifted and tapped her fingers against the bench. She turned back to her notes, flipping through her pages.

"We'll go to Nettleville afterward to get some photographs," she offered. "They won't be nearly as distressing but heaven knows they can use aid."

Brock sighed. "Are you sure they'll let us in?"

"He'll let us in," Amelia said confidently. "He's a friend of my aunt's." She was getting to know Ian Hayworth far better than she'd ever expected. He'd been stopping by almost daily to see Aunt Angie. Most times, he brought a small gift, intended to make her smile. He always asked if there was anything he could do. Amelia could see just how badly Aunt Angie's illness continued to shake him. Whenever possible, she joined in their conversations. One day, he asked how her article about the orphanages was coming along. She'd been pleased, and a little relieved, to be able to tell him that her article would be published soon.

She was startled out of the memory by Brock speaking.

"No offense, but I hope that neither of them grants us access," he frowned, playing with the handle on his camera bag. He looked considerably unhappy, and she felt it was all her fault. She had dragged him into this, after all. An apology would be of little use. Instead, she sought to reassure him.

"I'll interview him while you take photographs. We can meet at the carriage when we're done."

⌒‿‿⌒

"I appreciate you giving of your time, Mr. O'Nell, as well as allowing us to take photographs," Amelia said as she entered O'Nell's office. "I truly believe people's hearts will be touched by this endeavor."

"As long as they open up their pocketbooks, I don't much care if their hearts are touched or not, Miss Hughes," Mr. O'Nell replied. Amelia smiled uncomfortably.

"How long have you been the director?" she asked. The tall man leaned back in his chair, his coat unable to button due to his girth.

"Well now, it would be about ten years," he said, squinting at her. "Don't go writin' that I haven't done what's best for them castaways," he went on. "They've got a roof over their heads, and we teach them a trade so they can break the curse of their parents, if they have 'em, and become worthwhile citizens."

Amelia wrote quickly. "And what sort of trades do you teach?"

"Bricklaying…masonry…some others…the types of skills that will keep them out of the poorhouse, that you can be certain."

"A worthy goal, to be sure," Amelia said. "And how many children do you currently have?"

"Seventy five."

"You're only billeted to have sixty-five," Amelia said, looking up from her notebook. "Where do you put the extra children?" *And why are there so many here when Nettleville is low?*

Mr. O'Nell leaned forward, his thick eyebrows lowering. "And would you have me turn them away? We have them share bunks, of course."

"Forgive me," Amelia demurred. "I only meant that you have quite a large number, while other orphanages are lower than they are billeted."

"We've got the handful here, 'tis the truth. But we do receive some assistance." He frowned immediately after he said that. Amelia jumped on it.

"You receive assistance? From whom?"

"Now, Miss Hughes, I can hardly be speaking about…"

"Wouldn't it benefit your orphanage if the public knew where your support comes from?" She tapped her pen on the notepad, hoping it would come across as intimidating. She couldn't believe she'd pushed him like this! Mr. McFarce had been telling her that she needed to be bolder in her interviews. Here she was, actually doing it.

O'Nell glanced at her and shuffled some papers. "We have some sponsors, but they give little enough when all is said and done. It isn't cheap to run a place like this, you know." He waved his hand in the air. "Not only must we pay for the building each month, but there's a lot that goes into it, now."

"That's exactly why I'm here, Mr. O'Nell," Amelia countered. "I want to open the public's eyes to how much help the children require. What is your greatest need right now?"

As he answered, Amelia felt that the director wasn't being completely honest with her. But she couldn't decide if it was about the sponsors or something else. It upset her to think of those poor children being forced to work each day. She couldn't imagine Mr. O'Nell being as compassionate as Ian, which reminded her of another question.

"What are you teaching the children each day?"

"I told you already, bricklaying and other skills."

"I meant what other classes are you holding for them? Arithmetic? Reading? Writing?"

"There's no way we could possibly cover all those topics," Mr. O'Nell snapped. "Remember, we house seventy-five castaways! These children won't have much use for all that nonsense, anyhow."

Amelia bit her tongue to keep from pointing out that Ian Hayworth taught all those subjects. And she was sure he would do so even if he had two hundred children. She decided to move on to another topic. She wanted out of this man's office as quickly as possible.

The office door opened abruptly, startling them both. Brock stood with face flushed, one hand gripping the doorknob while the other clutched his camera bag.

"Let's be leaving, Miss Hughes." His words were clipped.

"Why, if that isn't Brock all grown up. I'm glad to see that you're working hard for your father."

"I've nothing to say to you, O'Nell," Brock said coldly. "I'm here for Miss Hughes."

An odd tension filled the room. She hesitated before nodding to Mr. O'Nell, grabbing her bag, and leaving the room.

They'd been in the carriage for several minutes when Brock spoke. "I should apologize for my behavior, Miss Hughes." Amelia recognized his expression as the same one from the day she'd overheard him talking at the diner. It hit her then, just why he'd be so upset. She had to swallow before whispering hoarsely. "That's where your father sent you, isn't it?"

Brock jerked his head forward. His eyes were red rimmed, but no tears fell. He seemed so immovable that she wondered if he'd ever cried about it.

As if he knew what she was thinking, he shifted uncomfortably. "I used to cry. That's what you do when you're ten years old and alone, expected to work like a slave for a measly meal at the end of the day. You cry until someone's had enough of hearing your sobs and beats you." He shook his head, his jaw working. "Crying doesn't change anything. It only ends up making things worse."

Tears ran down Amelia's cheeks, but she didn't wipe them away.

"Those institutions aren't there for the needs of the children, no matter what they say," he continued bitterly. "O'Nell…he's more concerned with his pocketbook than the children. He drives them like you wouldn't believe. And it's no different now than when I was there."

Silence roared in her ears as she desperately tried to think of something to say.

～⌣⌣⌐

As his guests entered, Ian stood, buttoning his jacket before shaking hands. "Mr. McFarce, it's a pleasure to meet you. I've heard about you from Miss Hughes."

"It's an honor to meet you, sir," the young man said. "Please, call me Brock. I've only seen a little of Nettleville, but already I can tell you genuinely care for your charges. As does Mrs. Lardish."

"Mrs. Lardish is truly one of a kind," Ian smiled. He motioned for them to sit. "She gathers these children to her, and mothers them until they flourish."

"That's a rarity," Brock said somberly.

"Indeed, it is," Ian readily agreed. "I aim to change how they're run across the city. Children need to learn more than a physical trade to grow into independent, active members of society."

"Mrs. Lardish showed me where they're building a set for a play," Brock commented.

Sensing he wanted more information, Ian obliged. "Thomas wanted to do *Robin Hood*. We've never done such a thing, but they've been learning a lot through it already. We try to encourage their interests when we can. Although this one is unusual, we're making it work."

They talked a little more until Amelia asked if they could take photographs for their article. Ian walked them to the room where children were busily working on the stage. He and Amelia watched while Brock engaged with the children and took photographs.

"How's Angela?" Ian asked her quietly.

"She's about the same," Amelia answered somberly.

"I'll come visit her as soon as I can."

"Thank you. She does love when you visit."

"Is she the only one?" he asked, suddenly desperate to hear the answer.

"No, I enjoy them too." Her voice and smile were soft.

His heart pounded. He bit his lip to keep from smiling too widely as Brock rejoined them.

"Thank you, Mr. Hayworth. It's been good seeing how Nettleville is run. I hope you're able to take over the other orphanages. They'd benefit from it."

"Thank you," Ian nodded. "You're welcome back any-time." They shook hands again and said goodbye.

As they left, two small boys ran up and asked Ian if he'd help them. He willingly obliged, glad to take a longer break from paperwork.

Early the next morning, Amelia sat in front of Mr. McFarce's desk and waited for his reaction to her article.

"This is impressive, Miss Hughes," he said around the pencil clenched in his teeth. "You've done a fine piece here."

"Thank you, sir. I worked hard on it." She tried not to smile too broadly.

"Mm hmm. Yes. I see you gave ample space to Mr. O'Nell's interview. That's good. Brock's photographs complement it well. Nicely done, Miss Hughes. I'm afraid there's a problem, though." He worked the pencil from one side of his mouth to the other.

Amelia winced at the sight. "Did I leave something out? I can work it in right away sir."

"This topic is a sensitive one, as you know, and the *Free Press* needs this publicity. So, it's not going to be your byline."

"What? Why not?"

"We can't afford to have a woman's name on it."

"But, Mr. McFarce, I'm the one who…"

He slapped the papers onto his desk and frowned at her. "I won't repeat myself. Now get back to work."

Amelia stared at him, biting her tongue. She went back to her desk and let it sink in that after all the work of interviews and research, as well as the time she'd put into the article, she wouldn't get the credit for it at all.

The glow of candles on the tree lit the corner of the room. The fireplace crackled and popped, sending out a cozy glow of its own while the gramophone played Beethoven. *The setting couldn't be more perfect for Christmas Eve.* Angie admired the greenery draped over the curtain rods and the bright red bows that tied the curtains back. She sighed in contentment. She always loved this time of year.

"This room has never been more beautiful," she said to her niece.

"It is charming, isn't it?" Amelia smiled. "It's my favorite spot in the house. There's something so wonderful about having the tree decorated and lit up. It makes me feel calm inside."

Angie didn't respond. She set her cup down and rested her hands in her lap. Suddenly, she felt anything but calm. She could not get enough air. Willing herself to relax, she closed her eyes.

"Aunt Angie?" Amelia's voice was pitched higher than normal. "I'll get Walter."

Angie stayed focused on her breathing. *Please, not tonight. Let me breathe. Please.*

"Mrs. Barrington? I'll send the boy for the doctor."

Her throat eased as air entered her lungs. It felt just as wonderful as always. She resisted the urge to inhale too deeply, knowing it would trigger a coughing fit. After several breaths, she slowly opened her eyes. Amelia and Walter were on their knees in front of her. She held both hands out to them. Amelia immediately grasped one, while Walter hesitated, then gingerly took the other.

"I'm all right," Angie said. She hated how small her voice sounded. Her reassurance didn't ease either of their expressions. She squeezed their hands, hoping that the little strength she had would convince them. "No need for the doctor."

"Please let Walter send for him?" Amelia pleaded.

Taking another deep breath, she shook her head. "He's coming in a few days," she said, then looked at Walter. "Have you any responses?"

Walter nodded, his brow still creased. "Yes, ma'am. The advertisement for your companion has generated a few responses Ms. Dean and I have believe worthy of your perusal." He tilted his head and stood. "I believe I hear someone at the door. Excuse me, ma'am."

"I think he just wanted out of the room," Amelia whispered to her conspiratorially as she stood.

"You're probably right," Angie agreed. They were both surprised when they heard a familiar voice greeting Walter. Angie breathed a prayer of thanks that the episode was over before Edith arrived, entering cheerily.

"Angie, dear, I had to come see you before service so I could give you this," she said, setting a bag on the couch, then kissing Angie's cheek.

Angie laughed weakly and peeked into the bag. "You won't hear me complain," she said and motioned to the chair next to her. Amelia poured their guest some tea.

Edith sat, arranging her deep purple skirt. "You're rather pale, Angie. Are you well?"

"Oh, I'm rather tired," she admitted, then decided to be even more truthful. "I've just had an episode, but I'm fine now."

"Did you call Dr. Martin?"

Angie shook her head. "But I've placed an advertisement for a companion with nursing experience," she said. "That way, I'll have help when I need it."

"That's a wonderful idea!" Edith said. "We'll all be so relieved if you have someone with you."

Angie smiled. "That's partly why I decided to."

"Mrs. Barrington," Walter interrupted. "Mr. Hayworth is here to see you." He bowed at the doorway.

Amelia briefly tensed and set her teacup clumsily on the saucer. All three women turned to greet the newcomer. Angie kept an eye on Amelia as Ian bowed to Edith.

"How are the Christmas celebrations at Nettleville coming along?" Edith asked.

"We had a party this afternoon, and another one planned for tomorrow morning," Ian smiled. "The children are excited about their gifts. Thank you for your generosity."

"I'm glad to be of assistance," Edith said. "Those little ones have enough trials. Christmas shouldn't be one of them."

"I agree," Ian said. "And thank you for your part as well, Angela."

"A pleasure, as always," Angie said. She paused for a breath. Perhaps she'd been too optimistic about feeling strong. "I'm glad you could come, Ian."

"I wouldn't miss it." His expression softened as he looked at her. "How are you?"

"Enjoying the day," she said truthfully.

He nodded and turned to Amelia. "The orphanage article and photographs were well done. Congratulations."

"Thank you," Amelia answered, her cheeks flushed. "Brock was very impressed with how you run Nettleville."

The three moved to sit, all facing Angie, the younger two of the company continuing to talk. Angie didn't want to get her hopes up, but could it be that they were growing fond of one another?

At the gong of the half hour, Edith set her teacup down. "I must be off," she said.

"I appreciate you coming, Edith," Angie said. "Tell the pastor I am sorry I won't be there tonight."

"I'll pass on the message. You know that we understand, don't you? Take care of yourself and have a blessed holiday." Edith hugged Angie gently. As she pulled away, she wiped her cheeks free of tears.

After she'd left, a hush fell over the room until Ian spoke. "Since we won't be attending the service tonight, how about we do a little something of our own? I could read the story of the first Christmas. Would that be all right?"

"That would be lovely," Angie smiled, touched by her friend's thoughtfulness. Ian retrieved a Bible from a nearby shelf, flipping to a familiar passage in Luke. He glanced at Angie, cleared his throat, and began.

"*In those days, Caesar Augustus issued a decree that a census should be taken of the entire Roman world...*"

Angie closed her eyes, letting Ian's soothing voice fill the room as he read the story that had been shared through generations. As the story continued, she felt a sense of calm settle over her—a moment of quiet reflection she hadn't realized she needed.

"*...But Mary treasured all these things and pondered them in her heart. The shepherds returned, glorifying and praising all they had heard and seen, just as they had been told.*"

"I've never thought about how hard it must have been for Mary," Amelia said quietly. "Leaving her home and family behind like that... she must have been scared."

The conversation continued as they awaited a fresh pot of tea. When Angie suggested a game of cribbage, Amelia stood up quickly to fetch the game and start a new record. Ian cleared the low table in front of them.

After their first game, Angie smiled as Ian and Amelia gathered the cards and prepared for another. "Thank you both for spending the evening with me," she said. "I know you would've liked to attend the Christmas Eve service. It means the world to me to have you here."

"You know we'd rather be here with you than anywhere else," Ian spoke, glancing at Amelia as he said it.

"Yes, Aunt Angie, you're practically a mother to both of us. What sort of ingrates would we be if we went off and left you? You know I far prefer your company to anyone I know."

Angie took Amelia's hand in hers. "You are more than I deserve, both of you."

They assured her that they were not…that they were giving her the sort of love and devotion she'd given them. They played another game until dinner was announced. Ian escorted Angie to the table, while Amelia held her chair out for her. So much love was in her expression that Angie felt tears fill her eyes. She was indeed blessed this year.

⌒‿‿⌒

Walter admitted a young woman who was likely in her mid-thirties, dressed stylishly but not ostentatiously. Her face was pleasant, her gaze direct.

Not wanting to get her hopes up on first impression, much less on her very first interview for the position, Angie greeted the woman cordially. "It's a pleasure to meet you, Miss Post," she said. "Thank you for meeting me."

"The pleasure is mine, Mrs. Barrington," Miss Post replied. "I've heard a lot about you since I came to Portland.

You're held in the highest esteem." Her voice was deep and pleasing to the ear.

"Oh, I'm no better than anyone else," Angie protested. "Please, have a seat." She motioned toward the chair opposite her and sat down carefully. Her joints ached terribly today. "Would you tell me about yourself?"

Miss Post began by relating how she'd attended the Women's Hospital of Philadelphia for nursing several years ago. Her most recent job in town had been for a matron who passed away sooner than anyone anticipated. Now she was searching for a new position.

"I'm in need of a nurse as well as a companion," Angie said, then paused to catch her breath. "I'd like to offset my niece's worries by having someone nearby to assist me."

"That sounds reasonable, and your niece sounds like she cares a great deal for you," Miss Post said. "May I ask what you're needing assistance with?"

Angie dredged up a small smile. "I've been diagnosed with consumption. Dr. Martin has said that with time…"

"Yes. I know all about tuberculosis," Miss Post said kindly. "I'm terribly sorry, Mrs. Barrington. How's the pain today?"

Angie hesitated. "It's pretty strong, especially in my joints," she finally admitted. "What would you suggest helping with that?"

"A warm bath can soothe the aches," Miss Post said. "As will applying magnesium lotion regularly."

As they continued to speak, Angie posed more questions, while Miss Post answered with confidence.

"This is rather sudden," Angie said eventually, "but would you be willing to have a trial period, to see if we are compatible?"

"I'd love to. Thank you, Mrs. Barrington."

"Please, call me Angie."

"In that case, I'm May," Miss Post said. "I look forward to working with you."

They scheduled for May to return in the morning at nine o' clock, then said goodbye. "We're going to have a trial period," Angie told Walter when he entered the room. At his look of concern, she added, "Let me know what you think of her after a few days, and we'll talk about it."

"Very good, ma'am." When Walter left, Angie sighed and closed her eyes. Even though she admitted to May how she was hurting today, she'd striven to hide her pain as best she could. Now that she was alone, she let the pain wash over her, and wilted into her chair. How she missed her pain-free years. Perhaps having May with her will help balance the loss of independence she felt.

Chapter Eighteen

The Ladies Aid Society had split into two sections, and Amelia was able to write a regular article on their causes. They were raising funds to help rebuild a church and were also starting to support the suffrage movement. Amelia found herself meeting with several ladies a week, interviewing them and anyone else connected to the causes.

Faithfully she sent her parents copies of every printed article. When she mailed the first one, her stomach was in knots. Her mother's answering letter barely touched on Amelia's accomplishments, but she did make sure and let her opinion be known: "*I don't know why you're wasting your time working like a commoner,*" her mother had written. "*I'm glad that you're at least part of this Ladies Aid group, although what they must think of you, traipsing around acting like you're a man...*"

She was pleasantly surprised when her father wrote almost two pages detailing everything he liked about the story. The postscript at the end of his letter caused her eyes to fill with tears. "*You've got talent, Amelia. I'm proud of you. Send more.*"

While her mother's response had been what she'd expected, it didn't hurt nearly as much with her father's words buoying her. She'd even asked him for advice in the last two letters. His years as an avid reader came in handy, she found.

After sealing her latest letter to her father, she glanced at the calendar—1899 was near. Most holiday parties were over, though elites still held a few. She smiled, reminiscing about dancing with Harrison and her youthful infatuation. Her life had evolved greatly since then. Now, with a job and spending time with her aunt, she didn't miss the days of parties and gossip.

She pulled out her journal and wrote about how things had changed in the almost ten months since she arrived in Portland. She closed her eyes, remembering how Harrison had looked the last time she saw him. She couldn't deny that she was still attracted to him. But another face came to mind.

What a different man Ian Hayworth is than I first thought, she wrote. *There's something about him that makes me feel content. Although I do seem to blush a lot when he's around. It's so embarrassing.*

Even just writing it in her journal made her uncomfortable. She was not interested in Ian Hayworth. It was just that she was seeing so much of him lately. She sighed.

I'm glad Aunt Angie has May with her, she continued writing. *I don't worry so much, going to work now. Her joints ache awful, and I heard her telling the doctor that she's barely sleeping most nights. It's so hard to see her like this. It makes me feel guilty, being so excited about having my stories published, but she says she loves reading them. Mrs. Grey often comes to tea. They embroider when Aunt is able to, but those days are becoming rarer.*

She set her pen down, her heart heavy. Seeing her aunt decline was heartbreaking. Writing about it just made it all the worse. Thus far, Angie had been able to avoid bed rest, but Amelia feared it wouldn't be long. She'd seen her aunt's frequent grimaces, and asked May to tell her when the medication wasn't as effective.

Amelia rose to check her reflection in the mirror. To keep her aunt from feeling shut off from New Year's celebrations, she was hosting a small dinner party. She'd planned the whole evening, from meal to decorations. Mr. and Mrs. Grey were coming. A fleeting wish that Ian had been able to come caused a blush. Needing a distraction, she rang for Grace so she could get dressed for dinner, even though it was still early.

A delicious feast ensued. Plump rolls with apple butter, roasted vegetables and fruit salad, and the side of beef. Looking around the table, Amelia loved the sight of the Lenten roses in small vases, the bouquets of lavender hung over the backs of chairs, and the candelabras that lit the room. Everyone admired the room as they were served. Even Pastor Grey nodded his approval. It was a wonderful evening that continued until Aunt Angie admitted exhaustion.

Walter entered the dining room and reached Amelia's side quickly. At his whisper, she flushed. "It seems Mr. James is here to see me," she said to her aunt.

"Let's greet him as we're walking the Greys out, shall we?" Angie suggested. Amelia felt the knot in her stomach ease as they made their way from the dining room and entered the hall as a group.

"Mrs. Barrington, Miss Hughes," Harrison said as he bowed. "Might I speak to Miss Hughes out in the garden?"

Amelia waited for her aunt's response. It wasn't fully dark yet, so it was still proper to walk out with him. When Aunt Angie gave her approval, Amelia accepted Harrison's offered arm, wondering what purpose he might have for coming unexpectedly.

"You look lovely, Amelia," he said.

She smoothed the velvet skirt with her fingertips. "Thank you."

"I hope you're not upset that I came unannounced," he went on, turning to look at her as they walked, the light from the house highlighting half his face.

"Not at all," Amelia admitted.

"I'd hoped you wouldn't be," Harrison said. "I came because I wondered if you would attend the Whitmores' party with me?"

Amelia hesitated, blushing. "I'm honored. But may I ask when the party is?" She was surprised when her voice was steady, as her heart was pounding. She had no idea who the Whitmores were. Perhaps she *could* take a break from the seriousness of life and go have fun for one evening.

"Tomorrow evening," Harrison said. Amelia frowned.

"So soon?"

Harrison admired the fact that she didn't scold him for the insult of such a late invitation. He couldn't very well tell her that his previous date had cancelled on him a few hours ago. He eyed her profile. She looked different than the last time he'd seen her. She'd grown more graceful, easily matching his pace around the garden path, her hand lightly resting on his arm.

"Say you'll go with me," he urged. "You haven't been to a proper party in weeks." He stopped walking so he could turn her toward him. She let him pull her closer, until he could tilt her chin up. He searched her eyes. *I'm not smitten with this girl, am I? No! She's just like any other girl.*

"Say yes, Amelia," he pressed.

"Why do you want me to go with you?" she asked softly. "We've not seen each other in weeks."

His smile deepened. "That's exactly why. I've missed seeing you lately."

She lowered her eyes. A flash of doubt crossed her face before she tried to pull away. He tightened his hold on her arm, hoping to change what he was certain would be a refusal. "I'm not letting you go until you agree. I'm very stubborn about these things."

"All right. Yes, I'll go with you," she said, flustered.

He grinned. "I'll be here tomorrow evening at seven o'clock."

Later that evening, Angie gathered Amelia's hair and picked up the wide bristled brush. "I used to love having my hair brushed," Angie said. "Your great grandmother had the gentlest hands." She paused to catch her breath. "Are you sure about this party?"

"Harrison wouldn't take me anywhere that wasn't proper, Aunt Angie," Amelia said confidently. Angie wished that were true, but rumors about the James boy had been circulating, and she wasn't comfortable with him escorting her niece anywhere. Still, what was she to do? Forbid Amelia to go? Remembering their last fight, Angie knew she couldn't bear another disagreement with her niece.

As she brushed Amelia's long red hair, the only other option came to her. She'd allow Amelia to go and discover for herself what Harrison was like. She only hoped she wouldn't regret it.

The Whitmore residence might not have been the grandest in the city, but its decorations certainly tried to compensate. Buntings, flowers, and lights adorned every corner, and waiters circulated trays of hors d'oeuvres and beverages.

Everywhere Amelia looked, there was a dense crowd of people. Their own presence was dwarfed by the sea of guests that filled the home. As Harrison navigated her through the throng toward the center of the main room, Amelia only caught fleeting glimpses of faces. Dazzling gowns and jewelry shimmered, while slender wisps of smoke drifted toward the ceiling. After a bit more jostling, they paused.

"Why does our hostess stand back here?" she asked, leaning closer so he could hear her. "Making people fight their way to her is absurd."

Harrison stopped waving at someone and turned to her. "You'll find that she likes to do things in her own way," he said. "From here, she can be surrounded by her admirers." He winked then looked around, frowning. "We should've had drinks by now. Simply unacceptable service when I'm parched."

"We've not been here that long," Amelia replied, slightly amused at his assertion, but thirsty herself. Without warning, Harrison dove back into the crowd, dragging her behind him. She decided that the appeal of being on a gentleman's arm was greatly diminishing. The crowd opened around them, allowing them to pass without too much hassle. Amelia still needed to straighten the lace ruffles on her sleeves when they halted.

"Harrison, darling!" their hostess called out. "I've been dying of loneliness without you!" Harrison smiled, bowed, and kissed the lady's hand. "Come tell me what you've been up to, naughty boy."

Stunning was the only way to describe their hostess. Her figure was one to be envied, her lips full, her eyes bold. And her choice of gown was daring, and not altogether proper. As Amelia's eyes flew to the woman's face, heat filled her cheeks.

"Celene, it's an absolute pleasure to see you again," Harrison said. "It's been as dull as tombs around here with you gone."

"I see you haven't been too bored. You've found a pretty young thing to amuse yourself with." Miss Whitmore raked her eyes over Amelia. "Are you going to introduce her, Harrison darling?" Her words dripped with an intimacy that made Amelia more uncomfortable, but Harrison didn't seem to notice anything amiss. "This is Miss Amelia Hughes, niece to Mrs. Barrington. Miss Hughes, this is Miss Celene Whitmore."

"You've chosen your diversion well," Celene smiled. "She's refined, yet with a hint of a backbone. Although, that might be an obstacle in this case. We'll see if she's able to handle our types of diversions. If not, the loss won't be so great."

Harrison merely smiled and nodded, much to Amelia's shock.

"Come, I would have another drink!" Celene called, her voice carrying over the crowd. At that announcement, a half dozen waiters arrived with full trays, offering them to everyone gathered around Miss Whitmore. Harrison took one, drank it then snagged two more from another passing tray. Then he returned to Amelia's side.

"She's something, isn't she?" he asked.

Amelia took a hesitant sip of her drink. "She's rather brash," she said.

"Celene just likes to shock people," Harrison said, laughing. "Come, let's get out of here."

They wove their way through the crowd again, ending up on the opposite side of the house. Amelia sighed, thinking longingly of the comfort of home. "How did you meet Miss Whitmore?"

"Celene? At some function or other I suppose. Do you want to dance?" When she hesitated, he stepped close, his gaze intense. "We haven't danced in months. You won't continue such maltreatment, will you?"

"Maltreatment?" Despite the warning sounds going off in her head, she couldn't help but notice how handsome he was, or how his deep voice reverberated.

"It's been pure torture," he said.

"Then I suppose we must relieve that at once. Lead on, Harrison *darling*," she teased.

"Now that is the sweetest thing you've ever uttered," he said, staring at her mouth as if mesmerized.

"I was only teasing." She bit her lip and took a step backward, hoping to escape the intensity of his gaze.

"Ah, if only you meant it." He offered something of a sad smile.

"As she means it?"

"No, Amelia. Not as she means it." His mouth twitched as he looked at her lips once more, then pulled her arm through his. "Now, I believe you promised me a dance."

As the party continued, Amelia realized something. Harrison still had a quality that drew her, even though she wasn't the same starry-eyed girl who had immediately fallen for him months ago. That change somehow made the extravagance of the party feel wrong.

"Why do you look like you just ate a lemon?" Harrison asked her. "Aren't you having fun?"

"I just was thinking of those children at the orphanage and, well, this all seems so…" Amelia looked at him, hoping he would understand.

"Would you rather we don't have fun, because there are poor in this town? You can't save them all," he said, grabbing her hand and leading her toward the stairs. "I know just the thing to distract you."

His cavalier attitude bothered her, but she tried to put it off as they reached the top of the stairs and turned right. The room was thick with smoke, only lit in the center, leaving the edges shrouded in shadows. It was hard for Amelia to make out everyone who was present. She continued to follow Harrison, even though she was getting nervous. All eyes were fixed on the center of the room. Calls and whistles regularly split the air. At first glance of the sight before her, Amelia looked away instantly, her cheeks burning.

"Harrison!" she hissed, outraged, already taking a few steps back.

"What?"

She stared at him, nonplussed. He didn't seem surprised or embarrassed. "You knew about this?"

"Celene always has something like this at her parties. It's her *pièce de resistance*, if you will." Aghast, she stared at him, seeing how thoroughly entranced he was by the woman, for the word 'lady' could not be applied, dancing in a lascivious manner beneath the spotlight. Hand going to her own neck, she clutched her collar tightly.

"And…you brought me here?" she stammered, so shocked she could barely think, let alone speak. Amelia took a deep breath, not believing this of him, even though he'd admitted it. Stepping backwards and mumbling apologies to those she bumped into, she realized Harrison wasn't the man she thought he was.

"Where are you going?" he asked. He reached out to take her hand, which she quickly pulled away.

"I want to leave. Now." But he'd already turned back to the entertainment and didn't seem to hear her. She waited a heartbeat longer, turned, and started making her way out of the room and down the stairs.

After retrieving her cloak, she waited by the edge of the driveway, still furious. *I'll not have anything more to do with him, ever again.* When the carriage driver opened the door, she paused. "Thank you. Once you've taken me home, you may return to the James' estate. Mr. James informed me that he has other transportation home."

Somewhat mollified at leaving him stranded, Amelia sat back for her ride home, determined to never again be put in such a position.

Chapter Nineteen

Early March came with a constant drizzle throughout Portland. On their way to the opening night of *Is He Dead?* Angie fingered her bracelet. She'd hoped she'd feel well enough for the whole play, after waking this morning with pressure behind her eyes. Her entire body ached in a way that felt different than usual. She was worried her condition was worsening. The one blessing of the day had been when May accepted her offer to take a permanent position.

"Cedric says his classes are keeping him as busy as could be," Amelia informed her. "He's worried about passing a few of them, but he loves it in Seattle. Campus is very nice."

"I'm glad to hear it. Did he mention anyone special?" Angie asked, thinking about the sparks she'd noticed between him and Grace.

"No," Amelia fidgeted. "However, he did ask me to give a letter to Grace," she confided. Angie smiled.

"That's good," she said. *Will anything come of that relationship?*

As they stepped inside the theatre's crowded lobby, Angie was relieved they weren't late. However, the clamor of the crowd instantly jarred her senses. She sighed in relief as they entered the hallway. She gave Amelia's arm a gentle squeeze.

"Slow down, please," she said to her niece.

"What's wrong?"

Angie shook her head, focusing all her attention on each successive step. When they made it to the auditorium, Angie paused and rested against the handrail. After a bracing breath, she started forward again, making her way past rows of seats. They settled into their spots, and she sighed softly. *It feels so good to sit down*! Walking had strained her far more than she'd expected.

Realizing Amelia was watching her closely, Angie smiled. "I'm just overtired today."

"We could have come another evening," Amelia admonished. "You know Dr. Martin told you to rest when you feel like this."

Angie didn't confess that staying in bed wouldn't have been helpful. "I didn't want to miss opening night," she said and patted Amelia's arm. "I'll be fine."

"Yes, because it's magical," Amelia smiled and leaned against her seat.

Because it is magical. Her eyes went to the lights above, and the wide expanse of curtains waiting to be drawn back.

Two hours later, as they left the auditorium, Amelia tried to talk over the noise of the crowd, exclaiming about the parts that had struck her fancy. Angie appreciated that they stayed near the wall, and how Amelia kept her arm securely tucked in hers, supporting her without appearing to. A wave of gratitude for her niece welled up in her.

Even as they lingered in the lobby, hailed by friends, Amelia never left her side. She insisted that people could come to them, adding that in this crush of bodies, no one would notice.

At the sight of Ian threading his way toward them, Angie smiled at how he seemed to be watching Amelia. *I wonder…*

When he and his friends reached them, he bowed over Angie's hand. "You're not feeling well, Angela. Shall I get you out of here?"

Angie was surprised when Amelia leaned close to Ian. "Please convince her that we can leave! She needs to rest, but she won't listen to me!"

Her frustration was evident, and Ian looked at her, obviously caught by her intensity. Angie swallowed, wishing she could tell them to stop fussing over her as if she were an old dowager. Still, as she looked at their youth and vitality, she felt every ache in her body. She leaned against Amelia and decided she was ready to go. Amelia and Ian talked a bit longer, and Angie wondered what they were planning.

She was surprised when Ian turned and introduced his friends to Amelia. They chatted pleasantly, but Angie wished she knew why they'd abandoned the attempt to make her go home. She kept track of the conversation but offered little to it, instead taking in the looks that Ian kept sending Amelia.

After a few minutes, Ian took Angie's free hand and pulled it through his arm. "Would you allow me to escort you to your carriage, ma'am?" he asked with a teasing smile.

"I'd be honored, sir," she answered lightly. They worked their way through the crowd, Amelia trailing behind. Once they were out of the building, Amelia took Angie's other arm again. The three of them waited for Henry to bring the carriage.

"Did you enjoy the play?" Angie asked Ian.

"I did. It's been a while since I came to the theatre, but my friends insisted I join them."

"Is that all it takes to gain your company?" Amelia teased. "I'm glad to know the secret."

"I'm not such a recluse as all that," Ian laughed.

When the carriage stopped for them, Ian waved for Henry not to climb down. He opened the door, unfolded the step, and handed Angie up, then Amelia. Angie sighed as she let the padded seat take her weight. She was so very tired. She didn't notice at first that Ian was still standing in the open doorway, watching her.

"Will you be all right, Angela?" he asked.

"I just overdid it tonight," she said. "A good rest is all I need." She ignored the doubtful look he shot toward Amelia, before he nodded and bid them farewell.

As the carriage pulled out, Angie leaned her head back. "Ian's a good man," she said. She smiled at the small sound of agreement Amelia offered from the opposite side of the carriage.

⁓⚮⁓

After having wrestled with his worry and overwhelming fear about Angela's health during the night, Ian woke with a lump in his throat. He felt a strong need to see her. He'd be working with Austin on estate business today, and decided to schedule a longer-than-usual lunch break so he could visit her. Unfortunately, his plan was waylaid just two hours later when Austin noted his employer's distraction.

"I'm sorry, Austin," Ian admitted. "I can't stop worrying about Angela."

"Perhaps it's an indication that you need to visit her, sir."

Relief filled him. "You don't think it's just my fear overriding my faith?" Ian asked.

"It could be. But that doesn't mean that God isn't nudging you to be a ministry to Mrs. Barrington."

A ministry to Angela. A blessing. "Can we put this on hold, Austin?" He was already standing, slipping his coat from the back of his chair. As he buttoned up, Amelia's image flashed before him. He paused. "Do you think a year is sufficient for someone to permanently change?"

"Depends on the year. And the person."

"She's young, sixteen." *It sounds even younger when I say it aloud.*

"Ah, well," Austin began. "My answer stays the same. It depends on the person's character. If they respond with compassion and fortitude as they go through something traumatic, then yes, I'd say a year is sufficient for it to be trustworthy."

Ian nodded, thanked Austin, and left as quickly as he could. He wasn't certain what had prompted his questioning, especially when he was so concerned about Angela. But Amelia had changed these past months. Indeed, she didn't seem a girl anymore.

⌒﹏﹏⌒

Walter admitted Ian into the salon, where Amelia sat directly across from the doorway, a book in her lap.

"Good morning, Mr. Hayworth," she said pleasantly.

"Miss Hughes." He ignored how appealing she looked and turned to see Angela reclining with a blanket over her legs. He sat on the edge of a chair next to her.

"Angela, how are you?" He scanned her face, noting she had more color in her cheeks than the night before. Her smile calmed some of his fear. "You look better."

"I'm feeling better," she said. "Amelia has been taking good care of me."

"Good," he said, suddenly at a loss for words. *Be a blessing to Angela. Don't be ruled by fear.*

"Are you all right, Ian?" Angela asked gently.

Embarrassed, he smiled. "I'll admit to letting my worry challenge my faith this morning. But seeing you has eased much of it."

"I've been feeling the same thing," Amelia agreed. "I was just going to read from the Psalms."

"The Psalms remind me that I'm not alone in my fear… that God is big enough to handle it," Angela said softly. Ian felt perhaps she was saying something beyond the words she spoke. He smiled in thanks. "Will you read to us?" Angela asked, turning to her niece.

"Of course, Aunt Angie," Amelia smiled. She darted a glance at Ian, then opened the Bible. For his sake, Ian liked the idea well enough. He settled calmly into his chair. No one had read to him since he was a boy. Amelia's voice, as she began reading Psalm 13, was comforting. As the words seeped into Ian's heart, he admitted to himself that yes, Amelia Hughes had grown up into a remarkable young woman.

***

"A letter has arrived for you, Miss Amelia," Walter announced later in the afternoon. Amelia absentmindedly accepted the envelope and returned to her seat. Aunt Angie looked terribly worn out again, and Amelia was about to ask her how she felt when she scanned the short letter. She gasped and began blinking in disbelief.

"Ian Hayworth has asked to call on me tomorrow evening," she said, her heart racing. She fingered the thick cream paper and looked at her aunt. "How should I respond?"

"How do you *want* to respond?" Angie asked in reply.

Amelia's mind scattered. She just stared at the note, her mouth agape. "Do you want him to call on you?" Angie continued, hoping to call back her attention.

"I can't think of a reason to say no." Her cheeks burned at the admission.

"What about a reason to say yes?"

Amelia sipped her tea and made a mental list of what she knew about Ian. Finally, she answered. "He cares for those around him…you, the children at Nettleville, Mrs. Lardish, his sister…I've never heard anyone say a bad word about him. He isn't caught up in society at all." She fell silent again, thinking of their encounters over nearly a year. Her heartbeat quickened. "I should reply quickly, shouldn't I?"

She set her teacup down and went to the library to pen her response.

Early the next morning, Amelia sat at her desk, trying to summon the courage to talk to Mr. McFarce. He'd changed over the last few weeks, coming in drunk and having irrational mood swings. She couldn't understand it, especially since the paper was doing well. After the orphanage piece, they'd gained more subscribers. As a result, he'd hired more newsies, as well as a boy to work in the back, which freed Brock to write obituaries and other news.

She eyed the two men, Brock hunched over his desk, the elder Mr. McFarce placing the letterpress. The scowl he aimed at the letters didn't encourage her, but she knew she had to try. The environment had changed enough that she wasn't sure how much longer she could work here. She'd come up with another focus piece as a last-ditch effort to bring back some enjoyment into her job. She'd even done preliminary questioning to gauge people's interest.

"Mr. McFarce," she said. "If I may, I'd like to cover working conditions of women in factories this month."

"You'll stick with the Society Page," Mr. McFarce grumbled, not looking up. "That's what we agreed upon."

"I thought that Brock and I could do another focus piece," she replied. "The last one did so well that…" As she trailed off, she realized he wasn't going to agree. Indeed, he wasn't even listening. She sighed. Writing about flower shows and boating events wasn't enough for her. She wanted to write about things that encouraged change…that inspired people. But McFarce had denied her the chance without even listening.

She stared at her typewriter, discouraged. *If I have to type up one more wedding announcement or dinner party description, I'll scream.*

Determined, she quickly finished her tasks and turned to the stack of papers to file. If she hurried, she could make it to the new millinery shop's opening, have tea with Aunt Angie, and still write up the article before Ian Hayworth called.

⁓⁓⁓

The parlor wasn't nearly large enough for her to pace out her nervousness. Pressing her hand against her stomach, she wondered if she should be doing this at all. *I feel so unprepared!* To make matters worse, she couldn't get her aunt's pain off her mind.

At the sound of Walter greeting Ian, Amelia checked her appearance. All was well, except she still held her long gloves in one hand. Glancing at the doorway, she started working them up her forearms, straightening each finger.

"Mr. Hayworth is here to see you, Miss Amelia," Walter announced. She centered the last seam as she turned.

His dark suit fit perfectly, showing off his broad shoulders. His white shirt contrasted with the blue vest that matched his eyes. His dark hair was, as always, combed to the side. One long-fingered hand briefly touched his watch chain. She blushed and hurriedly curtsied, embarrassed at having stared so long. When he remained quiet, she frowned, confused. Her expression snapped him out of his daze. He blinked and quickly bowed.

"I apologize, Miss Hughes," he said, and kissed the back of her hand. "You took my breath away, although I realize it's not quite proper to say so." He paused. "I seem to have gotten myself into a spot, haven't I?"

At his compliment and warm smile, Amelia's nerves eased. "Thank you. Shall we sit?" She motioned to the chairs, her heart pounding.

"Thank you for allowing me to come this evening." His deep voice held a touch of embarrassment over his blunder.

"Thank you for asking," she said. She sounded stiff to her own ears. Seeing his slight wince, she fell silent and bit her bottom lip.

"It was a pleasure to get your acceptance note," he said. "How's Angela doing?"

"Today has been a better day," Amelia confided. "She slept most of the afternoon. She's probably asleep again."

Ian nodded. "Has she told you how we met?"

"No, I've never heard."

"When I was newly head of my household, I believed that I had to accept every invitation that came my way. I was afraid to offend anyone." His smile was rueful. "I've since stopped caring about that. At one party, I snuck away for a bit of peace, and happened to choose the room where Angela was also hiding. We started talking and discovered that we'd both lost loved ones recently. Over the next months, we ended up at the same parties, and would spend most of our time together." He smiled. "I felt like I'd somehow found a friend who, well, became a mother figure to me."

Amelia felt herself relaxing, able to imagine how her aunt had taken him in. After all, Angie had taken her in, too. It was her nature.

"Are you close to your mother?" Ian asked her.

"No. We've never been close." Her words came quickly, as if all the hurt her mother had inflicted on her gave them strength. "Were you close with yours?"

"I was," Ian said softly. "She was a sweet woman, a pillar of faith. However," he shifted, and glanced at her hands. "I don't think your handkerchief can handle much more."

Shocked, Amelia realized that her handkerchief was twisted through her fingers. She blushed and clenched her hands, trying to hide it.

"Miss Hughes?" he said gently, but Amelia couldn't bear to look at him. She hadn't known she had been fidgeting, she was that nervous. "May I interest you in a stroll in the garden?" he suggested. "It's stopped raining."

Amelia took a deep breath, raised her eyes, and accepted his assistance to stand. She couldn't exactly go the whole night not looking at him.

"I hope I haven't bored or embarrassed you," he said. "I apologize if I have."

"You weren't…you haven't. I'm just not used to this."

"It does bring out the nerves, doesn't it?" he smiled. "I'll freely admit that I'm not used to this either."

As they passed through the garden, the smell of the early spring air calmed her. She confessed to spending hours out here. "I write there, under the tent," she pointed.

"The Society Page stories for the *Free Press*, isn't it?"

"Yes. I hope to do more someday. For now, it's enough," she added, lying slightly. Her last conversation with Mr. McFarce still caused her anxiety. She didn't want to think about it.

"I confess I hadn't paid much attention to the Society section before you started writing for them," Ian said. "Now I read them regularly, at least once a month." He shot a cheeky grin at her. She smiled back, liking this relaxed side of him. "May I ask what else you do?"

"Well, mostly I stay with Aunt Angie," she said. "If not with her, I'm writing…or attending events. I'm not very exciting."

"I beg to differ," he protested. "I know how hard you worked on that article about the orphanages. I'm sorry you didn't receive the credit."

Flustered, she sought to change the subject. "And what do you do? Or is your focus only Nettleville?"

"Nettleville does keep me quite busy, but there's plenty more," he said. "I belong to a group that is working toward creating a minimum wage for workers, and an eight-hour workday. I also manage my family's estates."

Unconsciously, Amelia started twisting her handkerchief again. *Did my question offend him?* Ian pulled her hand through the crook of his arm. "I don't offend easily," he reassured her, as if reading her mind. Then he went back to asking her questions. "When you said you'd like to do more, what exactly would that be?"

"I want to be a journalist. Like Nellie Bly and Margaret Fuller."

"Interesting role models," he said. "You know they've both been arrested."

"But they shouldn't have been!" she objected. "They were doing what they needed to for the story. Freedom of speech counts for journalists too."

"An admirable idea, but is the general public ready for such freedom in the press?"

"Probably not," Amelia admitted. "But I want to get out and see the world…and write about it."

"And ideally not get arrested," he chuckled. "I can see you doing it, though. I think you've got enough of Angela's tenacity to make it in such a rough field."

Amelia accepted his compliment with a smile. They walked quietly, arm in arm around the garden. Eventually, they went inside and sat just across from each other, eager to go on talking. Too soon, the clock chimed eight.

"Already? It hardly seems possible," Ian said. "I hope you've had a good time, Miss Hughes."

"It's been a lovely evening, Mr. Hayworth."

"Call me Ian, please. And I agree, it has been a wonderful evening." He paused. "Would you permit me to call again? Sunday, perhaps?"

"I'd like that. Thank you…Ian."

"Until then, Miss Hughes." He kissed her hand and strode out.

"That was completely unexpected," Amelia spoke softly, her hand against her cheek. She kept it there as she climbed the staircase. She would check on her aunt, then go to her bedroom to finish her story. Although, as she paused outside her aunt's door, she wondered if she'd be able to focus. She felt light all over.

Chapter Twenty

Amelia arrived early at the paper with her article. She was certain Mr. McFarce would be pleased with it. However, when he saw her he scowled and began complaining how she was barely ever there. *No matter how good the piece was, it won't offset his foul mood.*

"I don't understand why I should be here so often if I'm not needed," she protested. "You told me at the outset that it didn't make sense for me to be here every day."

"And now I'm saying that you should come in each day, just like the rest of us," Mr. McFarce barked. "You think every girl on the Society Page has it as easy as you? You have to work hard to make it in this job, young lady."

"I have been working hard, Mr. McFarce. Just because I'm not here every day doesn't mean that I'm not."

"Don't take that tone with me!" he yelled. "I'll have no back talk in my own office. Understand? You might come from posh surroundings, but this is my domain. My word is law." He stood up quickly, the crash of his chair punctuating his words. "If you work for me, you'll earn your wages how I say you will."

"I'm not used to being spoken to in such a manner, Mr. McFarce," Amelia lifted her chin. "No matter where I'm from, I would have expected you to give me every courtesy that you'd show a man. Clearly, I've been mistaken." She took a shaky breath. "You're nothing but a bully who's out to take what he can from the world, with no thought of what he can give. I refuse to work for someone like that."

On trembling knees, Amelia crossed the few feet to her desk and loaded her personal items into her bag. She'd just set the case for her typewriter on her desk, when a pair of rough hands appeared. Amelia gratefully moved aside as Brock settled and locked the typewriter safely in its case. Without a word, he carried it to the door and stepped outside. Amelia swiftly put her hat on, grabbed her bag, and followed Brock. Mr. McFarce's harsh voice stopped her.

"You'll not get another job at a paper, Miss Hughes," he hollered. "No one's in the habit of hiring women for more than recipes and gossip."

"I'd rather wait for a job where I'm respected than stay somewhere I'm not." Without a backward glance, she walked out the door, her steps steady and sure.

Outside, Brock had already hailed a carriage and loaded the typewriter. "I'm sorry you're leaving," he said, pausing before closing the door. "But I'm glad you stood up to him. Good luck."

He shut the door before she could respond, and the carriage rattled away, her future uncertain but her resolve unwavering.

***

Harrison reclined in the leather armchair, balancing a glass on his knee. The amber liquid shone in the morning sun. He squinted against the light, shifting so it didn't blind him. He groaned at the pain that moving caused and wished he'd been able to sleep longer. While sleeping in the parlor hadn't been the worst decision he'd made last night, it hadn't been a good one either. The maid had woken him as she built an early fire, then his father had caught him on the stairs and ordered Harrison to wait in his office.

That had been a quarter of an hour ago. Now, Harrison wondered if his father had miraculously forgotten about him. He swirled the liquid in the glass before savoring the last of it. He'd just decided to go change and find some coffee when his father strode into the room.

Despite his short stature, Francis James was imposing, commanding attention with the lean frame and fierce tenacity that had served him well as a jockey. He was determined to have his son uphold the family name and business. Harrison's lip curled just thinking about it. *The last thing I want to do is banking.*

His father walked past him and stared out the tall window. "I've given you a lot of leeway over the years, Harrison," he said, his back to his son. "Your mother is convinced that you must sow your wild oats first. Then you'll settle down."

Francis James turned from the window and jerked his coat taut. "I believe you're of an age where you should've settled down by now," he glowered. "You should at least be seriously courting some young woman, if you're not ready to come work in the bank?"

"No sir, I'm not courting anyone," Harrison said. "Nor am I working in the bank." He kept his face blank.

"Blast it all, son!" Mr. James exploded. "I've had enough of your frivolous, apathetic ways. You've forced me to take drastic steps." His thick eyebrows lowered, framing the anger in his gaze.

Harrison clenched his jaw, fighting to control his own temper. They'd been here many times in the past year. He'd learned that if he held his tongue long enough, his mother would talk his father around.

"Fine," Mr. James went on. "Don't respond, but you will listen. Your nineteenth birthday has come and gone. I'll give you until your next one to prove you've amounted to something other than…" He paused and waved his hand in Harrison's direction. "If you've still not made something of your life, then you'll no longer receive one cent from your mother or me. Am I clear?" Mr. James enunciated each word carefully, a habit Harrison hated.

Harrison swallowed, trying to dispel the rising dread. His father was serious. "How do you expect me to make something of myself in just a year?" he argued. "You're not being fair." He glanced at the decanter longingly.

"I've been more than fair with you, boy," his father snapped. "You'll receive a monthly stipend, and you'll still be able to live here, but only on the condition that you're working. I've even provided a way for you to start proving yourself." His father slapped a folder down next to Harrison, then he finally sat behind his desk.

Harrison picked up the folder and felt his life slipping away from him. *What's the harm of having fun?* He leaned over the folder, hoping the letters would focus, but couldn't understand what he was reading. The pain in his skull was severe. Comprehension finally dawned after reading it three times. He looked up at his father.

"A newspaper?" he spat. "You want me to run a newspaper?"

"This is your chance to prove your boast about being able to do better than what's out there," his father said calmly. Harrison scanned the financials in despair, then looked up again.

"This place isn't making enough to keep the doors open!" he cried. Thanks to the schooling he'd endured, he knew enough about business to know when an enterprise was dying. "This is ridiculous! Be reasonable. You can't expect me to run this shoddy paper and turn it around in a single year." He tossed the folder onto the table with disdain. "Is this a test to get me to see the light? If so, it worked. I'll be a good boy." He half bowed in his seat but regretted it instantly. A small groan escaped him.

His father grunted and looked down at his own papers. "Do it or be cut off. You're dismissed."

Stunned, Harrison stared at him for a moment, then rose unsteadily and walked to the door. "You raised me to be at the top of society," he said. "If I'm a failure, Father, it's your doing…not mine."

His father didn't bother looking up as Harrison walked out.

⌒﹏﹏⌒

Angie sighed, letting the hot tea soothe her. She'd spent the morning dictating responses to invitations and letters of business to Marie. She was pleased with their progress, along with the fact that she'd barely coughed all morning, despite all the talking. Marie had just left the room when Amelia appeared in the doorway, still shedding her jacket and hat.

"You won't believe what just happened! Ooh! Are there any sandwiches left?" Her attention snagged by the tray of treats next to the teapot, Amelia flounced onto the couch, and reached for a dainty sandwich.

"Amelia, please," Angie chided, setting her teacup down.

"I'm sorry, I'm just so hungry. I guess being upset does that." She wiped her fingers on a napkin and leaned forward to pour a cup of tea. "You won't have to worry about me leaving you every day anymore. I just quit my job."

"You what?"

"I just couldn't handle the way he treats his son! It's sad and awful."

"You quit because you don't like how he treats his son?" Angie questioned.

"No, that's not why," Amelia said. "He'd come in smelling like he'd taken a bath in alcohol. And while he was accommodating to me when I started, these past weeks he's been rude and just plain mean."

"Why haven't you told me?"

Amelia shrugged and avoided eye contact, reaching for a pastry. The answer dawned on Angie. "You didn't want to bother me when I've been sick. Is that it?"

Her niece nodded, taking another sandwich from the tray, holding it in the palm of her hand, along with the half-eaten pastry. "I didn't want to tell you," she said. "But today was the last straw. I hope you're not upset with me, Aunt Angie. I did the right thing, didn't I?"

"Do you think it was the right decision?" Angie asked, then watched as Amelia sat up properly and looked at her. Some of her stress seemed to have eased after the initial telling.

"It certainly felt right," she said. "But now I wonder if I should've stayed and seen things through." She shivered. "Aunt Angie, he really was quite a bully. I didn't like to be around him."

"If he made you feel unsafe, then leaving was the right thing," Angie agreed.

"Thank you," Amelia smiled. "The benefit is that I get to be with you as much as I want now." Truthfully, Angie was relieved that now she wouldn't have to wonder where her niece was during the day, or worry about Amelia going around without a chaperone.

"Do you think you should look for a new job to keep up your skills?" Angie asked.

"I hadn't thought about it," Amelia said. She sipped her tea and stared out the window. Angie let the subject drop. She was so tired, and trying to figure out how best to parent in this situation was exhausting.

* * *

"You have a visitor, Miss Amelia," Walter whispered, frowning as he glanced at Aunt Angie asleep on the chaise. Amelia followed Walter to the entry, then set a hand on his arm. "She's not in so much pain when she sleeps," she said. "I'm sure we'll want tea when she wakes."

"As you wish." His grave expression didn't ease as he turned to leave.

Amelia took a deep breath as she turned to her guest, smiling in welcome.

Ian's smile was warm but fleeting, his eyes stormy. "Please forgive my tardiness, I had an unexpected and unwanted guest arrive just as I was leaving."

"Is everything all right?" Amelia asked.

"For now," he said. "But Maddox won't give up his attempts to swindle me out of the family money. He's convinced that he has as much right to it as I do." He sighed and shook his head. "Forgive me, I didn't intend to be so negative when I arrived."

"You're upset, and rightfully so. Perhaps a walk outside will calm you," Amelia suggested.

"First, please tell me how Angela is doing. You sounded worried in your note."

"She's been in a lot of pain," Amelia said softly, a tremor in her voice. "May had to double her medicine last night, just so she could sleep."

"I'd like to see her, if possible."

"She's sleeping now," Amelia said. She glanced toward the salon, feeling the need to check on her aunt even though she'd just left.

"She should rest then," Ian suggested. "I think a turn around the garden with you would do me wonders."

Pain continued to show in his eyes, but the storm he'd entered with had receded. His smile lit something inside of Amelia as they headed outdoors. "And how are you today?" he asked. "Our last few meetings have been so rushed that we barely spoke."

Amelia nodded, thinking of the past week. "I'm not sure. I'm worried and confused, I suppose. But that isn't really anything new, is it?" She squinted in the bright sunlight. "I'm desperately worried," she went on. "Aunt Angie can only speak a few words at a time before she needs to pause for a breath. And some days she barely eats." Amelia sighed. "I'm worried for her…and for me. I'm glad to be home with her, but I wish I had a job to distract me from it."

"Mr. McFarce fired you?" Ian asked with anger in his voice.

"Oh, Ian! I haven't told you?" When he shook his head, she began to explain. They made several passes through the garden by the time she finished. "He really was getting awful towards me," she added at the end. "Besides, I'm not sure if I really can make it as a journalist. I think I should just stay home and take care of Aunt Angie."

It was the first time she'd spoken her fear out loud. She gulped at hearing the words leave her mouth. Still, something seemed right about staying home, which was safe and comfortable, and where she could be with her beloved aunt.

"Is that what you want?" Ian asked.

"I don't think so," she admitted. "But I'm not sure if I can do the job. It's so much more than I always dreamed of, and I was only at a small paper. What's it going to be like at a bigger paper, like the *Oregonian*? I'm not that good of a writer."

"Stop with that," Ian said. He pulled her to a halt and took hold of her shoulders. "If you want to spend the time with Angela, that's understandable…and commendable. But don't quit your dream because of fear. You'll learn what you need to know, and you'll do fine. You just have to keep your head up, and your feet in the right direction."

"There's no reason why I would get a job at the *Oregonian* anyway," she mumbled. "It will probably be a small newspaper again."

"That might be for the best," Ian suggested. "It will help you get experience. But there's no reason to think that you *won't* get a job at the *Oregonian*."

"I don't know, Ian. I just don't know." Amelia turned away from him, embarrassed that tears were threatening to spill down her cheeks. She hadn't meant to share these fears with him, and now she wasn't sure what to do. He turned her toward him again. She refused to meet his eyes, staring instead at his shoulder.

"Amelia, it's okay to cry," he said softly, rubbing his thumb across her cheek. She blinked at his tenderness, and a single tear rolled slowly down.

"I can't," she whispered. "I must be strong for Aunt Angie. She's in so much pain and tries so hard. I don't think I could bear to leave her every day, hoping that when I get home, she'll still be…with us."

Ian pulled her to him, resting her head on his shoulder. He wrapped his arms around her. "I know, I know," he soothed.

A long moment passed before the sound of someone clearing her throat drew them apart. Amelia pulled away, wiping her eyes.

"Your aunt is requesting you, miss," Grace curtsied. Amelia took a shuddering breath and wiped at the wet spot on Ian's shoulder.

"I hope I didn't ruin your coat," she said.

"I don't mind," Ian replied. "You don't have to do this alone." He caught her hand and kissed it, capturing her gaze. "I'm here for you, Amelia."

Amelia's heart skipped as they entered the house to join her aunt. Her burden felt a bit lighter now, even if nothing had changed.

Angie watched them enter with their hands linked and felt a cord of worry ease. *Amelia will be okay, and so will Ian. They have each other now.*

Amelia sat on a low stool next to where Angie lay on the chaise. "How are you feeling?" she asked. "Tea will be brought in soon."

"I'm tired," Angie said. Her throat ached, and breathing hurt terribly. As she started coughing, Amelia pressed a handkerchief into her hand. When the coughing fit eased, she leaned back against the pillow with her eyes closed. "Crying?" she whispered, her hand tightening around Amelia's.

"Yes, I was," Amelia admitted. Worried about sending herself into another coughing fit, Angie raised her eyebrows and looked at her niece. Amelia sighed. "I'm worried about you and…I don't know if I can make it as a journalist. It's much harder than I expected."

Angie desperately wished she had the strength to hug Amelia, but she had to make do with squeezing her hand. "You're strong," she whispered. "You can do it. You must try." The pain of talking, yet not being able to say everything she wished, was so strong that a tear rolled down her cheek. Amelia wiped it away.

"Are you in great pain?" she asked. "Do you want a dose now?" Angie shook her head, not wanting to sleep when her niece needed her. She looked over at Ian, who seemed to know what Angie was saying.

"I encouraged her to keep trying," he assured, "no matter what newspaper hires her. She'll learn…and she'll do well. I'll be here to cheer her on." His smile was brief. "She's not alone, Angela."

He understood her fears so well. She mouthed "thank you." He acknowledged her words with a nod. The sadness in his eyes tore her apart. *Do I look as awful as I feel?*

Once tea came, Angie allowed her mind to wander. It seemed like only yesterday she'd been wanting to plan a small dinner party. Now, she could barely function. She tried to be grateful that her mind was still strong, and that her niece was here with her, but she knew dark days were ahead. She'd done what she could to prepare Amelia for what was coming. Now she wondered if she'd done enough.

"Keep trying, Amelia," she urged through a faint and halting voice. "You can't give up. It may sound selfish of me, but I can't pass on with the thought that you've given up."

"Oh, Aunt Angie, don't talk like that! I can't bear it."

After a moment, Amelia took a shuddering breath. "I don't know that I will give up. It's just so hard. And how will I make enough to live? They barely paid me as it was. Besides, my mother will probably want me back when…"

Angie squeezed Amelia's hand and took as deep a breath as she could. Then she whispered to her beloved niece, "I've taken care of that. Don't give up."

Chapter Twenty-One

"Mr. Harrison James recently acquired the Starr Reporter *and commenced daily operations in April,"* Amelia read aloud. *"Mr. James is the son of Mr. Francis James, the brilliant founder and owner of Midwest Bank. When asked about why he chose the newspaper world over banking, the younger Mr. James said, 'I like the pace of it. It boils your blood, then leaves you cold. There's absolutely nothing like it.' We see a bright future ahead for this remarkable young man."*

Harrison smiled, raising an eyebrow at Amelia's questioning look. He wondered why she was so pale and had disappeared from most of society these past few months, but didn't ask. His main concern was what her reaction to the article would be. Indeed, that was why he'd come to her aunt's house.

"You bought a newspaper?" she prompted.

"I bought a newspaper," he agreed and leaned forward, resting his elbows on his knees. The weeks spent at the *Starr Reporter* had given him an unexpected drive to see it succeed.

"Congratulations…but why?"

"I was the editor's assistant at my school's paper for almost a year and quite enjoyed it. This was an opportunity I couldn't refuse." He smiled ruefully. "My father can't very well force me into the banking industry when I'm making a name for myself somewhere else, can he?"

Amelia agreed, eyeing the article. He could tell she was still uncomfortable with him after the New Year's party.

Turning on his charm, he decided he'd best amend things before he told her why he really came.

"I want to apologize for what happened at the party," he said. "I'm ashamed I took you there. And then…for what happened." In truth, his blood still boiled that she'd left him there without a ride home. No woman had so thoroughly humiliated him before. And yet…

"Thank you," she said. "I appreciate that." When she met his gaze with a small smile, Harrison cleared his throat, suddenly very aware of her beauty. He stood and moved to the fireplace, unexpectedly needing some distance between them. Hopefully, they could forget about that evening now. He didn't know why, but he couldn't stand the thought of never seeing her again.

Catching himself gazing at her lips, his eyes danced around her face to avoid their mesmerizing pull. "There are some good reporters at the *Starr*," he said, "but I intend on adding more. And I want the best. I want you to come work for me, Amelia."

A stunned look crossed her face. His gaze lingered, taking in the way her dress accentuated her figure. As she tilted her chin up, he realized two things: she would eventually agree to the job, and she had no idea what he was truly thinking.

He let out a breath and waited, hands in his pockets, trying to appear calm and indifferent.

"They won't stand for a woman journalist," she blurted after eyeing him for a moment. "I'd have to write under a pseudonym."

"Absolutely not," he objected. "You'll write under your name. And you'll get real stories, not fluff pieces and recipes."

Amelia felt a spark of excitement. This was more than a job. It was her chance to really write.

"What have you got to lose, Amelia?" he added. She hesitated, recalling her recent conversation with Ian and her aunt.

"Even if I agreed, I couldn't start right away. My aunt is very ill… I don't know how much time she has left." Tears welled in her eyes. Harrison stepped forward to offer his handkerchief. She accepted it, wishing Ian were there.

"I'm sorry," he said. "I didn't know. Perhaps this isn't the best time."

"I wasn't sending you on your way. I was just trying to explain the situation."

"That you're willing to come work for me as soon as you can?" he said hopefully. She laughed a little as she wiped the last tear from her eye.

"You're always so persistent," she remarked, folding the handkerchief and handing it back to him. After considering his proposal, she said firmly, with her heart racing, "It will cause a stir, no doubt, but I don't care. I'll do it."

Harrison didn't look surprised at all. He nodded, then quickly began telling her what he'd planned for her weekly column. She even went to fetch the articles she'd written while at the *Free Press* that Mr. McFarce had never published.

"I want to be known as the man who took a chance on Amelia Hughes," he said with a wink.

◦─◡◡─◦

"Tell me," Angie said, after reading the announcement about Harrison's purchase. She could already guess her niece's news, considering the pen behind her ear, and the ink stains on her fingers.

"He wants me to work for him," Amelia said in a rush. "He's going to have his editor read some of my work. I'm not going to be stuck on the Society Page either. I'll cover real stories under my own name! Can you believe it?" Amelia hugged the pile of papers she held, beaming.

"I'm excited for you," Angie swallowed, willing her voice to work. "Did he…?"

"Yes, he apologized."

"Work for him, but don't love him," Angie warned, holding Amelia's hand. Amelia sat down on the edge of the bed.

"I don't think I ever could, after seeing how he was at the Whitmore party. He was a different man that night. I'll never forget that."

"And Ian?"

"Ian would not have been there, or taken me there," Amelia smiled. "He's worlds apart from Harrison."

Angie wanted to laugh in delight at her niece's words, but a wave of exhaustion hit her. She groaned, closing her eyes.

"Aunt Angie! You haven't taken your medication yet," Amelia chided. "No wonder you look miserable."

Angie opened her eyes to watch her niece pour a dose of syrup. "I wanted to see you," she whispered.

"We'll talk more at breakfast," Amelia said. "You take your medication, or I'll tell May."

They shared a smile, seeing as May had become quite protective of Angie. Amelia helped her aunt sit upright enough to swallow the syrup, then guided her back to lying down.

"Chase your dream, Amelia Lynn," Angie spoke. She thanked God for this turn of events as the medication lulled her to sleep.

Amelia paused on the side of the street to straighten her skirt and get a good look at the building in front of her. The one-story brick structure was as common as any other. In the window next to the door, bold letters announced it as the home of the *Starr Reporter*, owned by Mr. H. James. Aunt Angie had been eager to hear about the place, so Amelia promised herself she'd be as quick as possible.

As she opened the door, she caught a glimpse of what appeared to be a separate office just after a tornado had ripped through it. She stepped inside and stopped at the nearest desk, where a large man was sitting, scribbling furiously.

"Excuse me, sir?" Amelia began, embarrassed by her shaky voice. "I'm here to see Mr. James."

The man held up a finger, his head bowed over his papers for a moment. He sighed and looked up, then abruptly rose. "Please forgive me, miss. Mr. James is out right now. Might I assist you?"

"I'm not sure," she shrugged. "I just stopped by to get a look at the place." She could see he was confused. She cleared her throat, attempting to sound more professional. "Mr. James and I talked about it last evening," she said. "I wanted to know more about the paper…to get a feel for things around here."

"I don't have much time, but perhaps it will be enough to satisfy?" he offered, shoving his pencil into an overflowing cup on his desk.

"That would be fine, thank you."

"We've got a reporter there," he waved toward a young man was stooped over a typewriter, a beat-up camera next to it. "Then our obituary writer over there." This time he waved at an older man with mussed gray hair. Both men were engrossed in their work, and neither acknowledged her. "Aside from Weist, that's the whole of the operation," her guide concluded. "Mr. James has plans to bring in more talent, and I expect he'll turn this place around quick."

Amelia smiled as she looked around the office space again. Despite its modest size, she liked it. "Thank you for your time, Mr. …what was your name?"

"Stanton," he said, and extended his hand. "It's been a pleasure, miss."

Amelia walked out, pleased with the visit despite Mr. Stanton's hurried demeanor. "Let's stop at the Nissen bakery before returning home," she told Henry as he helped her into the carriage. "I'd like to surprise Aunt Angie with some pastries."

"Yes, Miss Hughes."

Ian's nerves were wound tight as he paced Angela's salon. He traced the links of his watch chain as he debated how to approach the reason for his visit. Besides it being bad timing with how poorly Angela was doing, it touched upon his greatest fear…that he cared far more deeply for Amelia than he had for anyone ever, despite their brief courtship. As he paced, he worried his composure would slip. He didn't want to have this conversation to begin with. His pride was begging him to keep his fears to himself. But he had to know the truth.

When Amelia entered, he waited until she was seated before he asked the question that haunted him.

"Do you and Harrison James have an understanding?" He forced himself to look at her rather than divert his eyes. His heart dropped when a blush rose on her cheeks.

"No," she said quietly.

"That was convincing," he said, his voice dripping with uncharacteristic sarcasm.

"I'm going to be writing for his newspaper," she insisted. "That's all." Her voice had regained its strength.

He longed to believe her, but the gossips had done their job too well. He didn't like to be made a fool of. If she was secretly engaged…he didn't want to think of it.

"Do you want me to stop calling on you?" he asked abruptly.

"What? No! I don't understand why you're asking me these questions."

Frustrated, Ian sat next to her on the davenport and took her hands. "Don't you?" He winced at the pleading in his voice.

She held onto him tightly. "Ian, I'm just going to be working for him. I don't care for him." She hesitated a moment, then continued. "But I do care for you." Her soft words were a balm to Ian's anxiety. He exhaled deeply.

"Forgive me for allowing rumors to rule me…and for doubting you," he said. "I was foolish to think otherwise. I should have trusted that you wouldn't play games. I'm truly sorry."

He sighed again as his eyes fell to their intertwined hands. He caressed Amelia's knuckles with his thumb. "I've always had a distaste for society's subterfuge," he went on. "Years ago, I decided that I'd rather be single than be part of it. I've not courted before. I want a relationship like the one my parents had…something built on mutual love and respect."

His heart pounded at having been so vulnerable, but he knew that if their relationship was to succeed, he would have to let her see the parts of himself he normally kept hidden. A light panic seized him when she pulled her hands away.

"Thank you for telling me," she said in a wavering voice. She rested her palm against his cheek. "I promise, I never have and never will play games with you. You're far too important to me." Her hand slid away. "I understand the longing for a real partnership. I grew up watching my parents dislike each other every day, and decided I'd never marry if that's what marriage was. But you've shown me there's more...much more."

Her voice grew quiet. He leaned toward her, waiting for her to continue. Instead, he became captivated by her eyes. He knew he should pull away, but he couldn't. She held him with her gaze until she blinked and looked away. Just as he started to speak, a quiet cough brought his attention to the doorway of the salon.

"She's askin' for you, Miss Amelia," Grace said.

"Is she all right?" Amelia asked, standing abruptly, paling.

Ian stood as well. Grace answered softly. "She's in some pain is all. May is fixing more medicine."

Amelia would have flown from the room, but Ian caught her hand. When she looked at him, he asked quietly. "Am I forgiven?"

"Yes, Ian," she said, the slightest smile playing about her lips. Then she was gone.

He could only stare as she left, having completely lost his heart. And the lady had no idea.

～～～

Noting that the door stuck in the jamb, Amelia entered the large entry hall of the new building for the Nettleville Orphanage.

"Good morning, Miss Hughes," Mrs. Lardish said cheerily. "We're so blessed by all the friends who have come today."

"It's an honor to help, Mrs. Lardish," Amelia said.

"That's what I told her," a tall woman interrupted as she approached Amelia. "If we can't take time to help the poor, are we really doing our part?"

"I'm Miss Hughes, it's a pleasure to meet you," Amelia said with a polite smile.

"Mrs. Griffin," the woman replied. "Pleased to meet you."

"Excuse us, Mrs. Griffin," Mrs. Lardish interrupted. "I want to introduce Miss Hughes to someone." In only a few steps, Amelia was in front of Mrs. Griffin's exact opposite. "Miss Hughes, this is Miss Pond," Mrs. Lardish introduced before getting called away.

Amelia and Miss Pond exchanged a few words before Miss Pond hurried off, leaving Amelia to inspect the entry hall. Though it needed improvement, Amelia could imagine the spacious area bustling with activity. She smiled at the thought of spending time there, building relationships with the children.

"Are you looking forward to our activities that much?" Ian asked, walking up, looking handsome in a rough-spun shirt, sleeves rolled up to his elbows, collar unbuttoned to reveal his collarbone. His pants were somewhat worn but fit him well.

"I admit that I am," Amelia smiled, blushing. Ian smiled back, then grew serious.

"How's Angela?"

"She's having a better day today, but it was still hard for me to leave her."

"I'm sorrier than I can say, Amelia," Ian assured. "Are you certain you want to stay?"

"She said she doesn't want me cooped up with her," Amelia said, blinking back tears. "But I don't like being gone."

Angie moved restlessly in bed, the pain almost unbearable. Hardly a day passed that it wasn't. She'd spent the morning tossing and turning, even taking extra doses of the medication. In the midst of it all, she felt May gently take her hand.

"The medication isn't helping you anymore, Angie," May said. "I'm going to send for Dr. Martin." Her voice caught. "I'll get Grace to sit with you while I send for him. Is that all right?"

Angie nodded weakly.

Amelia was thankful for how sturdy the clothes were that Grace loaned her, even though the long sleeves kept unrolling. She enjoyed getting to know Miss Pond as they worked their way around the east classroom, cleaning walls and floors while Ian concentrated on cleaning the ceiling and windows. All the while, Amelia kept thinking about her aunt.

Toward the end of their work, a boy entered quickly and slid to a halt, gasping for breath. Amelia turned, still kneeling. "What's wrong?" she asked.

"May's called fer the doct'r. She says ya'd want to come too."

Amelia's eyes slid closed for a second, unable to move. *Oh, please no. I'm not ready.*

"Amelia…breathe." Strong hands cupped her shoulders. Ian knelt in front of her. His eyes were bright with unshed tears, and Amelia's eyes filled as she looked at him.

"Ian…"

"The boy said Angela is in extreme pain, that's why they're sending for Dr. Martin. It's not...it doesn't seem that..." He swallowed, unable to finish his thought. He helped her stand, then let his hands fall from her shoulders. She instantly missed his touch.

"I'll see you soon?" she asked.

"Yes, I'll come this evening," he agreed.

She barely had the presence of mind to pick up her hat before leaving with the messenger boy to hurry home.

"I'm sorry, Miss Hughes," Dr. Martin said. "She doesn't have much longer. I'll come by every day. She knows what's coming, and don't be afraid to talk with her about it." The doctor paused. "She worries about you, as any mother would. You've made her happy being here. And as her friend, I thank you for that."

Amelia murmured her thanks and watched the doctor walk down the stairs. Her mind racing, she clung to his phrase, "...*as any mother would.*" He'd given her a precious gift that she would hold onto for the rest of her life. Her aunt was dear to her, and she knew that anything she accomplished would be on account of Angie's guidance and prayers.

Aunt Angie isn't long for this world. She wrapped her arms around her middle, unable to hold back her tears. It took several minutes to regain control of herself. Once she did, she returned to Angie's bedside.

Ian gazed out the salon window, his heart weighed down by sorrow as twilight fell. *Grant me strength.* The rustling of skirts made him turn. Amelia stepped into the room. "You've been crying," he said, moving towards her.

Amelia nodded, a single tear falling. Ian brushed it away with his thumb, only for more to follow. She nestled her head against his shoulder as he held her close in his arms. His own tears threatened to spill. *How will we cope without Angela?*

He'd been trying to prepare himself, but how can anyone be ready to lose someone they love? When a maid halted in the doorway, he waved her off, not wanting Amelia to be disturbed.

Gradually, she stopped crying and leaned back. "Come and see her," she said softly. Holding hands, they walked through the house together. He took a deep breath, trying to steady himself as they entered Angela's bedroom.

"Angela," he whispered, heartbroken. How he ended up on his knees beside the bed, he didn't know. But he stayed there, resting his arms on the edge of the mattress, holding his friend's hand. The light in her eyes was still strong, but he could tell the illness had taken the fight from her. She was ready to go home. Tears rolled down his cheeks.

Angela shifted her gaze to the other side of the room, then back to him. He understood what she was saying.

"I told you I'd be here for her," he whispered. "I will be. I promise." He kissed her hand. As the others stood at the edges of the room, he decided to confide something.

"If she'll have me, I plan to marry her," he said in a low voice. "What do you think of that?"

She smiled, and he returned the expression. He was sure she'd say 'I told you so,' if only she could speak the words. His smile faded as she closed her eyes, and her breathing grew shallower. Panicked, he looked toward May.

"She's just had a dose of laudanum," she said gently. "She's sleeping."

Nodding, he looked back at Angela. She was a shell of who she'd been only a year ago. He couldn't believe things had come to this.

～〜～

Amelia felt there was something in the air all day, as if everyone was holding their breath. It was present through the doctor's visit, and as she read aloud to Aunt Angie. Exhausted, she sought refuge in the kitchen for a cup of tea before heading to Angie's bedroom. She left the door open, her bare feet silent on the rug.

Aunt Angie was sleeping fitfully again, and Amelia frowned. She donned her nightgown and climbed into bed. Seeking her aunt's hand under the covers, she found it curled tight against her side. Carefully, she straightened the stiff fingers, and held Angie's cold hand loosely. Her aunt's features slowly relaxed. When Amelia was certain Angie was deeply asleep, she allowed her own eyes to close, a tear rolling onto the pillow.

Amelia woke with a start to see May standing near her aunt. "What is it? Is she..."

"No, miss. Feel here." The nurse turned Angie's wrist towards her.

Amelia hesitated but took it, feeling a light pulse beneath her fingertips. She breathed a sigh of relief.

"But...I dare say it probably won't be long now," May added.

Tears welled in Amelia's eyes. "Oh, Aunt Angie. I'm not ready to say goodbye." She clutched her aunt's limp hand.

"Ame-lia," Angie whispered.

"Aunt Angie?" Amelia's heart skipped a beat. She lifted Angie's hand and pressed it against her cheek.

"I love you," Angie whispered tenderly.

"I love you too," Amelia said, tears falling.

"Be…happy," Angie spoke in the faintest of whispers.

"I'll try. I love you." Amelia's voice became a sob. She closed her eyes, her heart breaking.

Chapter Twenty-Two

Angela Barrington hadn't expected to see the door so soon. But here she stood, clad in her silk nightgown, in front of it. She was so close.

Carved into the door's center was a large, thriving tree. She stared, certain the leaves were moving, as if blowing in the wind. Surrounding the tree were the promises of God, carved in tiny letters. The door's handle glowed, beckoning her to touch it.

It was the most beautiful door she'd ever seen.

Still, she hung back. As beautiful as it was, she was afraid. She wasn't ready to pass through and into what lay beyond. Her eyes caressed the precious promises, and she couldn't resist running her fingers over the words, stroking them as a mother would her baby's cheek.

She read them aloud in a hushed voice, and a sense of peace settled over her. Her knees no longer shook. Her joints were no longer weak and aching. In awe, she took her first deep, full breath since the illness began. The air was sweet and filling. She closed her eyes, savoring it all.

Her fingers trailed the words down to the handle. She slowly turned it. When it was open just a crack, she heard a voice calling her. She hesitated, but then another voice from beyond the door called to her. "Come, my daughter."

With those words, a gentle wind that smelled of spring curled around and drew her in. Angela took a step forward, realizing that what she'd thought of as Death was truly Life.

Chapter Twenty-Three

With his Bible open to Psalms 23:1-6, Pastor Grey began to read. *"The Lord is my Shepherd; I shall not want. He makes me to lie down in green pastures. He leads me beside the still waters. He restores my soul. He leads me in the paths of righteousness for His name's sake. Yea, though I walk through the valley of the shadow of death, I will fear no evil: for You are with me; Your rod and Your staff they comfort me. Surely goodness and mercy will follow me all the days of my life and I will dwell in the house of the Lord forever."*

"Angela is at peace now, free from pain," the pastor said, his voice thick with emotion. "Though we will feel her absence deeply, we can take comfort in knowing she's no longer suffering."

As he continued, Amelia's focus drifted until they narrowed in on the tombstone. Despite being surrounded by friends and family, she felt a profound sense of solitude in the cemetery. When "Amazing Grace" began, she joined in, her voice soft but steady.

Once it ended, the group dispersed, heading to the Barrington house to share memories. Just as Amelia began to walk away, Edith gently slipped her hand under Amelia's arm, offering silent comfort.

"I desperately want to leave," Amelia admitted, "yet I don't feel able to. It seems wrong to leave her here alone."

"Remember her as she was," Edith said softly. "She's not really here, after all…not in this place."

As they drove to her home, Amelia did her best to focus on Edith's words. Inside the house, her sadness turned into a searing sting at the sight of her mother.

"You should've been here to receive everyone," Diane scolded, her eyes cold. Amelia didn't answer. Instead, she followed Edith's guidance toward the other side of the room, where Pastor Grey was standing. She accepted people's condolences along the way, her eyes filling with tears. She wished Ian were with her. As if he somehow knew, he suddenly appeared at her side. He didn't speak, just stayed nearby as people shared stories of her aunt.

By mid-afternoon, everyone had gone home, though Ian promised to return for a late dinner. The house was quiet. Diane, claiming a headache, went off to lie down. Richard was reading in the library, while Cedric and Horace had settled in the salon for a game of checkers. Amelia sighed in relief and closed her aunt's bedroom door behind her. Then, in a wail of sorrow, she flung herself on the bed and wept.

⌒◡⌒

Diane Hughes was incredibly wearisome. Ian felt that, even as she simpered at him, she despised him for his wealth. He hoped Amelia would join them soon. As difficult as it was to be here under the circumstances, dealing with Diane only made things worse.

"And you've been taking care of your family's estate for how long?" Mrs. Hughes asked.

"Two years, ma'am."

"So young to oversee such an estate!" she exclaimed. "Your father must be very proud of you."

"My parents have passed away, ma'am." His eyes darted to the door, hoping…*ahh, there she is.*

He stood, bowing. "Miss Hughes." He longed to embrace her until the ache in his heart eased, and the shock in her eyes had faded. Only the presence of her mother stopped him.

"You kept Mr. Hayworth waiting entirely too long, Amelia Lynn," Mrs. Hughes interjected. "If I hadn't been here to entertain him, he would've felt quite offended."

"It was quite all right, ma'am. It's been a trying day."

Mrs. Hughes cut him off with a huff, then glared at her daughter. Astonished by her audacity, Ian quietly retook his seat. Amelia sat in a nearby chair. Following several minutes of strained dialogue, Mrs. Hughes excused herself to summon her husband.

Ian took hold of Amelia's hand. "I don't believe that handkerchief can take much more," he whispered. Amelia gripped the cloth.

"Seems you are doomed to be always saving my handkerchiefs," she said, coming as close to a laugh as she'd gotten in days.

Smiling slightly, Ian reluctantly released her and leaned back in his chair. "At least now I understand why you do it," he said. Amelia folded the square and tucked it up her sleeve.

"Mother isn't someone to cross," she said. "It's easier to just comply."

"Forgive me, but even if it's to your detriment?"

"What?"

"I know this isn't the time, but…don't change who you are just because she's here," he urged gently.

She was trying to think of a reply when her parents entered. Ian fiddled with the gold chain of his watch, leaving the timepiece in his pocket.

~ ~

When dinner was announced, they moved to the dining room. Diane kept up the conversation throughout. Amelia longed for a quiet meal just with Ian, her father and Cedric. She glanced at Cedric, who kept his eyes on his plate, more withdrawn than Amelia had ever seen him. Horace, still so young, was eating as if nothing was amiss.

After dinner, Ian again offered his condolences and excused himself for the evening. When he was gone, Diane turned to Amelia. "You've made a fine catch, although I doubt you'll manage to keep him. You barely spoke to him the entire time he was here."

Amelia exchanged a glance with her father. Diane pressed on. "And making him wait like that! That's not ladylike, Amelia. I would've expected my sister to teach you better."

Mrs. Hughes continued her tirade, undeterred by the silence in the room. As Amelia struggled to maintain her composure, Ian's words echoed in her mind. She wondered whether she'd ever muster the bravery to confront her mother.

~ ~

The next morning, they settled in the spacious office of Mr. Hansen, Aunt Angie's lawyer. Amelia distanced herself from her mother as much as she could, and sat on the other side of Cedric.

"I'm genuinely sorry for your loss," Mr. Hansen began, looking between them. "Mrs. Barrington didn't want this to be a long ordeal, so I'll give everyone the general breakdown of her will. For each of her nephews, you'll receive a large sum on the day you reach your majority. It's to be spent either furthering your education, or toward starting your own businesses. Mr. and Mrs. Hughes, in addition to a large sum, you are to receive the family china, the silver, and the painting of your parents that currently hangs in Mrs. Barrington's bedroom."

He turned to Amelia. "Miss Hughes, she's left you the house and furnishings, as well as the rest of the estate in its entirety, aside from the items given to your parents."

Amelia stared back at him, stunned. The lawyer cleared his throat again. "Your aunt and I were in conversation with your parents about this," he said, and nodded to Amelia's father. "In the end, your aunt decided that instead of having your father be trustee until you reach your majority, as is common, you'll receive your inheritance today." He eyed her, ignoring the sputtering from her mother. "I encouraged Mrs. Barrington to tell you, knowing what a shock it can be, but she said it was best this way."

"Mr. Hansen!" Diane erupted. "You cannot be serious that the entire estate is going to be left to the hands of a young girl."

"Indeed not, ma'am," the attorney smoothly cut her off. "Mrs. Barrington left a stipend to the Nettleville Orphanage, the church, as well as donations to other local charities."

"Be that as it may, you cannot mean that you're going to allow a child to oversee such an estate!" Diane exclaimed. "Surely you can see that it would be better…"

"I understand your concern," Mr. Hansen interrupted. "But these things are occasionally done. Mrs. Barrington was firm on this point, ma'am. Miss Hughes inherits in total."

Amelia clenched her handkerchief, eyeing her parents. Her father put a hand on her mother's arm, but the woman brushed it off, glaring at Amelia.

"Tell Mr. Hansen that you wish to…"

"Madam, if you'll refrain from bullying Miss Hughes," Mr. Hansen interrupted. "I'd like to continue."

"Bullying! Well!" Diane stood, the feather in her hat shaking as she looked down at Mr. Hansen. "If my sister decided that *a child* has better financial sense than I do, then I see no recourse but to contest the will. Expect to hear from my lawyer soon, sir." She turned to her sons. "Come. We're leaving." She sailed out the door, with Horace on her heels. Cedric squeezed Amelia's hand before standing.

"Wait a moment, please," Mr. Hansen said before handing an envelope to Cedric. "Your aunt left this letter for you, as well as a sum of one hundred dollars in it. It will be taken from the sum you'll receive upon your majority."

Cedric stared at it a moment before leaving the room. Richard straightened his bowed shoulders. "I ask your pardon for the way my wife acted, sir. She's a determined woman. I'll see if I can dissuade her from contesting the will. As I see it, Angela knew what she was doing." While he didn't look at her, Amelia felt the knot in her stomach ease at his words. She stood to follow her father out of the office.

"Please wait a moment, Miss Hughes?"

"I'll wait for you outside the door, Amelia," her father said softly.

Amelia sat back down, hands shaking.

"I'm sorry that things have turned out this way," Mr. Hansen said gently. "Your aunt confided she was worried about your mother appropriating the money. I'll oversee your funds while you're underage, which is a required measure when a minor inherits. When you reach your majority, you'll have full control. I'll go over the details once you've signed the papers." He paused and picked up an envelope.

"I wanted you to know that you'll receive a generous monthly stipend until your majority," he went on. "You're a wealthy woman, and will want for nothing, just as when Mrs. Barrington was alive." He held the envelope out to her. "This letter is for you. She was a very special woman, your aunt."

As Amelia began to read the letter, all she could do was weep.

Dear Amelia,

I'm sorry for you to find out in this manner, but I didn't want to talk about money during my last months. You've been as a daughter to me, and I thank you for it. I wish Miles could have gotten to know the fine woman you've become. You've made me so proud.

Chase your dream of being a journalist, Amelia Lynn. Chase it with all you have, but remember to live as well. Sit in the garden and read. Attend the theatre with Ian. Go to Edith with the questions you would've asked me. You aren't alone, Amelia. You have a wonderful life ahead. The gift of the house and money is my way of easing that path for you.

And Amelia, about your mother...don't let her push you around. You are a woman of means now. Trust yourself.

With all my love,
Aunt Angie

Amelia had been telling her father about her new job at the *Starr Reporter* when her mother's announcement caused her to stop mid-sentence.

"Be sure and leave by noon today," Diane ordered. "I'll not have you missing the train."

Shocked, Amelia could only stare at her mother, while her father frowned.

"What do you mean by that?" he asked.

"I'm staying a while longer," Diane said calmly.

Amelia almost dropped her teacup in shock.

"When did you decide you were staying?" Her father's shock eased some of Amelia's. "Am I to transport your trunks without at least having your company? I'll not hear of it!"

"You'll do well enough with those trunks," Diane said dismissively. "Amelia can't be left here on her own."

"So, you mean to move here, do you?"

"Of course not!" Diane's tone, though belligerent, was uncertain.

"Well, she'll be on her own eventually," her father said. "It might as well be now."

"I'll stay a fortnight."

"You won't be staying," Amelia said, the words tumbling out of her. "I have friends to call on if I need. I've lived happily without you criticizing me. I don't intend for that to change."

"How dare you speak to me in such a manner!"

"Forgive me, Mother, but I'm not a child," Amelia said. "I've made a life here, one that made Aunt Angie proud."

"I'm proud of you too, Amelia Lynn," Richard said. "You'll do just fine."

Grateful for his words and support, Amelia smiled at him.

"I'll not stay where I'm treated in such an insolent manner," her mother shrilled. "But mark my words, Amelia, I will see this decision of my sister's changed. It's utter foolishness."

The silence that followed Diane's departure was deafening. Amelia took a sip of her now cold tea, her hands shaking.

"You know your mother's always been jealous of her sister," her father said, shaking his head. "I've never understood it." He squeezed Amelia's shoulder. "I'm sorry I didn't stand up for you children sooner, and especially when she sent you away. But seeing you now, it's clear that coming here was the best thing for you. You've become your own woman. I'll always be thankful to Angela for that."

Her heart full, Amelia watched her father leave. A moment ago, she'd been afraid he'd order her to apologize to her mother. Instead, he'd given her his support, love, and blessing.

~ ⚬ ~

Diane sent the pageboy to trade their tickets for an earlier train, then made them all wait in the salon until the boy returned. Cedric reminded her he was leaving the next day to go back to school, then joined Amelia on the opposite side of the room. Diane merely sniffed and glared at everyone until Walter announced their carriage was ready.

Diane led the group outside. She stayed silent and cold as the family shared goodbyes, and didn't speak until she was safely in the carriage. "Enjoy this while you can," she glared at Amelia. "It won't be yours for long."

Amelia hugged herself and didn't respond. She and Cedric stood on the porch, watching the carriage disappear down the street. She was glad her brother hadn't left yet. She felt less lonely as they settled once again in the salon.

"So, you're starting at the *Starr Reporter*," he said.

"Yes, but I'm not sure how soon," Amelia answered.

"I hear that Ian's your beau." Amelia blinked at her brother's abrupt subject change. Her cheeks flushed. "I thought I saw something between the two of you," he continued, chuckling.

Flushing further, Amelia decided to turn the tables on him. "Do you have a girl?"

His eyes lit up. "You already know the answer, sis."

"I just wanted you to say it."

"I'm not risking anything by saying it aloud," he said softly. "You understand?"

"I do. I'm happy for you, all the same."

Silence filled the room as they drank tea. Afterward, Amelia sought the solace of her bedroom. The events of the day, along with the absence of her aunt, had drained her. Despite her brave words to her mother, she didn't know how she'd survive on her own.

Ian's heart ached as he walked through the salon to the windows, looking out at the sunny afternoon before turning back to inspect the room. It was here that they'd taken lunch after church one day, and on those couches where he and Angie sat many times to play cribbage.

"I'm sorry for keeping you waiting," Amelia said as she entered. "How are you?"

He turned at her greeting. Her simple black dress accentuated her paleness.

"I'm all right," he said as he hugged her, feeling the ache inside ease. "And you?"

"Holding up."

Ian led her to the couch and sat next to her, wrapping his arm around her shoulders and pulling her close.

"It's been hard these past few weeks," she continued, resting her head on his shoulder. "But Grace has been such a comfort."

"I'm glad to hear that," Ian said. "Good friends are important during times like these." He then added softly, "I missed seeing you on Sunday."

"I'd planned on going, but the idea of facing all those people was too much." She took a shuddering breath. "I know they mean well. But I just can't imagine having them talk about her as if she's gone."

Rubbing her shoulder, he prayed silently for them both. Moments passed. When footsteps approached, Amelia sat up, pulling away from him. He understood the need for propriety but missed her warmth.

Grace set the tea tray down and immediately started serving them.

"Thank you, Grace. How are you doing?" Ian asked.

She finished filling the teacup and handed it to Amelia. "Thank you for asking, Mr. Hayworth. It's been hard, but Amelia has been a comfort. Not that my grief compares to hers, or yours, sir."

"She was dear to us all, Grace," he said, pleased and reassured that they were helping each other through this time. "Please, join us. I'm sure you could benefit from a bit of companionship and tea as well."

With a smile, Amelia rang a small bell. It wasn't too long before a maid arrived, curtsying in the doorway. "Yes miss?"

"Please bring a third teacup, Susan."

"Right away, miss," Susan curtseyed, glancing at Grace before leaving.

"Oh dear, Amelia," Grace said with a frown. "Ms. Dean won't like this."

Ian was pleased to see that even as Grace protested, she was straightening her rather drab uniform skirt over her knees. "Put the blame on me then," he interjected. "She won't have anything to chide you two for."

Amelia chuckled, the sadness in her eyes receding some. Grace kept her face averted when Susan brought another teacup and saucer. Ian was amused at how Grace drank her tea in pace with theirs, then excused herself as soon as she was finished. His gaze caught on the couch as she left.

Angela, it's only been a month and yet I miss you terribly.

"…do you think?"

Ian blinked, trying to dispel the image of Angela lying on the couch across from them.

"Ian, are you all right?" Amelia asked.

"I'm sorry. I just…" He motioned in the direction of the couch, unable to pull his eyes away from it.

"I do the same," she admitted. She leaned against him and slipped her hand into his.

"Being here today is harder than I expected."

"It's empty to me as well," she said as she squeezed his hand. "Although, not so lonely with you here."

He smiled. "I'm glad to hear that."

"I spoke with Mr. Hansen yesterday," Amelia informed him. "He said my mother's contesting of the will has been deemed unlawful. She doesn't have any legal grounds for it."

"Your inheritance is safe then?"

She nodded against his shoulder. "It is."

"That's good news."

"I received a letter from May," Amelia said. "She's started her new job in Meadowlark and seems happy."

Ian pulled his gaze away from the couch and looked at their joined hands.

"How's the orphanage? And Mrs. Lardish?" Amelia asked after a moment.

"Mrs. Lardish almost has us ready for the move."

"That's wonderful, Ian."

"Dorothy sends her condolences. She asked if she could call on you this week, but only if you're up for it."

"I'd enjoy that," Amelia said. "Tell her she can come any-time, and she can bring Raymond, if she likes."

"Thank you, Amelia. She could use a friend."

Amelia sighed. "I keep thinking Aunt Angie will walk through the door any moment. But then I remember…"

Chapter Twenty-Four

October arrived after a week of continuous rain. Harrison thought it was appropriate that their first day of sunshine was also the day Amelia started at the paper. Checking the time, he rolled his sleeves down and snagged a tie from a towering pile of papers. He slipped on his jacket, taking in the chaotic state of his office. His organizing skills had never been strong, but since taking over the paper they'd gotten worse.

The bell over the front door chimed and the noise of activity faded. Amelia stood just inside the doorway, a vision of femininity in the male dominated room. The room stayed quiet as Harrison walked toward her, although everyone made the appearance of going back to work.

Harrison motioned for her to precede him into his office, struggling to regain his regular calm manner. He cleared a chair for her, then leaned against his desk, carefully avoiding the stacks of papers.

"How are you?" he asked. Up close, he could see shadows under her sad eyes.

"Grace had me wear gray today."

"Yes, I see that," he said, his gaze skimming her becoming gown.

"I liked it at home, but now that I'm here..."

"It's more than proper to wear gray," he said. Seeing her worry lift, he resisted the urge to take her gloved hand in his and instead leaned back, crossing his arms. "Are you ready for your assignment?" At his words, some light returned to her eyes.

"What do you have for me?"

"Everyone must prove themselves to become a reporter," he began. "And while I feel you're good enough, you've got to prove it to yourself, to the readers, and to them." He pointed to the newsroom. "So, for starters, you've got the Society Page. Any event that's newsworthy, you'll report on. We'll get you moving up the ladder from there."

He grabbed a stack of papers from a far pile and handed the whole lot to her. "I want you to review these past editions. You'll get your assignments from Mr. Weist. If he doesn't like what you turn in, he'll rewrite it. Then you'll have to work hard to regain his trust. Do you have any questions?"

"You talk more than you used to," she observed.

"And you're quieter," he said. She nodded in agreement, which caused Harrison to frown. "I don't want to overwhelm you, but you need to know what to expect. If you have questions, ask me. O'Brien in Obituaries is a good man to turn to as well. Let me introduce you to everyone."

Soon they were in front of a desk that rivaled Harrison's own chaos. The man behind it, almost slovenly in appearance, looked up, recognition crossing his face.

"Miss Hughes, Mr. Stanton, our editor-in-chief. He keeps the place running."

Before either could speak, Harrison hurried her to the next desk. Ever since he'd told the staff of his plans, he'd received a weekly lecture from Stanton about hiring a female.

"This is Mr. Weist. Mr. Weist, Miss Hughes," he said. "Ah, here's Mr. Gregory, one of our reporters, and Mr. O'Brien."

"You write the obituaries, Mr. O'Brien?"

O'Brien laughed and pushed up his sleeves along his thick forearms. "Call me Obits, miss. Yes, I do them. Along with running that contraption back there. We're a small group, an' we wear many hats." He waved a hand toward Mr. Gregory, who hunched over a desk on the far side of the room. "Gregory there handles the blasted camera on his own, along with the interviews. That contraption gives him fits, it does. We're going to have to replace it soon."

Harrison watched Amelia fall for the simple charm of the older Irishman. He knew the odds were stacked against her, a young lady aiming to make it in journalism, but he also knew she had talent. He'd shared some of her work with a few friends in the business without disclosing the author, and they'd urged him to send the writer their way.

"Well Harrison, are you going to get this young lady a desk, or is she going to stand whilst she writes?" O'Brien quipped.

"You're right next to Gregory there," Harrison said, pointing to the other side of the room. "I'll grab those papers for you." He led her to the desk, then continued to his office, wondering why he felt so rattled.

⌒⌣⌒

Amelia lightly touched her desk. She was disappointed that Harrison had stuck her on the Society Page. Hadn't he promised her *real* stories? *Prove that you are too good for him to keep on the Society Page. He'll keep his promise.*

Still, as she looked around the room, the longing to go home almost overwhelmed her. For a split second, she was torn between staying and walking out. Only the slap of papers on her desk, and the way Harrison whispered, "You can do this," kept her in the chair.

Time ceased as she made her way through each edition, taking notes on the event coverage. When a reporter's pass landed on her desk, she looked up at Weist, who stood nearby, his arms crossed over a bulging middle. "You'll be going to the yacht race on Wednesday," he said. "I'll need your piece in by the following morning."

Amelia picked up the pass, smiled, and tucked it in her bag. Then she returned to her research. The previous writer's coverage was dry as bones. She knew she would do a better job…she had to.

In a few hours, she finished reading each paper front to back. Her shoulders ached. Before she even tried to stretch the stiffness out, her sudden awareness of being the only woman made her self-conscious. Instead, she tidied her desk and tried to check in with Weist. He simply waved her off.

She knocked softly on the doorframe of Harrison's office instead.

"Heading out?" he asked abruptly, continuing to pace.

"I was," she said. "You seem out of sorts."

"Newspapermen are a nasty lot," he said. "They think that because my background isn't as ink-stained as theirs that I don't know which end is up." His jaw tightened. "When this paper is the best, they'll be eating out of my hand," he added, his voice hard and cold.

Amelia quickly said goodbye and started for home, longing for silence and a cup of tea.

The weather was ideal for the yacht race on Wednesday afternoon. Harrison spoke with Mr. Messner, the event coordinator, then ambled through the crowd until he spotted Amelia. Her notebook opened, she was engaged in conversation with a young man in a sailor's outfit. Even from this distance, Harrison knew the expression on her face, the same she'd worn her first day at the paper…determined and focused.

As he drew closer, he admired how lovely she looked in her gray mourning dress. He nodded to the young man and waited for Amelia to see him. When she did, she introduced him to Captain Lea, a newcomer to the American Yacht Club who had grown up racing. Once Lea excused himself, Harrison stepped closer to Amelia.

"You're late," he accused.

"I arrived a half hour before Mr. Weist instructed," she said, frowning. "I wasn't aware you'd be here."

"I wanted to see the race."

"It isn't because you wanted to check in on me?" she asked, closing her notebook abruptly.

"That might have been part of it," he hedged.

"Thank you, but I'm fine," she said, then started to walk away.

He touched her arm to stall her. "That's not what I meant."

"I'm here to do my job," she said curtly. "If you plan to tail me to each event, maybe you should hire someone else."

"You're awful bossy today. What happened to the meek girl who came into the office earlier this week?"

Amelia sighed. "I'm sorry. I shouldn't have…"

"On the contrary, this is a cutthroat field," Harrison said. "I like that you're standing up for yourself…just don't forget that I'm your boss." He walked away briskly, irritated that their conversation hadn't gone at all like he'd wanted.

After an hour interviewing people and watching preparations for the race, Amelia's frustration from her interaction with Harrison had eased. At one point, he returned to introduce her to Mr. Messner, who'd arranged for her to climb aboard a yacht and receive a quick lesson on how to steer it.

With the start of the race just minutes away, Amelia headed to the cordoned-off area by the water, hoping to secure a chair. She was so focused on listening to the chatter of everyone she passed, she ran into Mr. Weist, knocking his hat off his head, causing what little hair he had left to blow in the breeze.

"I'm so sorry, Mr. Weist!" she said as she snatched his hat from the grass and handed it to him.

"Do you assault everyone in such a fashion?" he asked, jamming the hat back on and peering down his nose at her.

"No, of course not, I'm terribly sorry," she apologized.

"I told Harrison it was a mistake to hire a girl," he glowered. "This only proves my point. I'll be telling him about this incident, young lady." He stomped away before she could respond.

She was still upset when she found an unclaimed chair, sat down, and began wishing herself back home. Tears filled her eyes as she dwelled on various mistakes she'd made recently. She sniffled quietly, fumbling for her handkerchief when one suddenly appeared in front of her. She hastily accepted it and dabbed her eyes, peeking up to see who had rescued her.

Ian smiled compassionately. "It can't have been that bad," he offered.

A laugh escaped her as she motioned him to sit next to her. "Perhaps not, but your timing is impeccable. Thank you."

"Do you want to talk about it?"

"No. It's silly." She took a deep breath to calm herself.

"If you're sure," Ian said, then began regaling her with stories of his own yachting adventures. She took notes as he talked, and a firm idea of how to write about this event began to replace her weariness. In the water, the yachts slowly gathered at the starting line. The U.S. yacht, the Razor, lined up between France and Germany, while Switzerland, Great Britain, and the Netherlands completed the line.

At a shot, the boats were off, and the spectators rose to their feet. The crowd grew deafening when the Americans gained the lead. The excitement swept Amelia up with it as the yacht crossed the finish line, setting a record speed.

The whistling and cheering continued for several minutes. By then, Amelia was hunched over her notepad, eager to catch the moment before it was gone. When she finally looked up, most of the crowd had dispersed. Ian still sat next to her, watching her with a smile.

"You're still here," she said, pleased.

He leaned close. "I don't have any intention of leaving you behind, Amelia. You'd best speak now if you have any reservations about that."

She pressed her lips together, smiling.

His smile grew as well, and his gaze turned tender. "I'm glad to know that."

"Amelia! Here you are!" Edith called, walking up with her husband. "I was sure I'd seen you earlier."

"Miss Hughes, are we keeping you from your duties?" Pastor Grey asked. "It looks like you're on assignment."

"I am!" she said. "This is my first event for the *Starr Reporter*. But I have some time before I need to go."

"Splendid! Shall we venture closer to the boats?" Pastor Grey offered his arm to Edith, while Ian did the same for Amelia. The four of them made their way to the docks.

Chapter Twenty-Five

Amelia rubbed the ink stain on her finger and watched out the carriage window as traffic got heavier near South Park Blocks. It was late October, and the streets were damp from an earlier rain. When the stain didn't budge, she gave up on it and checked her watch. Two o' clock. She was a few minutes late, but there wasn't anything she could do about it.

The carriage slowed, drawing near the side of the street. Grabbing her bag, she accepted Henry's assistance down.

"Thank you, Henry."

"It's a pleasure, Miss Amelia. When shall I pick you up?"

Amelia smiled. Walter had given them strict orders that there was no reason for her to be stranded in the city.

"I shouldn't be more than two hours," she said.

Quickly, Amelia joined the gathering crowd. It was mostly women, as she'd expected, although there were several men in attendance as well. Her source was right where she said she'd be, wearing a tell-tale yellow suffrage sash, and carrying another one. Amelia sighed quietly. She'd been so careful to tell Miss Kempthorne she was only coming to interview her and to see the rally, not to participate.

"Miss Hughes!" Miss Kempthorne greeted her. "They're about to get started. I brought one for you too." She set the bright yellow sash over Amelia's shoulders, straightening it to lay flat. "There. That's perfect."

Her slight English accent was charming. "Thank you, Miss Kempthorne," Amelia said.

"Call me Thea."

"How long have you been part of the movement, Thea?" Amelia asked.

"Not very long. My family isn't progressive," she said apologetically. "Especially Edward. I'm afraid I upset him the most when I decided to join. But I must stay true to what I believe. Don't I?"

"Most assuredly," Amelia smiled. "Do you know what's planned for today?"

"I've heard rumors that Mrs. Stanton is speaking, but I'm really hoping it will be Mrs. Brown. She's got such a way of inspiring people! No matter what, you'll get a good idea of what we're trying to accomplish. It will change so many lives in the end."

Amelia nodded and looked toward the raised platform. "Shall we move closer?" she asked.

"Of course!" Thea linked their arms, and the two started through the crowd, wending their way to the middle of the park. At a cheer from onlookers, Amelia stood on tiptoe. A petite, older woman with gray hair and delicate features was climbing the stairs to the platform. Recognizing Lucy Brown, Amelia ran over the facts she'd researched and jotted onto her notepad. Lucy had earned her own money to go to college, and graduated when she was almost thirty. She'd helped form two suffrage associations, and only recently had cut back on her involvement in the cause.

Amelia took quick notes as Brown spoke, intent to catch as many important details as she could. After a few moments, a nearby disturbance drew her attention. Several women were screaming and attacking someone. Police waded through the crowd, and Amelia hoped things would calm down so they could get back to Mrs. Brown's speech. But the crowd and police were attacking one another, and the violence was spreading.

Fear coursed through Amelia as she stood on her tiptoes and searched for a way out of the melee. She was knocked into Thea when a nearby woman savagely attacked a man.

"Let's get out of here!" she yelled, her heart pounding. They tried to make their way through the crowd, but as soon as one area cleared, it filled again. They were stuck with nowhere to go. A line of mounted policemen surrounded the park. Others entered the fray, using their truncheons without mercy, subduing anyone within reach.

Her heart in her throat, Amelia reached for Thea's hand. "I don't see a way out," she yelled above the noise. "Do you?"

Thea shook her head, eyes bright with tears. "I'm scared, Miss Hughes!"

Holding tightly to Thea's hand, Amelia led them in a weaving line, ducking and sidestepping their way through the chaos. When she spotted an opening, she rushed for it, pulling Thea behind her, determined to reach safety.

Just when Amelia thought that they'd made it out, she went sprawling to the ground. She fought to get back on her feet, and realized she'd lost Thea's hand. Spinning, she looked for Thea and screamed her name, but it was useless. The yells of several hundred people drowned her out.

Feeling sick at the savagery, Amelia stumbled forward with tears streaming down her face. She pushed off and away from anyone or anything that got in her path, desperate to reach safety. Just as Amelia tried to evade a larger woman who was kicking someone on the ground, a startling pain lit the left side of her head. She fell into blackness.

Things were going well enough that Ian decided he could get some extra paperwork done before heading home that evening. He lingered over the last of his coffee while he read the newspaper, content and at ease. Then Mrs. Lardish entered the office in a fit.

"You've been called to…the precinct," she began, trying to catch her breath. "They have," she gasped, unable to finish the thought. Tears filled her eyes.

Ian frowned. "Whom do they have?"

"Miss Hughes."

He dropped the newspaper and rushed across the room to grip the woman's shoulders. "Tell me everything."

Amelia was just coherent enough to realize that she was in jail for having been at the park, imprisoned after the supposedly reserved, genteel women attacked the police. Sluggishly, she wondered if the officer at the front desk had taken her seriously when she shared her name, as well as Ian's.

The hours that passed in the large cell came and went with a shifting mass of pain and frustration. She was in her own world of agony. Her head throbbed relentlessly, and her whole body ached from the beating she'd received as she tried to escape. As soon as she found a position that minimized her head pain, her neck protested the odd angle.

She drew a deep breath, straightened her shoulders, and brought her head upright. The pounding intensified so much that her vision swam. She moaned and closed her eyes.

"Ye're lookin' peaked there," a wary voice said. "Ye aren't going to retch, are ye?"

Amelia opened her eyes. An old woman was peering at her. When she merely blinked, the woman muttered and scooted a few inches away. Her vision continued to swim, and she began to fall into the blackness once again.

A rough shove on her shoulder woke her. "Ye be Amelia Hughes, girlie?"

Amelia strained to open her eyes. "Mmhmm."

"She be here!" The woman hollered, shocking Amelia into sitting upright. The movement caused such a wave of pain that she immediately doubled over and heaved all over the washer woman. Startled oaths barely reached her ears, the pain was so severe. Someone wiped her face. "Careful wit 'er girls, this one's a lady."

A few hands reached out and worked to stand her up and pass her through the crowded room toward the cell door.

Ian couldn't recall ever having been so mortified and furious in his life. He gripped his cane as he watched Amelia being guided toward him, so disheveled he barely recognized her.

"Is this how you treat innocent women, officer?" he snapped. "Beat them up and leave them to rot in an over-crowded cell?"

"I assure you, we checked with each woman. Miss Hughes was coherent. She said her head hurt, but nothing more."

When Amelia reached the cell door, Ian brushed the policeman aside. "Amelia." He pulled her near, moving to tilt her head up. "Where are you hurt?" She cried aloud and pulled back from his touch, folding in on herself. Appalled at having hurt her further, he gently put his arm around her. "I'm so sorry. I'll take you home."

"Mr. Hayworth? I need to speak with you both before you leave."

"Officer Kempthorne, can you not see that she's in no state to talk?" Ian bit out, moving toward the doors of the precinct. The tall officer stepped in his way.

"Please, sir. It won't take long." His voice was low and urgent, with an undercurrent of anxiety. Resigned, Ian nodded and followed, keeping Amelia tucked under his arm.

Officer Kempthorne motioned for them to sit near a cluttered desk. "I apologize, sir, but I'll be brief. How long has Miss Hughes been a member of the suffrage movement?"

"She's not a member!" Ian sat down, still supporting Amelia. He became even more worried when she leaned against him.

"Then how do you explain her presence at the South Park Blocks? And the sash she's currently wearing?"

Ian hesitated, glancing at the ribbon. "That I couldn't tell you, officer. But I imagine she went there for an interview."

"Miss Hughes, did you see a Miss Kempthorne at the park today?"

"Thea?" Amelia said softly.

"Yes, Thea." Officer Kempthorne's eyes were suddenly alight with hope. "When did you last see her?" He leaned forward over the desk, waiting for her answer.

"I lost her. I tried to find her again, but I couldn't." Tears filled her eyes.

"So she was…she was there when…" He stared, turning pale.

"Are you all right?" Ian asked.

Officer Kempthorne seemed to shake himself out of his stupor and stood. "Thank you for your time, Mr. Hayworth. Miss Hughes."

Relieved at the dismissal, Ian helped Amelia stand. His sole focus now was to get her home and send for Dr. Martin.

⌒◡◞◟◠

"What in heaven's name were you thinking?" Harrison demanded. "You were supposed to be at an interview, not at some riot! You know how dangerous those have been getting!"

Amelia quietly watched him rant and pace back and forth, acutely aware of Grace sitting on the far side of her bedroom.

"Didn't you wonder at all why I gave you an assignment on the other side of town?" he asked, pausing near the bed, wincing as he looked at her again.

Earlier, when Harrison had first arrived, he'd looked so concerned that Amelia wondered at the change in him. He'd been so stern and challenging lately that she actually missed the arrogant youth he used to be. The only remnants of his younger self were the hard set of his jaw, and the glint in his eye.

"What would I have done if something had happened to you?" Harrison asked, his voice hoarse. "You could have…" He cut himself off at the sound of footsteps coming behind him.

"The very question I had planned to ask," Ian said as he returned to the room. His eyes cut back and forth from Amelia to Harrison. "Although I'm curious as to why another man is asking her that."

As silence stretched between the two men, a sharp throb pulsed in Amelia's temple. She rubbed at it gently, wishing it would ease so she could think and see clearly.

"I came to check on Miss Hughes," Harrison said stiffly,

his voice back to normal. Then he turned and bowed to her. "Good day."

Amelia watched him leave, then looked at Ian. She tried to focus on his face, but he abruptly turned and left the room as well. As she leaned back against her pillow, tears began rolling down her cheeks.

$$\sim\!\sim\!\sim$$

"Mr. James," Ian called. "A moment please." He strode down the hall.

Harrison waited at the top of the stairs. "What can I do for you, Mr. Hayworth?" His tone was one of polite disinterest.

"Being concerned for an employee doesn't normally include bedside visits, at least so far as I'm aware," Ian said stiffly.

"I meant nothing improper by coming to see Miss Hughes," Harrison said. "We had no idea she was at the protest."

"Are you in love with her?" Ian cut in.

"What?" Harrison froze. "No, of course not." Ian lifted an eyebrow. "There's nothing between us," Harrison went on. "We are colleagues…friends at most. That's all, I assure you." Harrison looked him straight in the eye, seeming sincere.

Ian debated for a moment, then sighed. "Thank you for that. Whether it's the truth or not, I don't know."

"Mr. Hayworth," Harrison interrupted icily. "I may disregard some of society's rules, but having a relationship with another man's intended is one thing I would never do."

Harrison turned and started down the stairs. Ian watched him descend, his mind in a whirl. The man seemed sincere, and after so many months of wondering, it felt good to know that much.

As the front door closed, Ian leaned on the railing and hung his head, mentally preparing himself to go back to Amelia. He'd just barreled in and bullied her boss. What would she think of him now?

~ ⌣ ~

Amelia sighed in relief when Ian entered the room. She held her hand out to him. As his fingers gently closed over hers, he cleared his throat. "I apologize," he said. "I just don't trust him. The company he keeps, the lifestyle he leads..." He hesitated, then added softly, "and how can I blame him for looking at you as if you alone can save him?"

Amelia pulled Ian closer, his coat brushing her arm as he sat on the edge of her bed. "You're forgiven," she whispered. She wished that her head wasn't hurting so badly. In fact, she wished for so many things in this moment. More than anything, she wished Aunt Angie was here with her.

A tear slid down her face. Ian cradled her cheek as she sighed again.

"You should rest," he said. "I'll be here when you wake up."

"You're not leaving?" she asked hopefully.

"No, I'm not leaving."

~ ⌣ ~

Why am I so upset? Full of an ache he didn't care to identify, Harrison's mind wandered as he waited to enter the Whitmore home. *Amelia had looked terrible...all those bruises against her fair skin. Of course Hayworth was right to be confrontational...visiting her in her sickroom like that. The man had every reason to be suspicious.*

His jaw continued to tighten even as a maid opened the door then immediately disappeared. Frowning, Harrison followed the sounds of revelry toward the salon, where a dozen people surrounded Celene, reclined on a couch. At the sight of him, she sat up.

"Harrison, darling! What with that dirty newspaper of yours, I imagined you'd quite forgotten me."

He breathed deeply at the sight of her, as if trying to take every bit of her in. Kissing the back of her hand, he asked, "How could I ever forget about you?"

"You've not been to see me in weeks," she complained. He took her drink out of her other hand and downed the rest of its contents. Her eyes narrowed at him, but he ignored her glare.

"I'm here now," he said. "And you look ravishing, as usual." He set the glass aside and took his time admiring her. Her hair fell down her shoulders in ringlets, accentuating the line of her dress. He leaned one arm on the back of the couch so he could wrap a curl around his finger. "How anyone could think of anybody but you…is beyond me."

"You seemed quite taken with your little pet a while back," she teased, drawing a run of tittering laughter from the others in the room. Harrison released her hair and stood abruptly. He made for the side table, stocked with glasses, ice, and bottles. He filled a glass with the nearest bottle of clear liquor, downed it, then refilled it, hoping to banish the image of a bruised Amelia that was haunting him.

"Ah," Celene said, sitting upright. "You've been discarded. Poor Harrison." Her voice dripped with sarcasm.

"You've got it wrong, Celene," he mumbled. He picked up another bottle, whiskey this time. *Perfect.*

"I've seen that look before," she countered as she walked toward him. Her fingernails trailed the back of his neck. "Not on you, of course…only on lesser men. I know full well what it stems from." She leaned closer to whisper. "A broken heart."

His heart ached, confirming her words. He downed another glass, then filled it again. His desperation was fading. Numbness was coming on.

He turned around and wrapped an arm around Celene's waist. "I do not have a broken heart," he slurred. "What I do have is a beautiful woman in my arms."

"Flatterer. You think you can come back and just…"

"Celene!" Harriet called. "You promised us lunch! I'm starving over here."

Celene laughed and kissed Harrison, then squirmed out of his embrace. "We'd better eat. Are you coming?"

He downed another drink, grabbed the bottle, and followed them to the dining room. If he was lucky, between alcohol and friends, he might forget the image of Amelia battered and bruised, at least for a time.

Chapter Twenty-Six

Amelia gasped as she spotted the bruises on her shoulder, a mix of swollen purple and green marks. "Grace!" she called. "You told me these weren't that bad!"

"Compared to how dark they were, they're looking much better," Grace said. Amelia carefully tucked her blouse into her skirt, then walked out from behind the screen.

"Is Mother up yet?"

"No," Grace said reservedly. Amelia sighed and wondered if she should push the issue with Grace or confront her mother. Choosing the latter, she headed downstairs for breakfast.

As morning progressed, she could tell the entire household was on edge. On a normal day, she could hear the footsteps of the staff going about their duties. Today, the house was unnaturally silent.

At afternoon tea, she found the necessary courage to confront her mother. "Mother, what prompted you to come for a visit?" she asked.

"You don't think I'd let people believe I'm a heartless mother, do you?" Diane asked. "Besides, the message we received from your housekeeper was unbelievably brief. The woman could have given us a bit more information," she sniffed. "I assume you're not going to be involved with that violence any longer."

Grimacing, Amelia knew that no matter what she said, she would not change her mother's mind. She sipped her tea, looking ahead to the next day. She'd been cleared to return to work, and hoped to cover a new play, *Cinderella*.

"It's not as if you need to work, Amelia," Diane said, picking up the thread of conversation. "Especially with Mr. Hayworth's income, you'll never have to lift a finger. I'm not sure how you hooked him. Perhaps it was the wealth you come with." Diane looked around pointedly. "If you persist in this silly notion of working, you'll lose him. Then where will you be?"

Amelia set her teacup down and stood, feeling the sting of her mother's words. "I think I'll go lie down," she said. "I want to be rested for dinner with Ian tonight."

"Oh, delightful," Diane said. "I didn't know he was joining us. I'll have my burgundy dress pressed right away." She eagerly rang a small bell while Amelia stared at her.

"Ian's taking me out tonight, Mother," she said, speaking slowly and deliberately. "We aren't eating here." Without waiting for her mother's response, Amelia left the room, ready for the silence of her bedroom.

⌒‿‿⌒

By the time Grace placed the last ribbon in Amelia's hair, the disagreement she'd had with her mother was in the back of her mind. Now, she was looking forward to her first outing since the rally.

She stood in front of the mirror and smiled. The cream silk and chiffon dress had long sleeves and a high neckline, and the bodice was exquisite with chiffon flowers and artfully placed pin tucks. "You did wonderfully with the powder on my bruises," she said to Grace. "I can barely see them."

Grace accepted the compliment with a smile. "You look beautiful," she said as she handed Amelia her gloves. "And your dress for tomorrow is ready as well."

Amelia thanked her and made her way down the stairs. In a flash, she remembered her debut. How awkward she'd felt, complete with shaking knees. She could not believe how much she'd changed since then, without even noticing. Along the way, she'd gained a sense of self that she'd always longed for.

She stopped abruptly at the bottom of the stairs, her joy dissipating at the sight of the woman standing before her. "What are you doing, Mother?"

"I'm ready for dinner," Diane said, turning from pinning her hat on. "Oh, that is a lovely gown."

"I told you earlier that you're not going with us," Amelia demanded. "Cook has a meal ready for you."

"You can't seriously think that I'm going to stay here while you go out on the town," Diane said, pulling her gloves on.

"You're more than welcome to go on your own if that's what you want," Amelia suggested. She moved to the mirror and began to pin on her hat.

"I should say not!" her mother cried. "I'll be joining you and Mr. Hayworth."

"No!" Amelia yelled, tossing her hat and gloves on the table. "You need to leave in the morning." Stunned that she'd said it, she let the rightness of her decision settle in the shocked silence that followed.

"You can't banish me from my sister's house!"

"Yes, I can," Amelia said confidently. "This is my house now, and I've had enough of your bullying. You've upset this entire household. You'll leave on the first train in the morning." Her voice was calm, nothing like she'd thought it would be when she finally confronted her mother.

She called for Walter and asked him to send a boy for tickets for the morning train. Then she turned back to the mirror, bolstered by the nod of respect Walter had given her before leaving the entry.

"I'll leave when I'm good and ready," Diane yelled, "and not one second sooner! I knew this wealth would corrupt you. Look what it's done. You've become unbelievably selfish and rude." Her voice echoed in the hall.

Amelia prayed for patience even as she spoke through clenched teeth.

"This has never been your home," she said. "And it isn't now. I've asked you to leave. Please leave gracefully."

A knock at the door stopped Diane from responding. In the heat of the moment, Amelia tore one of her gloves. As she pulled it off, she cast a warning glance at her mother, then turned to welcome Ian. As he stepped inside, Ian ignored the tense atmosphere and greeted both ladies. The looks that Diane sent Amelia were enough to make him want to evict her from the house, though he had no authority to do so.

⌒～⌒

Amelia and Ian sat across from each other in the carriage. They were on their way to a new restaurant they'd been wanting to try, an up-and-coming place with first-class food, atmosphere, and a large dance floor. From there, they planned to visit Dorothy, so Amelia could meet the new baby.

"You didn't feel like wearing gloves this evening?" Ian asked, amused to see Amelia glance at her gloves, as if she'd forgotten she was still holding them.

"They ripped while I was putting them on," she explained.

Rather than pry, he simply nodded then rapped on the top of the carriage. Tom, the driver, opened the small door through which he could speak to the passengers. "Yes, sir?"

"We need to stop by Macy's first."

"Yes, sir."

Amelia smiled then sobered. "I asked her to leave in the morning."

"You did?" Ian asked, surprised. *Was it enough to send her home though?*

"She's just so controlling. I can't take it anymore. She talks to me as if I'm still a little girl. Somehow, I thought she might have changed after all this time."

"That's because you see the good in people," Ian said. "It's a virtue. You just have to learn to balance it with a touch of reality."

"There wasn't a doubt in her mind that she was joining us tonight, even after I told her she wasn't invited," Amelia frowned. "She's still angry that Aunt Angie left the house to me. She can't move on."

"From what Angela told me, there was never any sisterly love between the two of them."

"You're right. Aunt Angie told me as much when I first came here. Mother was terrible to her even when they were girls." She fell silent, her gaze unfocused. "I suppose my mother has tried to love me...in her own way."

"True love isn't about directing another person's life," Ian countered. "It's about coming alongside and living it with them. It's cherishing and protecting them, no matter what."

The carriage stopped. Ian and Amelia darted into Macy's for gloves, then continued to the restaurant. Amid idle talk,

Amelia took notes, in case the *Starr* wanted a piece on the restaurant. Ian teased her about it but was glad to see her scribbling in her notebook again.

The Lancers' butler showed them in. To Ian's surprise, Maddox greeted them and instructed a maid to show Amelia to Dorothy's room. When Ian moved to follow Amelia, Maddox grabbed his arm and led him into his study.

"You shouldn't be courting someone like that," he said without preamble.

"Like what?" Ian stared at him, incredulous.

"She's a working girl," Maddox sneered. "She's even trying to get into crime reporting. As if women have any place in that line of work. She's no lady, Ian. It's a downright embarrassment that you're courting her. If you had any sense, you'd drop her tonight."

Ian scowled and, unable to control his anger, did the only thing that felt natural. He punched his brother-in-law square in the jaw.

Upstairs, Amelia held the infant close. "She's so precious," she said to Dorothy, completely enamored with the bundle in her arms.

Dorothy smiled from the bed, pleased. "I'm naming her after my late grandmother, Margaret."

"It suits her," Amelia gushed. "Oh! I never asked how you are. I'm sorry." She shifted the baby and looked at Dorothy.

"I'm doing well. I should be up and about in a few more days. Don't worry about forgetting to ask me. Hugh did the same thing the other night. He went straight for Margaret, and only remembered me when he'd finished his initial inspection."

Amelia smiled. "That's sweet of him."

"Ian at least came to see me before stealing her," Dorothy said fondly. "Then he disappeared for hours in the playroom."

"I can see him doing that. He's got a soft spot for your boys."

"For children in general. He'll be a great father," Dorothy said, then laughed as Amelia's face reddened. "I shouldn't have said anything. I'll immediately change the subject. How are you healing? I was worried when I read about the incident."

"I'm sore, but almost back to normal," Amelia said. "I'm ready to return to work."

The bedroom door opened abruptly, startling Amelia enough that she jostled Margaret, setting her to crying.

"Dorothy, are you well?" Ian strode to his sister's bedside, his jaw clenched.

"What's wrong?" she asked.

"I just punched your insufferable husband."

Both women stared at him in shock. Amelia rose from the rocking chair.

"He was…" Ian shook his head, struggling for words. "It doesn't matter. He's out cold in his study."

"It matters, Ian!" Dorothy said, moving to get up. She caught herself and sat back against the pillows with a sigh of frustration.

"I won't discuss it," Ian said abruptly. "Perhaps he'll have the nerve to tell you." He looked at Amelia. "Are you ready to go?"

The ride back to Amelia's was silent. Ian stared out the window, while Amelia was unsure what to say or do.

"Would you like to come in?" she asked when they reached her home.

"I don't think so."

"Come in and talk, please," she said firmly as she climbed from the carriage. Ian took a deep breath and started out as well. At the door, Amelia greeted Walter and asked him to have tea sent to them as soon as possible.

"And if I may be so bold," he said, "Mrs. Hughes has retired for the night."

Amelia thanked him and breathed a sigh of relief. Amid everything, she'd forgotten about her mother.

She and Ian removed their coats, then settled in front of the fire. A few moments later, they were warming themselves with tea.

"What happened?" Amelia asked him quietly.

Ian sighed. "He insulted you."

"Because I work like a common girl?"

Ian's head snapped up. "He said something to you?"

"No. But it's a typical sentiment among society."

"It's unacceptable," he said, shaking his head. "It's not as if you're off doing something untoward. I shouldn't have taken you there." Frustrated, he stood and began pacing the room.

"You can't protect me from everyone who doesn't think I should be a journalist," Amelia countered softly.

"Not from everyone, maybe. But from my own brother-in-law? Amelia, you must tell me when people..." Ian stopped himself and sat down next to her. "I'm sorry," he said, taking her hands.

"Did you really punch him?"

He nodded as she reached to move his hair away from his forehead. "I've never hit anyone." He turned to look at her. "You, Amelia Lynn, have gotten under my skin." His words came quietly, but each one went straight to her heart.

The next morning, Amelia sat down for breakfast and frowned at the thick envelope next to her plate. Her name was scrawled across the front. Seated across from Grace, they ate in silence, Amelia casting dark looks at the envelope. After finishing their meal and half of their tea, Amelia finally opened the letter, a full four pages in her mother's meticulous hand, signed with a curt "Diane" at the end.

"Oh dear," Amelia whispered. With a mounting sense of dread, she turned back to the first page and started reading.

Amelia,

You have no experience of how harsh the world can be. I was only trying to protect my daughter from the pain that is sure to come. I'm certain I can blame your aunt for poisoning you against me, filling your mind with all sorts of lies about me. She always was a vicious creature…

Disgusted, Amelia turned to the last page.

You've no right to kick me out of the house that was rightfully mine. I won't stand for it. The fact that a mere girl inherited it, along with all my sister's money, is ridiculous. I've also written to Mr. James about you working for him.

I have nothing more to say, other than that I am deeply disappointed in you. Until I receive a proper apology, I won't be corresponding with you.

Diane

Amelia dropped the letter on the floor and cried bitter tears. Grace tried to soothe her, but Amelia simply felt like a little girl again. Finally, she sat up and took a shuddering breath, wiping her eyes. "Send that to Mr. Hansen, will you? I've got to go." She took a sip of cold tea to fortify herself then left, hoping that it would be a short, uneventful day.

～⌣⌣○

"Amelia's mother demands she remain on the Society Page," Harrison snapped once Stanton entered his office. "Unless, of course, we decide to follow what she calls only common sense, and fire her outright." Irritation flooded him. *Did the woman care nothing for her daughter?*

Stanton cleared the chair and sat down. "She has a point, boss." At Harrison's sharp look, Stanton amended. "Not to fire her. Just keep her on the Society beat. It's already caused harsh criticism, her covering that rally."

"We didn't even send her!" Harrison yelled, then tapped the letter against his desk, trying to regain his composure. "Has it been that bad?"

"Letters are pouring in daily. Her mother's is just the first one you've seen. We haven't got a choice."

Harrison started to respond when the front door opened, admitting Amelia. Stanton shot him a pointed look and returned to his desk.

Harrison had gained the reputation of being a severe newspaper man, expecting and demanding perfection. But, as the redheaded young woman headed his way, he realized that his heart beat softer for her.

"You're stuck on the Society beat," he said stiffly, bypassing any greetings. "I don't know for how long."

"Is it because of my mother?" she asked with a touch of anger.

"Stanton told me we're getting a lot of flak for you being at the rally. I can't lose readers." He softened his voice. "I'm sorry, Amelia. As soon as I can get you off it, I will. This must settle down first. Weist has your next assignment."

"I understand," she said curtly, attempting a smile.

"It's nice to have you back," Harrison added. She paused to look over her shoulder as she left the office.

"It's good to be back," she agreed. "It's in my blood, you know."

Harrison leaned back in his chair and wondered where the peace from earlier had gone.

Chapter Twenty-Seven

Amelia was flustered after rushing across town to Huber's Café to meet Ian for dinner. The past few weeks had been terribly busy for them both, and now the holidays were almost here. This was the first day they'd been able to carve out time for each other.

When she entered the café, Ian had already arrived. She smiled and let him pull out her chair for her. He rested his hand on her shoulder for a second before sitting across from her.

"How's Nettleville?" she asked, taking off her gloves. When she looked at him, his face was lined with worry. "What's the matter?"

He motioned toward the menu. "Decide what you want to eat first."

"But…"

"It's waited this long. It can wait a few more minutes."

The sadness in his eyes made her stomach clench, but she did as he asked, deciding quickly on stew with sourdough bread. She felt the need for something warm and hearty to offset the chill of the rainy day. After they placed their orders, Ian sighed and extended his hand. She grasped it, her worry increasing.

"Maddox banned me from the house," he said.

"What?" Amelia gasped. "What are you going to do?"

"There's not much I can do. The butler inferred that I could get messages to Dorothy, if someone else were to write them."

"I can write to her," Amelia offered without hesitation. "I'll use plain paper, not my personalized stationery."

"Thank you, Amelia. It means a great deal. I've hated not knowing how Dorothy and the kids are." He sighed. "How have you been?"

"Oh, Ian," she said softly.

Once their food arrived, she started sharing what she'd been doing since their last real talk. "I went to talk with that policeman today," she said after a short pause.

"What policeman?" Ian asked, leaning against the table.

"Edward Kempthorne, the one who talked to us that day. He's Thea's brother."

"Oh, that's right," Ian recalled.

"It's been bothering me that I didn't know what happened to her. I dream about it sometimes…losing her in the riot like that." She shuddered, feeling the fear all over again. "She's at the hospital…in a coma. I went to see her."

"Is she expected to recover?"

"Edward didn't sound very hopeful. The doctors wouldn't tell me anything since I'm not family. I sat by her and prayed for healing. And," she hesitated, hoping it wouldn't sound boastful. "I paid for her medical care and told them that I'd cover any further costs as well…anonymously."

"That was a kind thing to do."

Over dessert, Amelia shifted the topic of conversation again. "I really want off the Society Page," she said. "I'm tired of going to these stuffy events and interviewing people that don't understand there's more to life than their status."

Ian quietly agreed while Amelia eyed him. He was more relaxed than he'd been at the beginning of the meal. *I could get used to having dinner with him every night. Talking about our days and planning our weekends.*

"Well?" he prompted.

"What?"

"It seemed like you stopped halfway through what you were saying."

"Oh," Amelia said, flushing at getting caught daydreaming. "Yes…well, I want some real stories. But Harrison…" She hesitated, noticing the sudden tension in Ian's shoulders. *I shouldn't have mentioned Harrison…not tonight.* There was no avoiding it now. "He's been more driven lately, and it makes me hesitant to ask him. And though Stanton doesn't hate me anymore, I don't think he'd give me more than Society events."

"Would it hurt to ask?"

"I don't think so, but with the holidays coming up, I'll probably wait until spring."

Ian nodded. "That sounds reasonable." He motioned for the check. "But I'd say if it bothers you too much, just ask. All they can do is say no."

***

The salon was decorated splendidly for Christmas. While Amelia loved the ambiance of the room, it was so much like last year's décor that she kept picturing Aunt Angie on the settee. The bittersweet memory made her heart ache.

Cedric arrived a few days ago, and brother and sister had been enjoying their time together. Now, however, Amelia waited downstairs alone while he was getting ready for Christmas festivities. She was already dressed, having chosen a dark green velvet dress and sprigs of holly pinned in her hair.

Standing by the window, Amelia watched the light mist that looked like snow, her thoughts shifting to the past several weeks. As promised, she'd written to Dorothy and shared every letter with Ian. She also invited Dorothy and her children over for Christmas, praying that Maddox would allow it. She'd even gathered her courage and asked Weist about transitioning to more important news assignments. Even though she received a flat no, she decided not to give up simply because he refused her this time. Instead, she would work hard, and maybe have a chance at something more interesting early in the coming year.

Hearing a quiet sound behind her, she turned to find Ian. She smiled, admiring how he looked in his navy-blue suit, and took his outstretched hands.

"Merry Christmas," she said, leading him to the chairs. "Cedric should be down any moment. How are you?"

"Seeing you helps with the loneliness," he said. He sat next to her, keeping her hand in his. "I know today is harder for you, though."

"I don't want to get swallowed by my grief today, Ian," Amelia said. "I want to enjoy this time with everyone."

Susan and Sarah entered the room, burdened with boxes stuffed with beautifully wrapped gifts.

"Trying to buy out the stores, Ian?"

"I went a little overboard, didn't I?" he laughed. "I couldn't help myself. They're only young once." He sobered. "Although Hugh isn't all that young anymore. He's grown up too fast. If they don't come, I'll drop the gifts off this evening on my way home."

She squeezed his hand. "I'm hoping they'll come, Ian."

"So am I." His voice was rough.

As the maids began unpacking gifts, Ian tugged Amelia's hand. "Let us take over," he suggested. "You two should take as long a break as you can manage. It's Christmas, after all."

Amelia laughed, encouraging the maids to follow his advice. She settled on a low stool near the tree and began helping Ian arrange presents. Once they finished, they returned to the couch as Cedric entered the salon with a few gifts of his own.

"Good to see you again, Ian."

"I'm glad you're able to be here," Ian said. "I know it means a lot to Amelia."

"I could probably say the same to you," Cedric said and winked at his sister.

"I can see that you're going to be a problem today," Amelia teased. "So, I'm going to distract you. We've got cocoa, tea, and coffee waiting. What will you have?"

"Coffee. Thank you."

Amelia served him and settled next to Ian again, a quiet warmth spreading through her.

In the middle of a game of cards, Ian's breath caught when he heard Dorothy's voice. *They're here.* He dropped his cards on the table and stood to greet his sister.

"Uncle Ian!" The overlapping voices filled him with joy. Raymond launched into Ian's leg, hanging on tightly, while Leo and Carl grasped his waist. Ian laughed and hugged them all as well as he could. When he looked at Hugh, who was smiling, he noticed a shadow in his eyes.

Dorothy made waving motions with her hands as she drew near. "Allow me to hug your uncle too, boys." She wrapped her arms around Ian, ignoring Raymond, who still clung to Ian's leg. "I've missed you," she said to her brother.

"I've missed you too," he whispered, holding her gently. "Are you well?"

"I've missed you," she repeated, causing his worry to spike. When she pulled back, she smiled brightly. "The children are so excited, and I'm eager to see Amelia again."

"Come into the salon," Ian said. He motioned toward the open doorway, then draped an arm over Hugh's shoulders, noticing that the boy wasn't much shorter than him these days.

After introductions, the three younger children gathered around the tree, pointing out the gifts that bore their names. Hugh sat down and unwrapped the baby from her blankets.

"I'm delighted you're all here," Amelia said warmly. "If you want it, there's a bassinet for Margaret." She motioned toward the brand-new basinet on the side of the room. Ian smiled, touched that Amelia had thought of it.

When refreshments were served, the younger boys reluctantly left their posts to sip from teacups.

"How is Margaret?" Ian asked, eyeing the small cheek that stood out above the curve of the baby's blanket.

"Oh, Hugh, let your uncle hold her," Dorothy said to her eldest son. Hugh handed the baby to Ian, who splayed one hand along her head, the other behind her back. All he wanted to do was drink in the sight of her sweet face.

The afternoon passed lazily. The children opened their presents, exclaiming over each one. The adults played a game, laughing their way through it. Just before dinner, Amelia sighed in contentment. The day had gone well so far, and she was famished.

Dorothy and Susan led the boys off to wash, and Cedric made his way to the dining room. Amelia waited for Ian, who was setting Margaret down in the basinet. He straightened and stared at the sleeping babe. "Have you noticed how protective Hugh is of her?" he asked. "I worry what's prompted that." His mouth tightened.

"We'll do what we can to help," Amelia said. "For today, they need to see you happy. They need good memories."

"Speaking from experience?" he asked.

"I suppose," Amelia sighed. "Aunt Angie was the first person to give me a calm, happy Christmas. I'll see if I can get Dorothy to visit again soon."

He turned from the baby and pulled Amelia close. "Thank you."

After they ate, the boys played with their new treasures, while the adults opened their gifts in a small group. Dorothy surprised Amelia with a gold-edged copy of *Wuthering Heights*, while Cedric gifted her a new set of gloves. Amelia was pleased that Dorothy seemed to like the small painting she'd purchased from a local artist. Finally, when Ian held out a small velvet box, Amelia's breath caught at the beauty of the pearl necklace looped inside.

"It was my mother's," he said. At his words, Amelia looked immediately at Dorothy.

"It's his to give," Dorothy assured. Amelia smiled and turned back to Ian.

"I'll treasure it."

He settled the pearls around her neck. "It suits you."

"Thank you," she blushed, drawn by the tenderness of his gaze. The spell between them held until Raymond launched himself at his uncle, declaring that Ian needed to come play with them. Ian kissed Amelia's cheek, then moved to the floor to play with the boys.

Chapter Twenty-Eight

On an unseasonably warm spring afternoon, Amelia served iced tea and fresh fruit to her unexpected guest. "How was your trip?

"It was lovely. I can't believe all that we did, or that we were gone for so long." Georgia laughed, although it seemed forced. "I was sorry to hear Mrs. Barrington passed away."

"Thank you," Amelia said quietly.

"I also hear that you're not out in society anymore."

Amelia ignored the curious look the other girl gave her outfit and smiled. "I'm writing for the *Starr Reporter*. I've found this style more suitable."

"I've been seeing that style more often these past few months," Georgia said, casting another glance at Amelia's outfit. "Gibson Girl, is it?"

Amelia nodded and smiled, pleasantly unconcerned about Georgia's opinion. Mostly, she found herself at a loss as to what topic to bring up next. Before she could say anything, Georgia leaned forward and held out a small package.

"I thought of you when I saw these items," she said somewhat hesitantly. Amelia opened the package and pulled out two gifts, a scarf from the Netherlands, and a small painting from a street artist.

"Thank you very much, Georgia. It's extremely kind." Amelia fingered the soft scarf, then looked at her guest. "I hope this doesn't offend you, but you seem different from the last time we saw each other."

"I believe I am," Georgia shrugged and attempted a smile. "I met someone who made quite an impression on me."

"Who is it?" Amelia asked.

"Philippe Durand," Georgia said. "He had so many dreams for his life." She smiled wistfully. "I want to have that same zest for life. And then…" Georgia paused, a tear falling. "He died. His parents said his last few years were a miracle. He wasn't expected to live that long. We stayed for his funeral and then went to Italy. After a short while, my parents forbade me from mentioning him again. They began introducing me to potential suitors."

"I'm so sorry to hear this," Amelia said, shocked by Georgia's news. "That must have been terrible."

"Let's talk about something else," Georgia said sadly. "How are you doing with the loss of Mrs. Barrington?"

"The best I can," Amelia said, deciding to confide a little more than she would have a moment ago. "Between working at the *Starr*, Mrs. Grey calling once a week, and spending time with Ian, I stay busy, which helps keep me distracted."

As they talked, they moved to the ballroom. Georgia wanted to show Amelia some of the fencing moves she'd learned in Italy. They fetched Uncle Miles' old set of foils, and soon the ballroom was filled with laughter. They only stopped at the unexpected sound of clapping.

"Bravo ladies. Remind me not to challenge either one of you to a duel," Ian said.

"I'm confident that your skills far outmatch ours," Georgia teased, "but thank you for your gallantry, Mr. Hayworth."

Amelia smiled but flushed, realizing she'd forgotten her date with Ian. Before she could say anything, however,

Georgia took both foils and excused herself to return them to the library.

"Ian, I'm so sorry," Amelia said. "Would it be acceptable for Georgia to join us tonight?"

"I don't mind," Ian said cheerily, "especially if it means we get to eat that much sooner. The meal smells delicious."

~⁓~

Amelia was surprised at how much they all were enjoying themselves. She'd dreamed of such an evening when she was younger, but this version of Georgia was someone she felt she could genuinely be friends with…if the change was real, anyway.

"Your name came up at a meeting today, Amelia," Ian said. "Mr. Fletcher was saying you've got the skill to write 'real pieces about real news.' He wished he had a dozen writers like you. And, when someone mentioned your being a woman, he about blew his top. Then, he dared anyone to disagree with him. Of course, at that point, everyone readily agreed."

"Really? I can't believe it," Amelia shook her head in wonder.

"You're on your way up," Georgia said. "One day, I'll be able to say that I knew you before you were famous."

"Well, it hasn't happened yet," Amelia said in frustration. "I'm still stuck going to silly events that I have no interest in. Like the Stein party in a few nights."

"Those parties are wild," Georgia said, "maybe not as crazy as something the Whitmores throw, but they aren't far behind. I've never gone to either. They're too far out of my scene."

"Oh," Amelia said, at a loss.

Ian shifted. "If you have to go, would you like me to attend with you?"

"I'm sure I'll be okay," Amelia said.

"I know it probably doesn't mean much coming from me, but I'd take him up on that offer," Georgia said. "You won't want to be in that crowd on your own."

Amelia eyed the black-haired girl. *She seems genuinely concerned.* When she looked over at Ian, concern filled his eyes as well.

"Very well. I accept your generous offer, sir. You may escort me to the party." She said it teasingly, and he smiled in response, but she could see the relief in his eyes.

⌒～ ⌒⌒

"Mrs. Lockwood, Miss Lockwood, a pleasure to see you both again," Amelia greeted the socialites as she joined them in their sunroom.

"Why, Miss Hughes!" the matron said, arching an eyebrow. "Whyever are you working like a commoner?"

"My aunt encouraged me to chase my dreams," Amelia said. "So, here I am." She pulled out her notebook and fountain pen, adopting her professional demeanor. "Congratulations on your upcoming debut, Miss Lockwood. Who's designing your dress?"

"Mrs. Bobbin, naturally," Miss Lockwood said exuberantly. "I wouldn't dream of having anyone else. Her creations are divine. We have the whole party planned and have ordered oodles of fresh flowers. Haven't we, Mama?"

"Vibrant beauties for my vibrant girl," Mrs. Lockwood said, briefly touching her daughter's cheek. "Miss Hughes, the date is the eighteenth of August. It will, naturally, be held here at the house."

Amelia listened, noting the important details while subtly assessing the two ladies' attire. They invested considerable time and money into their appearance. She noticed as the daughter cast a glance in her direction, scanning her outfit that was strikingly plain in comparison.

"Our special entertainment is a surprise," Mrs. Lockwood went on. "However, I can tell you that they're coming to town especially for the occasion."

"That sounds wonderful, Mrs. Lockwood," Amelia said, forcing herself to sound cheerful. *And how am I supposed to write that up? 'Mrs. Lockwood smugly references entertainment without revealing who it is…' That'll go over well.*

The daughter leaned forward conspiratorially. "I doubt we'll have a coup like yours, having Adelina Parri attend," she said. "But our guest list is quite extensive. Isn't it, Mama?"

"Of course, dear," Mrs. Lockwood gushed. "We've invited anyone who is anyone to attend." She paused and studied Amelia's reaction.

And by that, I take it that I'm to feel slighted. Amelia jotted down a few notes, buying time so she wouldn't have to respond.

"I also particularly want mentioned that after her debut, she'll be going on a European tour," Mrs. Lockwood said with obvious satisfaction. Her daughter clasped her delicate hands together in excitement. "You didn't go on one, did you, Miss Hughes?" Mrs. Lockwood asked pointedly.

"No, I didn't," Amelia confirmed, her frustration straining her voice. "But I've heard such wonderful things." *These women…*

"I want my daughter to experience everything she can while she's young. One can't put a price on experiences."

"Indeed not, ma'am," Amelia agreed mildly. "Was there anything else you wanted to mention?" She glanced at her pocket watch. "I'm afraid I'm running short on time."

"Did you have anything else, Mama?"

"No dear, we don't want to keep Miss Hughes. She's very busy, you know."

"I didn't mean that at all, Mrs. Lockwood. Please forgive me if I came across…"

"Oh, that's just her way," the daughter laughed, waving off Amelia's concern. "You can't deny it, Mama. You think everyone should always be available to you."

"What's the point of being rich if you can't control people's time?" Mrs. Lockwood said severely, cocking one of her eyebrows.

Amelia forced a smile and apologized once more. She stood, packed her paper and pen, then wished them a good day. She walked sedately out of the house, eager to be gone from their sight. Despite their friendly affectation, their pretentiousness made her want to tear her hair out.

⌐⌐

The next night, Amelia could feel Ian's tension as they entered the Stein house. The noise of laughter, talking, and loud music bombarded them as it filtered through the mansion.

He pulled her arm through his and patted her hand. "Let's leave as soon as your interviews are finished," he said, squeezing her arm tightly against his side. "I'm surprised you were sent here at all."

Amelia smiled nervously. *Perhaps Weist is punishing me for asking to get off the Society Page.* She scanned the room and caught a glimpse of their hostess. "I'll be as quick as I can," she promised.

Mrs. Stein was reigning over her guests when Amelia neared her. "Welcome!" the woman called, beckoning her closer. "You're Amelia Hughes, aren't you?"

"Yes, ma'am. I have a few questions for you."

Mrs. Stein laughed loudly. "Don't 'ma'am' me, Amelia. We're probably the same age!" The crowd around her echoed her laughter. "Enjoy the entertainment!"

Amelia attempted to speak, but Mrs. Stein interrupted her and called out to someone else. Shaking off the awkward interview, Amelia looked for Mr. Stein. She found him in another room, clearly intoxicated, and knew an interview was pointless.

Instead, she stood against a wall so she could make note of the most influential guests, the Fossits among them. As she slipped her pen and notebook into her bag, she scanned the crowd for anyone worth interviewing. *I wish I didn't have to care about society. It's so tiring.* They'd only just arrived, but she was ready to go home. The crush and noise of people was overwhelming.

It wasn't until she felt Ian's touch on her arm that she realized he was next to her. His presence calmed her. He took her hand and led her to the front of the house. As they waited for their coats, a jovial Maddox entered with Harrison and Celene. Harrison glanced at Amelia, wrapped his arm around Celene's waist, and walked past them without a word.

Maddox was not deterred by his brother-in-law's grimace. "Ian, I'm astonished to find you here. This isn't your crowd."

"It certainly seems to be yours," Ian said, his jaw clenched.

Maddox waved off the remark nonchalantly. "Come along tonight! We'll have a capital time. I've heard the entertainment is absolutely top-notch."

His suggestive look made Ian stiffen. "I'd never find pleasure in the goings on here."

"Your loss, I dare say." Maddox shook his head and left them.

~⌇⌇~

"Please tell me you won't go to any other parties like that," Ian said quietly. The carriage had just stopped in front of Amelia's house.

"I won't," she promised. "I'm not sure how to convince Weist, but I won't."

"Thank you," he said. He reached for her hand. "I don't worry much when you're out on your own, but I can't help thinking about how society is changing. It seems to be corroding faster than I ever imagined."

"I decided tonight that I don't want to worry about society anymore," she said. "It's such a farce, and so tiring."

"Then let's not worry about it any longer," he said, squeezing then releasing her hand. "I'll see you tomorrow?"

"You don't want to come in?"

"Another time, Amelia."

"Being around that many people wears you out, does it?" she teased.

"I always need time to gather myself after events like that," he admitted. "It didn't help that we ran into Maddox."

Amelia bit her lip. "I'm sorry. I thought you just didn't like crowds."

"I don't," he said. "I never have. Eventually I realized that part of my aversion is because crowds drain me. I end up falling asleep in front of the fire in my library." He looked closely at her. "I can tell I'm exhausted. I don't normally admit that to people."

"Am I just *people*?"

"No, Amelia. You're not people." His voice was tender. Amelia hesitated, drawn in by his gaze. His eyes flicked toward her lips. She drew a quick breath. He blinked, smiled, and bid her goodnight, releasing her to climb out of the carriage.

Harrison left the Steins' gaming table to refill his glass. His luck had deserted him, leaving him infuriated with every rotten hand. As he savored the whiskey, Amelia came into his mind's eye. Seeing her with that insufferable Hayworth had torn at him. She'd looked like a vision, but her arm through that self-righteous…

A rough hand on his shoulder pulled him from his reverie. It also caused him to spill the last of his drink.

"Hoping your luck will change with a shot of liquid courage?" Maddox taunted.

"Don't be ridiculous," Harrison growled, shrugging the hand away to pour and polish off another drink. He thought of heading home, then being up early enough to see Amelia as she entered the *Starr*. He imagined her smiling just for him when their eyes met, then pulling her close, his gaze intent on her lips.

"Harrison!" Maddox called.

He blinked and walked to the table, pausing to lean on the back of his chair. *What would she say if she saw me now.* It would probably be the same thing his mother would say. Women were all alike…no matter their age or their appeal.

He put his tormentor out of his mind and sat back down. To his annoyance, Peter Peal arrived with flushed cheeks, just as the next hand was being dealt.

"I hope you're ready to lighten your pockets. I'm feeling lucky tonight." Peal rubbed his hands together in anticipation. Harrison felt a flare of satisfaction when Peal greeted him with a cautious "James," followed with a nod.

"Peal," Harrison smirked.

Once play started, Harrison's hands were just as rotten as before. Adding to his dark mood was the fact that Peal was getting good hands. The man had never been much of a poker player. He couldn't keep a blank expression to save his life.

"You're scowling at your cards like your girl just dumped you," Peal scoffed.

"You're one to talk," Harrison fired back. "You've been grinning at them since you sat down."

"I'm just pleased, that's all," Peal said. "Has little to do with cards tonight." He smiled wickedly and made his play, slapping a card down on the table. He waved for a refill of his glass, keeping his attention on Harrison. "Any luck with that Hughes girl?"

Harrison ignored him, focusing instead on the upcoming play. He still had a chance at winning this round if only… *ah, there.* He made his move, smiling slightly at the groans it provoked.

"Hand goes to Mr. James," the dealer announced.

Maddox leaned in. "You know her too Peal?"

Peal smiled. "I knew her. Could've known her better if it weren't for him." He gestured toward Harrison.

"She gets around a lot for someone who acts so upright," Maddox sneered.

"Careful," Peal warned. "We can't discuss women in front of him. Right, James?"

"Are you championing ladies' honor now, Harrison?" Maddox laughed loudly.

Harrison gripped his glass, glaring as the crude jokes continued. Each one made his blood boil more.

Alcohol continued around the table as one hour passed into the next. When Harrison finally left, he had to run a hand along the wall to maintain balance. The floor seemed to heave with every step.

"Oh, she just needed a little convincing," he heard nearby. The satisfaction in the man's voice was sickening. "That's all they ever need, really. Just a little persuading that a kiss is okay." A low laugh rumbled across to him.

Peal. He'd been forcing another innocent to endure his touch. Harrison hurried out of the house, feeling the same rage that had fueled him almost two years before. *That rat had touched Amelia.*

His heart pounding, he took several deep breaths of the early morning air, ignoring the urge to pound Peal a second time. Instead, he remembered how Amelia had looked that night in her robe with her hair down. If her aunt hadn't interrupted them, he likely would've stolen a kiss. *Which would have made you just like Peal.*

He straightened. *No. I wouldn't have forced her. I wouldn't have needed to.* Feeling better, Harrison climbed into his carriage and let it take him home.

———

"Miss Amelia!" O'Brien's voice rang through the office the next morning. Redirecting her steps, Amelia headed to where he was seated on the floor by the printing press.

"Good morning, Obits," she greeted, unable to mask the fatigue in her tone. She was thankful for the kindly man's distraction. It wouldn't do her any good to get lost thinking about the day's significance.

"Ya feelin' alright? Ya look a mite peaked." O'Brien peered at her over a set of small, wire-rimmed glasses.

"It's my aunt's birthday," she smiled sadly. Then she pulled her gloves off, taking in the mess around him. "What happened?"

"Ah, what didn't?" he groused. "The blasted contraption jammed itself all up, an' I've half a mind to toss the thing into the river."

"You'd have to get it out the door before you could do that. And Harrison might have something to say about it."

O'Brien chuckled. "He might at that. This blasted thing drives me to distraction."

"Meeting starts now, people," Stanton called out. "We're already late."

O'Brien and Amelia joined the rest of the group at the table. Amelia struggled to focus as they ran through various assignments and objectives.

"Our sales have gone up significantly these past few months," Harrison said. "I've been told, repeatedly, that a large part of it is due to the Society Page. Well done, Miss Hughes."

Amelia nodded in thanks, but her smile was forced. *I shouldn't still be on the Society Page. I should be out scooping real news.*

The meeting ended shortly after that. Amelia settled at her desk with last night's notes and started drafting her article, hoping she'd be able to run across the street to the café after turning it in.

***

"She deserves to be here, Stanton," Harrison sighed at his editor-in-chief. "And frankly, I'm sick of your complaints."

"She's sick. Make her go home."

"What?"

"Have you even seen her today? She's not well." For the first time Harrison could remember, Stanton looked concerned. "I know it's my job to deal with staff, but if I tell her, she'll think she's fired. Tell her to go home."

Harrison nodded, too surprised to speak as Stanton left. While he'd been growing the reach of the paper, Amelia had gotten under the skin of her fiercest adversary.

When she entered, Harrison pointed toward the chair he'd been sure to keep clear lately. "Are you all right?" he asked.

"I'm just a little tired."

"Don't take this the wrong way, but you look even more terrible than I do."

"I'm fine," she said, defensiveness creeping into her tone as she stiffened.

"Stanton just told me to send you home to rest. He didn't want to upset you, so he asked me to do it." He paused. "You've won him over. I'm impressed."

"I thought for sure he'd come to tell you to fire me."

"You need to go home and sleep, Amelia."

"I still have to finish that article about the Stein party."

"All right. How about a compromise?" He steepled his hands, thinking quickly. "Finish the article, then go home for the rest of the day."

"He really didn't tell you to fire me?"

Harrison smiled. He hadn't seen this vulnerable side of her since she first started working for him. "He didn't. Now get it done and go home."

An hour later, Harrison watched Amelia gather her things and make for the exit. Acting on an impulse, he darted from his office in hopes of catching her. By the time he reached the front door, she was already gone.

Feeling dizzy from the rush, he realized how foolish he must have looked, chasing after her. At least he hadn't called out her name, which would have made his stupidity obvious to the entire office. He wasn't even certain what he'd planned to say.

Since when do you think of her this way? Cut it out and get back to work! Harrison sat down at his desk and stared at the piles of papers. *They'll keep me busy…anything to stop thinking about her.* Unfortunately, the pounding in his head had barely eased. Perhaps next time he gambled, he'd drink less.

Chapter Twenty-Nine

It was four in the morning when Amelia, half awake, reached the bottom of the stairs and paused by Walter's side. They faced the salon, where her unexpected visitor waited.

"Say the word and I'll send him off forthwith," Walter said quietly. "I wasn't sure if I should, since he's your boss."

"Thank you," she said. "I'll meet with him, but please stay close."

"I'll be right here if you need me."

Amelia slowly entered the salon. Only one lamp was lit, leaving most of the room in shadow.

"Is there something wrong at the *Starr*?" Amelia asked.

"The *Starr*? No, no." Harrison motioned toward the spot next to him on the couch. Amelia sat on the edge of a chair instead.

"It doesn't look like you've gotten any sleep," she said.

"I haven't…I can't." He ran a hand through his hair, mussing it. "When I close my eyes, I see you. What would I do if something happened to you? What if you were hurt again? I'm tormented that I won't be there for you, Amelia. You must marry me."

Amelia stood up abruptly. "Marry you?"

"Yes!" Harrison stood as well. "I love you. I think I always have. I want to be the one to protect you…the only one with the right to kiss you." His gaze lingered on her lips. He stepped closer.

"Are you sure you're not mistaking this for what it most likely is?" Amelia asked, shoving down the spike of panic.

"And what is that?" His voice was low, intimate.

"A reaction to having had too much to drink, perhaps?" Even as she said it, she realized his eyes were too clear, his stance too steady.

"I'm not drunk, Amelia. I'm just in love with you. I want to keep you safe."

His words reminded her of the last early morning visit from him. "Mr. Peal hasn't touched me again," she offered. "You already have kept me safe."

"I know you care for me," he said. He stood and edged around the table between them. "You have since we first met." He studied her. "You look much the same now as you did that morning…with your hair down, your cheeks flushed from sleep."

"Enough of that!" Amelia said sharply. "I'm not one of your flings you can woo and dump the next day."

"That's what I'm trying to tell you!" Harrison insisted. "You're so much more than any of them. I want to marry you, Amelia."

He stood there, looking as earnest as she'd ever seen. She realized this was exactly the declaration she'd dreamed of two years ago. She smiled at the childish fantasy.

"Just say yes, Amelia."

"I appreciate your sentiments, Harrison. And you're right. I once had feelings for you. But they have turned into a friendship…one I hope we can maintain."

"I've seen the way you look at me."

"I'm in love with Ian," she said firmly. She wanted the conversation to be over.

Harrison ran his hand over his face. "The impeccable Mr. Hayworth. Of course." He looked at her with sadness in his eyes. "If you need me, I'm here."

"I won't need you," she said. "You're my friend. That's all."

"What does he have that I don't?" he shifted, hands clenching at his sides.

She frowned at both the question and his tone. "I think you need to leave," she said.

"I'm not giving up. We're meant to be together."

"Walter?" she called.

"Yes, miss?" Walter said promptly.

"Please escort Mr. James out."

"If you please, sir," Walter said, motioning to Harrison.

"You can't send me away," Harrison growled, ignoring the butler. "I can't live without you. Don't you understand?"

Amelia nodded to Walter, who stepped forward to put a hand on Harrison's arm. "Mr. James?"

Harrison shook the hand off, scowling. "I'm going." He left the room quickly, anger radiating off him.

The door opened, and Amelia held her breath until she heard it close. When the click sounded, she collapsed in a nearby chair. *He's gone.* Sadly, she had a feeling this wouldn't be the end of it.

⌒⌔⌒

After Sunday lunch with the Greys, Amelia and Edith settled in the garden to enjoy the fine weather. "Something seems to be wrong, my dear," Edith said gently.

"Yes," Amelia confided. "I was hoping I could talk with you."

"Of course. There's nothing wrong between you and Ian, I hope?"

"Oh no. Ian is wonderful," Amelia blushed.

"It's been so good to see his faith deepen as he's grown. He's a good, godly man."

All Amelia could do was nod. She could only imagine what Edith would say if they were discussing Harrison. Certainly not what she just said about Ian.

"But I gather that you don't want to talk about Ian," Edith continued astutely.

"I had a surprising visitor yesterday morning, and I'm still deciding what to do," Amelia explained. "Harrison told me he loves me…and that he wants to marry me."

"That is a surprise," Edith said. "Did you have an answer for him?"

"I refused him. He kept insisting though, even after I told him that I love Ian." Amelia flushed at the admission.

Edith smiled. "I'm glad to hear that's how you feel about Ian, my dear. I'm sure Harrison didn't take that news very well."

"No," Amelia shook her head. "He was very upset."

"I'd venture to say that your real concern now is what to do from this point on."

"Yes," Amelia said hesitantly. "What do you think?"

"A man that you work for has professed love for you. Do you see any potential difficulties arising?"

"I believe I should leave the *Starr*," she said slowly.

"A spurned man can hurt the woman he loves in ways he…or she…might never imagine."

"And Harrison is not the type to forgive and forget," Amelia said with a frown.

"Pray for guidance," Edith advised. "You'll be shown what to do. Even if it's simply in the sense of doing what's right when you make your decision."

"Thank you, Edith." Amelia hugged her. In some ways, she felt as if she had been talking with Aunt Angie.

"I'm here whenever you need," she said. "I love you, Amelia."

The next morning in the kitchen, the calm she felt yesterday had turned into nervousness. Cook stood at the counter, working up dough, while a maid stoked the fire.

"Good morning, Miss Amelia," Cook said as she turned to face her. "What can I do for ye?"

"I'm craving a cup of hot cocoa, if it's not too much trouble," Amelia said.

"Ruby, fetch the chocolate tin and a setting," Cook called out. The maid moved slowly through the task, then continued out of the room. Cook looked at Amelia. "She's willing enough, but she's a bit slow in the mornings. I give her two more weeks."

"Perhaps she simply needs more time," Amelia suggested. "New things take a while to get used to."

"Ye'r a tender heart, just like Mrs. Barrington. The truth be that girls either cut out at two months or stay several years. Thems that can get to it in the mornings are the ones who stay." Giving the dough a final pat, Cook placed it in the gas stove before filling the china teapot with boiling water. The smell of the powdered cocoa made Amelia smile.

"Will you join me, Cook? This tastes better when shared." Tears formed as Amelia realized she'd unconsciously quoted her aunt.

"Well now, I think I have a few minutes." The older lady glanced around the kitchen, then settled across from Amelia. "Ye'r worried about today, aren't ye? To work with Mr. James."

Amelia nodded. "Edith said that I'll know what to do when the time comes."

"Tis good advice, indeed," Cook agreed. "If it won't be oversteppin' my bounds, don't forget ya aren't bound to that job for the money. Ye write there for the pleasure it brings ya."

When a clatter from the pantry interrupted them, Cook hurried across the room, muttering about girls with butter fingers. Amelia took her mug upstairs. She'd take her time getting ready before going into work.

Amelia greeted O'Brien then took a seat at the table just as Weist called the meeting to start. She ran through her notes from her latest interview, hoping no one noticed how uncomfortable she felt.

The meeting ran longer than normal. The knot in her stomach tightened as the minutes ticked by. When it was over, Amelia took a fortifying breath and knocked on Harrison's door. At his call, she entered and closed the door behind her. She hesitated. Should she really quit? Or dare she hope that his advances had been part of a drunken misunderstanding?

When he looked at her, the hope and heartbreak in his gaze strengthened her resolve. *I must do this.*

"I need to speak with you, if you have a moment," she began. Her voice was softer than she'd intended. *Be confident.*

"You know I always have time for you," Harrison said as he leaned back in his chair, tucking his pen behind his ear. "Always, Amelia."

"As things stand, I've decided that I must resign. I want to thank you for this…"

"Blast it all!" he snapped, cutting her off. "You can't quit!" He threw himself out of his chair, papers dropping in a heap on the floor. "There's no reason to throw away your career."

"I'm not throwing away my career," she refuted. "I'm simply going to a new paper. It'll be best for both of us. I've become a distraction."

"You're not a distraction," he said, taking her hands in his. "You're the woman I love. Don't you see the difference?"

Amelia pulled away and backed up a step. She could smell alcohol on him. "I don't, Harrison."

"You said you're going to a new paper. You already have another job?"

"No. But you've given me a good start, getting my name out there. I'm certain I'll find another one."

"Then stay until you've found it," he offered. He reached for her again, wearing a smile he often used to get what he wanted.

"No." She took another step back, keeping out of his reach. "I'm going to pack my things and leave now. I do thank you for this opportunity. You've been a great friend."

"Don't call me that," he growled in a low voice. Amelia had heard this tone many times, though never directed at her.

"Goodbye, Harrison. I wish you all the best." As she left his office, she hoped no one could tell how badly her knees were shaking. They were all watching. Obits looked concerned. Weist, Stanton and Gregory seemed baffled.

Harrison followed Amelia to her desk and spun her to face him. Desperation filled his voice as he pulled her into his embrace. "Amelia, please," he begged. "We can build the *Starr* into something great." He stepped back so he could cup her jaw, breathing in her sweet scent, his gaze on her lips. "You'll keep me honorable. I'll keep you safe. Nothing will stand in our way."

She started to push against him again, but he leaned in to kiss her. Surely, she just needed to feel how much he loved her and then she'd…

Suddenly he was struggling to regain his balance. He stared at her in shock. She'd pushed him away! Her eyes were blazing. "I thought you were a gentleman," she glowered.

"I am!" His defense was automatic, as was the way he reached out for her again. "I can't believe this is…"

"What? Can't believe that you're being rejected?" she accused. "That someone isn't enthralled with the *great* Harrison James?"

He flinched, pulling his hands back. "What?"

"You claim you want me to feel safe, but then try to kiss me without my leave? You'd do the very thing you lambasted your friend for?"

Her words were sharpened arrows, hitting him in the chest. "I'm nothing like Peal," he cried. She raised an eyebrow, then turned back to her desk and gathered her things. "Would I be asking you to marry me if I were? Would I be vowing my love? I can't live without you, Amelia."

She turned around suddenly, her satchel swinging on her shoulder. "It's all about you, isn't it? *Your* love. *Your* life. I won't be the next thing you obsess over and then drop, Harrison."

He frowned, shoving his anger down as best he could. "That's not true. I love you. Why won't you understand?"

She held a hand up, halting his attempt to step closer. "Please," she said. "I've given you my answer. Accept it and let me go."

He scowled. "I've built the *Starr* up so you could get the chance you deserve…the opportunity you've always wanted. And this is how you…"

"I didn't ask you to buy a paper so I could get my big break!" She glared at him. "I learned a lot working here, and for that I'm thankful. But that doesn't mean I have to marry you in gratitude. That's ridiculous. Besides," her voice softened. "I love Ian. I told you that."

"What can he give you, except money?" Harrison scoffed. "The man's weak."

"Stop it." Her voice was tight and angry. "This conversation is over. Let me leave."

"Best let her go," Stanton said calmly. "She looks mad enough to spit nails."

Harrison's anger was a furnace inside of him. "I'll never stop loving you," he said. As she walked past him, he pitched his voice as low as he could, so only she could hear. "I'm not giving up."

She didn't respond. She simply walked out of the building without a backward glance.

The Fossit home was as imposing as always, but it didn't affect Amelia today. Her mind was too full, her heart too confused. She wanted to go home and cry alone on Aunt Angie's bed. Instead, she took a deep breath and entered Georgia's sitting room. *I must talk to someone.*

Georgia greeted her enthusiastically, taking Amelia's hands in her excitement.

"Good morning, Georgia," Amelia said. She squeezed her hands but didn't try to match Georgia's enthusiasm.

"What's the matter?" Georgia asked as she led them to the dark green floral settee.

"I quit the *Starr.*"

Georgia let out an unladylike huff. "Harrison did something, didn't he?" She looked so sympathetic that tears sprung into Amelia's eyes.

"He told me he loved me…and then he…" Amelia paused, uncertain how Georgia would react. "He proposed!"

"Well, it certainly took him long enough," Georgia said calmly. "Perhaps he was worried, what with Ian calling on you."

Amelia stared at her friend in disbelief. "Ian's been calling on me for a long while now."

"Harrison's had his eye on you ever since you came to town," Georgia told her. "I'm assuming you refused him?"

"Yes," Amelia said. "I love Ian. I can't believe Harrison really thought I'd marry him. He's become harder in the last year."

"His father gave him an ultimatum…clean up his act or lose his inheritance. The newspaper was Harrison's way of showing his father he doesn't need him."

Harrison's determination over recent months suddenly made sense to Amelia. She watched quietly for a moment as Georgia poured tea, then cried out in dismay, "How am I going to tell Ian?"

After some thought, Georgia spoke. "Philippe would advise honesty with yourself and your loved ones. I believe that quitting the paper was wise. If you'd stayed, Harrison might have seen it as a chance to win you. He's not used to refusal." She paused. "As for Ian, he's a rare, good man in society. Not telling him could strain your relationship. Plus, how would you explain why you quit the *Starr*?"

"Thank you," Amelia said, more tears forming. Georgia smiled, her eyes misting as well.

"Philippe was a good man, like your Ian," she said. "He would have helped me become a better person."

Amelia leaned forward to hug her friend. "I'm sorry I never got to meet him. But he did help you, Georgia…even though you didn't get the ending you wanted with him." Pulling away, she smiled and wiped her eyes with a handkerchief. "Do you have plans for today?"

"No," Georgia said. "Honestly, I've been at a loss for what to do. Normally, I'd be at the Portland Hotel. But I just don't enjoy it anymore. It seems so shallow now."

Amelia nodded, having already come to that conclusion. She finished her tea and fingered the delicate pattern on the mug's edge. She was still confused about what had happened, though some of the rawness of her emotions had eased.

Harrison stepped into Celene's welcoming embrace, yearning for her to banish his inner demons. However, the moment they kissed, he felt a chill instead of comfort. "I can't do this…I simply can't," he muttered. He pulled back and paced, raking his fingers through his hair.

"Will you calm down?" Celene scoffed as she reclined on a chaise. "So do you deny that you love her?"

"Why would I deny it?" he shot back. "I'm not ashamed to be in love with her."

"Ha. You admit it readily enough now that she's shot you down so far you can't even think," she sneered. "Have a drink already, you're making me nervous."

Harrison rubbed his eyes, trying to dispel the image of Amelia leaving him. He wheeled around toward the liquor. "I'm not good enough for her," he grumbled, grabbed the closest bottle, and poured a shot. He paused then threw the shot back into his mouth. "When she was around, I knew I could do better…could *be* better. What am I going to do without her?"

"You're pathetic," Celene laughed cruelly. "So, a woman refused you. Who cares? There are plenty of us out there… some much closer than others."

Harrison ignored her suggestion. "I could've done anything, could have been anything, if Amelia had chosen me. Why did she have to choose Hayworth? What does he have that I don't?" Anger filled him. He looked across the room at Celene.

"Some women can't see what's right in front of them," she said lightly. "Perhaps she wouldn't have made you happy."

"She would have," he said stubbornly. "She's all I need."

"Perhaps you wouldn't have made her happy," Celene shot back. Her words stabbed him. He hunched his shoulders, letting the pain wash over him.

"I was never good enough for her," he said. "She was purity itself. She would've been my redemption."

"So, you'll remain with the rest of us in our sinful states," Celene laughed. "Join me for lunch then. Go back to your dingy paper tomorrow. Things will turn right, Harrison. Trust me." She stood and held her hand out to him.

Ian sighed as he sat down at his desk for only the second time since arriving at Nettleville early this morning. The day had been unusually full of distractions. Several looming deadlines were cause for concern…he'd have to take work home tonight.

A knock on his door made him sigh again. "Enter," he called. "I'll be right with you."

"That's quite all right," Amelia said. "We can wait."

His head popped up at her voice, his heart beating rapidly at the sight of *his Amelia*. She stood there with a shy smile. "Forgive me," he said. "I thought you were one of the boys pestering me for a soccer game."

"I promise not to pester you," she laughed. "I simply wanted to show Georgia around Nettleville."

At her words, he finally noticed Miss Fossit standing next to her. He stood and bowed. "Miss Fossit, my apologies…"

"It's quite all right," she laughed. "You were otherwise occupied."

He caught her teasing tone and smiled. "I freely admit that I was…by something that's been occupying my thoughts for quite some time now." He looked at Amelia, ensuring she understood. Her reddened cheeks were confirmation enough. "Would you prefer to give the tour, or shall I accompany you? I'm at your service."

"Having you with us would be more enjoyable," Amelia replied.

The looming deadlines hadn't disappeared, but this was an offer he couldn't refuse. "Absolutely. After you."

Nettleville had changed so much since Amelia's last visit. The new fireplaces would surely make the harsh winters more bearable. For now, the open windows invited a gentle spring breeze, and the sunlight spilling in cast a warm, almost joyful glow on the hallways. The atmosphere was at odds with the heaviness she felt.

She flinched at a sudden angry yell that came from one of the classrooms. Even though Mrs. Lardish's reprimand quickly smothered it, the moment lingered with Amelia.

As Ian guided them room to room, memories of her last visit surfaced unbidden. It had been the workday when May called for the doctor...the day Amelia finally understood with dreadful clarity that she was losing Aunt Angie.

Remembering it now, she blinked back the tears and took a steadying breath, then forced herself to join the conversation Ian was having with Georgia. She couldn't afford to be melancholy right now, considering the day's whirlwind of emotions.

Once home, Amelia wrote to Mr. Fletcher, requesting a meeting with him at his earliest convenience. Now as evening settled in, she waited for Ian to arrive. She was going to tell him everything. Putting it off would only make it worse. Still, she was nervous about how he would react. She remembered how he responded when he found Harrison in her sickroom. She'd never dreamed of finding a love like what she had with Ian and was scared this would ruin it.

A knock at the door coincided with the clock chiming seven o'clock. *You're fine...calm down.* She ran her fingers over her dress, the silk overlaid with chiffon soft to the touch. It was far too fancy for tonight, but she hadn't been able to resist wearing it.

Ian entered. He smiled when he saw her, but then it faded. "Is everything all right?"

Amelia nodded, attempted a smile of her own. She faltered. "I'm rather a mess," she admitted. "I'm sorry."

"What's happened?" he asked, guiding her to a chair. He sat beside her and took her hand.

"Oh, Ian, you're so wonderful." She blinked away tears that filled her eyes. "I love you."

A soft smile lit his face. "I love you too…although I don't know why that should make you cry."

"I wanted to say that before the rest." She dabbed her eyes with her handkerchief.

"You're not ending our relationship, are you?"

"No! Never!"

"Well then," he kissed her hand. "It can't be all that bad, can it? As long as we're together, we can handle anything."

Amelia smiled, finally able to draw a deep breath. "It's just that it caught me off guard, and I've not known how to process it," she admitted, frowning again. "Harrison unexpectedly visited me quite early the other morning." Heart pounding, she paused.

"To tell you he loved you?" Ian's voice was low.

"Yes," she whispered, avoiding his gaze. "And he proposed. I refused and told him that I loved you. And I quit the *Starr* today."

"You refused him?"

"Immediately." She looked at him, tears on her cheeks again. "I've never loved him, Ian."

"You don't know what it means to me to hear you say that, Amelia." Ian laced his fingers through hers. "I confess that I've been worried. His feelings for you were unmistakable. It's been difficult, knowing you were working with him."

"His proposal came completely out of the blue. I hardly knew what to make of it."

"And then you quit? That's why you were free to come see me this afternoon." Ian's smile was so tender that Amelia blushed.

"Georgia knew I'd feel better for seeing you," she said.

"I'm glad she did. It was a wonderful surprise."

Amelia hesitated, but knew she had to tell him all of it. "He wouldn't take no for an answer this morning."

"You mean he pressured you?" Ian asked, frowning.

"In front of everyone. He said that he's not letting me go."

Ian's hand tightened on hers. "This is your decision, but if I can suggest telling Walter that he's no longer allowed here…"

"That's a good idea. I hadn't thought about him coming again."

A knock on the doorframe surprised them both. "Dinner is served, ma'am."

After dinner, they returned to the salon. Amelia noticed Ian absently fingering his watch chain. "Are you all right?" she asked.

"Yes," he replied. "Just thinking." He slipped a hand into his jacket pocket and pulled something out, but before she could glimpse it, he closed his hand tightly around the object.

"Before I say anything else, I want you to know that I'd already planned this," he said. "I was only unsure about the timing because of the news you shared earlier." He exhaled deeply and showed her a small velvet box. "I love your adventurous soul, your tender heart, and the way you inspire me to improve. I can't imagine life without you. Will you grant me the privilege of your hand in marriage, Amelia Lynn?"

She stared at the delicate gold ring in the small box, and then looked back at him. "Yes."

The ring slid easily onto her finger. They both laughed breathlessly.

"Do you like it?"

"It's beautiful," she said. "Wait. What about me working?"

"Amelia, I've always known you wanted to be a journalist. I'm proud that you're doing just that. I would never ask you to give it up. It might be a little unconventional, but I know we can make it work."

She looked at their clasped hands, fears rushing through her. "I don't want to end up like my parents, always bickering."

"We won't."

"How do you know?"

"Because I love you." He leaned forward, bringing them just inches apart.

"I love you too."

"Then you'll marry me?"

She couldn't stop the smile that formed. "Yes, Ian. I'll marry you." And then she kissed him.

⁓⌣⌣⌐

Harrison woke with a pounding headache. He groaned as he tried to get off the bed. It wasn't unusual for him to be missing his shoes, jacket, and vest after a night of heavy drinking, but he was surprised to wake up in one of Celene's guest rooms. *How'd I get here?* He righted his appearance and left the room, trying to remember how he'd ended up staying the night.

He found her having breakfast at the end of a long dining table. She silently gestured to a chair, and he sat gratefully. A member of the house staff set a cup of coffee before him. He took a drink and grimaced at the taste. Celene sighed, taking the cup from him, and added cream and sugar.

"I don't remember anything after lunch," he admitted.

"Which was yesterday."

He took a drink of coffee as breakfast came. "What happened?"

"You drank yourself into a stupor," she said flatly. "I had you carried into a bedroom, so you didn't drool on my floor."

He sighed, gulped his coffee, and considered the food in front of him. Instead, he stood abruptly and bid her farewell.

Outside, he directed his driver to Amelia's house, desperate to see her again. On her front steps, her butler blocked him from entering. "Miss Hughes has made it clear that you're no longer welcome."

Harrison reeled briefly from this information. Then he took a step toward the door. *Some high-minded servant isn't going to keep me from…*

"She's engaged to Mr. Hayworth," the butler said. "Good day."

The door shut. Harrison stared stupidly at it. She'd refused him entry and gotten engaged since yesterday morning? Impossible! She was sweet and everything pliable. This had to be a mistake. He pounded on the door, but it didn't open.

Eventually, he climbed back into his carriage, his hand sore. *Amelia, what have you done?* His breath rushed through his chest. As the idea of Amelia never loving him sank in, he realized he needed to get away from it all. *Leave Portland for somewhere new.* He didn't care how long he'd be gone, at least until the memory of her became less of a mortal wound.

You're nothing but a failure who's spent too much time on whiskey and cards. Why would she accept you?

When he got home, he ordered his trunks packed and a ticket to the furthest destination money could buy. He wasn't staying in this awful city one more day.

Chapter Thirty

Amelia, Grace, and Ian caught the morning train to Riverside. As the journey wore on, Ian opened the window to let in some fresh air, then sat back down, gently tugging at the handkerchief Amelia was twisting.

"Nervous?" he asked.

"Yes," she admitted, putting her handkerchief away. Her mind had been drifting to her last trip, when she visited with Grace. "I know that I can stand up to her if I need to," she added resolutely.

Ian's hand sought hers under the folds of her skirt. "You're an independent woman now," he said. "She needs to respect that. Perhaps you'll find her changed. When I visited your parents to request their blessing for our marriage, both were exceptionally welcoming."

"Of course. You're everything Mother ever dreamed of for me," she said.

Ian smiled before changing the subject. "Have you heard anything from Mr. Fletcher?"

"Only that I won't get a response until next week," Amelia said. "He's out of town."

"Well, it's not a refusal," Ian offered. "That's something."

"You're right...not a refusal," Amelia agreed. "It was disappointing all the same. I thought I'd inquire at the *Bulletin* next."

"That's a good idea."

As Amelia watched the scenery pass, she mentally listed the newspapers she planned to inquire at once they returned home to Portland. That reminded her of something she and Ian hadn't yet discussed.

"Where are we going to live once we're married?" she asked, realizing they should have talked about it when they set the wedding date for next April.

Ian tilted his head and studied her. "If you want to live on Avery Street, I'll happily move in," he said.

"You'd move in with me?" she whispered. She was surprised he'd be willing to leave his family home.

His smile deepened and grew more intimate. "I'm not concerned about what house we're in, Amelia, as long as we're together…and you're happy. Those are my main concerns."

Amelia smiled, realizing anew how blessed she was by this man.

～☙～

Amelia's father was waiting for them at the station. "Let's get your luggage loaded," he said. "I'm to take you home directly for the party your mother is throwing."

Amelia hid her grimace and climbed into the carriage. *I should have anticipated this.* Her mother loved to throw parties, and this occasion certainly would be one she could not pass up…announcing her daughter's engagement to a wealthy Portlander.

While her father and Ian talked during the drive through town, Amelia's worries about the weekend began to mount. She was quickly losing confidence in her ability to stand up for herself. She tried not to let the worry show on her face, but the twisted handkerchief in her hands gave her away.

Ian grew concerned as Amelia slipped into what he termed her "reporter mode" as they greeted party guests. She was polite and proper as they mingled, but her eyes lacked sparkle, and her laugh had lost its sincerity.

The crowd was clearly the town's elite. When Ian saw a man he knew from business, he steered Amelia toward him. "Let's go greet Mr. Grote," he said to her.

"Mr. Hayworth, good to see you again," Mr. Grote said, extending his hand. His wide girth and short legs made him look something like a toad, while his neckcloth seemed to be choking him. "I suppose congratulations are in order!" he added, then turned to Amelia. "And Miss Hughes, the same to you."

"Thank you, Mr. Grote," she said. "It's good to see you again."

Ian was surprised, not knowing they'd previously met. *Although, Riverside is a small town.*

"It seems you've gone and grown up while in the city," he winked. "You couldn't do any better than this young man. Let's talk business in the morning, Ian. I have an offer you won't be able to refuse."

"This trip is for pleasure," Ian countered smoothly. "I'm sure you understand. If you'll excuse us."

"Of course," Mr. Grote said, his chin shooting upward.

Ian guided Amelia through the crowd and into an empty hall. "You're worrying again," he said.

"Aunt Angie said I liked to worry things to death," she said, forcing a laugh. "You might as well know about it before we're married."

Ian led them into the garden, welcoming the fresh air and sunshine. "I've known that for a long time. What's worrying you right now?"

"Mother," Amelia said with a sigh.

Ian spied a small alcove that was shaded from prying eyes and led her to it. Satisfied that no one was around, he turned to Amelia. Her cheeks were pale, and she was chewing on her bottom lip. Unable to resist, he pulled her forward by the shoulders, hesitating only until she tilted her face up to his, then kissed her.

Amelia's eyes were wide as Ian opened his slowly. It was difficult to breathe as he kept his hands on her shoulders, his face inches from hers.

"You kissed me," she whispered.

He smiled tenderly. "I did. Are you ready to go back inside?"

"No."

He chuckled and gave her another quick kiss before releasing her. "We'd best get back to the party. Maybe we can sneak away for a walk after dinner this evening."

"I'd like that," she said.

"You know you're not alone this time, Amelia," he reassured. "If your mother upsets you at all, we'll leave immediately. I'm here for you."

Amelia smiled, tears in her eyes at his tenderness and understanding, and followed him back to the party.

～✦～

A few days later, Amelia sat alone and read in the library, hoping Diane wouldn't seek her out. It was just the two of them in the house. Her hope had been naïve, apparently, as her mother appeared abruptly in the doorway.

"I've kept my peace since you arrived," Diane said sharply. "But I won't watch you throw away everything you've gained, Amelia. I'm certain he's here because of the money my sister left you. Don't you dare let him slip away, or else…"

"Or else what, Mother?" Amelia snapped. "What will you do? I don't live here anymore." Her voice shook with anger.

"You're too young to be living alone in the city," Diane said, distracted. "I don't know what my sister was thinking. I should've gotten the estate."

"That's what this is about, isn't it?" Amelia demanded. "It's not about Ian at all."

"If he looked past your fancy home and expensive clothes, what would he see? A silly girl who runs around unchaperoned every day," Diane sneered. "I won't have you blackening the family name. Marry that man, Amelia, as soon as you can." Diane's harsh voice echoed through the house.

No matter how many times Amelia tried to interrupt her, Diane charged on, obviously determined to have her say. Finally, Amelia was able to sneak a question in.

"Why can't you believe that he loves me?" she cried.

"Why would a man like him love you?" Diane shot back in a cold voice. "You must learn your place, Amelia. Women are to be in the home."

"Enough!"

Both women turned to the doorway where an enraged Ian and stunned Richard stood.

"You'll never speak to Amelia like that again," Ian announced. "I'm proud of her for chasing her dream, despite you tearing her down all her life." He held his hand out to her. "Come Amelia, we're leaving."

Relieved, Amelia followed him out of the room. They paused when they reached Richard.

"You're always welcome to visit, sir," Ian said. "But your wife isn't."

He ordered a carriage ready as soon as possible, and asked Grace to begin packing their bags. Amelia peeked into the library. Her mother stood stock still, her eyes wide. Her father stepped closer, his eyes bright.

"Thank you, Ian, for protecting Amelia better than I ever did." His gaze shifted to Amelia. "I'm sorry for not being a better father."

"Richard!" Diane's shrill voice rang out.

"You've grown into a fine woman," he continued, ignoring his wife. "I'm proud of you." He smiled before entering his study.

Amelia followed Ian outside, her arm in his.

"Has it always been that bad?" he asked quietly.

"I've never been able to do anything right," she said. "Mother wanted me to simper and laugh on cue, but I just couldn't do it."

"You told me how she was…and I saw a little…but I never dreamed it was this bad. I'm sorry for putting you through it again." His voice trembled with anguish and regret.

"It's not your fault," she said gently. "That's how she is. She's terribly angry about Aunt Angie leaving me the estate. She'd been good enough…until today."

"Because I was around," he said. "And then…I can't believe she said that about you." He stopped and turned to trace the curve of her cheek. "You're more than I ever imagined, Amelia Lynn. I'd lost hope of finding love. Then…there you were. I couldn't resist." He embraced her. "Never doubt my love. I would marry you no matter what."

Amelia leaned into him, feeling safe and loved. When she pulled away, they continued their walk, hand in hand.

"I only wish Angela was here," he said.

"And why's that?"

"I'd thank her for taking you in…helping you escape your life here. By doing that, she brought you to me."

The pages trembled from Ian's tight grip. His heart was breaking, yet there was nothing he could do. "Maddox is sending Hugh to that boarding school he mentioned a year ago," he told Amelia. He scanned the note from Hugh one more time. His brother-in-law had reached a new low with this development. "As if being part of the start-up mandates sending a son as well," he said bitterly. Taking a deep breath, he looked at Hugh's drawing of Margaret. "She looks just like Leo did as a baby."

"She's precious," Amelia commented. "And Hugh has real talent."

Focusing on the artistry instead of the picture, Ian agreed with Amelia's observation. The boy did have skill. He looked back to the note. His nephew also wrote exceedingly well.

Ian clenched his jaw and handed the pages to Amelia. "It's not good that Maddox is sending Hugh away. It's likely to do with the fact that Hugh's becoming a man who can challenge him." Anger burned in his chest. What would become of Dorothy and the other children without Hugh there?

"What about Carl?" she asked.

"Carl is only twelve. What can he do against his father?" Ian put his head in his hands. "I'm sorry, Amelia. I feel so helpless. There's nothing I can do."

Neither spoke for a few minutes, until Ian sat up, sighing. "I need to discuss something with you."

"All right," Amelia said.

"To tell you sooner would have been presumptuous, since we weren't engaged." He paused to gather his thoughts. "Should Dorothy ever leave Maddox, I've set up an account that she or Hugh can access. That way they're provided for. They'll never know about it until the time comes, if ever."

"I understand, Ian. Your concern is only for their betterment. And you're doing what you can for the future. It's a fine idea." She clasped his hand tightly.

"I've also set Hugh up as an heir. He won't take precedence to any children we might have," he said and swallowed hard, feeling a flush on his cheeks. "But if he oversees his siblings and mother, I want him to have the means to do so."

She squeezed his hand. "If I'm so unfortunate as to lose you too soon, I'd be glad to see that he's part heir. I'll also do all that I can to aid your family, Ian."

He hugged her, unable to stop his tears, relief and worry mingling as he held this dear, understanding woman.

Chapter Thirty-One

The Oregon State Fair of 1900 was the summer's highlight, drawing a stream of crowds. Among them were Amelia, Ian, Georgia, and the Greys, who gathered just inside the gates to plan their visit before strolling down the main pathway. Amelia was delighted to see a lamb following a young girl obediently

"Amelia!" A man's voice rose above the crowd's noise. She turned and smiled as Cedric and Grace hurried towards them.

"Sorry we're late," Cedric said. "Talking with Grace's parents took longer than I thought it would."

After they all exchanged greetings, they continued as a group down the broad pathway. Amelia stepped in pace with Georgia, Ian on her other side. "Well?" she asked Grace.

"They gave their permission for us to continue our relationship," Grace said excitedly.

"Oh, Grace. I'm so happy for you! Cedric was worried they wouldn't approve."

In her excitement, Amelia gripped Ian's arm. He pressed her hand against his side but continued talking with Pastor Grey. The men discussed possibly going to watch a horse race, while the women showed interest in checking out various crafts. They stopped at different booths and amusements that caught their attention before ultimately deciding to head to the horses together. Amelia was amazed by the speed of the race but couldn't help being concerned about the horses' well-being.

As the sun set, the new display of lights came on. It was the first year the fair had been lit by electricity, and fairgoers were in awe. Georgia and Amelia linked arms as the group headed for dinner.

"It's so magical," Amelia said. "I could see this every evening and not get tired of it."

Georgia nodded distractedly as a gentleman approached. "Do you know him?" she asked Amelia quietly.

Edward Kempthorne was wearing a worn-out suit. He looked quite a bit older than the last time Amelia had seen him.

"Officer Kempthorne, isn't it?" Ian said in greeting. "Good to see you again."

"You as well, sir," Officer Kempthorne said as he shook Ian's hand. "I read that congratulations are in order."

They accepted his well wishes, then Ian turned toward Georgia to introduce them. "Miss Fossit, Mr. Kempthorne."

Officer Kempthorne hesitated, then bowed over Georgia's hand.

"Have we met before?" Georgia asked.

"I'm not sure where that would have been, Miss Fossit. I'm an officer on the north side." He glanced at her dress. "And I'll venture that you don't go to that section of town." When she started to pull her hand away, he grasped it tighter. "I apologize. I'm not such a cad as I seemed just now."

"It's all right Mr. Kempthorne. I'm not quite the socialite that you've assumed I am. Not anymore, at least."

"Then we are both forgiven our assumptions?"

"I believe so," Georgia said.

Officer Kempthorne smiled slightly then abruptly dropped Georgia's hand, a flush staining his cheeks.

"Has your sister been able to go home?" Amelia asked.

Any animation in his gray eyes quickly faded. "She's still unconscious," he said, shoving his hands in his pockets. "Thank you for your assistance with her medical costs."

"It was the least I could do," she said. "Please keep me updated on her condition." She smiled but felt heartbroken to hear that Thea's condition hadn't changed.

Georgia gently set her hand on Officer Kempthorne's arm, but when he flinched at her touch, she quickly dropped it.

Once Kempthorne bid them goodbye, they joined the line outside a large tent that housed the fair's finest restaurant.

Standing outside the *Oregonian* building the next morning, Amelia adjusted her necktie and double-checked that her jacket was straight before opening the heavy door.

The paper had little in common with the *Starr*, except for the basic layout. The room was much larger and filled with disorderly desks. Amelia walked down one row, seeing Mr. Fletcher in his office.

"Are you Amelia Hughes?" A lanky man inquired, sitting at the last desk in front of Mr. Fletcher's office. He peered at Amelia from over his glasses.

"I am. I have a meeting with Mr. Fletcher this morning."

"He's only in with Morris, so go ahead." When she hesitated, he offered a wink. "I've never seen him eat a redhead…yet."

Smiling her thanks, she knocked and clutched her portfolio. The door opened, and a man rushed by her.

"Come in, Miss Hughes!" Fletcher called. "That was Morris Troble, my assistant editor. Have a seat."

"Thank you," she said.

"Now," he continued. "Most of the men will go rabid at the idea of working with a woman. But if you can handle it, it'll make you a better reporter. That's my opinion, of course, just my opinion. But…if you give me your best, I guarantee you'll become a household name. A star reporter. That's what we'll make out of you."

He paused, eyeing her. "But you've got to want it with everything in you. If you don't, you know where the door is. I plan to get you on the front lines, not hiding away in this office." Mr. Fletcher sat back and looked at her, waiting for a reply.

"I've wanted this chance since I was a child, reading about Nellie Bly," Amelia said. "If you hire me, I won't let you down, Mr. Fletcher."

"I'm glad to hear that, very glad. You've got to have a backbone to make it in the newspaper world. I have a few doubts about taking you on, young lady. Your aunt came to see me a few years ago, and you refused the opportunity I offered." He raised an eyebrow at her. "Your writing has improved, though, so perhaps it was for the best? My wife has been wanting to go back to the Portland Hotel lately. She still talks about the time your aunt took her."

Amelia supposed she should have expected the subtle request for a favor. "I'm glad she enjoyed herself," she said. "As for my experience, and drive to succeed, I've learned a lot, working at two small newspapers. But I'm eager to learn more here at the *Oregonian*." She smiled, hoping he'd take the hint.

Mr. Fletcher nodded slowly. After an awkward silence, he clapped his hands together. "Well, go to Mr. Troble's desk. He'll get you squared away."

"Thank you, sir."

The sun was shining when Amelia stepped outside, and the world continued just as always. It was as if the fact that she'd just gotten a job at one of Portland's most prestigious papers wasn't significant at all.

She climbed into her waiting carriage, told Henry where she wanted to go, and sat back to savor her accomplishment. Before she could celebrate, there was one person she had to tell…the one person she missed more than anything in the world.

As the carriage drew closer to the cemetery, memories of their time together ran through her mind…their first outing to the theatre…the hot air balloon…the first time her aunt had gotten ill…

By the time Henry opened the door, silent tears were falling. She wiped them away, with little success, and slowly walked to the gravesite.

"Aunt Angie, it's me," she said. "Remember when you told me I would write for the *Oregonian* someday, and I laughed? You were right." She let out a breathless laugh. "I got the job. I'm a journalist for the *Oregonian*."

Amelia fell silent, peace filling her. She took a deep breath. And just as she knew as a child that one day she'd be a journalist, she knew now that she would be okay.

The End

About the Author

LAURA STARR is an author and avid reader. She shares her love for literature on her blog, *The Start of a Good Life*, with monthly book reviews and updates on her writing journey. In addition, her poetry has appeared in a number of small poetry collections. *Amelia*, the first installment in the *City of Roses Collection*, is her debut novel, and a testament to her dedication and passion for storytelling.

Beyond writing, Laura enjoys spending time with family and friends, walking her golden retrievers and crochcting.

The Oregonian – founded in 1850 as a weekly newspaper by Thomas J. Dryer. By 1900, a daily newspaper that adopted new technologies, content and organization. Editor: Harvey W. Scott. Originally located at the intersection of First St and Morrison St. The newspaper is still active, and is located on First Ave.

The Free Press – founded by George Law Curry in 1848, however, it soon failed, but its declaration endured: "Here shall the Press the people's rights maintain, Uncowed by influence and unbribed by gain."

Portland Hotel – It stood between SW Morrison and Yamhill, on 6th St (now called 6th Ave), facing the Pioneer Courthouse. Opened in 1890 as a new standard in elegance for accommodations in Portland. It was an H-shaped design, 8 floors and 326 bedrooms, electrically illuminated throughout. It used to occupy a city block on which Pioneer Courthouse Square now stands.

Opera House – In reality, named The Marquam Grand Opera House that opened in 1890 – a five-story building. Portland's first opera house sat on the corner of 6th and Morrison St.

University of Washington – Founded in 1861. Originally called the Territorial University of Washington. It awarded its first bachelor's degree in 1876; opened its first dorms as well as a law department in 1899.

Women's Hospital of Philadelphia – Established in 1861. Providing treatment of women and children's diseases and obstetrical cases as well as providing facilities for clinical instruction for nurses. It's one of the earliest U.S. institutions to create a nursing program.

Is He Dead? Play – Written by Mark Twain in 1898, The play focuses on a fictionalized version of the French painter, Jean-François Millet, as an impoverished artist in Barbizon, France who, with the help of his colleagues, fakes his death to increase the value of his paintings.

Robin Hood play – Based on the Robin Hood legend, this was a comic opera with music by Reginald De Koven; composed during the winter of 1888-1889.

In Search of the Castaways by Jules Verne – published in 1867-1868.

Lucy Stone – While I strove for historical accuracy, I took some creative liberties for the sake of the story. One example was to include Lucy Stone in a scene set in 1899, though she passed away in 1893. She was a pivotal figure in the fight for women's votes, and I wanted to honor that in the novel.

Acknowledgments

My heartfelt thanks go to my parents for their incredible support and to my siblings for their encouragement along the way. To my editors, Jasmine Fischer and Dave Jarecki, whose enthusiasm for the characters and narrative helped shape it into something truly special. A special thanks to Lieve Maas of Bright Light Graphics for believing in my ability to self-publish and for bringing the final product to life so beautifully.

To Fili and the hobbit group for plotting assistance, proofreading, and encouragement. And to Abby and Rory, for insisting I take countless breaks to throw sticks for you.

Lastly, to my readers—your support makes every revision worth it. Thank you for joining me on this journey. Here's to many more stories shared and enjoyed!

CITY OF ROSES COLLECTION

Look for more stories in the collection, including:

Georgia
Harrison

COMING NEXT

FROM LAURA STARR:

Georgia

The next book in the *City of Roses Collection* returns to Portland, Oregon, where the story unfolds against the backdrop of social change brought by the suffrage movement of 1912.